DEATH AND THE CHEVALIER

DEATH AND
THE CHEVALIER

Robin Blake

This first world edition published 2019
in Great Britain and 2020 in the USA by
SEVERN HOUSE PUBLISHERS LTD of
Eardley House, 4 Uxbridge Street, London W8 7SY.
Trade paperback edition first published
in Great Britain and the USA 2020 by
SEVERN HOUSE PUBLISHERS LTD.

British Library Cataloguing in Publication Data
A CIP catalogue record for this title is available from the British Library.

ISBN-13: 978-0-7278-8920-1 (cased)
ISBN-13: 978-1-78029-672-2 (trade paper)
ISBN-13: 978-1-4483-0371-7 (e-book)

All Severn House titles are printed on acid-free paper.

Severn House Publishers support the Forest Stewardship Council™ [FSC™],
the leading international forest certification organisation.
All our titles that are printed on FSC certified paper carry the FSC logo.

Typeset by Palimpsest Book Production Ltd.,
Falkirk, Stirlingshire, Scotland.
Printed and bound in Great Britain by
TJ International, Padstow, Cornwall.

for Jasmine Rose

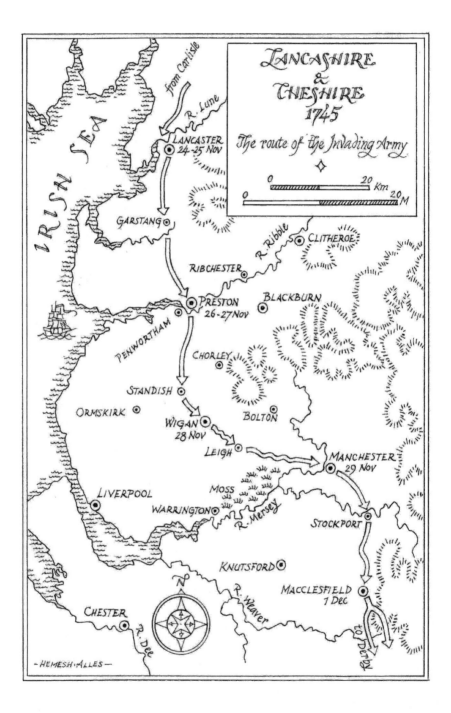

IRISH SEA

From Carlisle

R. Lune

LANCASTER
24-25 Nov

GARSTANG

R. Ribble

CLITHEROE

RIBCHESTER

BLACKBURN

PRESTON
26-27 Nov

PENWORTHAM

CHORLEY

STANDISH

ORMSKIRK

WIGAN
28 Nov

BOLTON

LEIGH

MANCHESTER
29 Nov

MOSS

LIVERPOOL

WARRINGTON

R. Mersey

STOCKPORT

KNUTSFORD

MACCLESFIELD
1 Dec

CHESTER

R. Dee

R. Weaver

to Derby

- HEMESH·ALLES -

LANCASHIRE
&
CHESHIRE
1745

The route of the Invading Army

0   20 Km
0   20 M

ONE

Rumours had been afoot months before the armies mustered. They made the Jacobites of Preston breathless with anticipation. The Whigs, too, whispered it amongst themselves. A reckoning was inevitable. War loomed. *He* was coming.

Who was he?

He had many names. His real ones were Charles Edward Stuart, but you rarely heard these spoken. His sworn enemies, the Whigs, preferred to revile him as the bedpan bastard's brat, foxcub Charlie, the girl-prince, the Knave of Jacks. They joked about his effeminacy, his cowardice, his baby face, as if no such feebleness could ever usurp the solid God-given rule of the manly German Georges. He may come, they were saying, but he'd have his little boy's bottom horse-whipped if he does.

His friends had more reverential names: God's appointed, the veritable Prince of Wales, the prince in arms to bring his father to his own again, the brave Chevalier. Sometimes the sentiments were coarser: the harrow of Hanover, a boot in the arse for the bloody Brunswickers.

But excitement and scorn were not the only responses. As the year 1745 advanced, our old ones told fearfully of what had happened twice before here at Preston, when Stuart armies had clashed with English forces and received a thrashing. These memorials of history were darkly underwritten by the repetition of prophecies and omens. The ominous words of the old-time seer Robert Nixon of Cheshire were on the lips of many Prestonians at this time. Nobody knew for sure who Nixon was, or when exactly he lived, but he had long been a favourite of the Jacobites. Then, after the disastrous 1715 rebellion, books of his pronouncements had been printed in London with the idea of proving that the Cheshire foreteller's prophecies were actually in the Hanoverian interest: that he anticipated, for example, the destruction of the Stuarts in 1649, 1688 and 1715.

Nixon's pronouncements could indeed encompass contrary interpretations. First, he would give a vision of some portent, as 'when the raven shall nest in the lion's mouth', which would be followed by some dire consequence, such as 'then it shall come to pass that a Grand Liar shall invade the land and come to destruction and be dragged behind the horse's tail'. The Jacobites hotly maintained that Grand Liar was George of Hanover. The men supporting Hanover were equally adamant it was the Pretender.

The vicar in his sermons denounced Nixon, setting him unfavourably against Jeremiah, the false against the true prophet. The former had clothed his words in ambiguities and insinuations, while the latter spoke the truth with a voice of brass: 'And the Lord came unto me saying, "What seest thou?" And I said, "A seething pot; and the face thereof is towards the north."' Prophecies of evil in evil times could not, he thundered, come forth as plainly as that.

So deep emotions were stirring. I was made strongly aware of this myself on a certain day in August, when I went across the river to Walton-le-Dale about the business of a will. My late client, William Entwhistle, was an unmarried mercer who had died from the flux aged fifty-two a few days earlier. Entwhistle had not been rich enough to turn himself into a gentleman, yet he had done moderately well in life. More than three hundred pounds in coin had been found at his house, as well as lots of material goods, such as silver, china and cut glass, as well as the stock of damasks and velvets of his trade. As there were no living Entwhistle relatives, I had come to Walton to assess the distribution of the testator's goods and chattels as stipulated by his will.

There was one particular clause that required circumspect handling. 'With regard to my objects appertaining to the cause of him that some believe to be Great Britain's true king over the water,' Entwhistle had written (under my advice), 'I direct they be given as one parcel to my friend Jonathan Parkinson the candlemaker, of Church Gate in Preston, and none other.' The wording (this being a legal document) was tricky because to adhere openly to the cause of the Pretender might be construed as advocating rebellion against the rule of King George. It might, in other words, be high treason, and to assist a person in any such advocacy might equally draw a charge of conspiracy. I remember drafting Entwhistle's testament with him. I had only with great difficulty persuaded him to drop the word 'just' in front of 'cause', and to insert the words 'him that some believe to be'.

I knew very well what kind of objects Entwhistle's will referred to. Passionate Jacobites like himself and Parkinson had got into the habit of expressing their loyalties through household objects embellished or inscribed with coded emblems and ambiguous quotations. Now the candlemaker's wife, Catherine, had come over to Entwhistle's place to help me find all such Jacobite keepsakes and artefacts in the Entwhistle house. These we assembled on his dining-room table.

'Eh, Mr Cragg,' said Catherine, as we surveyed the array of objects before us. 'It's a fine lot of goods, is that. And right handsome of Will Entwhistle to tip it towards us with his last wishes.'

I pointed to a wine glass decorated with a thistle and a rose within a wreath of entwined oak leaves. Below was inscribed a single word in Latin.

'*Fiat*,' I said. '"Let it be." Let what be, Mrs Parkinson?'

She gave me the kind of look a schoolmistress directs at a pupil fallen down at his arithmetic.

'What do *you* think, Mr Cragg? Not the Germans governing us for ever from London, any road.'

I now picked up a small leather-covered case and opened it. Nestling in its velvet lining were two bronze medals. One showed an enthroned king being crowned by a descending angel. The inscription gave the date twenty-third of April 1661 – close to the beginning of King Charles II's reign that followed the collapse of Cromwell's power.

'It's the last King Charles's coronation medal, is that,' said Mrs Parkinson. 'It was made on the day he was crowned.'

I read out the Latin inscription curving around King Charles on his coronation throne: '*Everso missus sucurrere seclo.*'

'I recognize the words, Mrs Parkinson. They mean some-thing like "Sent to set aright the time turned upside down", and refer, I believe, to a famous passage in the Latin poet Virgil's poem the *Georgics*.'

Suddenly, Mrs Parkinson was taken aback.

'I don't hold with any Georgics! I don't hold with the name of George at all, as you must know. A dirty old name, is that!'

'Well, you may change your mind when I tell you that the words – as far as I remember – come from a passage in the poem where Virgil speaks of the end of civil war, with everything tumbled down – or, more precisely, head over heels – and the coming of a prince who will get things the right way up again, and bring peace and plenty. That is what the young Emperor Augustus did in Rome, you know, in Virgil's time, all those centuries ago. King Charles considered *he* would do the same for this land on his return in 1660, which is why they put the words on his coronation medal.'

'"With the job of cleaning up the mad mess", you mean? Ha! Right enough, Mr Cragg. That's just what we need now when all's said and done, and here's another Charles that shall do the job an' all.'

I took out the second medal and turned it in my hand. Each side showed a young man in profile.

'Who are they?'

'William brought it back from Rome seven or eight years ago. On this side is the Prince of Wales – I mean the *true* prince, Charles Edward – and on the other side is his younger brother, Prince Henry. I don't know what the letters mean, Mr Cragg.'

I read the inscription around the head of the older brother.

'*Hunc saltem everso juvenem*. The words don't make complete sense on their own. They may also be a fragment from a line of poetry. *Everso* is on the coronation medal too – it's the word that means head over heels. *Juvenem* is "young man". I must see if I can find it.'

Having made a complete list of Entwhistle's Jacobite arte-facts, we packed them up in a box to be brought in due course to the Parkinsons' home. Catherine Parkinson then walked with me back to Preston, up the hollow way that led to the end of Church Gate.

'William Entwhistle was unshakeable in his beliefs,' she

said. 'And an inspiration. There was none more zealous in the cause than him. He travelled all the way to Rome in 'thirty-eight, you know, just like a pilgrim, all because he had to set eyes on the King. What a pity that he should be carried off just as we hear this beautiful news.'

'News? What news is that?'

'Why, the news that the Chevalier has already landed! Haven't you heard? He is in the Scottish Isles. He is coming, Mr Cragg. Truly, he is coming.'

'Are you quite sure about this, Mrs Parkinson?'

'There is no doubt, Mr Cragg,' she said, her eyes hot with zeal. 'So now it is *fiat*, after all. *Fiat* that the world is put back on its feet. *Fiat* that the foul Georges are sent packing back to their German rat-holes. *Fiat*, Mr Cragg!'

It was the first time I heard this rumour of Charles Edward's landing, but within a few days it was flying about the town like a flock of starlings. It remained a rumour, however, to be taken as an article of faith by some, and to be dourly doubted by others. One of the doubters was my clerk, Robert Furzey.

'It's all a fantasy, Mr Cragg. That lot, they shot their bolt thirty year ago. They'll not dare try it on again. He's not called the Young Pretender for nothing. It is all a pretence, but all so far away no one can see it.'

Furzey was forced to change his way of thinking when news came in from much closer at hand. A merchant ship, the *Ann*, inbound to Liverpool from the Baltic, brought information that she'd gathered just a week earlier. To escape a storm, the captain had taken shelter in a bay of one of the western islands of Scotland, and while they rode at anchor, a badly frightened schoolmaster, a faithful Protestant, had rowed out to them in the dark of night with a piece of intelligence he wanted trans-mitted to London. A French frigate, he said, had set ashore a small party of conspirators including the Young Pretender, whom locals called, in Gaelic, *Prionnsa Teàrlach*. This gang had proceeded to a gathering place on the mainland where thousands of clansmen had flocked to his standard. This had all happened just a few days earlier.

Despite hearing this from Liverpool, there were still many doubters. At Marcus Porter's Mitre Tavern on Fisher Gate,

Sebastian Beach the poulterer wagered his peruke against that of Paul Judd the tailor that it was all a wishful story, the like of which we had heard several times before, and which no respectable newspaper ought to print. Three days later Seb had lost his wig. The most recent printing of the *London Gazette* had reached us, and I was present at Porter's when the landlord called for silence so that he could read out a short government announcement printed in the paper.

'Mr Beach and Mr Judd to take notice,' Porter roared. 'The *Gazette* contains the following: "A report was received from Edinburgh that a French ship of sixteen to eighteen guns had appeared on the west coast of Scotland and had landed several persons there betwixt the isles of Mull and Skye. Amongst these there is the greatest reason to believe is the Pretender's son."'

Porter lowered the paper and waited for the laughter and jeers aimed at Beach to subside. Then he picked out the thin and plainly dressed figure of Archibald MacLintock, a merchant from Glasgow who traded in salted meat and tobacco.

'Archie!' said Porter. 'What do you make of all this? Is it to be 1715 all over again?'

'Not a chance!' said MacLintock, who was evidently no Jacobite. 'That boy'll no get very far south. It's nothing like 1715 in Scotland today. Have ye heard of Fort Augustus that they've just finished building? There's a chain of strongholds like that across the country that'll keep the foolish fellow bottled up in the Highlands for years. And serve him right!'

There was a murmuring of 'Hear! Hear!' from his companions at the table of Whig-minded Prestonians – who included Robert Furzey.

'They've built many a good straight road north to south, and east to west,' the Scotchman went on. 'So the army of His Majesty can move around as it likes and pounce like a tiger wherever the boy raises his snivelling little head. Oh, never doubt it. He'll be mauled in the end and run howling home to his daddy and his friend the Pope, if he isn't hanged first.'

Suddenly, Jonathan Parkinson, at another table, jumped to his feet.

'You speak of roads, MacLintock. You will allow me to address the same subject. Roads are there for marching on by anyone who chooses, not just the Elector of Hanover.'

This choice of words called forth a hubbub of protest from MacLintock's friends.

'You must call him the King!' they shouted. 'Jacobite blackguard!'

Parkinson stood his ground.

'I tell you, the Prince will not be slow to march down south along those roads. He will not be hindered, and if his cause be just, he and his army'll receive God's good grace and sweep all before them.'

This was too much for MacLintock, who also jumped to his feet.

'His army?' he shouted, shaking his finger at Parkinson. 'He's got no army! The best he can scrape together is a rabblement of savages. No discipline, no organization. They'll be destroyed in half an hour. They can't even speak English up there.'

'They don't speak bloody German, any road,' growled Parkinson.

But among the men of Preston, MacLintock's view – a hopeful view in the eyes of the Whigs – received widespread credit over the next few days. There was no need for alarm, they were saying. The Stuart prince could skulk around the Highlands and Islands to his heart's content, but he'd be hard put to penetrate into the civilized parts of the country, defended as they were by General Cope with his formidable force of redcoats and his line of forts and barracks. A few days later, however, when I came into my office after breakfast, I found my client Miss Colley awaiting me, and I heard the female view of the matter.

'Oh, Mr Cragg,' she said, as I ushered her into my inner sanctum. 'I feel sure I should review my will. The savage Highlanders are coming to slaughter us all, so I've heard. Mrs Bryce insists they make human sacrifice and eat human flesh.'

As always with Amelia Colley, her words were qualified by her tone. The lightness in her voice, that touch of irony, revealed she was far from overwhelmed by her friend Lavinia Bryce's forebodings. But disbelief in the tale did not mean disapproval of it. On the contrary, Miss Colley was charged with pleasure. Her eyes were sparkling. There was nothing she loved more in real life than a drama, and the thought that people were openly talking of massacre and cannibalism greatly excited her.

'I believe the provisions of your will are adequate, whatever the future may be,' I told her.

'But I have left all my money to my nephew Charles, and he is a sworn friend of the government in London.'

'What is wrong with that? It will not make his flesh taste any sweeter to the clansmen.'

She fluttered her eyelids.

'Oh, no, Mr Cragg. Rather the opposite, I should think. No, I do not fear Charles will be roasted and eaten, but at this time of emergency I prefer my last wishes to be those of a neutral observer, do you see? I would not desire to be either condemned or rewarded for them. I wish to sit on the fence and enjoy the fun.'

'What therefore do you propose?'

'To divide my fortune equally between Charles and his cousin Henry, who lives in York and is a notorious Jacobite. They hate each other, of course. I can't think of a better way to express my intense interest in this coming fight.'

'Very well, Miss Colley.'

I went to the door of the outer office.

'Furzey! Come through, if you please. There is writing to be done.'

TWO

Some weeks later I was standing in a field on the edge of a windypit a few miles east of Preston. Beside me stood Dr Luke Fidelis and Samuel Norris, constable of the parish of Ribchester in the bounds of which the field lay, and Andrew Ambleside who farmed the field. It was cold at this early hour of the morning. Our out-breaths puffed as steam in the air, and white frost crisped the grass. We were looking down at the frozen surface of the pond, whose ice was spiked around the fringe with the spears of numerous reeds. Its centre, however, was occupied by the large, naked and ice-rimed corpse of a man: a corpse, moreover, without a head.

Trying to describe the body's attitude I wrote that night in my personal journal:

> Imagine the classical marble statue of a spear thrower, in the act of running up to deliver his weapon. The head has been knocked off. The legs are spread, the left before and the right behind, both crooked at the knee. The feet are flexed. Meanwhile, the right arm is bent high above the shoulders ready to deliver the shaft, while the other points forward in the direction of the throw. And now imagine this figure tipped over and lain down on the ground. This was how the body appeared.

'Do we have any notion of who he is?' I said.

'Not one, Coroner,' said Norris, glancing at Ambleside. 'There's been nobody gone missing round here as far as we've heard.'

'So it's not one of your men, Mr Ambleside?'

The farmer pursed his lips and shook his head.

'Nay. He's none of mine.'

'And it was you yourself that first spotted the body?'

'Aye. I was out at first light and saw it as I rode cross-field.'

'The primary question,' said Luke, 'is where was it brought from? There was no blood-letting here, or we'd see blood.'

'What *I* want to know first off,' said Norris, 'is where's his head?'

'We know one thing at least,' I said. 'He was brought on a two-wheeler cart. The hoof prints and wheel tracks in the frost are clear. The cart entered by the gate from that lane over there, some time last night after the frost whitened the grass. It came up here to the pit and, after the body was thrown down, wheeled around and went back where it came from. Which I would wager is a neighbouring parish.'

'Aye,' said Norris.

'Where are the parish boundaries, Norris?'

The constable stood like a signpost pointing to the north with his right arm and south with his left. He extended his right forefinger.

'That way's Goosnargh parish. And the other way' – he pointed with his left hand – 'that's Whalley parish. It's even nearer.' He pointed to the west. 'And our nearest neighbour over there is Preston.'

'So we're right next to the boundaries with three other big parishes, none of which would particularly like the bother of a dead body and the cost of an inquest, or so I'm guessing. So did one of them remedy the matter by removing the offending corpse by dark of night to a neighbouring parish – this one? I've seen it before. Illegal, but effective as long as you don't get found out.'

We heard horse snorts and a squeaking axle. Three men from Ambleside's farm had arrived with a cart.

'What shall us do wi' him, master?' one said.

'You'll have a look over him, Luke?' I said. Fidelis was my unofficial adviser on the practical aspects of death. For a coroner to employ a medical assistant was unorthodox, certainly, but I had long found Fidelis's insight into the state of a corpse invaluable preparation for an inquest.

Fidelis walked over and cast an eye over the body.

'Get him under cover,' he said. 'I'll want the frost off him before I take a proper look.' He turned back to Ambleside. 'Is there a barn where he'll be safe?'

The farmer nodded and walked across to give the order to his men, who immediately went down to the pond to drag the rigid body to the shore and then up to the rim of the pit, where they heaved it with a thud on to the bed of the cart. As they handled it, I caught a glimpse of the severed neck – a hole between the shoulders clogged with coagulated blood.

'I'm going in search of his head,' I said to Fidelis. 'Without it I can do nothing. I doubt the law will allow me to inquest a headless corpse. The thawing out'll take time, so why don't you come with me?'

'Where to?'

'We'll take the lane towards Simmy Nook. If Mr Headless was carted here from some part of the Whalley side, it was likely from somewhere like Simmy Nook, or if not, it came through it. Abraham Pilling's the constable for that part, and not only does he live in Simmy Nook, but he's idle and corrupt enough to lay off any corpse he stumbles on to the neighbouring parish, if he can. And I'll tell you something else: Pilling is a thatcher. He'll use a horse and cart every day of the week.'

'Is he indeed?' said my friend with interest. 'We must certainly go and see him.'

It was a ride of half a mile to the boundary with the parish of Whalley, and another half to the village of Simmy Nook. Pilling's house – a well-maintained cottage, whose roof was testimony to its owner's craft – stood across the street from the village inn, a run-down establishment called the Black Cat. Pilling's cart was tipped up with its shafts leaning up against the side wall of his house. His old horse chomped grass in a small neighbouring patch of field. Pilling had evidently not yet begun this day's work of roof-making.

We dismounted and I knocked at the door while Fidelis strolled towards the side of the house where the cart was propped. No one answered my knock, so I turned away and looked up and down the street. A fellow bent under a loaded sack was making his wobbly way towards me.

'D'you know where I'll find Constable Pilling?'

He may have been deaf or mute, or simply a churl, but he went straight past me without breaking stride.

'I said, have you seen Abe Pilling?' I called after him.

'Try the Cat.'

I crossed the road to the inn. Pilling was the only customer, sitting in his work clothes over a pot of ale. His breakfast, no doubt.

'Mr Cragg!' he said. 'Whenever I clap an eye on you, I know by day's end I shall regret it.'

'They've found a naked man over in Ribchester parish, lying on the ice in a windypit.'

'Drunk, was he?'

'No, dead.'

Pilling raised an eyebrow, then sniggered. He was a small wiry fellow and thin in every way except for the roundness of his belly.

'Dead drunk maybe, if he fell in a windypit and cracked his noddle on the ice.'

I heard a horse galloping away and glanced out through the grimy window. I saw the back end of Fidelis's horse as he rode off in the direction we had come from.

'Noddle, you say?' I asked. 'What noddle is that?'

Pilling looked at me boldly.

'His own.'

'Ah! But his noddle was off, Pilling. And it was missing, you see. Do you know anything of this, such as its whereabouts?'

He maintained his lofty assurance.

'How would I, Mr Cragg? I am not informed of evil happenings that go off at Ribchester, or anywhere else outside this parish. My duty is only here, as you well know.'

'I wonder, however, if you perceive your duty as including the removal of dead bodies from your parish to avoid the expense of an inquest.'

He did not blink but looked me steadily in the eye.

'But that would be contrary to the law, Mr Cragg.'

The flat tone of his voice and his impervious demeanour told me there was no purpose in continuing the conversation. I went outside, wondering what had taken Fidelis away in such a hurry. His actions were often impulsive and abrupt when he conceived a particularly clever idea, though perhaps in this case he had simply gone back to Ambleside's farm to proceed with his examination of the corpse. I returned to my horse, mounted and set off by a more direct route across the fields, thinking I might get there before him.

With the wide eyes of child as she tells a ghost story, one of the milkmaids at Ambleside's explained how to find the stone barn where the headless corpse had been taken to thaw out. As I rode towards the building, which stood at the end of a cart-track a half mile away, I saw three or four farmworkers standing around the door. Before I could reach them, I heard a horse catching me up from behind. It was Fidelis.

'I have it,' he said, holding high a bulging hempen sack.

'What have you?'

'The errant head, of course.'

'Good God! That was fast work. Where did you find it?'

'A ditch. It wasn't hard. The track was potholed, and Pilling's cart had no tailgate, you see. All I had to do was go back looking for a bump in the road big enough to dislodge it.'

'It rolled off the back of the cart, you mean?'

'Exactly. Heads roll. This one did so a quarter mile after he left Simmy Nook.'

'You're sure the cart was Pilling's?'

'There were scrap ends of thatching stuck to the body, which it must have picked up from lying on the bed of the cart. I noticed them when they brought it up out of the frozen pit. There was even some lodged in the crack of his bottom. I was certain it was his cart as soon as you mentioned Pilling was a thatcher, though I can't say if Pilling himself did the driving.'

'I'll stake my best wig on it. He must have tried to find the head on his way back after leaving the body, but couldn't see it in the dark. He may have thought he had plenty of time to retrieve it in the daylight this morning – more fool him. Shall we reunite it and find out how he died?'

'That will not be easy. The body has no visible sign of any wound, and nor has this head.'

The men made way for us a little fearfully as we went into the barn. A wintry light was admitted to it by a single window, feebly helped by the flames of a fire someone had lit in the hearth. A table had been fashioned by resting an old door on some straw bales. A sheet of sailcloth had been stretched across it, underneath which lay our naked and beheaded corpse. Fidelis approached and drew away the covering. The body, no longer iced, lay on its back as if finally at ease. Fidelis drew the severed head from the sack and, placing it face upward, laid it down in such a way that its neck was aligned with that of the body.

'Now that is curious,' said Fidelis in a wondering way. 'And it explains the absence of any wound.'

Without explaining himself further, he took a candle-stump off a shelf attached to the wall and lit it while I crouched and peered at the dead face. It was that of a young man who had been about twenty and no doubt good-looking in life. His fair hair, plentiful on the crown, sprouty on the cheeks and chin, was matted with dirt, and possibly with dried blood. The eyelids were closed. As Fidelis brought the flickering candle-light to bear, the features seemed less rigid, less dead. I put my thumb on one of the lids and drew it up: the eyeball glittered in the light. The iris was blue.

'What is curious?' I said at last, unable to stop myself.

But Fidelis seemed not to have heard. He was passing the candle over the body, paying particular attention to the legs.

'These knees also have much to tell,' he said.

I looked closely. The knees seemed to be of a darker colour than the skin of the thigh and of the shin.

'They're muddy,' I said. 'But you just remarked that you knew why there are no visible injuries. Please tell.'

'They don't match.'

'What don't match?'

'The head and the body. They belong to different individuals.'

'Surely not! How can you tell?'

'For one thing the hair colour isn't the same: on the head it's more fair, on the body more ginger. But there is another much more definite sign that these are two people.'

He pointed to the truncated neck below the head.

'Do you see the thyroid cartilage, here? That's the Adam's apple to you.'

'Yes, I see it.'

He moved his finger round so that it pointed to the shorn-off portion of neck above the torso of the body.

'Strangely, there's one here also. So, unless this man was born a freak, equipped with a brace of Adam's apples, I'm saying we have before us the remains of two different men.'

I looked back and forth between the two severed necks. The evidence could not be contradicted.

'Can you tell how they died?'

'By having their heads cut off would be a strong possibility.'

'Shall you make an examination to decide the matter?'

'With the greatest of pleasure, but I will have to do the job outside. There is not enough light here.'

Calling for the men to come in, he directed them to remove the human remains, and the makeshift table, into the open air. While they did this, he fetched the leather bag that hung from his horse's saddle and drew out the roll of canvas in which he kept his surgical knives and bone-saws. Then he took off his coat and rolled up his sleeves, at which Ambleside's men exchanged bashful glances and began to edge backwards until there was a safe distance between themselves and the operating table.

'As you mentioned, Luke, there is still much to do,' I said, 'and I must go about it. The most pressing matter is to question Pilling again, and I fancy I might find him in the lane looking in vain for what you have already found. Will you give me your report later in town?'

I found Abraham Pilling, as expected, walking his horse and cart slowly along the verge of the lane while staring fixedly into the passing ditch.

'Have you lost something, Pilling?'

He eyed me biliously.

'Nothing to concern you, Mr Cragg.'

'On the contrary, since I know you're searching for the same missing head as I mentioned earlier, which you told me you know nothing about. That very much concerns me.'

Quite suddenly, the fight went out of the man as air from a punctured bladder.

'Aw, Mr Cragg,' he implored, 'I were only tidying up. We are a poor enough parish without having to stand the cost of your inquest court landing on us.'

'You will pay more dearly than that if you don't tell me exactly what happened last night prior to your taking that head and body away to the next parish.'

'All right, Mr Cragg. This is how it was.'

Pilling told how the corpse had simply appeared in the dark of night, deposited by persons unknown on the ground between the road and the door of the Black Cat Inn. One of the inn's customers, Jerome Wharton by name, had come out late in the evening the worse for ale, and seeing the head lying there in the dark of a moonless night, he mistook it for a football and gave it a mighty kick, which unbalanced him and he tottered sideways and toppled over the naked headless corpse, the fright of which left him crying and jibbering for some time afterwards. Coming out of the Black Cat in response to Wharton's cries, Pilling and other customers put their heads together and concluded that the man had been killed outside the parish, as no one in Simmy Nook had seen anything or could name the fellow. They determined that the remains must be carted away immediately to avoid the taint and expense of an enquiry, and that no one would say a word about it thereafter. They all agreed that the dead man had surely been brought across the parish boundary by the men of Ribchester, and that he should therefore be returned to them.

The thatcher had carried out this task alone – somewhat resentful that no one would assist him – and had reached Ambleside's field before he discovered he had lost the head in transit. Leaving the body on the ice of the windypit, he had made unavailing efforts to find it on the road back before deciding he had better wait until daylight when he would be sober and able to make a more effective search of the ditches.

I gave him a stern talking-to. I said that unless he could provide me with information about the origin and identity of the remains – I didn't let on that they came from two bodies – he would face the task of organizing an inquest. I added I would be making a full report to the magistrates with regard to any criminal conduct on his part. I left him with an expression on his face like that of a ship's mutineer watching the rise of a desert island on the horizon.

These events had unfolded as if part of the usual everyday duty of a coroner, of the kind that he performs at any normal time. But these times were far from normal. By the end of summer there cannot have been many who had not heard of the Young Pretender's dangerous activities north of the border. The earlier scraps of rumour out of the mountains and glens had given way to solid reports. In early September the Prince broke out of the Highlands. To the astonishment of all England, he had marched his men unopposed – thousands of them – through the Pass of Killiecrankie and into the supposedly fortified city of Perth.

A week later my barber Gilliflower, a highly reliable source of news, told me, 'They say he marches ahead of his army on foot and never rides, and always a-wearing the Highlander's garb of tartan and a blue bonnet. And when there's a ford to be crossed, he's ever the first to lead his men in.'

'Do I detect a note of admiration in your voice, Gilliflower?' I said.

This was a surprise. Like all trusted purveyors of news, Gilliflower had never been known to take sides in politics.

'I give respect to any man that makes a brave show.'

This fascination with the person of the Pretender – or Chevalier – reached a crescendo when he walked into Edinburgh, held court at Holyrood and then sortied with his army to smash to pieces the government force led by General Cope at Prestonpans.

'The question now is this,' said a wiseacre politician in the Mitre Tavern. 'Why should he not be content with Scotland? It's the historic land of the Stuarts and a Stuart is lord of it again. He will stop there.'

'Aye. He should be satisfied,' said another. 'He'll make his position solid and fight off the English until they're forced to make terms.'

But a third wiseacre would have none of it.

'You think he'll be satisfied with that poxy country? No,

the lad'll be down here to knock on the door of King George's palace. You may count on it.'

As history relates, the third wiseacre was right: on the feast of All Saints, the Jacobite army marched out of Edinburgh and began to make for the English border. Then, a couple of days before Ambleside's discovery of the headless corpse, some news broke in Preston more sensational than any yet heard: Carlisle was under siege. If and when it fell, the road into England would be open.

On my return from Simmy Nook I went straight to the Turk's Head where Fidelis was waiting to report on his examination. But first he had other news to relate.

'There are reports that the garrison at Carlisle castle will not be relieved, Titus. If the rebels take it, they must come here. They must come to Preston.'

'They may cross into Northumberland yet. That is where General Wade is. Surely the Jacobites will want to engage Wade as soon as possible.'

'They are not going to do that.'

'How can you be sure?'

'Because of what we saw in Ambleside's field this morning. The remains of those two dead men.'

I laughed.

'You're not serious. What possible connection do you make?'

He frowned, disapproving of my levity.

'If I am right, it's an incontrovertible one.'

'What, then?'

'I think these men were Highlanders, Titus. I think they were an advance party of the Chevalier's men.'

THREE

'Highlanders? How do you make that out?' I said.
Languidly, Fidelis took a pear from his pocket and
examined it as if it were a medical specimen.
'Consider this,' he said. 'You remember I mentioned that the
fellow's knees told a tale. You suggested, somewhat foolishly,
that they were muddy, but in reality they were sun-browned and
weather-beaten, while his thighs and shins were not. What does
that tell you?'

'That he had holes in the knees of his breeches?'

'No, Titus! Think! The knees were like that because he wore
the highland kilt.'

'Is that all the evidence you have – brown knees?'

He bit into the pear and chewed reflectively.

'In the stomach, oats,' he said at last. 'That's their staple.
Healthy teeth, strong bones – that's typical of people eating
a simple sufficiency of food.'

'People do that all over. If they were Highlanders, how ever
did they end up in a windypit near Ribchester?'

'There is a larger picture we must look at. As most people
now believe, the rebel army is set on marching down the
western road, just as it did in 'fifteen. They cannot be sure of
success unless supplies are gettable. How do they find this
out?'

'I see what you're getting at. They send out scouts.'

'Precisely: big strong men who can look after themselves
and bring back the bacon – or at least the whereabouts of the
bacon. Hence, two Highland men descend through the country
between Lancaster and Preston, ranging one side or other of
the road, in advance of the main force. They make contact
with supporters, they find stores of food and fodder, sources
of ale and wine and horses.'

I thought for a moment. I was warming to Fidelis's theory.

'It is a persuasive picture, Luke.'

'It is even more persuasive in the light of this.'

Luke laid his pear down and drew a folded sheet of blank paper from his pocket, in which was enclosed a second paper, also folded but more tightly. He handed the latter to me.

'Be careful not to tear it – it is damp. I fished it out of the throat.'

I unfolded the paper with caution and read out loud the writing that I saw there.

To whomsoever shall find this severed head, know that it is the head of a traitorous evil-doer who came into this County of Lancashire solely to serve the interests of the Papist Pretender, against those of his Protestant Majesty King George. Joining battle with this traitor and his confederate, we loyal covenanters of Lancashire have put them to death, and submitted both to the traitor's indignity by cutting off their heads. (signed) Loyal Covenanters of Lancashire. Let it be noted: this was an act of legitimate warfare and not subject to the civil laws of the peace.

It took me a few moments to absorb this extraordinary piece of evidence.

'They do not declare who they are – just "covenanters".'

'Did Pilling tell you anything to the purpose?'

I relayed Pilling's story, which I believed more or less. There was nothing about the people of Ribchester that suggested they were fanatical covenanters ready to lay down their lives for King George.

'There's something of the extreme in what happened,' I said. 'These covenanters claim there was a fight. But that may be a story to cover the truth – to cover a crime, in effect.'

'Or it may be that there really was a battle between the Scotchmen and these covenanters. But if there was, why remain anonymous? And why were the bodies moved and abandoned in the way they were?'

'Because the rebel army is much closer at hand than the Lord Chief Justice, or any assize judge. The killers' first thought was of what kind of justice the Prince might mete out, if he were to come here and discover the truth.'

The pear had been reduced to its core by now. Fidelis raised it above his head and lobbed it across the room. It landed cleanly in the waste basket.

'Summary and savage, I would think,' he said. 'The kind of justice that in war goes under the name of reprisals.'

It was now late in the afternoon. Having a patient to see, Luke Fidelis left me while I went back to the office. My clerk was at his desk, drooping over a bit of writing.

'I have a question about my powers and duties, Furzey.'

Furzey became immediately alert. His demeanour was in general that of a hangdog, but he much enjoyed showing off his superior knowledge of coronial law – and no one had a more complete knowledge of the coronership and its powers than he.

'Yes, Mr Cragg, how may I inform you?'

'I appreciate that we do not inquest on a body part – I mean a finger or a toe or even a limb that may be found, for instance. But we've today found a head detached from its body and, separately, a headless body.'

Furzey looked at me suspiciously.

'Well, you have all you need – it doesn't matter if they're detached. You have parts adding up to a whole body – that is the minimum requirement.'

'But, you see, I have parts that don't add up. Or, more accurately, they add up to two. I have, to be precise, the parts of two different bodies.'

'How do you know?'

'There are two Adam's apples.'

Furzey looked down for a moment, then perked his head up again.

'Ah! I see. The necks are cut in different places.'

'Yes.'

He pursed his lips in thought.

'You need all parts of a whole body essential to life. Therefore, you must find the missing headless corpse and the missing chopped-off head, and then you will have two bodies to inquest for the price of one.'

'Thank you, Furzey. We shall endeavour to do so. There is another conundrum you can help me with.'

'And that is?'

'At the moment a question in theory, but it might become real at any time. Let us suppose a rebel army such as the one presently besieging Carlisle sends scouts south in pairs ahead of its advance and these scouts are killed. However, their deaths are brought about not by soldiers but by people who call themselves loyal covenanters – signatories of some document like the one we have seen going around this town in recent days. What do I do?'

'Killing in the course of warfare,' said Furzey, 'killing involving soldiers, is outside the scope of your duties. If there is any law in such a case, it is military law.'

'We don't know it was warfare. The victims are or may be soldiers, but the killers are civilians.'

He considered for a moment, then frowned.

'That is indeed a ticklish one,' he said.

'You mean you don't know the answer?'

'I mean I don't know that there *is* an answer. But let me mull it over. There may be precedent from your father's time.'

'The Fifteen? Yes, it's quite likely, though there was also real military fighting then.'

I was a lad when the last invading Highland army occupied Preston. They had been soundly beaten, but I had no memory of the occupation, or the action, as I'd been sent away from town with my mother to the countryside.

I used the connecting door to make my way into the house. Elizabeth was out visiting, but from the kitchen I heard the babble of little Hector and found our girl Matty trying to coax the lad into taking his first steps. But, mighty crawler though he was, his legs were not quite strong enough yet to support him.

'Pap! Pap!' he shouted as soon as he saw me come in, and then, 'Up! Up!'

This meant I had to lift him by his armpits and whirl him around as giddily as I could. I performed the office twice, making him laugh with delight, which was one of the gladdest sounds I knew.

It was raining now, a sleety drizzle. I threw on a greatcoat against the weather and went out again.

*   *   *

If literature is the best teacher in morals, I prefer history for guidance in practical affairs. Anyone investigating a death is helped if he can inform himself about a similar event from the past. Precedent is one of the most powerful persuaders in a court room, but its usefulness is not confined to the law. Precedent is also very handy in everyday life.

Fond as I am of a book, I know that the best source of history is living memory, and as far as the history of Preston was concerned, this was embodied in our oldest inhabitant, Wilfrid Feather. He was universally known as Old Methuselah, a man whose ninety-two years and continued mental lucidity lent his voice unrivalled authority, backed up by the rumour that he was writing a history of Preston. No one had ever seen this work, but it was generally agreed it must be monumental and full of the antiquarian learning in which Feather had immersed himself since his retirement as Town Clerk. It was to Old Methuselah's house in Marsh Lane that I now made my way.

It was a small and old-fashioned little cottage, much humbler than would be expected of a former senior official. But Feather's clerkship had been decades in the past and most of the money he had saved was now spent. His granddaughter, Mrs Farrowby, who looked after him, sat me down across the hearth from Old Methuselah's rocking chair and placed a blackened kettle on the fire between us. Then she went on to the back to gather the necessaries for tea.

Feather was nearly blind and his voice was flutey, but his memory was in as excellent condition as his abundant white beard.

'I am hoping you can tell me about the rebels in 1715.'

'Only yesterday, was that! There's scores of Prestonians alive can remember what happened.'

'None so thoughtfully as you, Mr Feather. None so reliably, I'm thinking. In some people, memory plays tricks, does it not? But not in you.'

'That's very soft of you, Mr Cragg. Very kindly soft. What do you want to know?'

'How Preston was affected. We have new rebels already entered into Cumberland, just as there were then.'

'Oh aye, and it was just at this time of year an' all. November.

They had no royalty with them, not then. General Forster was one leader and the Earl of Derwentwater was another, and they led this raggle-taggle army of Jacobites marauding down the road from Scotland, with a few from Lancashire joining up with them as they came along. It was here in Preston that they met up against the forces of the newly arrived king from Germany.'

'And before the main body of rebels arrived here, how much did Preston know? How prepared were we?'

'We were unprepared. We should not have been. We'd heard the news of this army coming down the north road. Scouts and pioneers had been picked up here and there around the northern part of the county.'

I sat forward in my chair.

'Scouts, you say?'

'Yes, they were looking out for how they could fodder their troops and animals. Some collected money on behalf of the Pretender – lawful taxation, they called it; distortion, we called it.'

'What happened to these scouts?'

'A few were taken up. They were sent away to Chester, or to London maybe.'

'Were any that were taken up attacked by the people? Were any killed?'

Old Methuselah paused for thought.

'I think I do remember a case, not far from town. It was maybe a week before the rebels came in. A Highlander was caught in the Fylde and beaten to death. They brought his body next day to show it off in Preston Market Place.'

'Were these men prosecuted?'

'No. There was no appetite for that.'

'And when the Scotch came, what did they do about it?'

'They gave the body a burial.'

'Did they not seek out those that had done it? Did they not exact reprisals?'

'There was talk of it as a possibility. I don't think there was anything done. The Scotch were having too much of a good time, drinking our taverns dry and dancing our ladies to exhaustion, and then the King's army came up.'

'What happened after that?'

'The Scotch were in a fix. They were bottled up and then the government army forced its way into the town and gradually battered them into surrender. There were no defences, see? No walls, no castle, no more than there is today. Just barricades at the town bars, which any cannon could dismantle with a few well-aimed blasts.'

'So there was no siege?'

'Oh no, nothing like that. It was an invasion, street by street, house by house. Then the King's men started to set fires. They didn't care about Preston; they just burned any building they thought the Scotch were in. More than half of poor old Preston was lost at the end, and what wasn't was looted. Some girls and boys were raped, one or two young apprentices were put up to a wall and shot. Spoils of war. At the end, when the Scotch were beat, them from round here that joined the rebel army were publicly hanged, drawn and quartered on the Moor. It was all part of the price we paid for having hosted the Pretender's men, Mr Cragg. We'd done it none too willingly, but that made not a scrap of difference. They punished us for it.'

I was aghast. Fighting in the streets. Half the town burned. Public executions. Looting. It had been much worse than I knew, and now the same perils were facing our town again. And what were we doing to prepare ourselves?

I gave Old Methuselah sincere thanks and took my leave.

I deviated from my way home, in spite of the rain, to call at the Mitre Tavern. I thought I would have a smoke and hear what the people were saying about the events at Carlisle. As usual, the wiseacres were drinking and picking away at the latest news as one picks at the carcass of a roasted bird.

'I don't like to hear the man called Pretender,' said the blacksmith Adam Clark. 'Why should we take sides in the argument? Whoever has the grace of God will prevail. Let us keep out of it and await the outcome.'

'Don't be so daft,' said William Sowerby who had a cooperage near the Fisher Gate bar. 'How can we keep out of it? The Pretender, Prince or Chevalier – whatever you want to call him – is at Carlisle, and when he's taken that castle, he

will march to Lancaster and he'll take that castle, and then
he'll come to Preston. And it'll be just the same as in 'fifteen.'

'And we've not even got a castle,' observed Aloysius Hutton,
who kept a tobacconist's nearby.

'That's right,' said the printer Anthony Buckler. 'And the
King's force will come again to fight them here. They say
the King's son the Duke of Cumberland is sent for to take
command.'

'Fatty Cumberland?' the cooper hooted. 'That hogshead of
lard. He'll never get here in time. It's said a horse lasts less
than an hour under him before its spirit is broken.'

'But the rebels – if I may call them that, Adam?' said Seb
Beach the poultryman. 'They may yet avoid Cumberland and
sheer off to the east and after General Wade.'

A heated argument blew up over this last point, as it was
popularly hoped that Preston would indeed be sidestepped by
Prince Charles in favour of Northumberland and Yorkshire. I
regarded it as a delusion. This was his most direct way to
London. It was his way to glory. I snapped my clay pipe and
left.

Later, sitting up in bed with Elizabeth, I gave her an account
of the day. She had brought a jar of pickles up and was eating
them one by one, generously giving the odd one to me. I
allowed myself the pleasure of withholding until last the information that the headless body they'd found in Ambleside's
windypit and the head Fidelis found in the lane did not match.
I then added that Luke Fidelis had convinced me there had
been two murdered Highlanders from the Pretender's army,
and that the head of one and the body of the other were still
to find.

She said nothing for a few moments but spooned another
pickle into her mouth while she thought.

'Which leaves you with a dilemma, Titus. What does the
County Coroner do in such a circumstance?'

'Furzey says I can't lawfully inquest either a headless corpse
or a stray head. I need the corresponding parts of both bodies.'

'That is not the dilemma I mean. As Coroner, you are servant
of the crown. But which crown? The crown that the victims
gave their allegiance to – the Old Pretender – or the crown

that the murderers support, which we can assume is Farmer George's? If the rest of these two bodies are found, and you insist on an inquest, you will have to decide in whose name it is done.'

'So you think I should do nothing about the Highlanders.'

'I know you, Titus. You have a way of storm-chasing in search of justice. But there is an argument for keeping your head down once in a while and allowing the storm to pass over you.'

As if to underline her remark, there was a howl of wind and a battering of rain on the window.

FOUR

All night it stormed. Across the county, rills became rivers, and streams torrents. Trees were lifted as easily as carrots, loose thatch was ripped out, scaffolding was scattered. Carcasses began to appear in the river, drowned sheep and cattle, a dog or two; and then, in the afternoon of the next day, a human body, naked, was spotted as the spate rolled it under the bridge at Ribchester. A fisherman found these grisly remains early in the morning a few hundred yards further downstream, entangled in roots under the southern bank. When they pulled it out of the water, they found it was headless.

The weather had resolved once more to a steady drizzle by the time Fidelis rode out with me along the eastern road to the village which, as antiquarians tell us, had once been a camp of the Roman army. Ribchester's importance had long ago faded, but it still boasted a twice-weekly market, a church dedicated to St Wilfrid and a population of clogmakers and handloom operators.

Norris met us in the parish rooms, a stone building like a barn where meetings and get-togethers were held. Here the head and body from Ambleside's farm had been brought, as had the corpse newly discovered in the riverbank. Norris had placed the bodies beside each other for comparison on trestle tables. The river corpse's neck had been cut through low down, close to the shoulders and below the thyroid cartilage, which meant that when Fidelis placed the windypit head atop the body, there was no doubt that they belonged together.

As Fidelis began to work on his examination, a group of local gawpers drifted into the building, mainly old ones and children, all of whom were raggedly dressed and barefoot, or wearing wood-soled clogs.

'It'll be best if you turn them out, please,' said Fidelis to Norris. But no sooner had Norris done so than they reappeared at the window, or clogged up the doorway, trying to see what was what. They were not threatening or active in any way, and in the end they were allowed to return as long as they kept well back from the anatomical proceedings. I noticed that the individuals in this group continually changed as people came in for a lingering look at Fidelis at work before going about their business again, but that one little girl of perhaps ten, with a lot of dark curly hair tied back with baling twine, stubbornly remained with us.

I never assist Fidelis with the more visceral of his physical investigations, though I like to be on hand while he works. So I was loitering about, talking idly with Norris, when the dark-haired little girl came up and tugged at my sleeve.

'Well, well!' I said. 'What do you want, my dear?'

She looked up at me boldly.

'Our Margery, she knows where something is. She's seen it in its hiding place.'

'Wait a minute! First things first. What is your name?'

'Susannah.'

'And who is Margery?'

'My little sister.'

'So what has Margery found in its hiding place?'

'She won't say.'

'That could be anything, then, couldn't it?'

'Well, it frighted her. That's why she won't say.'

'And why are you telling me, Susannah?'

'I think it's what you want to find.'

'Which is?'

She nodded towards Fidelis bent over the table, plying one of his tools with considerable force.

'He's got two bodies and only one noddle, which he needs two of, don't he?'

This was a child who didn't mince her words.

'What exactly did Margery tell you?'

'She just says she's seen this man hiding. She said it were a buried man, all except his noddle staring at her, and she thought he were left over from Halloween. She were that frighted she won't say more about it.'

'A buried man? Where was this?'

'Well, I think it's not buried at all, me. I think it's the
noddle you want that goes with the rest that they got out of
the river.'

'Won't she say where it is, this, er, noddle?'

Susannah shook her head.

'And where is she now?'

'With our mother. At home.'

'Perhaps you had better take me and Mr Norris there.'

She took a step backward and pointed at Norris.

'I won't take him.'

I took Norris by the elbow and turned him away from the
child for a moment.

'Who are they, Norris?'

'Family called Bruff. He's a farmworker, casual. She works
a hand loom.'

'Is this child reliable?'

Norris shrugged.

'Well, the family's honest enough, though poor. But she's
a child. They make things up, don't they?'

'Yes, but I'm going to have a word with the mother anyway
and perhaps we can get little Margery to spit out some more
detail or show me the place. You stay here in the meantime
and keep the curious off the doctor's back.'

With pride of possession, Susannah took my hand and led
me out into the street.

The Bruff cottage lay about a hundred yards down the street
and up a muddy weind. The interior was as clean as a house-
proud woman could make it, but however hard she scrubbed
and besomed, she would never give it the appearance of prosperity. There was almost no furniture and a pitifully thin turf
fire in front of which we found Mrs Bruff kneeling and brushing
the hair of another little child – Margery, I supposed, as she
was a smaller edition of Susannah.

'Hey, mother!' said Susannah from the door. 'I've brought
a man with me that wants to see our Margery.'

Her mother stood up and faced us as Susannah led me in.
Awkwardly, I took off my hat.

'Mrs Bruff, I believe. I am Titus Cragg, the County Coroner.'

Mrs Bruff was not above thirty, with a somewhat boney

face and a glint of intelligence in her eyes. She shook her head dubiously.

'Nay, Mr Cragg, I hope you've not been listening to our girl. She's that full of fancies she'll see faces in the floor and make a horse of the wind, so her father says.'

I smiled, as I thought, diplomatically.

'Nevertheless, Mrs Bruff, she insists she has information that will help me. A body which we believe to be that of a stranger turned up early this morning in the river downstream from here. But the body as it was found was unfortunately, er, decapitated. It was without its head.'

'I know what decapitated means.'

There was impatience in her hand-on-hip stance. She was the opposite of the village busybody or the gulper-down of sensational news.

'Your daughter Susannah here believes that her sister knows where the missing, er, part is.'

'She's said nowt to me.' She turned to the little girl. 'What's all this, our Margery?'

Margery began immediately to cry and her mother went down on her knees to mop the tears. Mrs Bruff and her younger daughter then held a secret conversation directly into each other's ears. Finally, Mrs Bruff rose and took her younger daughter's hand.

'She'll show us where.'

All four of us proceeded to the village street and turned down it in the direction of the riverbank meadow.

'She says she were playing on the riverbank just this morning,' said Mrs Bruff. 'Her father will give her a leathering for going down there by herself so soon after the flooding, which is why she's so shy of telling.'

We'd left the last village house two hundred yards behind and were now walking along the riverbank. The entire meadow had been flooded only a few hours earlier, but the stream, though still much swollen, had already withdrawn to its normal confines, leaving large puddles, patches of silt and rafts of imported reed and other detritus in the middle of the meadow. We soon came up to a pair of willows spreading over the river, their trunks joined together as they emerged from the bank.

Margery pointed at them but would go no nearer than twenty yards. Susannah was told to stay with her sister while Mrs Bruff and I approached the trees.

The fused bases of the willows, coming out almost horizontally from the sloping bank, formed a natural receptacle in which water could collect, making a summer bird bath, say, or a hedgehog's drinking bowl. Today a great quantity of sticks and other debris had piled up around the tree and its roots, entirely covering this declivity. But when we looked more closely at the heap of flood deposits, we saw something else was there, within the detritus. It was a human eye staring out.

'There's a head in there all right,' said Mrs Bruff, as stating a matter of quite ordinary fact.

Together we began lifting the covering matter away until we could clearly see the object as the flood had left it, right way up but askew in the hollow of the two willow trunks. To me, though I have seen most of the extreme manifestations of death, a sight like this never loses its aspects of horror and woe. The eyes seemed to protrude maniacally, the forehead and cheeks were streaked and smoothed with grey river mud, and the muddy hair had dried to form itself into stiff little worms. It might have been a Medusa head had it not been for the abundant russet-coloured face-hair of a fellow who, from the weather-beaten lines that creased his face, might have been forty years of age.

'Eh, it's a fright to look at is that,' said Mrs Bruff. 'You'll be wanting to reunite him, I'm thinking.'

Indeed, I did want to reunite him, but one cannot openly carry a severed head up a village street on a Thursday afternoon for all to see.

'What are we going to wrap it in?' I said.

I was, a little reluctantly, about to take off my coat when I felt another tug on its sleeve and turned. Susannah was pointing to a muddy heap in the middle of the meadow.

'There's a blanket, mister. Shall us fetch it?'

She didn't wait for my say-so, but ran across to the place, with little Margery scampering after her, and returned in triumph, dragging a sopping, filthy piece of broadcloth. Mrs Bruff and I took the cloth by its corners between us and gave it a shake to remove twigs and pebbles, then twisted it to squeeze out some of the river water. Finally, Mrs Bruff spread the cloth on the ground and we saw it was a Highland tartan, though very muddy and indistinct. I lifted the head by its ears and put it down to be wrapped.

So we returned to Fidelis in the parish rooms. He was too absorbed in his almost finished task to pass comment on our discovery of the severed head. But a few minutes later he had finished sewing up his incisions and I was able to offer him the dripping bundle.

'So you have the head. Excellent. Let's see if it fits.'

He placed it down, severed neck to severed neck, and we saw at once that it was a match for the body found on Ambleside's land.

'First of all, this second body is smaller and slimmer,' said Fidelis. 'Less mature, though a young man rather than a youth.'

'The head confirms it. He looks about twenty.'

We were riding back to Preston, having left Norris with instructions to secure the two bodies and draft a jury for an inquest to be held in two days' time. I was not sure what Elizabeth would say, but if we were indeed going to be overwhelmed by armies of Highlanders and redcoats, I wanted to get this business over first.

'His hands are younger too,' Fidelis went on, 'but even so they look less used. And I don't think that he wore the kilt.'

'No tell-tale brown knees, then?'

'No. Lily-white, they are. However, the most important new evidence from these bodies comes in the form of the wounds.'

'You mean we have some wounds to inspect at last?'

'We do. We have a bullet hole in the chest of the younger man and a great crushing at the back of the skull of the elder – he was struck hard on the back of his head. Both injuries, I think, would have resulted in immediate death.'

'Was there anything else?'

'Yes, there were two other indicative differences between these two men. One is in their stomachs.'

'Neither man had a fat belly as far as I could see.'

'Exactly. As far as you could see. But I've seen inside their bellies and they ate different food. This young man had dined on some sort of game in a ragout, perhaps pheasant. His stomach also contained traces of nuts, dried fruit and sweetmeats, and he had been drinking wine. Different from his companion, who had dined off boiled oats mixed with offal and the blackest of black beer.'

'So, if they were this supposed scouting party travelling together, it does not seem they were eating together.'

'And what they ate doesn't look like two foragers living and eating rough. The old one might possibly have been fending for himself, but the last time the youngster was victualled it was by a chef.'

'Were they maybe travelling as a young master and his servant?'

'Or somebody's precious callow sprig and a muscular bodyguard appointed by his doting dad. You have the cloth from the riverside that you carried the head in, I hope.'

'I have it. I'll get it washed and we'll be able to see it better tomorrow. You mentioned a second difference between the two heads. What is it?'

'In their mouths. The second head, the one found by the river, had nothing in its mouth.'

'No note from the loyal covenanters?'

'No. There may have been, but if so, it was washed away.'

'Do you have any other observations?'

'I saw no new injury marks or wounds in the remains found here at Ribchester. But there is something about the beheading in both cases. It was done with a saw, and rather a delicate one.'

'Not a woodsman's saw?'

'More like one of my own instruments. The cut edges were hardly rough at all, and the work was done with precision. Whoever did it knew what they were about.'

'A butcher, then?'

'Yes, that's possible.'

I could tell that he regarded the manner of the cutting as a significant detail, but he said no more about it, turning instead to a more general conversation until we reached Preston.

My horses were kept at Lawson's Livery in Old Shambles, and as I turned into the yard, Old Lawson himself came out to speak to me.

'I am holding a meeting of all my customers, Mr Cragg, to tell them about certain dispositions I must make with all this scrowing and dicking about up north. Please will you be good enough to attend? It's tomorrow morning at ten, here in the stable yard.'

'Very well, Lawson, I'll be there.'

Over supper I told Elizabeth of my proposed inquest in forty-eight hours. She listened attentively.

'If this dead lad's as precious as you say, there may be consequences for whoever killed him, and for anyone thought to be helping his killers.'

'I am wondering if he was a messenger. The killers left a note claiming both dead men were rebels from the Pretender's army. Fidelis believes this, based on his finding of a pair of sunburned knees.'

Elizabeth grasped at once what this meant, and laughed.

'Of course! Because their men wear skirts and go bare-arsed, as it's said.'

'The common soldiers go bare-arsed, I think, my dearest. Not the officers.'

'Bare-arsed or not, they have a fearsome reputation. The word around the town is that they do not stop at beheadings.'

'Have you been talking with Miss Colley? Well, whatever the truth, the events that happened the last time they were here don't make for a pretty tale. No wonder people are trembling in their beds.'

She grasped my hand across the table.

'But we do not tremble, do we, Titus? We do not huddle under our blankets and cover our heads for fear of civil war and bare Scotch arses. That will do no good. Surely not all of them are savages. Some may be like the sergeant in the Sergeant's Letter.'

That night in my library I took down a volume of *The Spectator* and read again the celebrated 'Sergeant's Letter' with the editor's approving remarks on it. This sergeant had

been at the battle of Blenheim and his letter to a fellow soldier
relates the slaughter of comrades and his own head wound
(which he makes light of), and goes on to promise he will
send the contents of a dead comrade's purse to the man's
grieving widow – seven shillings and three pence in total. The
letter has a stoicism and nobility about it, despite the fact that
it was not the writing of any officer or gentleman, but a fellow
from 'the Heap of the Army'. I tried to take heart from *The
Spectator*'s assurance that the common soldier, for all that is
said of him, is a man of natural gallantry and generosity. And
I tried to believe that the Highland soldier would be no different
from this sergeant in Marlborough's army. But the image that
Miss Colley and Elizabeth had left in my mind, of beheadings
and anthropophagy, and Scotchmen in skirts with bare arses,
would not go away.

FIVE

awson's Livery kept its own riding and coaching horses, but also housed the mounts of many townspeople – such as me – who did not have their own stables. The majority of horses were boxed in a large yard on the edge of town and brought to the smaller stables at Old Shambles when needed by their owners. The proprietor was a staunch supporter of the government, and what he had to say to the thirty people who gathered in his yard the next morning didn't please all of them.

'I have above fifty horses in my care,' Lawson told us, 'and I'll be damned if I'll let them fall into the hands of the rebels. They must go into the country for safety. You will all have to do without your horses until the danger is past.'

There were a few cries of dissent.

'They're not yours to do with as you please, Jack Lawson. I make my own mind up what's to do with my gelding.'

'It won't be up to you – it'll be the soldiers when they take him and give him to a dragoon who will flog him to death. I remember 'fifteen. The only things they were desperate for were powder and horses, and they helped themselves until this town was stripped bare.'

'Don't forget girls. They stripped them bare an' all.'

There was some laughter, but Lawson was in no mood for jokes.

'I will let the old horses stay in town – any over twenty years – as they're no use in warfare. The rest are coming away.'

'Where are you taking the horses, Jack?' someone called out.

'The lesser number that knows that, the less likely the bloody Scotch'll find them out. You may trust me. The Corporation does, isn't that right, Alderman Grimshaw?'

Heads turned to locate Ephraim Grimshaw, a former Mayor of Preston who was still the most formidable power on the Corporation. He had been standing at the edge of the meeting. Now he shouldered his way to the front and held up his hand.

'Mr Lawson has given his assurances that the horses will be cared for as well as ever, and will, of course, be returned to their owners. But I want to emphasize – please! – it would be unthinkable to let half a hundred prime animals be added to the rebels' strength. Lord Derby, who has himself (I am sure) already dispersed the stables at his own house, would be scandalized. And the figure this Corporation would cut in London – well, we'd be a laughing stock. So we consider this a capital idea.'

The meeting broke up, with the numbers of men grumbling being roughly balanced by those who welcomed Lawson's scheme.

'It's a precaution worth taking, I suppose,' said Nick Oldswick the watchmaker, as we left together. He was a notorious Jacobite. 'It's a hard choice for one like me: I can't afford to lose my horse, but I don't want the Chevalier to lose the war – or his life.'

'Then you should prepare yourself. History says he will lose the war, at least.'

'Not the latest history. The battle near Edinburgh wasn't even a close heat. General Cope got a thrashing. We must wait for the next and that'll decide the issue.'

'But where will that be?'

Oldswick shrugged.

'Not here, I hope.'

Everyone I spoke to gave a different opinion, with no one sure where the decisive engagement would be fought. The gloomiest considered that history would be repeated and it would be here in Preston. Others saw the rebels crossing the Mersey into Cheshire, where they would be cut to pieces by Cumberland's army – or vice versa. Yet others considered the rebels would give Cumberland the slip and press on to London, where they would batter the militia and trained bands on Finchley Common. Or vice versa.

Lawson looked after three horses of ours: Goody, a sober mare of fifteen, the eight-year-old gelding, Patrick, and old Jones, who was now twenty-two and fit enough, though a little stiff about the legs and cloudy in the eyes. We never sold Jones or sent him to the slaughterhouse because we were too fond of the old fellow, but nowadays I only rode him to picnics and the like. However, it meant that while Goody and Patrick would be whisked away to the country, I would still have a riding horse available, if only a very slow and thoughtful one. 'It is a good precaution,' said Fidelis when I told him of Lawson's move. 'If the Prince is to win, it had better be by fair play and not stealing horses.'

We were at the Turk's Head Coffee House and I had given him a concise account of what occurred at Lawson's. Fidelis had not been at the meeting as he stabled his own two hacks at his bachelor house on Fylde Road, which he called Scrafton's Roost, having built the place from the winnings of a particularly fierce gamecock called the Sultan of Scrafton. Having your own stable was more expensive than paying Lawson's monthly fees, as he had to employ a handler, and in bargaining for oats and hay he had none of Lawson's advantage. Yet a doctor could not put in hazard his ability to ride out to a patient at a moment's notice. Fidelis needed his horses close at hand.

The customers at the Turk's Head were not like those at Porter's. This was generally a wittier, wiser constituency, sceptical about politics and more interested in opinion and literature, art and music. But the atmosphere even here was loaded with the suspicions and secrecies that attend these moments of high national uncertainty. Customers were talking in quieter tones than usual. Their neighbours at the next table may not be trusted and those on the other side might be plotting. Such were the times.

'By the way,' I said, 'that piece of broadcloth – Matty washed it last night and it is dry now.'

I had it folded up in a linen bag, which lay on the table between us. Fidelis took it out. The tartan was a chequerboard, each square the same size, a symmetric arrangement of pale orange, pale green and muddy brown.

'Congratulations, Luke,' I said. 'If this is part of the costume of one of the dead men – the older one, I suppose – then your deduction from the fellow's brown knees has been vindicated.'

'It looks as if the killers, while throwing a body and a head into the Ribble, also threw in some of their victims' clothing.'

'My understanding is that all the Highland families have

their own pattern. If so, this can help us identify the dead man. Who is there near at hand and might know one pattern from another?'

'William Douglas?'

'Let's try him.'

Douglas's butchery was a few doors from the top of Turk's Head Court, at the corner of School Lane. The butcher spoke with a pronounced, but not impenetrable, Scotch accent, and hewed his meat with a ferocity to match, so that Fidelis and I walked up there in high hopes that he would provide us with the clan name of the tartan.

Douglas put down his cleaver and looked attentively when I showed him the blanket, which he told us was called a *plaid*, pronounced 'pladd'.

'I believe all the Highland families or tribes have different designs,' I said.

'You must call then clans, Mr Cragg.'

'Very well, *clans*. Do you know which one this belongs to?'

Douglas pushed out his lips and shook his head.

'I'm from Musselburgh,' he told us, 'a fair way from the wilderness. This *is* a Highland plaid, I'm fairly sure of that. But I don't know the clans' codes. I'm sorry, gentlemen, but as you are here, can I interest you in a cut of this lovely brisket – perfect for braising?'

Politely declining, we left Douglas picking up his cleaver to return to work. I suggested that we try MacGowan the cartwright, whose yard was outside the Fisher Gate bar. This was an even worse idea as MacGowan told us he had been born and learned his trade in Dundalk in Ireland.

'Where is a genuine Scotchman in this town?'

We were strolling back along Fisher Gate when the answer appeared in the shape of MacLintock emerging right in our path through the door of the Mitre Tavern. He looked in some way disorderly, as if making an escape.

'They're building up to fisticuffs in there.' he said to us while knocking the dust off his hat. 'Nobody knows a bloody thing and they're all in a panic and firing questions at anyone they think might give them answers. And when you say you can't, they bloody turn on you. They menace you.'

I knew that, being a Presbyterian from Glasgow, MacLintock did not take kindly to the Highlanders. But that might not preclude some knowledge of their ways.

'May I fire a question of my own at you, Mr MacLintock?' I said. 'I promise you I won't menace you if you can't answer.'

He nodded and I showed him the plaid.

'Can you identify the clan?'

He looked over it judiciously.

'How did you get this?'

'It was in the river.'

'With that headless body of yours?'

'It was merely found washed up nearby. I am curious.'

He shook his head.

'I know some of the tartans, but I cannot be sure of this one. In Glasgow we prefer the Highlands to be contained *in* the Highlands, if you understand me. How they like to live is foreign to us and most rebarbative.'

He put on his hat and then doffed it with a small bow.

'I would be interested to know how this Highlander and his garments came into the River Ribble. And so, I am sure, would the Lord Lieutenant. Good day, gentlemen.'

Fidelis and I exchanged a sharp glance. That reference to Lord Derby. What did it mean?

'Is *he*, MacLintock, presuming to inform his lordship of events in Ribchester?' I said as MacLintock moved off down a side street. 'It's none of his business.'

'It might be if he happened to be a confidential informant of Lord Derby.'

'I don't believe it. We are falling in too much with general suspicions. Not everybody is a spy.'

'So MacLintock was only advancing a course of action – that you apply to Lord Derby for intelligence in this matter. It is not a bad suggestion.'

This was true: it was by no means a bad suggestion and, parting from my friend, I went directly to Patten House, Lord Derby's residence in Church Gate. I had reasonable hope of finding him in residence. Although it had no soldiers, Preston was a more central headquarters for directing the defence of

Lancashire than Derby's country seat at Knowsley, for it sat at the heart of a natural web of news and information.

If you wanted to meet the Lord Lieutenant at Patten House, you had to do so on his own terms. You craved an audience; he graciously inclined his head, or shook it, according to his own decision. There would often be a long wait in the room beside the entrance reserved for supplicants.

But I was in luck. The Earl invited me to go up to him directly. I found him in his shirtsleeves leaning over a map table. He was plotting a line with a pair of compasses.

'I hope this is important, Cragg. I am very busy.'

'My lord, two naked bodies have been discovered in the country around Ribchester. Both were decapitated.'

'Well? You are the Coroner. You know what to do.'

'I have an interesting problem of identification, with a possible bearing on the military situation. There was a tartan plaid nearby, and Doctor Fidelis's examination has shown evidence that one of the men may have been a wearer of the kilt.'

Still bent over his map, Derby half turned to me.

'Highlanders at Ribchester?'

'There was a note with one of the bodies – in the mouth, as a matter of fact. It was an exculpatory note, claiming that the men were killed by covenanters loyal to King George.'

'Do we know when this was?'

'We believe the victims may have come two days ago.'

'You are holding an inquest?'

'Tomorrow.'

'And this note in the mouth – an unusual procedure, I must say – was it signed?'

'It was unsigned, my lord, except that the author claimed to be a loyal covenanter.'

He straightened his back and laid down the compasses.

'Run through the facts in a little more detail, would you?'

Lord Derby listened to my account with close attention. I could see how the strain of the political and military circumstances showed on his face.

'So you have no idea of who these supposed covenanters were?' he said at last. 'Was not this man Pilling one of them?'

'I don't think so. His story is that the human remains were

foisted on him from another parish and I am inclined to believe him. His own reason for removing them again was that he didn't want the parish to bear the expense of an investigation. So he carted them secretly elsewhere.'

'But not secretly enough, evidently. As far as that goes, you have done well, Cragg. But I am wondering what brought these two men into Lancashire in the first instance.'

'Were they scouts for the rebel army?'

'The rebels are still at Carlisle. I don't think they would yet be sending scouting parties as far south as this. But letters are another matter. I am beginning to think that these two men must have been messengers from the Pretender to his supporters in this county.'

'And instead of delivering their message, they ran into trouble and met their deaths.'

'Precisely.'

Lord Derby moved from the map table to his writing table, on which were heaped numerous pieces of paper. He sifted through these until he came upon one, which he abstracted from the pile.

'Here is a list of the more prominent Jacobites in Lancashire, compiled by my zealous deputy, Sir Henry Hoghton. He has the tendency of seeing traitors in the cracks of his own boots, and there is no proof that all on the list intend to join the rebels, but never mind. Let us just see who we've got that the Pretender might write to, and where they live.'

He moved back to the map and planted his finger on the town of Blackburn.

'Townley Hall. They are rank Jacobites there, unquestionably. But I fancy we are looking for a house north of the Ribble.'

He looked again at the list and his finger came down much closer to Preston.

'This is the only one, I think.'

He was pointing to a spot north-east of Preston, not far from the village of Goosnargh. I moved to his side and read the name.

'Barrowclough Hall?'

'Yes. Do you know Sir John?'

'I know he's a member of Parliament – a Tory of the old school, by repute.'

'Just so. He's exactly the kind of fellow the Pretender would try to contact. Sir John is very rich and was in his younger days a courtier of Queen Anne. He's still active in certain parts of London society, and keeps a town house in Grosvenor Street, though one doesn't see him at court. And, of course, he is an outright Jacobite.'

'Then if my two dead men – one of them at least a Highlander – had been to Barrowclough Hall, how and why would they have met their deaths? If Sir John's politics are as you describe, one would expect them to have been received civilly at the very least. Instead, they were killed, and their bodies savagely mistreated afterwards.'

'But suppose Sir John happened not to be at home at the time. They would then have been received by Mr James Barrowclough – a fish with a very different look in his eye.'

'They are brothers?'

'Father and son. James is unmarried and lives at the Hall.'

'And you imply that he doesn't quite agree with his father's point of view on everything?'

'That is putting it mildly. They hate each other.'

'Suggesting that Mr James Barrowclough would be no supporter of the rebels.'

The Earl gave me an ironical smile.

'James Barrowclough is a rich subject of study in himself, Titus, as you must find out.'

The Lord Lieutenant was impatient to return to his maps, so I took my leave, after promising I would inform him if anything material came out of the inquest. Back at the office I mentioned to my clerk in passing that I was interested in the affairs of the Barrowclough family, and especially in the character of Mr James Barrowclough.

'Do you know who minds their legal business?'

'Rudgewick and Tench,' he said. 'I'll find out what I can.'

He clapped his hat on his head and went out. An hour later Furzey was back, with James Barrowclough's whole life story at his fingertips.

'I've spoken with Chapman, the head clerk at Rudgewick's,' he said. 'Young James was always athwart his father. He refused to go near either Oxford or Cambridge but took himself off to Europe where he made the Grand Tour as far as Rome, then looped back to the Low Countries and settled for a year at Leiden to study the science of medicine at the university there.'

'How could he do all that without his father's support?'

'Because James is rich in his own right. An uncle on his mother's side left him ten thousand pounds while he was still a schoolboy.'

'And yet he lives with Sir John at Barrowclough Hall.'

'Well, they live in the same house, but James is in the east wing and his father's in the west, with comical results. When they meet in the rooms between, Chapman says they agree on nothing. Sir John likes to employ a keyboard musician; Mr James detests the sound of the harpsichord. Mr James revels in chemical experiments; Sir John abominates the smell. Sir John loves the hunt and maintains his own pack of hounds; Mr James favours shooting and keeps a pair of Belgian pointer dogs. And so on.'

But according to Chapman's report to Furzey, it was politics and religion that caused the deepest rift between the Barrowcloughs. Sir John hankered after the Stuart restoration, but Mr James, having observed the Old Pretender at his papist rituals in Rome, found nothing to recommend the fellow. As far as religion was concerned, Sir John was a High Anglican with an unshakeable devotion to church ceremonial and the sacred hierarchy stretching down from kings, bishops and cathedral deans to the beneficed clergy, with their tithes and their parish courts. Mr James, on the other hand, had been a year in the Netherlands, where he'd caught the contagion of enthusiastic religion, and a passionate hatred of everything resembling Roman Catholicism. On his return to England he was entranced by the preaching of George Whitefield and John Wesley. He hosted them during their preaching tours of Lancashire and, to the great annoyance of his father, built a Calvinist chapel or meeting room in the grounds of the hall.

'But what's he like in himself?' I asked.

'He's quick to anger, and it's impossible to change his mind. If messengers from the rebels did come to the Hall, and fell into his hands, they might be in some serious difficulty.'

SIX

M y father, who was Coroner before me, used to reflect that our office is only that of a humble tax collector. The job, after all, is to assess whether dues are owed to the Crown in cases that may or may not be murder, treasure trove, shipwreck and the like. If committed by one who happened to be wealthy, murder can be very lucrative indeed, since all the murderer's worldly goods are forfeit – lands, properties, securities, beasts and valuables of all kinds – so a murder by one such as James Barrowclough is exactly what the First Lord of the Treasury likes to hear about. Ten thousand pounds poured straight into his coffers would finance a regiment of horse for a year.

After my meeting with Lord Derby, and much enlightened by Furzey's report, I was quite seized with the idea of Barrowclough as a guilty man in the two murders. The only questions I still faced were how to prove it and who else was in it with him. It was hard to see how one man could ever have done this alone.

The inquest was to be held the next day so, if I were to go out to Barrowclough Hall and look into the matter, it would have to be done straight away. There being only four or five hours of daylight left, I immediately sent word to Lawson's to saddle old Jones.

At Jones's tranquil pace it took more than an hour to reach Barrowclough Hall. Built in the time of the first King James, the house had hardly been altered in the years since, and its face of undressed stone with diamond-paned windows and nail-studded doors, the wings extending to the east and west of a low central tower, was somewhat forbidding. In the event, however, I did not get further than the pair of iron gates that faced the public road, through which could be seen a mature beech avenue a quarter of a mile long leading to the house. A pair of lodge cottages stood at each side of these gates, with columns of wispy smoke rising into the still air from their chimneys. They were exactly alike in the way that something is alike to its reflection in the mirror. I approached the door of the right-hand lodge and rapped on it.

My knock was answered with a flurry of barking. Presently, the door was opened by an ill-shaven, elderly man wearing a greatcoat that hung open, showing a dirty undershirt and breeches.

'What do you want?' he said, with not a hint of welcome in his tone.

The yapping mongrel got a cuff around the head, whimpered and fell silent.

'To see your master.'

Gloom filled the lodge behind him, and a fetid smell gusted out.

'On what business?'

'Coroner's business. You may be aware that two bodies were found this week in or near the parish of Ribchester. I am Coroner Cragg and I would like a conversation on the subject with Mr Barrowclough.'

The lodgekeeper raised his finger and pointed across the way to the opposite lodge.

'I serve Sir John. If it's *Mr* Barrowclough you're wanting, apply over there.'

He shut the door in my face.

I crossed to the corresponding lodge on the other side of the gates and knocked there. The door was opened promptly by a younger man, a man of striking good looks – I put his age at thirty – dressed in clean livery and a simple house-cap. A black cat performed a figure of eight around his ankles.

'I regret Mr James is not at home,' he told me when I'd named myself and stated my business. 'He's gone to market at Clitheroe with the dairyman. One of the milk cows has died and they've gone to get a new one.'

'And you are?'

'Abel Grant, sir. I have the honour of being Mr James's personal valet.'

'May I perhaps come inside? I find I am thirsty.'

The valet stood hospitably aside, and I walked into a small

lobby that opened on to an orderly parlour, its flags freshly
swept and fireplace glowing warmly. Abel Grant went into an
inner room and came out with a cup of ale, which he placed
in my hands.

'Of course we have heard about the murders at Ribchester,
Mr Cragg.'

Carefully, as servants do, he watched me drink.

'It is not surprising that they are talked about everywhere,'
I said, lowering the cup. 'I wonder if anyone hereabouts knows
who the dead men were, and who may have killed them.'

'Not that Mr Barrowclough's heard, sir. Mr Barrowclough's
on the magistrates' bench, so he's forced to take an interest.'

'You mean he's investigated the matter?'

'Mr Barrowclough is a gentleman. He does not investigate.
He requires others to do so and to report their findings to him.'

There was a commotion at the front door, and then it crashed
open. A voice called out at a pitch a little louder than strictly
necessary.

'Abel! Are you there? Come out and see what a fine milker
we've fetched from Clitheroe.'

A man, who might have been close to forty, burst in,
stopping short when he saw me.

'By heaven, Abel! You have company.'

'This is Mr Titus Cragg, sir,' said Grant. 'He is the County
Coroner, looking into the murders at Ribchester. Mr Cragg,
this is Mr James Barrowclough.'

Barrowclough extended his hand and we shook.

'How do, Cragg? You are a Prestonian, I believe. A
disgraceful town given to riot and debauchery, it seems. I never
go there. I suppose Grant has told you that we can tell you
nothing about the matter of these murders. They came, and
then they were gone, and it was the last we saw of them. I
did not—'

Abel Grant stepped forward and shot out an arm in warning
between Barrowclough and me.

'Mr Barrowclough, sir! I never mentioned that.'

Putting my hand on Abel Grant's arm, I gently pressed it
down.

'The two men,' I said, 'the murdered men – are you saying

they were here, Mr Barrowclough? At your house? Mr Grant has told me you didn't know who they were, yet you imply you saw them.'

Barrowclough frowned. The momentary uncertain glance he flicked in the direction of his valet told me that they might be more than a master and his servant. It hinted at some sort of confederacy between them.

'Well, what I meant to say was they *may* have been here.'

'Abel here says you have taken an interest.'

'I must, as a magistrate.'

'Have you found out who they were?'

'Who they were is of less interest to me than what their business was. They were not local men.'

'Perhaps they were passing through, as wayfarers, you know, and were assaulted. Have you heard of any highwaymen active hereabouts?'

'I doubt it was highwaymen.'

That was a reasonable doubt. Highwaymen did not behead their victims.

'Well, then,' I said, 'the inquest is at ten tomorrow morning. You are welcome to attend.'

'Very well,' he said.

Hearing this, Abel Grant seemed agitated.

'I wonder if that would be altogether wise of us, sir.'

'I do not see why not,' said Barrowclough.

'Mr Grant,' I said. 'I would be obliged if you would attend also.'

Grant seemed uncertain how to reply.

'I do have the power to compel, you know,' I added.

He exchanged a glance with his master.

'Well, er, yes, since you put it like that, I reckon so.'

'Then I will have both your summonses sent here.'

Grant walked me to the door of the cottage and held it open for me.

As I mounted Jones, I could hear from inside the men's voices raised in argument, but nothing of the subject at issue. I urged the old horse into a reluctant trot, and as we got going, I saw, a little way ahead of us, the dairyman proceeding along the muddy lane astride a bony mule. He was huddled in a greatcoat against the cold and wore a misshapen felt hat, its brim drooping wearily. Behind him, on the end of a rope halter, ambled a brindled cow, her milk-bag blown up with milk. The dairyman clicked his tongue to encourage her along. It took even old Jones only a short time to catch them up.

'How do?' I said as we drew alongside. 'That's a half-decent milk cow you have there.'

'This 'un'll do. There was a better, but Master wouldn't pay the price.'

'Oh? Tight with his money, is he?'

The fellow raised his head.

'He's careful with his money, Mister. But I say there's such a thing as being too careful. I say a man must spend high for the honour of the herd. He's got the money, has Mr Barrowclough, but his religion stops him. His religion is a hard religion. I don't hold with it.'

'They're saying there were two Scotchmen seen hereabouts and they met with accidents leading to their deaths. Have you heard this?'

'Aye, I've heard. But it were no accident.'

'What happened, then?'

'They knocked at the wrong door.'

The dairyman's laugh was somewhere between a wheeze and a run of hiccups.

'Should've gone to t'other lodge, old Jos Wrightington's door. Jos'd've told them Squire's not at home and sent them safe on their way. He's Sir John's man, is Jos, see? But damn my onions, they tried their luck at Abel Grant's door instead, and look where it fetched them? Abel Grant being Mr James's man, if you follow.'

His last three words came out of the side of his mouth, insinuatingly – *if you follow.*

'So Sir John Barrowclough is away from home?'

'He is that. In London, so they tell me, since last month. Parliament business. Them two Scotchmen might've had a welcome from him, but not his son. Not Mr James.'

'Did you see anything of the two Scotchmen? Do you know anything of what happened to them?'

The dairyman shook his head.

'No. And those that do, why should they tell?'

'You must have heard something. Tell me.'

I had overplayed my hand. The dairyman gave me a shrewd look from under his hat brim.

'Damned if I know anything, Mister Whoever-You-Are.'

We had come abreast a muddy yard surrounded by low, untidily thatched buildings, from which I could hear the moaning and shuffling of cattle.

'I'll bid you good day,' said the cowman. 'I must get this one milked or she'll burst.'

Without another word he directed his mule through the gate with the cow in tow. I rode on.

As Jones took me sedately home, I asked myself what I expected from the next day's inquest. A solid verdict was my usual answer to this question – the cause of death and the naming of the responsible party, if there was one. When someone kills someone, it is normally murder, manslaughter or self-defence. Neither of the last two had ever in my experience concluded in a beheading, so I reckoned the appropriate finding must be murder, and strong hints received from the servant Abel Grant and the cowman were telling me James Barrowclough might know more about it than he'd told me. Yet he had agreed to attend the inquest. If he was complicit in the deaths, why would he poke his head above the parapet like that?

In the evening before supper I put my head into the Turk's Head. Luke Fidelis was there, in close discussion with Adam Clark and a couple of men dressed in the sober clothing of nonconformists. As I took a chair at a vacant table, one of these puritans wagged his finger at Clark and my friend, and I could hear fragments of the threatening biblical quotation one of them was deploying in the argument.

'"So then because you are lukewarm and neither cold nor hot I will spue thee out of my mouth." So says Scripture, my brothers. So says the Good Lord.'

Catching sight of me, Fidelis made no reply but detached himself and came over. We sat down together. I noticed the two men moving on to join a group of shopkeepers gathered at another table. They had a paper and were showing it to them.

'They try to browbeat us with the Bible,' Fidelis told me. 'We must take sides, they say. We must all join this covenant against the rebels that is in circulation. I refuse, however. I am not sure this is my quarrel at all. Whether the King is from Italy or Germany is all the same to me. Did you learn anything from your visit to Barrowclough Hall?'

'I never entered the hall proper. I reached no further than the lodge cottages.'

'You saw Sir John?'

'No. Sir John is in London. I met Mr James Barrowclough – I do not like him, by the way. He is supercilious.'

'Apart from that, what did you learn?'

'I heard rumour from one mouth, and hints from another, that the two Highlanders were indeed at Barrowclough Hall around the start of the week. It is possible that they did fall into the hands of James Barrowclough or his men. Barrowclough is a passionate opponent of the Pretender, so he may have had to do with their deaths.'

'If the dead men were emissaries from the rebels, I can believe it. But we should ask, does that fit the facts as we know them, Titus? Pilling moved the body and the head that turned up at Simmy Nook. But why was it put there in the first place?'

'Yes, and what about the other one that was found in the river? It would have been better simply to bury them some-where and have nothing more said. And why were the heads matched with the wrong bodies?'

'If the killers were in a hurry, the exchange of the heads was probably an accident – a muddle – and needn't trouble the jury at your inquest. The key question remains: why were the bodies left where they would be found?'

'I can only pursue the question at the inquest tomorrow. If James Barrowclough gives evidence, it will be interesting, that's certain, though I wonder if he will show his face after all.'

Now we heard a degree of commotion by the main door of the coffee house. A fellow had come in, his face red from running. Soon he was surrounded by other patrons and it was evident he had something important to say. But instead of telling it to all and sundry, he went to the proprietor Noah Plumtree and spoke into his ear. Plumtree nodded his head sagely, moved into the centre of the room and climbed ponderously on to a table.

'Can I have a bit of hush, gentlemen!' he intoned, and the hubbub drained away. 'Jerome Plint here has come from the post office. There is news just come in and, I must tell you, it is grave news.'

He paused, savouring the moment of suspense, until someone shouted out, 'Tell us, then, Plumtree.'

'Carlisle has surrendered,' said our host. 'The castle is taken by the rebels. Within days they will march south and all will be just as it was last time, in 'fifteen. Therefore it would seem we must all prepare for the worst.'

I spent the evening in my library reading about war and power in Shakespeare, and when I shut the book, I decided to have a turn in my garden as the rain had now stopped. Reaching the far end, I heard the sound of a spade turning earth on the other side of the wall that divided my house from that of Lionel Burroughs. As midnight digging is one of the most suspicious activities a person can be doing, I determined to see what I could see. We had a stone seat beside the wall and on this I stood so that I could peer over.

The digging was being done by lamplight, and the digger was Lionel Burroughs himself. He was in his shirt and had completed a hole three or four feet deep. I could hear him panting and muttering curses to himself as he worked. This was unaccustomed toil for a man of his standing. Burroughs was a cabinet maker but he was well-to-do enough by this date to have delegated all work of the hands, let alone of the muscles, to his men at the Burroughs workshops.

'Lionel,' I called out. 'What are you doing digging your garden at this strange hour?'

We were never close to the family but had usually kept cordial relations. On this night Lionel, who was always inclined to bluster, answered me with no cordiality at all.

'The devil, sir! You gave me a start. What do you mean by prying? I am going about my own business in my own property and you are spying me. Get down from there and mind your business!'

'I mean no harm, Lionel,' I said. 'I am relieved to see it is you with the spade, and not a villain intent on making away with your box hedge.'

Burroughs did not find this funny. He shook his finger at me.

'These are dangerous days. I have already sent Emmy and the girls into the country. I would advise you to mind your business, Cragg, instead of mine. Those who don't take precautions will pay a price, I warn you.'

Later, when I told Elizabeth of all this, she laughed.

'So he has sent his women to safety, Titus, and is burying his treasure. Should you not do the same?'

'Where would you like to go, my love?'

'In the country? Last time we went there, well . . .'

In the summer of the previous year we had spent an eventful few weeks in a primitive village in east Lancashire.

'Exactly,' I said. 'Sometimes it is better not to act too impulsively. Fear is the devil for driving rashly. We shall stay put for the moment.'

'Yes. It would be a pity to miss all the fun.'

'If there's a battle, it won't be fun.'

'There may never be a battle. We must wait and see.'

SEVEN

The inquest at Ribchester convened at ten o'clock, with a panel of jurors half made up of gruff countrymen from the farms thereabouts, and half from among the little town's population of qualified men, owning a dwelling or patch of yard valued at five pounds or more. No such qualification was required of the audience, who were men and women in every condition of life, from well-to-do to ragged, and not a few of their children.

Before we began, I had a short, backs-turned conference with Constable Norris.

'Have any more of the clothes from these bodies been found?'

'Not a stitch, Mr Cragg. There's just the blanket thing you brought in yourself from the riverbank.'

'And has no one come forward with more information, such as where the killings took place and, of course, who was responsible?'

Norris's honest face now looked flustered, as if I had accused him of hiding pertinent information.

'I assure you, Mr Cragg, there is no further intelligence on the matter.'

'Well, I'm glad to say I have some bits and pieces, though whether they add up will become clear only as the inquest proceeds.'

Norris arched his eyebrows in surprise.

'What is it, Mr Cragg?'

'You must pay attention to the evidence, Norris, and you may learn.'

'You know who did it, sir?'

'I did not say that. Please do not spread that as a rumour.'

I left him and, as I went to my chair, the church clock could be heard striking ten. I called the room to order and went on to swear the jurors one by one to bring a true verdict and so on and so on. I then took them into the adjoining room where the corpses were arranged on trestle tables for the traditional viewing. Removing the covering sheets, I showed them the manner of severance of the two heads and they whispered together, variously expressing wonder, shock or disgust. We looked at the other wounds and noticed any signs of interest, such as the weather-beaten knees of the one compared with the lily-white knees of the other.

In less than a minute we were filing out of the side room and back into the main hall, where the jurors took their places again on the jury bench. I called the assembly to order and explained how we would proceed. I told the jury that even though the bodies were found in different places, we must examine the two deaths together, since it was obvious from the evidence they would hear that the men were associated and had been killed at the same time and for the same reason. We would therefore start with the first finders of the headless bodies and the severed heads.

We began as ever with the narrative of how the bodies had been discovered. A shamefaced Abraham Pilling came first. He admitted that he removed the corpse that he and others had found that night outside the Black Cat at Simmy Nook, and had taken it by cart into Farmer Ambleside's field. He swore he had done nothing to the body – it had been naked when he'd set eyes on it and he had nothing to do with removing its clothes, nor did he know where those clothes were. I asked him why the head had not been found along with the body on the frozen windypit, and there was much laughter when he told how it had rolled off the back of his cart and gone into the ditch in the dark without his minding it. I let the constable off lightly, with only some mild words of reproof, as his former cocky manner had disappeared and he seemed thoroughly chastened, not least by being the butt of jokes.

Luke Fidelis then told how he'd found the head lying in a ditch half a mile from Simmy Nook, after which it was the turn of the fisherman who had spotted the other body after it caught in reeds below the bridge at Ribchester. This had been on Thursday morning just as the light was breaking, with the river in full spate after the night's heavy rain. He had first seen one of the arms just below the surface and had taken it for a dead pike, hooking it with his pole gaff in the hope of a good supper of broiled fish that night.

'And did you turn Caliban and eat the arm?' shouted someone from the room. There was more laughter. The people of Ribchester were in a humour to enjoy themselves at this unexpected entertainment.

The mood became more serious as the last of the finders, little Margery Bruff, came forward. She was brought by her mother but could not be persuaded to speak until I granted she could sit on Mrs Bruff's knee and whisper her answers into the ear of her mother, who then related them out loud for the benefit of the room. By this means we found out that Margery had been looking for fairies in the water meadow when she had seen what she thought was the face of a troll caught in the willow tree, which she told her sister about. I then completed the tale, describing how I'd later accompanied the child to the place and so recovered the severed head.

Next I called Luke Fidelis to return to the stand. He summarized his own medical findings, including the significance of the wounds, and what had been in the stomachs, and went on to show how he had matched the heads to the appropriate bodies, after explaining the careful way in which the cutting-off had been done.

'Do you remark anything about how the heads were severed?' I asked. 'With what instrument, perhaps?'

'I would hazard that it was done by someone used to cutting flesh, with an appropriate instrument.'

'A surgeon?'

'Anyone from surgeon to experienced butcher.'

'Now, doctor, in our viewing of the bodies we noticed a difference in the legs, and in particular around the area of the knees, of the two victims. Can you confirm this and tell us what it might mean?'

'Yes. The older man almost certainly wore the Scotch Highland kilt – a skirt worn by the common people in that part of the world. The younger victim wore breeches, as we do. I could tell this from the weathering of the skin around the knees of the older man.'

'What did it suggest to you?'

'Well, it suggested two things. One is that they were Scotch and that the older man was a Highlander wearing his traditional dress – the kilt.'

A tremor of excitement ran visibly through the audience. Everyone knew that the Pretender's army was made up of Highlanders, and many believed that they were savage brutes.

'And the other thing?'

'That the two men were probably from different ranks in society. Hypothetically, they were a young master and his older servant.'

I now stood, unfolded the tartan cloth we had found in the water meadow beside the river and held it up to be seen by all.

'This is part of the Highland dress,' I said. 'It is a "plaid" – that is, a kind of blanket worn around the upper body. The kilt worn with it would have displayed the same pattern of colours, rightly called a tartan, and there is a different pattern of tartan for each of the Highland clans, or families. Now this plaid was found near the river where one body and one head were found on Thursday last. Its tartan is therefore a clue about the identity of the one who wore it. I wonder, does anybody present know the name of the clan that wears this particular one?'

I looked around the room. There was a general murmuring, but none had a suggestion.

'Well, Doctor Fidelis,' I went on, 'did your examination yield any further discoveries?'

'Yes. I found a communication from the killers – a letter inside the mouth of one of the severed heads.'

The audience gasped.

'Is this the letter?'

I held the paper up for all to see, then handed it to Fidelis, who confirmed that it was.

'Then please be good enough to read it out loud.'

In a clear voice Fidelis did so, to a room absolutely quiet and attentive apart from a baby or two, and an old man who had fallen asleep and was snoring into his beard. After he had finished, I heard a few low whistles of surprise from the audience, followed by a burst of chatter. Suppressing this, I called James Barrowclough, who came to the witness chair and took his oath with an air of puzzlement.

'Did you see two strangers, one in Highland dress, on or near your land on Tuesday?'

'No. And I must say I am at a loss to explain why I have been called here.'

'It is because you told me that the two Scotchmen were on your land last Tuesday.'

'So they were, as I myself was told, and as I told you.'

'Ah! But you did not see them yourself?'

'I did not tell you I had seen them.'

'That is not my question.'

'It is my answer. You are under the impression that I admitted to having seen them. I am saying I did not. I merely told you that two strangers were seen – by my estate workers, as it happened – riding across my land.'

'When was this?'

'In the afternoon of Tuesday, I think.'

'Did they visit you at the Hall?'

'I have already answered that.'

'I mean without you seeing them?'

Exasperation altered his voice.

'No. No, they did not, sir.'

'Mr Barrowclough, are you a signatory of a covenant sworn to oppose the Pretender and his forces?'

'I am, along with hundreds of others.'

'And you signed the covenant because you are a passionate opponent of the cause of the House of Stuart.'

'I am a passionate patriot. I do not acknowledge the claims of the Pretender; it is why I call him by that name.'

I passed him the letter Fidelis had found.

'Is this your handwriting?'

'No. I write with my left hand and therefore form my letters differently.'

'Perhaps you had this written by another, then, at your dictation.'

'I did not.'

'Is it not the case that you learned surgical skills during

your time in Holland, and that these skills came in handy
when you were dealing with the two dead Scotchmen?'

'Yes, I did, and no, they didn't, and your second suggestion
is an outrage.'

I took him round the subject once more and Barrowclough,
with varying degrees of irritation, parried all my questions.

Finally, I said, 'I put it to you one last time that these two
Scotchmen came to call at your house, thinking they would
find your father in residence – your father who differs from
you about the legitimacy of the House of Stuart – and that
when they discovered their mistake, they tried to get away but
you killed them and then, using your surgical skills, cut off
their heads. Is that true, Mr Barrowclough?'

'No, no, no! This is a lie and slanderous. Neither did I
do those things, nor shall you ever prove that I did. And I say
this: those who speak loosely on this subject shall answer
for their recklessness. I give my word on it.'

We'd travelled no further from the ground he had established
in replying to my first enquiries, so I relieved him and called
his man, Abel Grant.

His evidence took us no further, however. Grant knew of two
riders being seen on the roads. He gave no sign of knowing
anything else. Nor could he throw light on the covenanters'
letter. He was not a covenanter, and he did not recognize the
handwriting. He had answered me in a controlled, smooth tone.

'Is there any man or woman present who can give testimony
to help us in this matter?' I asked the room once Grant had
been let go.

I looked around the hall and waited twenty or thirty seconds.
No voice was raised and no one came forward. So I rose and
turned to the jury.

'Gentlemen, there will be no further evidence given in this
inquest. We must proceed to a verdict, but first I have a few
remarks. We have here a case unique, I think, in my long
experience of inquests. Two men are killed and then beheaded.
The bodies and heads were left to be found in different places,
and the heads had been switched so that they did not match
the bodies they were found with. The two dead men, we have
reason to presume, are Scotchmen acting as some sort of

advance party of the army that has lately descended from
Scotland openly in arms against the King. Our presumption
is supported by the finding of plaid clothing typical of a
Highlander which was (again presumably) washed up out of
the river at the same time as human remains that had been
likewise washed up not far away. It is further supported by
the extraordinary note found inside the mouth of one of the
heads, that had been found earlier beside another headless
body on Mr Ambleside's land. The contents of this note,
purporting to be written by subscribers to a loyal covenant,
has been read out to you.

'What can we make of this? It is for you gentlemen to
decide the nature of this killing. I would only add, by way of
guidance, that killing in war is certainly exempt from the
charge of criminal murder, but this exemption is usually
restricted to soldiers. Can whoever did this deed be regarded
as a soldier, just because they signed a covenant swearing to
defend the realm? Such covenanters have never been constituted as a military force. They have typically been civilians.
Meanwhile, a soldier knows his duty without signing any
covenant. So you must ask, does the fact of signing this
covenant excuse this act of killing?

'Finally, please consider whether you believe the contents
of the covenanters' note. As we do not know who they are, it
is impossible to test their truthfulness. That is all I have to
say at the moment, but tell me if I can be of any further
assistance in this difficult task. I now ask you now to consider
your verdict.'

It was a frowning jury that huddled together in a corner of
the room to confer, while the audience debated the question
amongst themselves, some of them heatedly. After ten minutes
the foreman, a sensible fellow named Eastwood, came back
to me.

'We cannot decide the question of whether it was a justified
killing, Mr Cragg. We know not a scrap about these so-called
rebels for sure, bar their taste in clothing.'

'They were killed, however,' I said. 'Your decision hangs
on whether to be a covenanter gives you the right to kill a
rebel.'

He looked at me shrewdly.

'We're bamboozled about that, Mr Cragg. It's a question for a lawyer, is that.'

He was right, of course, and even I – as a lawyer – could not give him the answer he wanted.

'Very well, I propose you set it aside,' I said. 'State the fact as you see it, Mr Eastwood.'

'That they died by one or more unknown hands, justified or not.'

'Strike out "justified or not" and that seems the only possible verdict at our present state of knowledge. If you all agree on it, I shall allow it.'

Eastwood returned to his colleagues and I saw them nodding their heads. They returned to their bench, and the verdict was given: killed by an unknown hand or hands. I discharged them with a few words of thanks and brought the hearing to an end.

Fidelis and I rode back on the road to Preston, with Furzey mounted uncomfortably behind me on old Jones's rump.

'You pushed Barrowclough hard,' said Fidelis.

'But not hard enough. He is holding something back, I'm sure.'

'He owns to being a covenanter. He might also be a murderer.'

'Or is it a hero, Luke? A defender of the realm.'

'Did I not say it was a ticklish question?' said Furzey into my ear. 'Whether this is a criminal matter is far outside the competence of simple-minded Ribchester people.'

'Which Mr Eastwood acknowledged,' I said. 'But it is disrespectful to call a jury simple-minded, you know.'

Fidelis laughed.

'And yet I have heard you many times curse the stupidity of the panel,' he said.

'Separately, they may be stupid, Luke, but we must always respect them as a body. My father has many times dinned into my ears that the jury is the rock on which our law stands. Without it, we are barbarians or live under tyranny.'

'Yes, and not least the tyranny of lawyers. The foreman admitted only a lawyer could settle the question of murder. What does the lawyer say, then? Was it murder?'

'You must ask one of more proficiency than me. But without the knowledge of who did it, I doubt even he would give a safe answer as to whether it was murder according to the criminal law. But I do know this: by the moral law, that was a beastly murderous act by someone.'

That night I lay a long time awake. I had told myself before the inquest that I hoped for a solid verdict. I had not got one and now I couldn't get the two dead Scotchmen out of my head: their names unknown, their deaths unaccounted for; their families far away and all unaware.

Inconclusive inquests are the bane of my profession, but they are impossible sometimes to avoid. There is the lack of evidence, the mendacity of witnesses, and the slippery operation of evil by which the innocent are so often struck unnaturally dead, and the guilty go free. Yes, death unappeased weighs heavy.

EIGHT

The next day was Sunday and in Preston they would talk of nothing but the fall of Carlisle and the impending descent of the rebel army upon us. Our vicar being a great loyalist, his sermon that morning dwelt on the evils of revolt. It told of how the Lord ordered Saul the King to rid the world of the Amalekites, starting with their king and ending with their best sheep and oxen.

'But Saul disobeyed,' said the vicar. 'He slaughtered the Amalekites quickly enough, but spared their king and kept the livestock. Angrily, the Lord stripped Saul of his kingship saying' – here he intoned his text in a ringing voice – '"For rebellion is as the sin of witchcraft, and stubbornness is as iniquity and idolatry. Because thou hast rejected the word of the Lord, he hath also rejected thee from being King."'

Many quailed under the vicar's eye as it raked the congregation, not unlike the eye of the eagle into which his lectern was carved.

'These words of the Book of Samuel are extraordinarily prescient, my friends. Here in our own time we have a man – the Pretender in Rome – whom the Lord has rejected not once but again and again as king of this realm. And yet now we have his son stubbornly coming back here in arms to make another rebellion against the Lord's anointed king, His Majesty King George. I will only say this: in the hour of trial do not yourselves be tempted into rebellion. Do not fall into a sin as wicked as witchcraft. And for those of you already fallen into that sin, abandon it. For "stubbornness is as iniquity and idolatry". Abandon it, I say, and you shall be saved. Abandon it not and you shall be cast away by the Lord and suffer the dire perdition of all who are stubborn against Him.'

Lord Derby had attended worship with his wife and son, Lord Strange. Afterwards in the melee outside the church his lordship sought me out.

'Good day, Cragg. Clever sermon from the vicar, I thought. Should put the fear of God into anyone thinking of throwing in their lot with the rebels. By the way, I have written to you, in which connection I'll expect you tomorrow in the morning. It is a matter that bears on your recent inquest. Yes, my dear?'

Lady Derby had come to his side and was plucking his elbow. She drew him away.

I found his lordship's letter on the hall table when I returned from church. It had been written the previous day.

Cragg, he wrote, *from reports I have heard it seems you suspect who killed and beheaded those two Highlanders. I will not write his name, but the fellow's lawyer has been bothering me. Will you come to Patten House on Monday to talk the matter over? The lawyer has new evidence for you. Derby.*

The next morning, then, as the many clocks in Patten House were chiming nine, I sat outside the Lord Lieutenant's business room. Through the door I heard voices raised in argument, and when at last the door opened, half a dozen men from the Corporation of Preston filed out. Each of them gave me a grim glance as he passed.

'Those are not happy fellows,' said Lord Derby as I went in. 'They are frightened and want me to bring the militia here and summon a regiment of dragoons. Well, the militia is useless – not enough officers and a paltry ragbag of men. And how in God's name am I to procure a cavalry troop? I told the Corporation I had more to think about than Preston. The whole of Lancashire is at the mercy of the Pretender now.'

'There are others who say we are better off undefended, my lord. They mind what happened last time there was fighting here, when the town suffered so grievously.'

'Well, if it should come to a serious fight, open ground is always better from a civilian point of view. Ah! Rudgewick! Please join us.'

Richard Rudgewick, who had appeared at the door, slid into the room. He was one of those small dapper men who thought themselves devilishly alluring but who, in fact, had very little charm and a good deal of self-importance.

'Perhaps you know that Mr Rudgewick is the legal

representative of James Barrowclough,' Lord Derby said. 'He brings word from Barrowclough Hall. Say your piece, Rudgewick, and be quick about it. I am extremely busy.'

Rudgewick cleared his throat and addressed me directly.

'Before I impart the important information entrusted to me by Mr James Barrowclough, I have something on my own account to say to Mr Cragg. Mr Barrowclough considers your handling of Saturday's inquest to be an outrage, sir. Your examination of him was tantamount to an accusation of murder and he is minded to bring an action.'

'He has no grounds,' I said. 'It was our duty to examine the facts as best we could. The hearing dealt only with those facts. And they did not in the end lead us to name any killer or killers.'

'We are concerned not with the facts but with your words. Your accusations of murder.'

'Accusations? Suggestions at most, I would say, made in the normal course of questioning. That is entirely proper. And by the way, I am and was not even certain it can be called a murder, and nor were the jury.'

'Come, come, gentlemen,' interrupted Lord Derby. 'The substantive business, if you please. Mr Rudgewick, you told me your client has new evidence of interest to the Coroner, and to me. Well, we are here. What is it?'

'Very well, my lord. It is a letter come into the hands of Mr Barrowclough which is addressed to friends of the Pretender in this county. Mr Barrowclough believes it was carried by the two deceased rebels. The letter asks for help both in funds and in volunteers to the rebel army. This letter is in short a gross incitement to sedition.'

'Who signed it?'

'The pretended prince, my lord.'

'And which friends are addressed?'

'It is not specific as to names. It is a general letter.'

Lord Derby extended his hand and snapped the fingers.

'Show me the letter.'

'I don't have it, my lord. Mr Barrowclough keeps it at home, for safety.'

Lord Derby's features clouded in displeasure.

'That is unfortunate. And you have not even a copy of it?'

'No, my lord.'

He considered for a moment, then said, 'Oh God. I had better go and see Barrowclough myself. It is a great bother as I have very much business in hand, but I want to see this letter with my own eyes. Be so kind as to send to him, Rudgewick, and tell him I will wait on him in the morning at nine. Cragg, you had better come with me, as this touches on your inquest. Be so good as to come here at eight, and we shall ride together. That concludes our business for now. Good day, gentlemen.'

James Barrowclough received us in the stone-flagged great hall of the old mansion in which he lived with his (at present) absent father. Towards the Lord Lieutenant, Mr Barrowclough cringed deferentially; of me, he took as little notice as possible.

Our host and the Earl exchanged small talk while a handsome pair of twin footmen (I assumed twins as they looked extraordinarily alike with vivid ginger hair) brought in refreshment. His lordship, as soon as the footmen left us, pressed on directly to the point.

'I am here to look over the letter that Mr Rudgewick has told me about. The one that came into your hands purporting to be from the rebel camp.' He gave Barrowclough a transfixing look. 'The one that sought contributions of money and men.'

Barrowclough met his lordship's gaze for a moment, then wilted and looked away. He lifted his arms from his sides in a gesture of haplessness.

'It is gone, my lord. I deeply regret. It is destroyed.'

'Destroyed?'

Barrowclough now waved towards the great stone fireplace, where a heap of logs blazed.

'It is burned. In that fireplace.'

Lord Derby was momentarily lost for words. He swung around and stared at the flames in an accusatory way.

'You had better explain yourself, man,' he said, his eyes now more raptorial than ever. 'From what I have heard, that letter is of considerable importance to the state. How did it come to be burned?'

A pair of oak settles faced each other in front of the

fireplace, with a low table between them. Barrowclough
gestured at this table.

'The letter was here, you see. I had been reading it and laid
it down as I was obliged to ease nature, and so went outside.
A gust of wind from the open door must have blown the letter
into the fire. When I returned, the last of it was being consumed
in flame.'

Lord Derby sat down on one of the settles and gestured to
us that we both sit with him. His face looked pained, with an
edge of anger.

'And you have made no copy?'

'I regret, my lord.'

Lord Derby was agitated in a way rarely seen in him.

'By God,' he said, 'that is damned careless, Barrowclough.
That is damned . . . So I have come all the way out here on
a fool's errand!'

He flexed his fingers, making and unmaking a fist. His jaw
tightened. For a full quarter of a minute he said nothing,
appearing to be attending only to the crackling of the fire.
Then, mastering himself, he sighed.

'Very well, there is nothing to be done. You had better tell
me how and when you got this letter.'

'It was on Sunday, my lord. It had been delivered during
the night. No one saw the person. It was pushed under the
front door and found by my man when he came in the morning.'

'Do you mean Abel Grant?' I put in.

'Yes, of *course* I mean Abel Grant,' he said testily, and
without looking at me. 'Anyway, my lord, the people who had
killed the two rebels must have recovered the letter from one
of their pockets, or a bag, and thought fit to deliver it to me,
as local magistrate, since it was clearly seditious.'

'Was there any indication who it was addressed to?'

'No. The letter was headed something like "to all English
men and women who would rejoice at the restoration of the
true monarchy under King James III", or some such treason-
able twaddle.'

'And how was it signed?'

'It was signed Charles Edward by the Grace of God . . . I
am sorry, my lord. I can hardly say the hateful words.'

'By the Grace of God what?'

'Regent of Scotland and Prince of Wales.'

Derby smiled tightly.

'So that is how he styles himself. He has nerve, I'll say that. So tell me what you can of the letter's substance.'

'He announces in the most pompous terms that he has come to restore his house to the crowns of Scotland and England. He then asks for all who love his cause to rally to his standard with men, horses, arms and money. These men who died were carrying this wicked message all around the county. What happened to them – well, I myself had nothing to do with it, but they deserved to die, so I do think.'

'They suffered a hideous cruelty, nevertheless,' I said.

Now, for the first time, Barrowclough turned to me.

'Look here, Cragg: "An evil man seeketh rebellion: therefore, a cruel messenger shall be sent against him." Will you cast doubt on the Proverbs of the Lord? And will you allow evil to prosper?'

'Much as you may prefer it, we do not live in biblical times, Barrowclough,' said Lord Derby. 'However, it is not the manner of these deaths I regret so much as the missed opportunity. Those men should have been taken up and brought to me for questioning. Valuable information has been lost about the Pretender's intentions and the strength and morale of his army, and so on. We know little enough about all that, and this whole business has been a pitiful train of carelessness and waste.'

He stood up.

'Well, I can see nothing useful about prolonging this conference. I must get back now. Much to do. Good day, Barrowclough.'

The Lord Lieutenant strode towards the door and I followed him.

'Cragg,' said Lord Derby as we rode through the gate and out on to the rutted road, 'your horse is such a dawdle; I must leave you to wend your way alone. I have a heap of work to attend to.'

He applied his spurs and the horse leapt into a trot and then a canter as the Lord Lieutenant hurried on his way back to Preston. As for Jones and me, we continued on at the old horse's desultory pace.

*　　*　　*

After leaving Jones at the stable, I was crossing Market Place when I saw a fellow standing on the steps of the monument. A small crowd had gathered to hear him rant against the Highlanders.

'Barbarous, they are, both in their clothes and language, believe me. And also in their way of fighting. They like to hack at you with a bloody big sword they call a claymore before they close with you and take you on hand to hand using a stabbing knife they call a dirk. Their joy in slaughter knows no bounds, my friends, and likewise their appetite for rape and eating human flesh. And now they come. They come. And all they seek is to destroy us and ruin our just society and agreeable customs, all because we love decorum, speak civilized English and wear coats and breeches.'

Listening to this rant, I was reminded of Michael Montaigne who laughs at those that think everything abroad is barbarous, while all at home is done perfectly. It is in the essay on cannibals. This suspicion of foreigners and their habits was called by the Greeks 'misoxeny', which is a rare word in English. Only recently I had maintained to Fidelis that those who manage their justice without a jury are barbarians. Am I then a misoxenist? In the evening I asked the question of Elizabeth and she said not, unless it counts that she had many times heard me cursing the barbarous people of Wigan.

The events in that time – exciting to some, dreadful for others – have a way of crowding together in the memory, so that what happened seems to have occurred higgledy-piggledy, as in a dream. Reference to my other, more orderly memory – I mean my journal – allows me to put them in order.

Wednesday November the Twentieth.

The thermometer shows the weather colder. No news of the rebels.

I found Matty in tears while using the smoothing iron. She is afraid of the Highlanders.

Hector is walking without tottering now & claps his

hands. He points to all sorts of objects & gives them names, but only approximations of their real names.

I delivered my inquest report to His Lp this morning & found Patten House in a fluster. He is locking up & will remove himself and his family to London. I asked does he advise that I take my own family out of Preston & he said, 'I will not counsel you either way. But it is an important consideration that it is I not you that is Lancashire's Lord Lieutenant.'

Later I discussed this question with Elizabeth. We agree it is no good to go on the roads when times are uncertain, the weather is cold and wet, & the only horse on hand is Jones. We shall face what comes.

Thursday November the Twenty-first.

The rebels are still at Carlisle. News has come from there saying they forage the farms thereabouts & tax the merchants, but do not move. The Prince holds daily council & supervises manoeuvres.

It sleeted today & little more happened except business. Many are reviewing their wills & we are plagued at the office by requests from anxious clients to have their title deeds & other muniments back, that they might make sure they are safe.

Others are filling their storerooms with food and fuel. I have scoured the town for sea coals & firewood. Supplies are scant & prices increased by three times. Elizabeth has already secured a large ham, a shoulder of pork for pickling, much salt, butter & flour, & plentiful turnips & potatoes. She is a rare housewife. At night we kissed each other, & so on. Her love is my delight, & my comfort. & mine hers, I hope.

Friday November the Twenty-second.

In the afternoon a rider came from Kendal, less than fifty miles to the south of Carlisle. The Mayor questioned him & it is proclaimed that nothing of the rebel army has yet

been seen at Kendal. At Preston the town-talk is all, what
to do? The people watch each other like spies, trying to
discover inner intention from outer action. The excitement
of all the Jacobites here is palpable & the fear in the others
ditto.

Saturday November the Twenty-third.

A clergyman travelling out of Lancaster reports that word
has come there from the north of the rebels being on the
move. Some Prestonians that swore they would never
flee to the country are now preparing to sheer off. Others
who swore they would quit the town are still here. I am
reminded of the time I watched a beheaded chicken
running hither & thither.

Sunday November the Twenty-fourth.

Scotch outriders have been seen in the roads between
Penrith & Kendal. The main body must be in Penrith
itself. The town-talk is all disputes between our Jacobites
and the rest.

Monday November the Twenty-fifth.

We have word that the rebels are marching fast & are in
Kendal. There is a report confirming that the Prince does
not ride but walks at the head of the army. No one doubts
now that we must expect them here in Preston within the
week.

I had a conference early with Furzey. We picked out
the most important documents in our keeping at the office,
& locked them in a strongbox, but now I don't know
what to do with the strongbox.

Later, I drank with Luke Fidelis at the Turk's Head.
We spoke of my day's work as follows:

LUKE: You have brought everything of large value
together & put it into one box?

ME: We have. So if the office were looted or burned, we would not lose anything irreplaceable.

L: It is a mistake, Titus. If you concentrate all your valuables in one place, you can easily lose all. If you scatter them, you will probably miss only a few.

M: I don't want to miss any.

L: What are these valuables?

M: Title deeds, marriage contracts, deeds of entailment, old charters.

L: But if the rebels come here, they'll only want ready money & valuables. They will find your box &, naturally thinking it contains money & jewels, what will they do?

M: Force it open?

L: Of course, & finding no money or jewels they will be enraged & likely destroy the lot.

M: Then I shall not let them find the box. Those papers have enormous value.

L: To a looting Highlander they will be good for nothing but fire-lighting & wiping their bottoms.

Fidelis's reasoning is not always stronger than my instinct, but this time it prevailed. I took all the papers out of the strongbox & replaced them where had been before in the cellar, much to the disgust of Furzey who prophesied ruin.

The rebels are at Lancaster. The town-talk has turned apocalyptic. Will they be here tomorrow?

NINE

First thing next morning a message came that I was needed on coroner's business at Penwortham, which lies on the southern bank of the Ribble. Glad to have employment on this anxious day, I immediately went down to the ferry, crossed to Middleforth Green and walked along the bankside path to Penwortham. It is a sizeable village with a very imposing parish church, once, I believe, a Priory church. My mission was to a house in which lived Horace Limmington, a retired gentleman of much reduced means.

I was ushered in by a serving woman of unknowable age, with a discontented twist about her mouth.

'He's in the parlour.'

She opened a door and I entered. It was a gloomy room with little furniture and no fire in the grate, so it was also very cold. Sitting at an oak table was a down-at-heel figure in a skull cap, shabby greatcoat and woollen gloves, reading a newspaper with the help of a single candle. I had known the man professionally, as in more prosperous days he had been a client for whom I had drawn up several contracts. He had had a considerable business in linens and cottons.

'I am right glad you are here, Mr Cragg,' he said. 'Well, before we proceed to business, you must tell me: has His Highness arrived in Preston? Have you seen him?'

His eyes were shining, by which I perceived that Limmington was cast from the same mould that produced William Entwhistle and the Parkinsons: a true believing Jacobite.

'No, we haven't seen him yet,' I said. 'We expect him hourly and hope there will be no fighting. No army approaches to oppose him, which gives hope they will occupy our town peaceably.'

Limmington looked pleased. He lowered his voice.

'As the song says, he is coming into his own again. That is what *I* believe. Are you with him or against, Mr Cragg? Which side?'

I replied briskly enough, not wanting to have another discussion about this matter, being (I must confess) a little out of patience with the endless chatter and speculation about it.

'I do not take a side, Limmington. Now, tell me, what is the matter you want to discuss?'

'I've something wonderful to show you.'

He picked up the candle and took me into another room, as dark and bare as the other but which, from its mostly bare bookcases, appeared to have once been a study or library. Here, on a table, lay a bulging leather purse, which Limmington snatched up. In some excitement he loosened the string, pulled the purse's mouth open and tumbled a stream of its contents bouncing and ringing on to the tabletop.

'Golden guineas, every one of them,' he crowed. 'At last I have a little good fortune. Life has been painfully cruel in recent years. As you know, I once enjoyed considerable means.'

'I remember,' I said. 'May I ask what happened to your business?'

'It prospered, sir, until my warehouse burnt to the ground, and when I applied to the insurance company, I found them utterly insolvent and unable to fulfil their obligations. Soon after that Mrs Limmington took her leave of me and went to live with her sister in Macclesfield. I hoped she would return after I'd obtained the collectorship of the turnpike road to Liverpool. But she never responded and then the whole scheme failed. Never a penny of the tolls did I collect, and I am near destitute now, with no one but my housekeeper Griselda between me and cooking for myself – and she threatens daily to leave me. You will take a drink?'

Before I could answer, Griselda had returned and banged a jug down on to the table, with a pewter mug beside it. She splashed some small beer from jug to mug.

'I fear we can run to nothing better than this,' said Limmington. 'Once it would have been a good claret.' His voice took on a wistful tone. 'And neither, regrettably, can I offer you tobacco.'

I took the hint and brought out my own tobacco pouch. Offering him a fill, I tipped my head towards the pile of gold.

'But it seems your fortunes are on the rise again, sir.'

'I wish I could be sure,' said Limmington, eagerly stuffing his pipe. 'You see, I found this purse and do not know who ,it belongs to. Squire who is magistrate here told me the gold is perhaps treasure trove and must be given to the King. He says the only one who can decide the matter is the Coroner.'

I sifted the heap of supposed treasure with my fingers. It consisted entirely of guineas and five-guinea pieces.

'This must amount to the best part of two hundred guineas in gold,' I said.

'It is more. It amounts to exactly two hundred and twenty-seven guineas.'

'Where did you find it?'

'Beside the Liverpool Road.' He put the pipe to his mouth. 'Ironic, you must call that. The road that ruined me may now be my salvation. It would put me back on my feet, would that money.'

Limmington applied a spill to the candle and was soon puffing clouds of smoke.

'It was all inside this purse?'

'Yes.'

'It is important to know how the purse lay. Was it buried at all?'

'No, it lay in the ditch just where my eye happened to fall as I walked past.'

'Treasure trove must have been deliberately hidden with the intention of recovering it. So I am happy to tell you this is unlikely to be a matter over which I have jurisdiction. Is there no indication as to who it belonged to?'

'Some traveller on the road accidentally dropped it, I must suppose.'

'Have you made any attempt to find this person?'

'I asked the vicar to say something after his sermon on Sunday, but no one came forward. Happen the owner's long gone, the reverend says. Happen it was perhaps a criminal – some thief or highwayman – who would never come back looking for it, or not publicly.'

'Have you advertised in the newspaper?'

He looked a little crestfallen.

'Is that what I should do? Eh, Mr Cragg, but if he should turn up, I'd be done down again.'

'There would surely be a reward for its return. In any event, if the owner appears within a reasonable period of time, that money is not legally yours and must be returned.'

'Is there no finders keepers, then?'

'That applies if the first owner of the property really cannot be found. But you must make the effort before you can lawfully lay claim to the goods you found.'

Limmington scraped the coins together in a heap and began dropping them ruefully in handfuls back into the purse.

'I will put a notice in the *Journal*, then.'

'Yes, do so,' I said, 'but guard against dishonest claims. Don't let on how the money lay, how much the amount or what it is contained in. Any claimant must give that information to you before the magistrate or go away empty-handed.'

He shut his eyes tight and whispered.

'I will do it but, Lord Jesus, let him be long gone and far away.'

I finished my beer and took my leave. Walking back, I thought how well Limmington's honesty became him. There's many in need who would have simply kept that money without a word. The incident was also a reminder of the fear seizing the people at this time, for I felt certain that the purse of two hundred and twenty-seven guineas was money that its owner hoped to save from the Pretender. I imagined what might have happened: in a surge of panic a man had mounted a horse and fled the town with that purse containing all his money tied to the saddle. But, making too much haste, he had not properly secured it. And the more miles he covered before he discovered his loss, the more he would despair of ever regaining it.

I was two hundred yards from the ferry's landing stage when I noticed three figures loitering there. At first I took them for children, as they wore bonnets and skirts and were bare-legged. But soon I saw they were hairy muscular men in tartan plaid, and that they were armed with swords, pistols and pikes. In a word, Highlanders.

The three soldiers spoke no English. One of them gestured that I must raise my arms and in that position he patted me down my sides and legs. Satisfied – but a little disappointed

– that I was unarmed, he merely took my purse and extracted a silver sixpence before handing the purse back. Then he signed to the waiting ferryman Robert Battersby that he could take me across.

'How long since those three turned up?' I asked when Battersby had pushed us off from the bank.

'Arrived about an hour ago, Mr Cragg. An officer was with them when they came; told me the rebel army (though he didn't call it that) had come down the road from the north. They'd secured the bridge at Walton-le-Dale, and he'd been sent to post those men down here to control the ferry crossing.'

'And rob the passengers! But why didn't they just take my purse and everything in it?'

'You've not been robbed; you've been taxed. The officer told me every passenger has to pay. It's the same on the bridge. Sixpence per person to cross, no more and no less. Mind, you still owe me tuppence for your fare.'

Walking up Fisher Gate and into Market Place, I saw most houses were shut up and very few townspeople were to be seen. There is no Tuesday market, so I expected Market Place to be mostly deserted but found instead groups of armed Scotchmen clustered together, consulting papers and detaching by squads of three and four in various directions. I went into my house.

'Well, Titus, they are here,' said Elizabeth simply. I had found her spooning pease porridge into Hector's mouth.

'Yes. Battersby says some of them have crossed by the bridge into Walton already, and my own eyes have seen them guarding the ferry. Has there been fighting?'

'No, it has been all quiet.'

'The main body has not yet arrived. We have so far seen only the advance party. And is everyone safe here?'

'Furzey's in the office. I said he should go home, though he wouldn't. But there was no stopping Matty from running out. She's gone to the Friar Gate bar where the main army is expected any time. That's where everyone is that's out of doors – waiting for the Prince.'

'Dear God, are they all coming into the town? Where will they sleep? There might be ten thousand of them, so I've heard.'

I was standing at one of the windows, overlooking Market Place to our left and the west side of the Moot Hall to our right. Suddenly, Elizabeth gave a shrill cry.

'Titus! Oh, Titus! Look!'

I turned. She was pointing at Hector who had grasped the spoon in his fist halfway down the shaft and was attempting to get porridge into his mouth.

'He is trying to feed himself! It is wonderful! Just like when he took his first step on his own feet.'

Elizabeth thought for a moment.

'How fast he comes on,' she said. 'Before we know it, he will be fending for himself entirely, and have no more need of us.'

I kissed her on the forehead and said, 'Well, well, it is quite a day, wife! The Young Pretender is on our doorstep and Hector feeds himself for the first time. Which is the more earth-convulsing novelty of the two?'

She laughed merrily.

'I would not swear as to that, Titus.'

The troops in the advance party stayed mostly out of town, camped around the bridge. Some came into town to visit the taverns in and around St John's Court, searching, as all soldiers do, for the cheapest liquor and the cheapest women. This was nothing like an armed incursion. The Scotch soldiers strolled around as if they had come here for their health.

I stopped one kilted fellow wearing a tartan that was not the same as Ribchester's dead Highlander. I asked if he spoke English. He did.

'Are you a Highlander?'

'Aye.'

'May I ask what tartan you wear? What clan?'

'Clan MacDonald.'

In the afternoon Matty came in, flushed and breathless.

'I've *seen* him! I've seen the Prince. Oh, he's young and fair and so tall. All the girls think he's handsome and brave.'

'Is it true he marches at the head of the column and does not ride?'

'Yes. Everybody says what a fine brave thing it is.'

'And what did the army do?'

'They marched up to the Friar Gate bar and formed up. I mean they lined up in ranks just where the road is wide outside the bar. We were ready to run but they didn't attack or anything like that. They just stood there. Then they were given instructions, which I couldn't hear properly, but it must have been to scatter themselves around in the town fields either side of Moor Lane, because that's what they all did. They lit fires and some put up tents. They are enough to scare a person's socks off just to look at, but they did nothing bad, not like people said they would.'

'I have met some myself,' I said. 'They only took sixpence off me, when they could have had the entire purse, and they were perfectly polite. What did you see the Prince do?'

'I saw him walking up Friar Gate, and I ran back to fetch you out. He comes slowly because of the crowds. Many are cheering him, and he makes himself friendly and speaks to people that are waving his flag or holding up his picture.'

'Is he not afraid someone will attack him?'

'He is afraid of nothing, I reckon.' Her eyes were sparkling, like a person overwhelmed at the sight of a triple rainbow, or a shower of shooting stars. 'Come and look. He'll be in the Market Place any minute.'

We went back to the window, looking this time to our left towards the entry of Friar's Gate. Word had got around by now, and Prestonians had come out of their houses in great numbers to witness the young prodigy's appearance in our midst. After a few minutes we saw a party of people moving through the crowd, attended by a dozen cavalry clearing the way ahead of it and guarding its flanks. Somewhere in the middle of that knot, impossible to see at this distance and with this many intervening onlookers, walked the Young Pretender himself. Dancing up and down in excitement, Matty tried to point him out – there! and there! no, there! – but I myself saw nothing of him amidst the cheering crowd.

'They have taken leave of their senses,' I said. 'Not twenty-four hours ago everybody was waiting to be raped, murdered and set fire to. Now look at them.'

'Shall we go out, Titus, and have a proper look?' said Elizabeth.

I could tell she wanted to, but I preferred my family should stay at home until we knew more about how the rebels would act while occupying Preston.

'No, I am going into the office to speak with Furzey.'

I found my clerk at the open window gossiping with a man whom I recognized as another member of the clerks' fraternity, the chief writer for Preston's wealthiest lawyer, Edmund Starkey. As I came in, Furzey closed the conversation, and then the window.

'What did Mitchell from Starkey's have to say?' I asked.

'That all the best private houses are being visited by soldiers. They will forcibly be made to give accommodation to the senior officers.'

'Who are the leaders of this army? Have you heard any names?'

'Mitchell has just given me some. There's Lord Elcho and his regiment of Lifeguards. There's the Jacobite scoundrel the Duke of Perth. And there's Lord George Murray who's rebelled before. He was here in arms in 'fifteen but got away, more's the pity. Perth and Murray are lieutenant-generals under the Pretender himself, who is pretend general of the whole rabble.'

'Did you hear anything of Starkey's inclinations? Is he for or against the rising?'

'Mitchell refused to be drawn on it. Starkey keeps his counsel, just like you.'

This last remark was spoken with some bitterness. But I did not have time to reprove Furzey because now there was a hammering at the office door, which he opened cautiously. A young Scotch officer stood on the step, carrying a paper on which was written a list of addresses. He was flanked by two soldiers in kilts and with ragged hair. They carried muskets and had vicious-looking knives in their belts, just as described by the fellow in the Market Place. After a glance at the paper in his hand, the officer removed his hat.

'I wish to speak to lawyer Cragg.'

Furzey said he may come in but 'those two ruffians' must wait outside. Taking not the slightest notice of this, all three men shouldered their way past my clerk and in. The common soldiers then kept guard by the outer door, watching Furzey's every move, while I invited the officer into my business room. There seemed no point at all in giving resistance. The rebels had arrived and that was a fact I could do nothing about.

'You are Mr Titus Cragg?' he said. His voice had a touch of primness, and a light Scotch accent.

I confirmed that I was he.

'I am Captain Angus Lucas of the quartermaster's company, under the command of Major-General O'Sullivan. I present General O'Sullivan's compliments. He requires the use of bedrooms in this house for quartering purposes. I do not refer to servants' bedrooms or outhouse quarters. They must be rooms fit for occupation by guests of high rank.'

'I see. And what if I happen to refuse?'

'I'm afraid, Mr Cragg, you happen to have no choice.'

I kept my eyes looking squarely into his. There was no cause for grovelling.

'Allow me to bring you inside, where we can confer with my wife.'

I showed Captain Lucas through the door that joined the office to the house, where we found Elizabeth sewing in the parlour. She took this rebel incursion calmly, just as if she had foreseen it, or something like it.

'We have only one bedroom unoccupied,' she said.

'How many have you in all?'

'There are four, and the attic.'

'Please show them all to me.'

We led him upstairs and showed the guest room. The captain poked his nose into the dressing-room wardrobes, then said, 'Please draw back the covers and sheets of the bed. I must examine the mattresses.'

Elizabeth crossed her arms, eyes flashing.

'Captain Lucas! Do you think this is some slovenly dock tavern in Liverpool, that you must inspect our bedding for bugs? For shame, indeed!'

He was taken aback, which he covered by straightening his shoulders.

'It is my duty, madam, by orders of Major-General O'Sullivan. The covers, please!'

'You may do it yourself, because I won't,' she replied.

The captain looked at me, but I made no move. He distrustfully trailed his fingers over the bed cover, as if it might conceal a mantrap or landmine. Then he stepped back.

'Well, I suppose in this instance we may take the mattress as examined. Your next room, please.'

He went out and, crossing the landing, seized the handle of our bedroom door. It was a double-sized room, as it extended over the office on the ground floor below.

'That is our own bedroom,' I pointed out.

He opened the door and went inside.

'Good,' he said, looking quickly around. 'Very good. And upstairs?'

He ventured to make no further bed examination as we showed him the rest of our accommodation – Hector's and Matty's rooms on the floor above and the attic rooms which were at the moment unoccupied.

'We will require the two bedchambers on the first floor and the front one on the second. Please have them prepared immediately.'

'May we ask the names of our guests?' I said.

'As I've already said, they are of high rank. I can't tell you their names.'

'Then can you tell us how long we must expect these patricians to stay?'

'You will learn all these matters in a very short time. Now I bid you good day. There is very much to do.'

While leading him back into the office, I said, 'I hope the men are under discipline, Captain. I hope there will be no outrages here.'

'We are a well-found army, sir, and do not tolerate outrages; you may be sure of that.'

From my own encounters with the soldiers, I was ready to accept this. Furzey was less sure. He had been sitting at his desk while fixing the Highlanders with a rigid glare. Referring again to his paper, Lucas said something in Gaelic, and all three marched out into Cheap Side. I stood at the door and watched them ascend the next steps to rap the knocker of Burroughs's house.

I returned within and found Elizabeth sitting on the stairs.

'So!' I said. 'We are officially a billet. Even our own bedroom is pressed into the Prince's service.'

She laughed. Her ill humour had left her, though her opinion of the Captain had not changed.

'That is a bad-mannered fellow, but young. He may learn how better to present himself one day. Meanwhile, we must make the best of it. Shall you and I sleep in the attic and Hector with us? It will be an adventure.'

'The beds up there are single and so narrow. I'll miss having my wife beside me.'

'And I my husband, so we shall push them together. Now, Matty and I must get on with changing the beds.'

A few moments after she left me, there was a knock on the door and I went to open it. Luke Fidelis stood on the step.

'I am turned out of my house!' he said. 'It is to be filled entirely with soldiers. They are milling around at my end of town in their thousands, complaining that they do not have enough tents.'

Fidelis's house was on Fylde Road, outside the Friar Gate bar where the Pretender, on entering the town, had left most of his troops.

'Then you must take refuge with us,' I said, standing aside to let him in, and then leading the way into the parlour. 'We have a full house except for an attic room with a flock mattress and a feather pillow. I'm afraid you will not be extremely comfortable there, but it is dry and tolerably warm.'

'I am grateful, though I fear for my chemical laboratory with its glass vessels. Soldiers have a habit of breaking things. But I accept with gratitude your attic and lumpy bed.'

'We are having to remove to the attic ourselves. A captain from the rebel army was just here, and has pressed all our bedrooms except for Matty's, which must be too mean. We have been led to expect grandees.'

'I suppose they shan't stay for long. Preston is far from being a stronghold, as the rebels found in 'fifteen. They will not want to fight the government here – not again.'

'Which I imagine is why they have crossed the river and secured the bridge. They mean to cross it and press on south.'

Matty came in with an offer of tea, which Fidelis refused, saying he must go out again. 'I have a patient in Penwortham in a bad way after an injury. He is lucky he lives as near as that, as I have no mount. I hid my horses before the rebels invaded the house. I will not allow them to be taken as a tax.' 'You will be taxed anyway if you go over to Penwortham,' I said. 'Make sure to have two silver sixpences in your pocket.'

I returned to the office and found Furzey fretting. Being unmarried, he lived with his widowed mother, whom he now imagined under siege from marauding Highlanders. I sent him home to repel them.

Looking once more into the Market Place, I saw that the Prestonians who had greeted the Prince so warmly were still out there, talking excitedly and in some cases singing Jacobite ballads and songs such as 'When the King comes to his own again'. Here and there, Scotch troops had joined them, and I heard the wheedling sound of bagpipes. One or two peddlars were also plying their trade, patrolling the area with trays that displayed goods of interest to a soldier with a few pennies to spend.

I went back to my writing table and tried half-heartedly to sift through some affidavits in a civil case I was pursuing on behalf of watchmaker Oldswick, a notorious litigant. But my mind continually wandered, dwelling on the present danger and on the uncertain future. How split and splintered our country had become – and how enraged so many of our people were. Who would be governing us come Christmas, and what bloodshed would have decided the issue? The old political battles between Whigs and Tories, which had once seemed implacable and destructive, now felt a comfortable, even benign, natural state. The eruption of Prince Charles Edward in our midst signalled something newly dangerous and dismaying – the stirring of a more atavistic conflict, previously half hidden and now showing itself in full view, armed with battle standard, musket and sword in hand.

Restlessly, I went back into the house, where Elizabeth and Matty were still putting the bedrooms to rights for our enforced guests. I took Hector into the parlour and distracted myself playing peep-oh and other simple games with him. We were halfway through Ride a Cock Horse – with him bumping up and down astride my knees and laughing uproariously – when I had to answer another hammering at the front door – the door of the house rather than the office.

In the fading light a woman confronted me, accompanied by a young officer in full uniform. She wore a riding costume with a large hood shadowing her face.

'Mr Titus Cragg?' said the officer.

I said that I was, and, without another word, he pushed past and displaced me at holding the door, then bowed to the lady. I can only describe the way she entered my house and lowered her hood as stately. Her chin was up, her back straight and her gaze steady. I raised the candle in my hand so that I could see her face. It was possibly one of the most perfectly beautiful female faces I had ever seen.

TEN

The escorting officer – a sturdy fellow of about thirty – introduced himself as Captain David Brown.

'I have the honour of bringing this lady to her billet. You will also be providing a room for me, and another gentleman – a most important gentlemen, I will add – who you may expect to come here soon. We are all very tired after a long day on the road, and we desire above all to eat and rest.'

The lady entered. I knew little enough of armies on campaign, but the last person I expected to be billeted in my house was a female rebel – and not only a beautiful one but an important one, to judge by what we had been told by Captain Lucas. I covered my surprise by making a deep bow.

'May I ask your name, madam?' I said.

I was answered with nothing more than a twitch of her lips.

'This is Madame Manon Lachatte,' said Captain Brown, in a tone of voice suggesting I must surely have heard the name.

She was, I guessed, about twenty-five. Covered with neither powder nor face-paint, her skin was unblemished and unlined. Her eyes were a deep and liquid green, and her hair was a rich red. Suddenly, I felt awkward and out of my depth. I called for Elizabeth to come down to us.

'Oh!' said Elizabeth. Immediately getting over her surprise, she smiled in welcome. I repeated our guests' names and said they were tired and would like to see their rooms.

'Which room would you prefer, Madame?' Elizabeth asked the woman when we had shown off the three rooms that Captain Lucas had picked out and were standing on the first-floor landing. Madame Lachatte had said not a word during the tour. 'This room here is normally our own bedroom. It is the largest but overlooks the market and you may find it noisy. The other rooms are smaller, but both have a pleasant quiet view over our garden. The one above is our child's room but we have removed his cot. The bed in that room is rarely slept in.'

Those perfect lips still didn't open, and it was not even
clear that she had understood. Brown pointed to the room
across the landing and said a few words to the lady in French
– firm words, I would call them, though I did not know their
meaning. She replied with the faintest nod of her head.

'Madame Lachatte will take this room,' said Brown,
indicating the same room. 'The larger, with the aspect over
the market, has already been reserved for the use of your third
guest. I myself shall take your child's room upstairs.'

Captain Brown soon left the house, saying he must arrange
for the baggage to be brought. Elizabeth and I retreated downstairs, leaving Madame Lachatte to settle herself. The identity
of the rebel who would be occupying our marital bed was still
unknown to us.

'Oh, I am sure it is the Chevalier himself,' said Matty when
we had gathered in the kitchen. 'What a splendour that'll be!
I won't know where to put myself, I won't.'

'Matty, you must contain yourself,' Elizabeth said. 'He will
certainly not come here, as there are many better-appointed
houses in Preston, starting indeed with Patten House. If that's
good enough for Lord Derby, it is suitable for the Prince. I
expect, however, we might be receiving one of the generals.
What do you think, Titus? Have you heard the names of the
leaders of the army – the cavalry, infantry and so forth?'

I gave her the names Mitchell had told Furzey.

'There will be many other senior officers, of course, who
make up the Pretender's council.'

'Lords and Dukes!' exclaimed Matty. 'Have ever such titles
been seen under this roof before?'

'And may not be now,' said Elizabeth crisply. 'But the lady
upstairs, Titus: what are we to make of her? When I asked
which room she would take, the captain translated it as an
instruction that she could not take the larger room but must
have the smaller at the back.'

Elizabeth's advantage over me here was that she had much
better French, having spent almost two years at school in Belgium.

'I did not catch what he said to her, but he seemed perfectly
polite,' I said.

'Indeed, he was polite. But he would not be argued with, all the same. As to Madame Lachatte, I wonder what she is doing with this army. I wonder indeed if she is somebody's—' Elizabeth mouthed 'mistress' to avoid Matty's blushes.

'This important gentleman's, perhaps,' I said. 'I wonder who he is.'

'We must wait and see.'

We did not have long to wait and see, as Captain Brown returned out of the darkness half an hour later, in company with Captain Lucas. The latter told us to prepare for the arrival of 'the Marquis', and to make sure to provide a meal for him, as well as for our other guests.

'A *marquis*, is he?' said Elizabeth. 'What is his name?'

'He is Alexandre de Boyer, Marquis d'Éguilles,' said Lucas. 'As a French nobleman, he will expect the food to be hot. See to it, please.'

As Lucas hurried away, Brown went up to his room. Elizabeth clicked her tongue.

'"See to it!"? That boy gets even further above himself every time he opens his mouth.'

'So we have a marquis to entertain,' I said. 'A real French nob to be politely polished.'

'Don't be coarse, Titus. Anyway, where he comes from, marquises are two for a penny. *La France* is enormously overstuffed with nobility.'

She had considerably greater knowledge than I, who had been only the shortest of times in France. However, whether he was minor or major nobility, Lucas was making much of this fellow and had earmarked our best room for him.

Twenty minutes later Lucas was back again with a man a little younger than me, dressed in riding clothes and wearing his natural hair under a tricorn hat. This was the Marquis d'Éguilles, who strode in with a trooper carrying his box. The Marquis was rubicund and brisk of manner, and his coat was cut in a somewhat military style. He wore a sword and pistols on his belt, yet, for all that, he did not quite persuade as a soldier. He looked more of an excise officer or a gentleman-farmer on his way to attend militia drills. I showed him up to his room in person, followed by the trooper and box.

At the beginning it was an awkward, over-polite gathering around our dining table that night. Elizabeth laid out a more than serviceable meal of potato soup, thick slices of pickled pork and a beautiful cheese, and I decanted some of last year's excellent elderberry wine. But the meal began unfortunately. I noticed the Marquis eyeing the wine decanter avidly, so I quickly poured him a full glass. He raised it, held the ruby liquid to the light and made pompous exclamations to Elizabeth, who was beside him, as to its virtues. But the Marquis was evidently expecting a good Burgundy, for when, in what may have been a further gesture of appreciation, he drained his glass in one tip, the results were extraordinary. As soon as the wine hit his palate, his eyes popped and he began to choke. He clamped his mouth shut, heaved once, then again, and the elderberry wine began to spurt back out through his nose and on to his shirt and the table.

Elizabeth exclaimed, and then burst out laughing while saying something to him in French. The Marquis was stiff with embarrassment, but as she picked up her napkin and dabbed at his shirt, still laughing but also apologizing, his discomfort melted by degrees and before long he smiled. Taking his own napkin, he wiped his face and, catching Elizabeth's hand, he kissed it and indicated he would be willing to give the elderberry wine another try.

I found it difficult to read the true relations between him and the woman sitting beside me. Both had a certain hauteur. I supposed she was his mistress but, if so, the two were noticeably cool towards each other. My companion's coolness, indeed, may have had something to do with the fact that the Marquis showed every sign of being much taken with my wife. He talked to her almost exclusively and looked fondly at her, with more than the suspicion of a rolling eye.

'I am sorry, madam,' I heard him saying laboriously, 'I do not speak English very good.'

'Then we must speak in French,' Elizabeth said gaily and began chattering away in that language. Before long the pair were freely talking and laughing together, occasionally including Captain Brown in their discussions, so that I was left to attempt conversation with Madame Lachatte.

'*Vous avez fait un voyage confortable, j'espère?*' I said.

There was a fugitive movement of her lips, which might have been the wisp of a smile. How fatuous my question was! *Of course* she had not had a comfortable journey. I was speaking to her as if she were a clergyman's wife just come in by the Lancaster coach. Madame, by contrast, had been with an army, in the middle of a war, surrounded by hairy-armed men in tartan plaid. I tried once more, this time on the safer subject of our dinner.

'*La soupe vous plait?*'

With spoon halfway between plate and mouth, she nodded fractionally while widening her eyes. Was the ice melting at last?

'*Voulez-vous du vin?*' I ventured.

She had already sunk one glass, but I wasn't sure how to say *more wine*. Nevertheless, she nodded again and I poured. Then, fluently and with not a trace of a French accent, she said, 'I adore elderberry wine. You can't get it in Paris. They turn their noses up at anything that isn't grape juice.'

'Madame!' I said in relieved surprise. 'I did not suspect you of speaking English!'

'Well, why wouldn't I?' she said brightly. 'Am I not from Bandon in County Cork, where the elderberries are the juiciest you ever saw?'

'Oh! You are Irish?'

Another clot's question! I bit my lip.

'I was Mary Flarty,' she said, 'though now I am called Manon. My father took the notion of serving King Louis and we left for France when I was quite small. He went into one of His Majesty's Irish regiments.'

'Can you remember Ireland?'

'A little. My family kept cows, so I still have the smell of the dairy in my nose. It had a sweetness for me. After he stopped soldiering, my da become a merchant in milk and butter in Paris. He used to say that in God's eyes drawing the white stuff is better than drawing the red stuff. Anyway, it pays more, and he soon got enough money to give my sisters and me schooling and manners so that we could find suitable – as he thought – husbands.'

I replied with another question even dafter than the previous ones.

'And your husband is well, I hope?'

She took another sip of wine.

'He's dead, I'm happy to say. Lachatte was an old fool, a born drunkard and a spendthrift.'

So much candour in so short a time, whether or not it was provoked by wine, was disarming. And now that we could speak freely in English, I began to lose my awkwardness and relish our conversation as much as they were enjoying theirs at the other end of the table.

We did not broach military affairs, such as the rebels' strength and final objective, while delicacy prevented me from probing into what had driven Madame Lachatte to throw in her lot with the Jacobites' invasion of England. We stuck instead to everyday observations and anecdotes while, at the other end of the table, the French conversation flowed in a similar manner.

Towards eleven the party came to an end, by which time I had completely forgotten that the three guests were part of an army come to conquer us. As they withdrew to their rooms – the Marquis with notable reluctance – I threw on a great-coat and called Suez. The dog bounded up to me, his tail thrashing, and led me joyfully out for his nightly promenade. Groups of rebels were wandering the town or warming them-selves around open fires in Market Place under a light snowfall. As we approached the shop of Curtis the cutler in Fisher Gate, my ear picked up the scream of his whetston, and only then did I notice the quiet file of men, extending to thirty or forty soldiers, who waited patiently, past midnight as it was, to have their claymores and dirks sharpened.

As on many evenings, I took the dog on to the green south of Fisher Gate where the playhouse was. Here we found more fires scattered around, more groups of soldiers huddled in their plaids around them, smoking, arguing and sleeping. Passing one of these, I saw that they wore the same tartan as that of the murdered Highlander at Ribchester and I approached them. I addressed a lanky fellow that sat on a box beside the fire.

'Please excuse the question,' I said. 'But what is your plaid? What tribe, I mean?'

Every firelit eye turned towards me.

'Tribe? We are no tribe,' said the tall soldier.

He spat into the flames in contempt at my ignorance.

'We're Clan MacGregor. Ya'll have heard of Rob Roy?'

A large hound swathed in russet hair arose from the fireside. The dog would have looked menacing any time, but in this flickering firelight its cavernous mouth, great teeth and yellow eyes appeared almost demonic. Suez turned towards this drooling marauder and began heartily yapping.

'Bawty!' the soldier growled at his dog. I grabbed at Suez's lead to drag him towards me, but it turned out that the Scotch monster did not want to fight or, if it did, it was a play-fight. Without so much as a growl, Bawty nosed Suez's backside then bounded back, making three or four lolloping circles, before adopting the canine come-and-play posture, with his chest and forelegs flat to the ground and his backside and beating tail in the air.

'That's a marvellous dog you have,' I said, reaching out and scratching the animal behind its ears. The soldier obviously did not think so.

'Bawty, ya bloody girl. Ya stupid cur, come here.'

He darted towards the dog and, seizing its collar, administered three sharp knuckle-raps across its broad nose. With a whimper, Bawty sank down in submission.

'Well, we will be on our way,' I said, embarrassed at this unnecessary display of cruelty. 'I wish you goodnight, Mr MacGregor.'

I raised my hat and started to retreat. After half a dozen strides, I turned and saw Bawty's eyes following us. I had the sense they were imploring us. Then I heard another sizzling spit.

'It's Sergeant, ya bloody Sassenach.'

I let myself in, expecting the house to be in darkness, but saw that there was a light in my library. Letting Suez run into the kitchen, I opened the library door to find Madame Lachatte sitting beside the embers of the fire with a candle and a book open on her knee.

'You are a reader, Madame?'

'Am I just! Only romances and stories of adventure.

And fables. I am devoted to them, but I find I have read all the ones I brought in my luggage.'

'I have little of that kind, I am afraid. Have you found something to your taste?'

She showed me the book: *The Adventures of Robinson Crusoe*.

'It is an old favourite of mine, but I have read it so many times I had much rather have a new story. Perhaps there's another by this author, Defoe. Do you have one?'

'I regret, no. But if you will allow me to conduct you in the morning to my bookseller, Mr Sweeting, I am sure he will be able to supply something suitable.'

She agreed to be guided to Sweeting's shop after breakfast, then yawned and, rising, bade me goodnight.

I was about to go up myself when I heard the front door opening and found Luke Fidelis with his medical bag, shaking snow from his greatcoat.

'A late call to a patient,' he told me. 'And there is another from the house of one you may know – Mr Limmington in Penwortham. It is a pro bono job as he is a pauper. I shall attend him in the morning.'

'Good heavens! I saw him only today. What ails him?'

'He was struck on the head. His housekeeper wrote that a party of Highlanders came to the house demanding money and cracked his skull.'

'How is he?'

'Unconscious. I am hoping he will have awoken when I go to him first thing tomorrow.'

'If he dies, I suppose I shall have to inquest him. That will be a tricky matter if rebel soldiers were responsible.'

We went up the stairs and said goodnight on the landing outside our temporary attic bedrooms.

Later, lying beside my sleeping wife, I closed my eyes and found Madame Lachatte's flawless skin, rich red hair and, above all, her eyes appearing unbidden to my mind's eye, and fell asleep thinking of them.

ELEVEN

'Will you take a snuff, Madame?' said Sebastian Sweeting when I had introduced him early next morning to Madame Lachatte. He flipped open the lid of the big snuffbox that he kept on the counter for his customers, and we both took a pinch.

'How may I help you?' he said.

'I would like to purchase a novel for my entertainment,' she explained, after she had indulged in a hearty sneeze.

'I have some of the kind.'

He retreated into the dusty and shadowed rear of the shop and came back with several volumes, which he placed on the counter. He picked up the first and opened it at the title.

'Here is one of a serving girl called Kitty O'Mara.'

The lady's interest was piqued.

'Irish?'

'Evidently.'

He read out the information under the title.

'"Being the History of a Young Woman from the Country taken into the Home of a Noblewoman as a Chambermaid who doth Wantonly Steal from her Employer her Dresses, Jewels etc. and after Numerous Vicissitudes is discovered and doth repent and accept as the Will of God her Condign Punishment at Tyburn Gallows."'

'Oh, Mr Sweeting!' she exclaimed. 'Don't tell me the ending, please! To know the ending of a story before you begin – it's like swallowing a cake without tasting it.'

Sweeting laid this volume aside and picked up another, glancing at the title.

'This concerns a lad whose family is suddenly cast into hardship and he is made apprentice to a notorious highwayman.'

She shook her head.

'I have no taste for it. It smokes of boys who think they are men, and of men no better than boys.'

Sweeting opened a third volume from his pile. Glancing at the title, he quickly closed it again and laid it aside. But Madame Lachatte saw what he had done and took up the rejected book for herself.

'Ah!' she said, opening it. 'This looks more the sort that I like.'

'Madame,' said Sweeting, alarmed, 'I am not sure it is quite suitable.'

'No, Mr Sweeting, I cannot agree.'

She read the title aloud.

'"The Fortunate Mistress or, A History of the Life and Vast Variety of Fortunes of Mademoiselle de Beleau, Afterwards Called the Countess of Wintselsheim in Germany Being the Person Known by the Name of the Lady Roxana in the Time of Charles II." This promises to be good. I'll take it.'

By his face, I could see Sweeting was put out. He valued his reputation for perfectly matching customers and books, and yet here was one rejecting his recommendation. Still, he made a parcel of *The Fortunate Mistress*. She handed over half a guinea and tucked the parcel under her arm.

It was only a few steps back up Church Gate to Cheap Side and the Market Place. Friday market was in progress, but a troop of soldiers had cleared away all the stalls surrounding the monument, while half a dozen of their fellows set to work turning some traders' tables into a platform. Trading in the market had almost ceased as people gathered around the small stage to see what was going to happen.

'You may find this of interest,' said my companion. 'Shall we watch?'

We took our place at the back of the crowd and waited. Soon, from the direction of Friar Gate, we heard the sound of bagpipes and drummers, and a path was cleared through which a body of troops marched up and formed up around the monument. A number of standards were now raised on poles around the platform, the largest being a red flag with a white square at its centre. The clock on the parish church struck eleven. At once the music stopped as a tall young man dressed in white breeches and a blue coat trimmed with gold braid, a white cockade in his hat, jumped on to the stage. This caused some cheering, ragged at first but gaining confidence until he had to raise his hand to be heard. He held a paper in his hand from which he began to read.

I strained to hear but we were at the back of the crowd and the words were lost under the buzz of the audience, which was punctuated by cries of 'Huzzah!' and 'God save the Prince!' The young man's voice rose to try to overcome the noise. I heard odd words from which I gathered he was denouncing the Elector of Hanover as a false and illegitimate king. He continued speaking, but his words were whipped away by the wind. As he finished, there was a climactic cheer, which he acknowledged by flourishing the paper. He then jumped down and mounted a horse, from which he continued to wave the proclamation in the air as he rode through the throng.

'There you have it,' said Madame Lachatte. 'This is done in all the towns we pass through. King James the Third is proclaimed the undoubted King of England and all its dominions, and the Elector of Hanover denounced for a usurper.'

'That was the Prince himself who spoke?'

'Yes. Is he not handsome? And how the people acclaim him!'

The acclaim I could not deny, as the many convinced Jacobites in the town had turned out to cheer their hero, while the rest kept indoors. As to the Prince's good looks, I was not close enough to see his face as anything but a blur or a fog. But there was something familiar in it, I supposed, from portraits I had seen, and this led in turn to thoughts of my conversation with Mrs Parkinson at the Entwhistle house, when we had examined the medal with the Prince's portrait. I had never looked up those lines in the *Georgics* to which the inscription *Hunc saltem everso juvenem* may have referred.

We had reached the steps up to my front door when I saw Luke Fidelis rounding the corner from Fisher Gate. He raised his arm and shouted, and having handed the lady into the house, I waited for him.

'You must come with me to Penwortham,' he said.

'Is it poor Limmington?'

'Yes. His housekeeper has sent word. He died in the night.'

'Then I will come.'

*   *   *

They say that a house in which someone dies is colder by the thermometer three days continuously, and then the temperature returns to normal. Limmington's house in Penwortham was certainly cold, though it seemed no colder than when I'd visited the previous day. Cold, however, sharpens the nostrils, and as soon as the housekeeper let us in, I smelled pipe smoke. We were not admitted to the parlour – from where the smoke seemed to originate – but taken immediately up the stairs to Limmington's bedroom. It was a good-sized but Spartan apartment, the bed without hangings and the chandelier lacking candles. The corpse of Horace Limmington lay on its back with eyes closed as in sleep. His arms were neatly crossed over his chest, the hands palm down.

Fidelis immediately went to the bedside. He removed his hat, pulled off his gloves and opened his medical case. He first lifted the eyelids and flexed the fingers and arms.

'Rigor mortis is already well advanced,' he remarked. He looked at his watch. 'And the time is half past ten.'

He turned to the mouth.

'Is there no candle?'

There was none, so Fidelis took a tinderbox and small oil lamp from his bag, and lit a match to fire the wick.

'Hold this, will you? Bring it close to his mouth cavity.'

Fidelis levered the mouth open with finger and thumb, and I held the oil lamp as requested while Fidelis bent to peer inside. After this he put down the lamp and took a thermometer from his case. This was to measure the corpse's temperature (I will leave the reader to imagine where he'd be putting the instrument), which he would note down in a notebook against the time of its taking. No doubt he would then roll the body on to its side to see the condition of its back before turning to the wound on Limmington's head, which he would measure, smell and palpate, then put his eye close to it for minute inspection. These were things I had watched him do with many previous corpses.

My own job was not a physical examination but a verbal one – of the housekeeper. She had left the room, and hearing her voice in the hall, I followed her. From the stairtop I could see the open front door, where she was conversing in a low

voice with a man I could not see. A neighbour who had come
to condole, I supposed, and no doubt the author of the tobacco
smoke. I coughed coming down the stair, upon hearing which
she closed the door.

'May I have a word?' I said.

She led me into the parlour.

'What time did Mr Limmington breathe his last?'

'In the night. A half hour before morning light.'

'Five o'clock, then?'

'Happen.'

'Had he been able to speak?'

'Just huffs and snorts and wheezes. He never came round
after he was hit.'

'And you were there when he died?'

'I watched by the bedside all night.'

'That is commendable. Why did you not have his doctor to
him, from here in Penwortham?'

'Thomas Ross won't so much as snap the catch of his
doctor's bag without a fee. And I have no money. I sent to
Doctor Fidelis in town because I've heard he'll doctor you for
nowt.'

'Did Mr Limmington have no family you could appeal to?'

'Not here. His wife has upped and left and gone to
Macclesfield. They'd no bairns that lived.'

'Tell me how Mr Limmington came by the wound that felled
him.'

'The rebels did it. They rode in, four of them, collecting
money. They came hammering at the door. Well, I let them
in, not knowing what else to do, and showed them in to the
master. Pay up, I heard them tell him, by order of the paymaster-
general, or face military execution. They'd got his name down
as being a collector of excise taxes, they said, and those taxes
belong to the King – him that should be king, not him in
London, so they said.'

'You were listening at the door?'

She sniffed.

'I do not pry, sir. I wouldn't lower myself to prying. They
were in the study and I was in here, cleaning. I could not help
the hearing of it.'

Cleaning? My eye flicked involuntarily at one of the dusty cobwebbed corners of the room.

'How did your master reply?'

'Mr Limmington said he was never excise collector but would have been turnpike collector, only it never came about, so he didn't have a brass farthing to give them. He shouted, angry-like. He said even if he had, why should he? It was then that the soldiers, or one of them, attacked him.'

'With what weapon?'

'Oh, an axe, Mr Cragg. A terrible big axe such as those savages carry into battle.'

'What clan were they? What regiment?'

'I know nowt about regiments and clans.'

'And what time did they come? When was the attack itself?'

'Before dark. Happen half three.'

'And they went away with nothing?'

She smiled grimly.

'No. They went away with a lot. After they'd axed Mr Limmington, he lay there on the floor gasping and groaning. And as I was attending to him the best I could, those devils were searching the house. They found them golden guineas as Mr Limmington came upon on the Liverpool Road. The ones he was asking you about when you came Wednesday.'

'Well, that was quite a sum. Those rebels will have gone away highly gratified.'

'When the devil's abroad, murder eats dainties, as they say.'

'Poor Limmington. Luck was not his friend. However did you get him upstairs to bed?'

'I managed.'

'But he was unconscious. Did you have no help?'

'He was dazed. He could almost stand, and I found the strength to support him. I scorn help.'

Fidelis appeared in the doorway, hatted and gloved once more.

'There's no need for me to cut him open, Titus. It's the blow to the head that killed him. I will give you a report later. Meanwhile, I shall visit my patient here.'

'And I must speak to the constable about a jury.'

So we left Griselda and parted in the street.

*   *   *

'Yes, the rebels were here yesterday,' Constable Gibbins told me at the door of the Swan Inn, which he kept. 'A party of four rode through, looking for money by what they called lawful authority. Thievery, more like.'

Gibbins was a good, fat man – not rich, but comfortable enough from what he earned as innkeeper.

'Did you see them?'

'Aye, they came to the inn first. They were drinking ale and warming themselves.'

'Could you identify them in any way? The regiment? The clan?'

'No, I couldn't, Mr Cragg. I'm sorry.'

'Did you hear them talking?'

Gibbins beckoned that I come inside, where he pointed to the fireplace.

'They sat there talking in their own language and looking at a list on a paper they had with them. Then one of them called me over and asked me in English where they could find Ezra Potter, John Wilkinson and Horace Limmington. They showed me the names on their list, which they said were names of tax collectors, and I reckon they'd been copied from receipts in the tax and excise books in town. They promised to burn down the inn if I didn't tell them.'

'Ah! It seems the rebels have taken over King George's tax revenue for themselves.'

'It's a strange way to gather taxes, threatening to burn down a man's business.'

'They are soldiers, who are hard men, and many act without scruple.'

'Any road, they must have been copied, those names, from old excise books, see? Not the present ones.'

'Why do you say that?'

'Because, while it's true Ezra did work for the excise, he's been dead two years, which I told them. And I said they wouldn't find Big John here either. He was an excise man an' all – how d'you think he got so rich? – but he's been gone to Ormskirk since last year and built a fine new house for himself.'

'I suppose they could not get hold of the current receipt

books. They would've been hidden away. What about
Limmington, though?'

'That's the odd thing. He was never a tax collector at all,
not with the King's excise. He was made tolls collector for
the new road, but that was never finished. Limmington never
collected a single toll.'

'But you nevertheless said where he lived?'

'I did, God forgive me, because I thought he would explain
and they'd believe him. But they didn't, it seems. Am I not
therefore the cause of his death?'

'You had no choice, man,' I said consolingly. 'You might've
lost the inn, or even your own life. But they were thwarted
here in Penwortham by their out-of-date intelligence and they
killed Limmington in a fit of frustration, I think.'

So we turned to our arrangements for Limmington's inquest.
I told him it would be on Monday the sixth of December –
five days' time. Gibbins offered the use of his inn for the
hearing and engaged to have a panel of jurors recruited in
time.

'We shall need the servantwoman Griselda to give evidence.
What's her surname by the way?'

'She is Mrs Bigelow, a widow. Came here from – I can't
remember where, Yorkshire maybe – to marry Simon Bigelow
who had a pie shop. He died within a year and, seeing no
future in pies, she went as a servant to Limmington.'

'Please inform her that I shall require her to attend.'

We shook hands on it.

I dined with Elizabeth and Madame Lachatte. The latter had
spent the morning within doors reading *The Fortunate Mistress*,
which she was sure was a story of real life and not some
invention. She relayed the details to us with so much enthusiasm that, throughout much of the meal, it was 'Roxana this'
and 'Roxana that', exactly as if she was telling of the goings-
on of a favourite sister. Afterwards I retired to the office, where
Furzey and I drew up Griselda Bigelow's statement based on
what she had told me in the morning, and which I would be
sending over to Penwortham for her signature once Furzey
had produced a second fair copy.

In setting down my summary of Griselda's evidence about Horace Limmington's death, a number of questions had come to me. One was that of the weapon: a great big axe, she had said. Why an axe? Griselda may have believed the Highlanders fight with battleaxes, but I did not.

None of our guests were present at the supper table that evening. The Marquis had spent all afternoon at the Prince's war council and, on coming in, had ordered bread, cheese, fruit and wine in his room. Madame Lachatte, escorted by Captain Brown, was visiting the lodgings of one of the other ladies in the company, Mrs MacSheridan. So Elizabeth, Fidelis and I sat down together and were able to talk freely about the case of Limmington, which was to the fore in our minds. I had shown Fidelis Griselda's statement but had not heard any conclusions he may have drawn from his examination of the body. But first I raised the question of why the Highlanders had used an axe for this attack.

'On consideration,' I added, 'I wonder if they were carrying the axe to get into premises, if necessary by breaking down doors.'

'Or perhaps she meant a pike,' suggested Elizabeth.

'If she did,' said Fidelis, 'it does not help matters, for neither an axe nor a pike killed Horace Limmington.'

'How do you know that, Luke?'

'It is not the right kind of wound, Titus. Surely you could see that for yourself!'

'I did not look so very closely.'

'If you had, you would have seen that his skull wasn't split open, as by an axe blow. It was crushed like the shell of a boiled egg when you tap it with your spoon. It was something flat and wide that killed the man – something like the flat of a spade.'

'A *spade*? So why would Griselda say they used an axe?'

'She did not see the attack, but only heard it.'

'And yet she was so definite about an axe. And if they'd had a spade with them, she would have seen it.'

'I didn't say it *was* a spade, Titus. I referred to something that would have the *effect* of a spade.'

Fidelis's exasperation was showing in his face, but Elizabeth laughed.

'Not many things have the effect of a spade without being a spade,' she said.

'Shall we put that aside?' I said, 'Something else has occurred to me that is hard to square with these details of the rebels. Griselda says that Limmington shouted at the soldiers and defied them. But when I spoke to him the same morning, he was unmistakably sympathetic to the Pretender's cause. Why would he then have behaved so provokingly to the Pretender's men, even at the cost of his own life?'

'Obviously, dearest, Griselda may not be telling the truth,' said Elizabeth.

'And if she isn't, it's not the only thing she's been lying about,' said Fidelis.

'What else has she lied about?' I said.

'The time of death. I don't think Limmington gave up the ghost just before dawn. I think the man died hours before that. Possibly at the moment he was struck, or quite soon after.'

'What makes you think so?'

'Rigor mortis. What time was it we saw him? Eleven o'clock? That would be only four hours after sunrise, and in a house as cold as that I would not expect the stiffening of the body to be so well advanced. I would say he must have died more than ten and less than fourteen hours earlier.'

'But why would Griselda lie about that?'

'That is not a medical question. Talking of which, I have another suggestion. Go and see Limmington's doctor. Ask him about his patient's overall state of health, which I have reason to believe was not good. I saw certain signs of morbidity.'

'He was sick?'

'The doctor who saw him alive is best placed to answer that. It is probably old Tom Ross at Penwortham. A slave to the Almanack and astrology, like most older medical men, but not a complete fool.'

Madame Lachatte had not come home by the time we rose, and Elizabeth went up to the Marquis to bring down his tray. After five minutes, when she had not reappeared, I went up to the bedchamber door and found it closed. The Marquis could be heard speaking low, crossed by Elizabeth's voice rising in strength and pitch. Most of what they were saying I could not understand, until I heard her cry out.

'*Mais non, Monsieur le Marquis! Laissez-moi, s'il vous plait!*'

I hesitated for another few moments. Were the cries made laughing? Was this banter? Then I heard her again.

'*Non, je vous en pris, non!*'

I burst through the door and saw the Marquis using his weight to pin Elizabeth down on the bed, with his hand beneath her skirt as she struggled to get out from under him, twisting her head to avoid his attempts to kiss her. Then he knew he was discovered. He sprang up to face me, red-faced and alarmed, his penis visibly protruding from his breeches. I took three strides towards him and, swinging my arm, punched him on the nose with all my strength.

At exactly that moment Madame Lachatte walked in.

'*Mais q'est-ce que s'y passe?*' she asked in a shrill voice.

TWELVE

I sat alone in my library, making entries in my journal and seething with rage and loathing. Above me the house was glacial. Fidelis had taken a brisk look at the whimpering Marquis's injured nose and pronounced it broken, for which there was no remedy except time. He then went to bed. Madame Lachatte, herself furious at the Marquis, slammed the door of her room behind her. Captain Brown, on the other hand, took the path of cool discretion – that is, he said nothing and kept out of the way until morning.

Elizabeth took straight to her bed, having removed the sleeping Hector from his cot and brought him under the covers with her. She needed the kind of comfort that only his warmth afforded.

As for the Marquis d'Éguilles, we heard nothing more from him. He skulked as only an unmasked would-be rapist can skulk.

I was going over in my mind all that I had seen in that room and I thought about what might have happened if I had not been there to discover it. If I had gone out of doors – to the coffee house perhaps. Or what if Fidelis had not been there to keep me alert? I might have dozed off in front of the fire and slept for an hour, which I often did do after supper. What then?

The thought of Elizabeth being touched by that man's hands, his lips, simply seared me. It seared me and yet I thought it, I pictured it, unable to stop. Over and over, on the edge of tears, my heart beating, over and over.

I thought of what I would like to do to that man in vengeance. My first impulse – simply to kill him – had passed. The second was to arrest him and haul him before the magistrate, as one would do in normal times. What a feeble idea that seemed now, with our constables impotent, our magistrates fled, and all our law suspended. As matters stood, with a Prince and a whole army at his back, the Marquis was legally untouchable, and I was without recourse. It grievously wounded me that, as Elizabeth's husband, I could not punish him or see him punished in the courts. Any hope I might have of going to the Prince himself and denouncing the man directly was equally forlorn. After all, d'Éguilles was a member of his high council, and what did the Prince know of me?

I went up and squeezed in beside my wife and child. Both were sleeping and so, at length, was I.

In the morning the Marquis did not dare show his face, while Luke Fidelis had a full day ahead visiting country patients and set off at dawn. So it was only Madame Lachatte and Captain Brown taking breakfast with us – an almost silent meal. Elizabeth would not discuss with me the events of the previous evening and evaded all my attempts to talk to her alone. She saw to Hector's needs, gave household instructions to Matty and went about the house with even more than her usual bustle, all the time tight-lipped and narrow-eyed.

The whole of Preston was also in a bustle because, as we learned very early, the rebel army was everywhere striking its camps and quitting its billets prior to moving on. Market stallholders were pushed aside to form a wide diagonal passage across Market Place from the mouth of Friar Gate to the Old Shambles. Captain Brown explained what would happen. At the central cross, where he had proclaimed his father King, the Prince and his immediate retinue would greet the leading regiment as it came up. He would then take his place at its head and lead it on foot, just as he had led it into Preston, and so they would march away. Behind him the Highlanders, Lowlanders, French and Irish, who made up the motley army, would file through Preston in a continuous snake from the top of Friar Gate to the bottom of Church Gate until the last of the stragglers, the baggage train, the women and the hangers-on had entered the hollow way that led down to Walton-le-Dale and the road south.

Furzey came to the office telling how a couple of Highlanders had slept on his cottage's parlour floor. Their bare knees and incomprehensible language had terrified his old mother, but

Furzey, to my surprise, had nothing bad to say about his unbidden guests. They had been courteous, sung songs and even performed a dance for the entertainment of Mrs Furzey.

Our own guests departed in a manner rather different from their arrival. The Marquis crept away silently and was hardly noticed, with Captain Brown taking charge of his box and baggage. Madame Lachatte, on the other hand, said a very full farewell to Elizabeth in the kitchen, and then to me in the office.

'I feel you and I have become friends,' she told me, 'and I'm grieved we shall probably never meet again. I am also terribly sorry about the Marquis's behaviour last night. It was bad enough him looking goats and monkeys at your wife all through dinner yesterday, but now trying to . . . Well, there's no excuse. I have no control over him. He is a beast. *C'est tout!*'

She patted her bosom.

'I've told him he won't lay a finger on *this* body for a week, so I have. He can go whistle else.'

I found it hard to devise a response to this last remark, so I changed the subject.

'How are you travelling? Do you ride?'

'I have a seat in the coach of Lady Ogilvy. Mrs Murray of Broughton, the wife of another of the Prince's great generals, is with us also. She is a most beautiful woman.'

'You need fear no comparison, Madame,' I said.

'Thank you, sir, you are gallant. Now I must say goodbye, I think, or I shall have to run to catch up with them.'

As she leaned to touch cheeks with mine, her perfume filled my nose and I became hot and a little stammering. In spite of my concern for my wife's treatment by the lecherous Marquis, I had not become proof against his mistress's charm and face. And I thought now, as we said goodbye, that the fact she *was* the Marquis's mistress only showed the extent to which last night he had insulted not one but two beautiful women that I cared for.

I pulled myself together and gave her a bow.

'It has been an honour and a pleasure to know you, Madame.'

She extended her hand, and I kissed it.

*   *   *

By nine o'clock, while there were still many running around tidying up after the army, the main body of men had begun to move into Friar Gate and advance towards Market Place. As the first rank reached there, a cheer went up: the Prince had arrived to take up his station. Pipes played, drums drummed, banners streamed, and the townspeople hurried in their thousands to line the route. Many cheered and wished the soldiers victory, others tried to make one last-minute sale or get one last-minute kiss.

With all this tumult it was impossible to see the Prince himself, and I realized that I had still never had a proper look at him, apart from that distant view during the proclamation. So, with this in mind, I threw on my greatcoat and was about to go out when I was forestalled by a furious hammering at the office door. I opened it myself, as I was nearest, and found myself face to face with the Highlander that I had spoken to two nights before on Playhouse Green – the one with the huge dog.

'Good morning – Sergeant, isn't it?' I said politely. 'How can I help you?'

'You're Titus Cragg?'

'Yes.'

'I have orders to bring you with me.'

'Bring me where?'

'You'll find out.'

'But you can't just—'

'Aye, we can. I see you're in your coat already.'

He took a firm grip on my upper arm and pulled me down the steps. Once I was in the street, a second soldier seized my other arm and I was marched away. Twisting around, I saw Furzey standing in amazement at the door and Elizabeth at one of the upper windows. From the movement of her mouth I could tell she was calling my name. I attempted a smile of reassurance.

I was taken – or dragged – to the House of Correction in March Lane, which the rebels had been using to detain a few Prestonians who had offended them. I was immediately brought to the business room of Arnold Limb, who in more normal times was custodian of the place. Sitting behind Limb's writing table, an officer with a clerk alongside him was dealing with the release of the detainees, who stood in a file outside the door, guarded by a pair of armed soldiers. One of the prisoners hoping to be liberated was Arnold Limb himself; another was Sergeant Oswald Mallender, with three days of stubble on his chin and an aggrieved look about his eyes. Seeing me pushed forward ahead of him, this at once changed to suspicion. I had many times crossed swords with this law officer, who was ignorant enough to believe a sergeant took precedence over a coroner.

I was presented to the man in charge, a grizzled Scotchman with a weathered face and thick beard. He exchanged a few words in Gaelic with my escort while looking me gravely up and down. Switching to English, he asked my name and I told him. He spoke to the clerk, then snapped his fingers and held out his hand, into which the clerk smartly delivered a paper, which he looked over before turning his attention back to me.

'You are Lawyer Cragg?'

'Yes. And I would be obliged if you would tell me why I have been seized. You have no legal authority here. As a lawyer I know this.'

He pointed to the prisoners waiting outside the door.

'We had authority enough to lock them up. We call it the authority of the Regent of Scotland and England, Prince Charles Edward. Do you deny that authority?'

'Most certainly I deny it, if it deprives me unjustly of my liberty.'

'We'll see about "unjustly". We hear you have been party to, or are privy to information on, the deaths of our comrades William Sinclair and John MacNab. These men disappeared after coming to this area with letters from the Prince greeting his supporters. Our information is that they were killed. D'you ken what I'm talking about?'

'Yes. Yes, of course I do. You see I'm coroner and I—'

'Good. Then you may stop your blathering, because you're coming on the road along with us.'

I was shocked into silent gaping. The Highlanders that had brought me here received a couple of curt instructions, upon which they turned me smartly around and we marched out to the House of Correction's courtyard. A large cart stood near the gate, in which two rows of men sat facing each other. The soldier guarding the cart dropped the tailgate as we approached, and I was pushed up to join them. Arnold Limb's stock of leg irons had been looted from his storeroom and each of the prisoners wore a shackle around his right ankle, which was attached by a chain to one of the links of another much heavier chain – I would call it a nautical chain – lying on the cart bed. I was duly shackled to it by the guards in the same way. It was a simple arrangement that made the prisoners' individual escape impossible and their collective escape unlikely.

Most of my fellow prisoners sat with their heads bowed, deaf to everything but their own thoughts. There were two among them that I recognized. One was a very loud-mouthed fellow called Bellasis who was often heard in the Mitre bringing verbal brimstone down on the heads of all Jacobites. The other was Archibald MacLintock, and it was he that I was sitting next to.

'For what have they taken you up, MacLintock?' I said.

'Some daft idea they've got.'

'How is that?'

'They found letters in my house. A very nasty neighbour of mine suggested that they make a search. Well, I do correspond with Glasgow, you know, but only on matters commercial – purely commercial. I also write to Manchester, Liverpool and London. And now the rebels threaten me with their military punishment as a spy. My wife's afraid it means they want to shoot me. What do you think, Cragg? Surely they won't go so far.'

'I'm sure they will only interrogate you and let you go.'

'Which they could've done in Preston. For what reason did they arrest you, Cragg?'

'They think I know something about the murder of the two Scotchmen who were found dead near Ribchester with their heads off. They are quite right. I do know something about it, but, like you, I'm not sure why they haven't simply questioned me in Preston. Perhaps there is another reason for this.'

I did not enlarge on the thought – not out loud. I preferred

not to pour all the details of why I had broken d'Éguilles's
nose in public. And, in any case, the thought depended on the
extent of d'Éguilles's power and influence in the army. No
doubt he bitterly resented my assault on him. I had been in
the right, but that would not stop him from hating me for it.

In my own head I thought it over. Suppose the matter of
the Ribchester attacks had been raised in the rebel war council
on the previous afternoon. If so, d'Éguilles would know my
own connection with the matter and this would give him an
idea of how to get revenge. He had no doubt spent the night
dwelling on it. It would just be a matter of sending a message
to the MacGregors that I had been concerned in the horrible
death of their comrades to ensure my arrest.

Our cart bumped along two or three hundred yards behind
the rearmost of the main body of soldiers, one of three dozen
vehicles loaded up with baggage, victuals, arms and sick and
wounded men, and at least one carrying prisoners like
ourselves. In front of, behind and alongside us trudged the
camp followers – hawkers, mountebanks, ballad sellers,
ragged whores, soldiers' wives (a few with their children in
tow) and others who tagged along with the army for some
reason or another, or none. Geese, goats and donkeys
were led or driven. Dogs padded this way and that between
the traffic, their tongues lolling. Chickens squawked in wicker
baskets.

The army's plan, I heard, was to rest for the night in Wigan.
The advance guard must have reached the town before noon,
but it took the oxen and spavined draft horses of the baggage
train ten hours to complete the seventeen-mile journey. Along
the way Bellasis bought a flagon of ale from a table outside
a wayside mughouse.

'Give us a wet, man,' the prisoners around him said, and at
first, with his flagon still pretty full, he handed it around. But
his liberality diminished as the level of ale in the flagon sank,
and soon he was sharing with no one as he became lion-like
in drink, roaring his defiance at the rebels in a continuous
stream of slurred oaths and profanities.

'Have my horses, would ye? I'll have ye, ye rebel bastards.

I'll have your balls boiled and your arses for bacon. Arrest a
Bellasis? Steal my colt and mare? Wait till I have ye, ye
mangy-bald, crooked-cock dogs.'

After receiving a few cuffs around the head from our guard,
he was forced to tone his tirades down until they were delivered under his breath, with occasional louder outbursts.

'Bloody shabby, scabby, scratchy, beshitten, lousy rebel
bastards. I'll have ye. I will.'

We rode into Wigan, a town much given to metal smelting,
where we were brought to the house of the constable, a fellow
called Terence Pitt, whom I knew to be more corrupt than a
rotten bucket. We were each put into one of Pitt's pinder cages
since, as well as being constable, he was the taker-up of stray
animals, which he returned to their owners only after the
payment of fines, from which he took a cut. Not unlike John
Wilkinson, late tax collector of Penwortham and now of
Ormskirk, Pitt had built himself a splendid new house out
of these profits. To the rear of the house lay a large compound
behind a high fence – the pinfold – in which stood a
scattering of about twenty cages and coops.

It was thus that I found myself sharing an ignominious,
draughty accommodation with two calves, whose large rolling
eyes followed my movements with grave curiosity. The cage
was some ten feet square and enclosed by walls made of
stout, close-set ashwood staves, which I could see would be
difficult to break down and impossible to squeeze between.
Two kilted soldiers guarded us, patrolling the cages at ten-
minute intervals.

Those of us in the cart with a few pennies in our pockets
had eaten on the road, buying bread and ham or cheese – at
grossly inflated prices – from shops or taverns we passed along
the way. But by the time we had been imprisoned at Wigan
for three hours, I, for one, was hungry again, though no one
seemed to have considered the matter of feeding us. I could
hear the voices of my fellow prisoners calling out to our guards
for food and water. They got nothing but orders in Gaelic,
which I supposed meant the equivalent of 'button it'.

*   *   *

At eight o'clock by my pocket watch, the sergeant of the MacGregors came for me, attended by another man. He removed my shackle and pushed me out of the cage. The pinfold lay just on the edge of Wigan, some twenty yards back from the highway that led to and from the town. With the sergeant leading the way and holding a lantern, and the other walking behind with his musket prodding at my back, we came by that road to a house which, from its size and furnishings, seemed to be that of a tolerably rich citizen. Here I was brought before two officers sitting at a card table in the lobby, men no older than twenty-five.

'What this one's name?' said one to the sergeant as he consulted a list that lay before him.

'Titus Cragg, sir. May we go and have our wet, sir?'

'Yes, go on. It's through there. You may sit, Mr Cragg.'

I sat down in the upright chair that faced the two men across the small table. The lobby had several doorways leading from it, a double one beside the foot of stairs and two or three at the back, behind the staircase. My escort disappeared through one of the latter as the second young officer addressed me directly.

'Your wife is Elizabeth Cragg,' he said.

'Yes – how did you know that?'

'Never mind. You had under your hospitality last night the Marquis d'Éguilles, I understand.'

The accent in his voice – in both their voices – was softer and more refined than the Highland tones I had grown used to.

'Yes.'

'Monsieur le Marquis makes a complaint against you. He says that you accused him falsely of rape against Mrs Cragg and that you yourself then gravely assaulted him, breaking his nose. What do you say to that?'

He looked very serious.

'Well, yes. I mean, I didn't in fact accuse him of rape—'

'You *didn't*? He says you did.'

'*Attempted* rape. I accused him, and I *still* accuse him, of attempted rape. I interrupted him before he could . . .'

'Before he could what?'

'Do any lasting harm.'

He snapped his fingers.

'What did you see, then? Tell!'

'I went into the room that we had given the Marquis to sleep in and found Elizabeth with him.'

'*With* him?'

'Yes, but only because she went in to collect his tray.'

'But in doing so she became intimate with the Marquis?'

'Certainly not!'

'Well, then, what is your complaint?'

'That the Marquis . . . that he was trying to force her, sir. He had her down on the bed and, well, he was lying on top of her, attempting to kiss her.'

'She was fully clothed?'

'Yes, *of course* she was fully clothed! She was collecting his tray!'

'But apparently had time to become intimate with the Marquis?'

'No! As I just told you—'

'And you became suspicious of her because, of course, the witch had done this kind of thing before, behind your back, so you went up there—'

'*Damn you, sir!* It was no such thing!'

'It wasn't?'

His eyes widened and the brows arched in surprise. As I grew angrier, the serious mask of the young fellow's face very slowly, almost imperceptibly, began to dissolve. His lips twitched. But even as he was trying to control his mouth, he could not prevent the hilarity showing in his eyes. He glanced at his companion and suddenly they both burst into laughter.

'Mr Cragg, shall I tell you something about the Marquis?' he said.

'I doubt I want to hear it.'

'Oh, I think you do. It is this. In every town we have stopped in, the Marquis has tried to take advantage of at least one woman in his host's household. Everyone knows he does it – he can't help himself. And you broke his nose because of this behaviour – and good for you, sir. He deserves it.'

'Then why have you . . . What am I doing here?'

'For a much better reason. You must reassure yourself, Mr Cragg. You should know we don't put a civilian in irons and haul him along in the baggage train lightly. We have more important things to deal with than the complaints of a cuckolded husband.'

He held up his hand to forestall my objection.

'All right! An *almost* cuckolded husband. No. It is a very serious matter that you've been taken up for.'

'What, then?'

He wagged his finger at me.

'It is a matter of a murder, Mr Cragg, for which this army does not shrink from exacting the penalty of death. To be precise, it is a matter of ascertaining whether you did it and are therefore deserving of a military execution.'

THIRTEEN

The two young officers were merely gatekeepers to the ordeal which lay ahead of me. I was made to wait in their company for a further twenty minutes, during which they played cards and took no further notice of me except to give me, at my request, a drink of water. At last a bell was rung within and they took me through to a panelled room where three older officers sat behind a long table littered with documents, and with them a civilian clerk equipped with paper and writing equipment. Towards the front of the tabletop a heavy cavalry sword was laid, to lend military authority to the meeting. My escorts were dismissed, and the older presiding officer rose and growled.

'You are Titus Cragg of Preston?'

'Yes.'

'The MacGregor.'

'I'm sorry?'

'The MacGregor.'

'What MacGregor?'

'Myself, man! The MacGregor. Are ye stupid?'

I twigged him then. He was introducing himself, MacGregor being not merely his name, but his rank. As *the* MacGregor he was the top man, the MacGregor that represented all the other MacGregors – and that included the dead MacGregors. And I had every reason to believe, based on the plaid, that those dead MacGregors included at least one of the murdered and headless men that we had inquested at Ribchester.

'I demand to know what this is all about,' I said. 'I have been unjustly taken away from my home and family, starved and imprisoned. I must know why.'

The MacGregor sighed, as if he were tired of explaining painful matters.

'This is a military tribunal. I hold the rank of colonel and am enquiring into the deaths of twae of our men, who were brutally killed and their heads taken off while they were visiting Lancashire, one of them being a clansman of mine, Jock MacNab. Jock was a very strong man who could only have been overcome by tricks and connivance or being grossly outnumbered. Under his protection was a young laddie, William Sinclair, who was carrying dispatches under orders of my commanding officer, the Duke of Perth, and he is the other victim. This tribunal has the power and authority of a military court. So now to the point: based on this evidence . . .'

He selected a sheet of paper from the table in front of him and, after quickly looking it over, wafted it in my direction.

'Based on this paper here, you, Titus Cragg, are accused of the responsibility for their deaths, which is a capital crime.'

For a moment the power of speech deserted me. I was thunderbolted. Incredulous.

I said at last, 'Who has accused me of this? Some lying person must have given perjurous testimony.'

'In saying that, you only accuse yourself of lying and perjury. And though you are innocent of perjury (in my estimate), you are guilty of the other far worse crime.'

'I am bemused. Perjury? What perjury do you mean? I demand an explanation for all this.'

'Are ye no listening? Like I just said: as you admit your guilt, there is no perjury. No man in his right mind admits to murder unless he did it. I shall read out your confession.'

He balanced a pair of ancient spectacles on his nose, cleared his throat and read in a ringing voice. '*I am it must be admitted the man who ordered the killing of the two Highlanders, and all that is the essence of villainy however one views the military situation. (Signed) Titus Cragg.*'

He looked up at me over the top of his reading glasses.

'There is more about you being coroner – whatever that is – but that's the meat of it: your admission that you ordered the killing of those two men, and that you know full well the evil you have done. You claim this writing is the work of a liar. Well, sir, that liar would be you, as you have signed it. It *is* your hand?'

'Let me see.'

'You may read it but not handle it. Come forward.'

I stepped up to the desk and he held the paper before my eyes. It had only three lines of writing and I could see straight away they were in the legal hand of Robert Furzey, except the signature, which was my own. After a few moment's thought my confusion cleared. I knew what this paper was.

'Where did you get this?'

'Is it your hand?'

'The signature? Yes, of course. I repeat: where did you obtain it?'

'We searched Lord Derby's house and there it was, under some piece of furniture. The man had been burning papers before he ran away, but your confession slipped the flames.'

'It is not my confession. It is very far from being my confession.'

'And yet that is your signature.'

'Yes, but you have misread it. You have misunderstood the whole thing.'

'D'you think we're stupid? No, sir, it is as plain as day. You confess here it was you that gave the order.'

'No, no. It doesn't say that. Look at the punctuation. You've read it wrong. You must see, this is the last page of a much longer document. It is, in fact, the end of my inquest report.'

'Inquest? What do you mean?'

'Coroner's inquest – surely you know what that is!'

He did not like my 'surely you know'. He frowned.

'Explain what you mean and be quick.'

'It is an inquiry into a death.'

'Ah! You mean by the Procurator Fiscal?'

'Yes, a person like that.'

'Looking into the deaths of our comrades?'

'Yes.'

'And you told the fiscal—'

'It's the coroner, here in England.'

'You told the coroner that you were the guilty one?'

'No, no. You miss the point, sir. I *am* the Coroner. This is my own report, or part of it.'

'And in this report you accuse yourself. I would say that is quite conclusive of your guilt.'

'No, it is not, sir. Why, how and under what circumstances

would I have cause to kill your kinsman and the other young man, and then confess it in my coroner's report? It does not make any sense.'

'I know that. The sense is what we want to find out – before we shoot you.'

'But look!' I said. 'Look at the punctuation. Here after "I am" you have a full stop. Then a new sentence: "It must be admitted the man who ordered the killing et cetera." Do you see?'

'I see it is written here "I am the one",' said the MacGregor. 'You are owning to the crime.'

'It is a loose page, the last one. There was more matter – much more – on previous pages, no doubt burned or taken away by the Earl. "I am" are the last words of the previous sentence, don't you see?'

He frowned more deeply.

'Step back, if you please,' he ordered.

I did so and watched as the MacGregor showed the paper to his colleagues. They conferred in whisper and, after no more than a minute, he turned back to me.

'We are nae satisfied by your explanation, sir, and as you cannae produce the supposed other pages you mention in your defence, this tribunal is in agreement. Your signed confession is in our hands and we consider that enough to condemn you. There is nae time for further investigation. You are therefore sentenced, by the authority of His Royal Highness, to die under military law by shooting.'

'Shooting?' I gasped. 'Are you mad? This is . . . I cannot take this seriously!'

'You had better,' he said, ringing his little handbell. 'And give thanks in your prayers you won't be hanged. It's a much nastier death.'

The sergeant appeared in response to the bell.

'Take him back to his cage, Sergeant. We'll make the necessary arrangements for first thing in the morning.'

Fifteen minutes later I was back with my fellow prisoners, the two calves. Feeling low, frightened and queasy in my stomach – all thoughts of hunger had disappeared – I went to them where they lay together in a mound of straw, pulling my greatcoat closely around me and sinking down beside them. Patiently, the young animals put up with my company, which was lucky because the air was freezing hard and the warmth radiated by their bodies was almost luxurious.

Surely the MacGregor had been bluffing, I thought. He had to be. But why? For what possible gain?

And if he had not, I was to be shot, first thing in the morning, with no chance of appeal. Well, I could understand why they would want to shoot the person who had ordered the nasty deaths of their comrades. I myself regarded it as a heinous crime and I sincerely hoped – I still hoped – someone would be punished for it in due course. Just so long as it was not now, and not me.

But perhaps there was still time to make them see sense. I thought very hard, trying to remember the wording of the last few remarks in my report to Lord Derby. If I did not remember them right, I would have no chance of defending myself – even if it was not too late, and I very much feared it might be. There was a copy of the whole document at the office back in Preston, but that was no use to me now.

To the best of my recall, I had ended by saying, despite the verdict of the jury, that I personally thought James Barrowclough was the one who commissioned the crime. I had written something to the effect that I expected him to absent himself for a while, and be difficult to find, particularly given the present military situation of the country. But what precisely had I written in that penultimate sentence ending with the words 'I am'?

That such a religious, outwardly decent man should engage in such a villainous killing, and specially on these victims at this particularly dangerous time, nobody is more surprised than I am.

Yes, it was something like that. And I went on to write: *It must be admitted, the man who ordered the killing of these two Highlanders, and all that, would be the essence of villainy however one viewed the military situation.* The commas around 'and all that' were also ignored by my accusers. How could they not see that the commas and full stops governed the sense? Of course, they would if the complete report was under their eyes, but it wasn't, and I would be shot dead before it could be.

Having rested for a while with the calves, it occurred to me for the first time that the soldiers had forgotten to reapply my leg-iron. Small mercies. I got up and prowled in the dark around the perimeter of my cage, testing the bars. They were strong. Without a tool of any kind, I stood no chance of penetrating them. And the ground was frozen hard: there was not the slightest possibility of digging my way out. I was as helpless as the two calves, but unlike them I could have no hope that someone would arrive to pay my ransom.

What would it be like to be shot? Wearing a blindfold, if I was lucky. Some sort of stake that I'd be tied to. Would there be one shooter or more than one? I had the idea that it was customary for a military execution to be by a troop of gunners, so that no individual could accuse himself of being the unique *one* that did the killing. It was a combined effort by comrades, and if there be any doubt afterwards, it would be a shared doubt.

I wished I had a light and writing material, to put down some thoughts on the solemn occasion of my facing death. I remembered once our schoolmaster reading to us from a book of Raleigh's melancholy poems those he composed in the Tower before his execution. We had been made to learn one of them by heart, but now I could remember just three lines. They ran, more or less:

> Such is time, which takes in trust
> Our youth, our joys, and all we loved,
> And pays us back with age and dust.

These were not words likely to brisk me up.

I have never been much of a poet – not much of a Raleigh, come to that. But I still wished I could write a letter, for Elizabeth, for Hector, to be something left of me after I'd gone. Not the possessions I would leave in my will, though there were plenty of those (and how meaningless!). And not my journal, which is mostly a dull daily record. No, I meant something of my thoughts on saying farewell, and my love for them. Otherwise, my family would only have rough memories for things I had said in affection, and many times only half said, as well as some few of my better actions. Such things live on in human memory, but only for a while. Memories erode, lose their shape and definition, and eventually disappear entirely. And when they disappear, one disappears oneself. That was the regrettable side of what I learned from a great friend of mine in childhood, Jerome Greatorex, my father's clerk. Jerome was an old man by the time I knew him, and I treated him as a kind of additional grandfather. We held long philosophical discussions together and once, speaking of death, and the fear of it, Greatorex told me, 'Remember, boy, you're never dead until the last one that knew you is dead. Until then you live in memory.'

Once I reached manhood, like Greatorex at the same age, and partly through his influence, I lost belief in the soul – or, at least, in its immortality. Greatorex told me that he did not consider there was a single soul in hell. I challenged him (as still youthfully credulous) by asking, 'What about the truly wicked people such as murderers, who surely can't go to heaven?' He told me he did not think much of heaven either.

'We come on to this earth inexplicably, and we leave it the same way. One day you may believe this too. It is not an opinion you want to go around shouting about, but it is one I believe educated people increasingly share in these days. Sir Isaac Newton and Mr Locke have shown us the mechanics of the universe and of society. They have nothing to say of the soul.'

So that was it. I was looking annihilation directly in the face. I thought of those Calvinists who believed in predestination; it didn't matter now if they were right or wrong. If life itself is the interval between nothing and nothing, all theories of God and his intentions are equally ridiculous.

I heard the scrabble of a rat and what sounded like gnawing. I shuddered. That I was spending my last night on earth in the company of young cattle and rodents was not cheering. The other prisoners they had brought here were in other cages, and none of them close by. The nearest thing to human company was when a shadow passed before the bars of my cage – one of the soldiers on sentry duty. I got up and crept to the wall. I could see him through gaps in the cage wall, stamping his feet and blowing on his fingers. Steam plumed from his mouth as he breathed out into the freezing air. I did not feel like speaking to him, even if he had been able to understand English. After all, he might be the one to put a bullet through my heart in the morning. I watched as he moved off to do the rounds of the other cages, and it became quiet again.

The rats resumed their gnawing and scrabbling, louder this time. Were they trying to get in? Or out? Suddenly, there was a mighty crack, like a pistol shot. I froze. The hairs on my neck bristled. Then the scrabbling became louder, fiercer, and I began to doubt my original rodent hypothesis. The noises were too loud.

'Who's there?'

There was a second cracking sound, multiple compared with the first, and all at once moonlight came into the calf-cage. An aperture had opened up in its far back wall, blocked now by a dark figure that was forcing its way inside. Having succeeded, it stood up on two legs.

'How d'you do, Titus?' said Luke Fidelis. 'And how in thunder did you get yourself into this pickle?'

FOURTEEN

I am not ashamed to say that I embraced him, and that tears welled up in my eyes. Perhaps I would have saluted any deliverer in this way, for I was certainly in a distressed and feeble state. But Fidelis being my close friend, and frequent colleague, made it impossible to suppress my emotion.

Fidelis, however, was the same as always – rational and cool in the face of physical danger. At other times he displayed a warmer side, usually in connection with a beautiful woman, for in love he was woundable and perhaps even capable of weeping (though I had never seen it). Also at certain sporting contests – boxing, or a cockfight, or (as I remembered) one particularly barbaric football game – he might become extremely heated about the money and honour that lay at stake. But at times when an entirely cold calculation was needed to face extraordinary jeopardy, Fidelis was your man.

'We must leave,' he said in a low voice as he disentangled himself from my arms, 'and be quick and quiet about it. The sentries should have reached the far side of the compound by now. They'll be stopping there ten minutes for a smoke.'

'How do you know that?'

'I've been watching them. You go first.'

He pressed me down by my shoulder and I sank to my hands and knees, then crawled towards the narrow opening that Fidelis had somehow created in the ashwood wall. As I pushed through it, my hand touched a tool, which proved to be a hand axe, and another, which proved to be a short crowbar. Then I was outside. I stood up in the lee of the calf-cage, pressing my back against it, and sucked air deep into my lungs, drawing tremendous breaths of freedom and escape. Fidelis came out immediately behind me and, as soon as he stood, crept to the corner of the building and peered round it.

'Come on, Titus! You must run if you can.'

The moonlight made the frosted grass of the compound

glitter. To anyone watching, there was enough of it to pick us out as two black shadows flitting across the whitened ground. But the sentries must have been fully engaged with their pipes for we heard no cry of alarm or sound of feet running towards us across the frozen earth.

But as we neared the gate, there was a new danger. I made out the silhouette of a large dog kennel, and from it a huge, shaggy, drooling hound emerging to greet us. He gave out a low growl, his gigantic mouth agape, and we both pulled up and stood facing him.

'Is it chained?' whispered Fidelis.

'I don't know. Didn't you meet him on the way in?'

'I came over the fence on the other side.'

'Then why don't we go back there now?'

'Because Towser here will run after us if he can. He'll certainly bark and probably bite. Even if they've chained him, he'll make a lot of noise and bring the sentries down on us.'

'I don't think he will,' I said. 'We can easily get past this dog. And *he* isn't called Towser. She's a bitch.'

I had suddenly understood who the dog was.

'I have met her,' I went on, 'and she's nothing but a softling.'

I went towards the dog, and she moved her massive head up and down, sniffing the air around me. Her memory stirred and she in her turn knew me – as the owner of that pleasant little buffle-dog that she'd met in Preston and had wanted to play with a few nights back.

'Bawty,' I said, softly.

I placed my hand on her broad head to scratch it in a friendly way, as I had before. She wagged her tail and very quietly whined, as if pleading for a favour. I now saw the screw-clip that attached her collar to a long trailing chain which, at its other end, must have been locked on to an embedded ring inside the kennel. For some reason of pity for the dog, or defiance of her master, it came into my head to set her free. In just a couple of seconds I had unscrewed the clip, unhooked the chain from Bawty's collar and thrown it aside. Knowing she was free, the dog then began capering around, as I had seen her do on Playhouse Green when she had tried to press Suez into a game.

'Come on,' pressed Fidelis. 'Leave the mutt. We must go.'

We crept out of the pinfold and past Pitt's house, which lay in darkness, before taking to our heels along the track that led away from the house and towards the road. Bawty bounded joyfully after us.

'Bawty, no!' I whispered sharply when we reached the road. 'Go back! Go back!'

I pointed the way back, but Bawty sat on her haunches and looked at me from the depth of her soul, her tail thumping the ground.

'Titus!' said Fidelis sharply. 'I have a horse tied to a tree in that copse over there. Forget the dog and come on, or we may never get away.'

With Bawty still in close attendance, we hopped over the stone wall that lined the other side of the road. The rebel army was camped on the other side of town so that the field we landed in was deserted. It contained a small stand of trees about fifty yards back from the road, and here we found one of Luke Fidelis's horses haltered to a tree and patiently awaiting us.

'So your horse wasn't discovered by the rebels?' I asked.

'No indeed. I concealed him just in time. My neighbour luckily has an unusually capacious pigsty.'

He patted the horse's flank.

'The poor fellow didn't much like the stink, but it stopped the rebels from having him for their cavalry, which he would have hated much more. Here. Take this. You must be thirsty and hungry.'

He had unbuckled a saddlebag and now pulled out a flask, a lump of bread and another of cheese. When I had devoured them, Fidelis mounted the horse, a large, strong animal easily capable of carrying the two of us without strain. Fidelis pulled me up behind him and we started off, taking roads that skirted the edge of the town at a distance of about a mile. Some way north of the village of Standish, we met the Great North Road and were soon making strong progress towards Preston. Bawty, who had raced around us in boisterous circles at the start, soon settled down in our wake at a steady and contented trot. She was now a confirmed deserter from the rebel army.

'So how the devil did you find me?' I asked.

'Mr Freckleton at the Bear's Paw Inn here in Wigan. I'd been calling on patients around Preston all day, but when I returned and Elizabeth told me you had been taken, I set off at once to follow. I made a reckless promise to Mrs Cragg to bring you back. Well, Freckleton knew the pinfold had been put to use for prisoners and directed me there. I was watching as they brought you in. You looked extremely depressed.'

'I was depressed. I was a condemned man. The early hours of the morning had been set aside for getting me shot and I could see no way out.'

Waking to a new day, Preston found it had a sore head. The rebels' stay had been brief enough, and the soldiers had been more or less well behaved, but no one sees the backs of more than six or seven thousand uninvited guests without there being much to set right, repair and clear up. Also the occupation had given the townsfolk a heady intermission from reality, a spree if you like, and they were now crapulously out of sorts as they went about this business. As we crossed the bridge at Walton and rode up to Church Gate, we passed the time of day with a few men and women along the wayside. They growled rather than spoke and did not walk erect, but shifted along with heads bowed, as if to avoid suspicion or accusation.

While the political division of the town was by no means healed, it was clear that neither the Whigs nor the Jacobites knew quite what to make of matters. Had the Chevalier (or Pretender) proved his honour or his shame? Was the Pretender (or Chevalier) scuttling down the road to miserable defeat or marching towards refulgence and glory? No one was quite sure of anything.

My own first concern on opening the door of my home was with my family, and most particularly how Elizabeth fared. I called loudly to her from the doorstep, and she came into the hall with a look of incredulity mixed with wonder.

'Oh, Titus! I had quite made up my mind they had killed you.'

'They wanted to, and might have, but for this man.'

I turned sideways to show her Fidelis, astride his horse in

the street. He raised his hat and she went down the steps to give him grave thanks. I did not hear exactly what she said – something along the lines that she was sorry if he had put himself in danger on her account. Well, I thought, Fidelis might have gone to my aid in any case, but an appeal from a beautiful woman had always stirred his chivalrous soul, compelling him to respond at any cost to himself.

Suez came out and barked in a friendly way at Bawty and ran circles around her, which she seemed delighted with. I had suggested during our ride that as we had Suez already, Fidelis might like to take the big dog into his own establishment. After some thought, he liked the idea, and now a rope was found by which Bawty was towed away behind Fidelis, protesting a little at the parting from Suez, to her new home. Before he left, Fidelis raised a matter that had escaped from my mind as completely as I had escaped from the pinfold.

'We must talk about Horace Limmington,' he said. 'I suppose you will not change the date of tomorrow's inquest.'

So we arranged to meet next day at the coffee house after Divine Service and I returned indoors, where I gratefully allowed myself to be pampered by Matty. A warming pan was put in my bed and a great fire lit in the bedchamber; meanwhile, a hot breakfast was prepared for me. By ten o'clock, when I had eaten my fill, the warming pan came out and I slipped into its place. I slept deliciously through the rest of the morning.

By Sunday the town had been more or less set to rights, but many waited eagerly for news of the rebels' progress. Word had come in that the Duke of Cumberland, the King's third son, was returned from service in Flanders to take command of a government force now in Staffordshire and would undoubtedly (according to some) intercept the Pretender and bring him to battle. In church on Sunday the vicar's sermon praised the young military Duke, with a text from his favourite prophet, Jeremiah: 'The lion is come up from the thicket and the destroyer of the Gentiles is on his way.' In his ringing (but long-winded) way he went on to foresee the lion's imminent mauling and disembowelment of the Jacobite army.

My own attention went elsewhere. I had the Limmington inquest to conduct at Penwortham the next day, in preparation for which I decided that after dinner I would ride over to Penwortham on Jones – the other horses having still not returned to Lawson's – and follow Luke Fidelis's advice by paying a visit to Limmington's doctor, Thomas Ross.

The doctor's house showed the man's considerable prosperity, the kind more likely to be found in a physician of Preston. Mrs Ross, a lean, fine-boned woman with an anxious look in her eye, received me. She became noticeably agitated when I said who I was.

'Oh, Mr Cragg, we are honoured, so *honoured* to receive you. Please forgive my husband as he is in his laboratory making up some powders.'

'No matter,' I said. 'Will you show me through to him?'

'Oh no! No. Oh no! He would not like that at all. Not at all. I must fetch him to *you*.'

I waited for five minutes in the hall before Ross himself appeared, a man even bonier than his wife, and with intense staring eyes.

'This way,' he said, opening a door into what I could immediately see was his consulting room. 'I have heard of you, Cragg.'

He said this in such a way that I felt as if he had shaken a warning finger at me. He now pulled a watch from his vest pocket and, noting the time, laid it on the writing table. Then he continued in abrupt style.

'I am a busy man. Kindly state your business.'

Before I could do so, Mrs Ross flitted in, offering me refreshments of currant-breads, shortcake and tea. Her husband gave her a stern glare.

'Don't be foolish, woman. We are in the consulting room. This is not an occasion of biscuits but of business. Leave us.'

When she had gone, I asked if he had heard of the death of Horace Limmington (he had) and whether he knew anything of his last hours (he did not).

'I haven't seen the man for a number of months. He lacked the funds, it seemed, so I closed my books to him. I cannot afford patients that are non-payers.'

'I see. And how was he when you last saw him in a professional way?'

'Very unwell. On the last occasion I noted many signs of decline in him – his spleen, his liver and his stomach were all somewhat disordered, and his heart was weak. He had allowed his troubles to overwhelm him. He had succumbed to poverty and loneliness, and these make very deadly companions, I find.'

'Yet his fortunes had recently turned somewhat. He had found a large sum of money which, he told me, if he could make good his claim to it, would set him back on his feet.'

'Too late,' said Ross, wagging his head sagely. 'He had dizzy spells, tingling in the limbs, cloudy urine and a morbid itching in the testes.'

'Which might mean?'

'That the man would never live long to enjoy the money. In my medical opinion.'

'It appears he was visited by a party of rebel so-called tax collectors on the day he died, who may have attacked him. How would his body stand up to such an unpleasant surprise?'

'It would not. I am not surprised he died if what you tell me is true. Even the slightest provocation would have likely been the death of him.'

'His servant says he was struck on the head with an axe.'

'Ah! Well, that would account for any death, of course.'

'But she may not be a reliable witness. I am wondering if perhaps he might in reality have fallen and struck his head.'

'An unexpected intrusion or threat leading to faintness, loss of consciousness and a fall. That would have done for him all right, in my *medical* opinion.'

He picked up his watch and looked at it, then drew a sheet of paper from a drawer and began to write on it.

'Now, sir,' he said, continuing to write, 'you have had a full ten minutes of my time. Is there anything more?'

'Well, no, I don't think so, unless you can shed any further light on this case.'

'Have I not shed sufficient light on it? The fellow was moribund; that's all there is to it. Here you are.'

He handed me the sheet of paper, which proved to be his bill for five shillings.

'I'm sorry?' I said. 'You are . . . You are *charging* me for this?'

'Certainly I am, sir. My time costs. If I gave it away free, I would be a pauper like Mr Limmington. I am therefore obliged to sell my time, and I do so at a rate of half a crown for every five minutes.'

'But I am not a patient. I merely asked for your valuable help.'

'If my help is valuable, then you must pay for it.'

I was incredulous. I couldn't remember this ever happening before. Briefly, I considered refusing to pay, but then I saw Ross's grim, implacable eyes.

'Oh, very well, I suppose I have it.'

I found the money in my pocket and handed it over. Ross whipped the bill from my fingers, endorsed it as paid and gave it back to me. He immediately began ushering me towards the door, but I stopped him.

'One moment, Doctor Ross. I in turn have a paper for you. May I use your pen?'

I brought the paper from my pocket. It was one of our printed draft summons forms, and I laid it on the table so that I could write Ross's name over the appropriate line. I then filled in the place, time and date, signed my own name and handed it to him.

'It is a summons for you to attend tomorrow's inquest as a witness. It is legally enforceable, and I am afraid you will not be permitted to charge the court for your time. I look forward to seeing you there. Good day, sir.'

The affronted look on his face gave me a certain satisfaction as I left the room.

A little later Fidelis and I met in Preston, as we had arranged, to discuss the testimony he would give the next day.

'How much did Thomas Ross skin you for?' he asked as we settled at our table at the Turk's Head.

I told him and he laughed.

'Two and six per five minutes? The man is a bloodsucker.'

'He has grown rich from it. His house is splendid.'

'And what did he say about Limmington?'

'That he has been mortally sick for weeks, or even months. I had the impression Limmington might have died at any time, from any number of causes.'

'A sudden shock?'

'Yes. I asked particularly if threats from rebels might have alarmed him so much as to cause him a fatal fall, and he confirmed it. What do you think?'

'I have no reason to contradict that diagnosis. The floor of the study – was it of stone?'

'Yes.'

'Then I think we may discount Griselda's axe. A flight of fancy caused by her hearing but not seeing the event happen. The fall, and hitting his head on the floor, might be enough to kill him.'

'There is the other anomaly in her statement, as you pointed out: the time of Limmington's death. She will be the first witness. I wonder if she will maintain her original account of it.'

'We shall have to see.'

He drained his cup of coffee and poured us both another.

FIFTEEN

'Ladies and gentlemen, we are here to look into the sudden death of Horace Limmington of this parish,' I said at nine o'clock the next morning at the Swan Inn, addressing those few good people of Penwortham who were there to give testimony, and the many more who had been drawn by the magnetism of curiosity. 'We shall hear tell of his last hours and some medical evidence also. Shall we begin with the formalities?'

Half an hour later these were complete. The jury had been sworn and taken to view Limmington's body. We solemnly measured the head wound and Furzey made a note of it. We examined the body in its nakedness for any other signs, of which there were none of any salience. I said little, but I felt compassion for these shrunken remains. In spite of Dr Ross's prognosis, Limmington had developed unexpected hopes just before he died, which had just as suddenly been extinguished. Well, I thought, at least he would no longer be bothered by the itch in his testes.

We returned to the courtroom, which was the inn's large parlour. The tables had been cleared away to the walls, except for the one Furzey and I sat behind, and the chairs and forms had been ranged in rows before us, most of them being now occupied by the said good people of Penwortham. The jury sat on a single form to my left while facing them to my right stood an empty chair for the use of the witnesses. I consulted the timetable of names Furzey had drawn up, rang my handbell and called to the chair the first of these.

Griselda, a hunched and shrunken figure in shawl and drugget skirt, shuffled forward and took the oath.

'What is your full name?'

'Griselda Susan Bigelow.'

'And you are a widow who worked lately as servant to the deceased gentleman?'

'Yes.'

'Please tell us what happened at Mr Limmington's house on the day he died.'

In front of this audience it proved difficult to prod and nudge her into telling the story of that night, but in the end she got it out more or less as she'd originally told it to me.

'And are you quite sure,' I said, 'that the bag of money that was found by Mr Limmington was discovered by these soldiers after he was struck down?'

'Yes. They turned the house over and found where it was hidden.'

'Where was that?'

'He'd made a secret hole in the wall behind the wainscot that even I didn't know about. I found the panel pulled away, which was how they found it.'

She also maintained the tale of the axe and did not change her story when I taxed her about the time of death.

'Just before dawn it was, when he gave up the ghost,' she insisted.

'Where did he die?'

'In his bed. He never rose again after I'd got him upstairs, put his nightgown and nightcap on him, and pulled the covers up over him. I sat up beside that bed hour after hour, I did, listening to his groaning breath, hoping for the better and a-fearing the worse, until the groaning stopped.'

'And did you then call in the usual women to lay out the body?'

'No. What do I need to call in the women for? I know what to do. I don't need their or anyone's help.'

'But you had already sent word to Doctor Fidelis of your master's accident.'

'Aye, well, it's what you do, isn't it? Calling the doctor. And like I told you, I knew Doctor Fidelis wouldn't charge.'

'And then in the morning you sent further word that Mr Limmington had died.'

'I thought to spare the doctor his journey. He'd be no use, would he?'

'However, as we shall learn in a few moments, he was of use to me when we came along together.'

I told Griselda she could leave the chair. As she tottered back into the audience, there was a disturbance at the far end of the room. A young female voice was raised to a high, and highly indignant, pitch.

'Give me back-word, would you? Yes, you! You dodger! You son-of-a-bitch of a swike! Crack on all evening and then have your cock's way and sneak off, you rat, leaving me like this? You bastard. You thorough cheating bastard. How dare you show your dirty feak's face here?'

I stood up, ringing my handbell. 'Now then! What is this disturbance?'

A young woman, fair-haired, red-faced and big-bellied, was standing at the end of a row of chairs almost at the back. By how she was pointing and jabbing the air, her torrent of words was meant for someone in the middle of that row. Those in front turned to see how the abuse was received, and in so doing identified her target as a dandified black-haired fellow, who was staring straight ahead, affecting to take no notice. A complacent smile was smeared across his handsome face.

The woman paused, as if to give him time to respond; when he didn't, she flounced from the room and slammed the door.

After the buzz of comment over this incident had fallen away, I asked Dr Ross to come forward. He swore his oath in a cold, resentful voice, and answered my questions in much the same style.

'Yes, I was for some time Limmington's medical adviser . . . No, I had not seen him for several months . . . That is correct. He had multiple disorders . . . No, I did not think he would recover. I considered him a hopeless case . . . A few more months at the most . . . He would quite likely have been killed by an unforeseen unpleasant surprise, or reprehension of the senses – what we doctors would call an *incursus improvisus* – or even a blow to the *corpus*, or the head. Such a knock would lead in all probability to a cordial insult.'

'I'm sorry, Doctor?'

'*Insultus cordialis*, sir. What many call an attack to the heart.'

'Leading to immediate death?'

'Oh, yes – in the state of Limmington's health, I would say so.'

I let him go. He'd spent ten minutes in the chair – time, by his reckoning, worth five shillings, a sum (I was happy to reflect) he would never get.

Next to the chair came Luke Fidelis. He gave a succinct summary, entirely in English, of his physical examination of the body.

'So what do you consider to have been the cause of this unfortunate death?' I asked.

'A blow to the head which may have led to bleeding in the brain. If so, he would have fallen unconscious and died within a few minutes.'

'What about Doctor Ross's suggestion of – what was it? – an insult to Mr Limmington's heart?'

'That is possible also, if his health was as Doctor Ross described. Supposing the injury to the skull did not kill him instantly, it might very well have caused the heart to fail.'

'Let's turn to the question of when Mr Limmington died. You mention the stiffness of his flesh when you examined it. Do you draw any inference from this as to the time at which the death occurred?'

'Stiffening begins in the eyelids no less than five hours after death. It takes a matter of a few hours to become general across the entire body. If the body is kept cold, that would be longer – ten to fourteen hours.'

'And stiffness was indeed general by the time you saw it?'

'It covered the whole of the body.'

'And the temperature of the house was . . .?'

'Very cold. There had been no fire in the room.'

'And what time was it when you made your examination?'

'Half past ten in the morning.'

'Our first witness stated that Mr Limmington had died just before dawn. Are you saying that is incorrect?'

'It must be. I would be very surprised if Limmington was still breathing when that night began.'

'Twelve hours earlier than we have been told?'

'Yes.'

The jury were nudging each other and whispering.

I then called Constable Gibbins, who confirmed that the four Highlanders had come to his inn and sat by the fire to warm themselves while poring over a handlist of names. This time he remembered a little bit more about them than he had told me beforehand.

'They were very jovial. Laughing and joking. I was concerned that they might drink too much and start a fight, but no, because just as the noise they were making came to a head, one of them said something very sharp to the rest and all at once they became quiet. I am guessing he was the officer, the leader. Mark you, until this moment he had been joshing and jesting as much as anyone but, as I say, he suddenly put a stop to it.'

'And all this was in Gaelic?'

'Yes, I suppose so. Not English, any road.'

'And was this leader the one that spoke to you about the whereabouts of the three men on his list, that he hoped to take taxes off?'

'Aye.'

'Was Mr Limmington's name on that list?'

'It was.'

'And did you tell the rebels where Mr Limmington lived?'

'I did. Like I said, they told me they'd set fire to this inn else.'

'And what time did they leave you to go, presumably, to Mr Limmington's house?'

'Three o'clock, I suppose.'

'And at this point did you, as the constable of Penwortham, do anything to prevent them?'

'No. What could I do? Get the Watch out? In daytime? They'd never turn out before nightfall, even if they thought it was to catch a boy that picked a pocket. And if I told them it was to go up against a gang of Highlanders . . . well! You may forget that!'

This caused an outbreak of laughter and rib-nudging.

'Then I shall,' I said. 'Thank you, Mr Gibbins.'

I now summed up all we had learned, in such a way as to invite the jury to choose a verdict between murder at one extreme and natural causes at the other. The jury then put their heads together and reached its verdict after only twenty minutes of debate. Supporters of the government evidently outnumbered Jacobites on the panel and were able to browbeat them into acceding to the view that, since all Scotch rebels were savages and killers, this party of them must have been the killers of Limmington. In spite of Fidelis's testimony about the victim's head wound, they were so taken with the idea of his skull being cloven by an axe blow that they wrote it into the verdict: *Death by undoubted murder by four unknown Highland rebels, and no others, by cleaving the skull of the deceased using a military axe.* Luke Fidelis would be highly displeased, but I decided not to interfere. It scarcely mattered, I thought, feeling unusually detached from the problem, and quite happy to allow the verdict to stand. Not very much was at stake in this inquest, I thought. There was no one who mourned Limmington, none who suffered by his death, and no likelihood that the killers the jury had identified would ever be arrested and held to account. The rebel army had marched away. That was all there was to it.

Or so I thought at the time.

Outside, it was snowing heavily, and Fidelis and I decided to dine at the Swan before attempting the journey back to Preston. He was, as I had predicted, simmering with anger.

'Those country clodpolls!' he said as he dissected a cutlet. 'They shape their ideas of events only according to how dramatic they can be made. You showed them Limmington's skull, did you not, Titus? It was obviously not cloven. But how much more purple, how much more interesting, when it has been carved apart by a rebel axe!'

'Let it go, Luke. It is not worth bothering about.'

Fidelis shook his finger at me.

'There is much more to this than you think, Titus. Look at the woman Griselda's evidence. There are so many gross anomalies and even lies in it.'

'Are you certain she lied about the time of death? She may have been simply mistaken – or, more probably, deluded. The aged mind plays tricks, and more than ever in time of crisis. No. I see this as the fantasy and confusion of an old woman.'

'She lied, Titus, and for a reason. Take this nonsense about getting the dead man to bed. She could never have got that corpse up the stairs by herself. Therefore, she had help. So you should ask yourself, why does she not say so? And who helped her?'

'But if Limmington was already dead, why did she send for you?'

'I don't know. But if she thought he was alive, she's a half-wit.'

A shadow fell across the table and we both looked up. It was the same handsome, complacent fellow that had been denounced by the pregnant girl at the back of the audience. He was carrying a bottle of wine.

'May I join you?' he said. 'There's a matter I would like to talk over.'

He placed the bottle on the table and made a help-yourself gesture. He sat down.

'It seems you have made a young lady angry,' Fidelis said, 'having first made her something else.'

'I hate to see a slut putting on airs. She was willing enough in the bedchamber, I do recall.'

'She said you gave back-word. I suppose you told her you'd marry her.'

'Marry her! That's improbable. And I'm not here to comb through that doxy's entanglements, though I'll say in my own defence that where I've been is a well-trodden path. I doubt there's a month goes by when that little Pertylott's not been feathered by one Chantycleer or another.'

'That's as may be,' I said. 'What *have* you come to us for, sir? To tell something or to hear something?'

'A little of both.'

'Telling before hearing, I think. Pray go ahead with your side of the bargain.'

'Very well, gents. Mention was made in the proceedings this morning of a certain sum of money that the rebel soldiers went away from Limmington's house with. Am I right?'

'Yes. The purse of golden guineas found by Limmington in a ditch. After the rebels attacked him, they found it in his house and claimed it, quite spuriously, as tax due to them.'

'Quite so. Would it surprise you to learn that those were my guineas?'

Fidelis, who had been lying languidly in his chair, sat forward and began to listen more intently.

'How did you lose them?' I said.

'I tied the purse strings through a saddle strap that some boneheaded stable lad never properly latched. After bouncing up and down for several miles of the road from Preston to Liverpool, the strap opened and the accursed purse slipped off. It evidently fell into the ditch.'

'On the Liverpool Road, you say?'

This detail had not been mentioned at the inquest.

'Yes, I'd covered thirty-five miles or more before I missed the money. I rode back but couldn't find it. Only yesterday night did I learn it was picked up some time later by another. Near two hundred and thirty guineas, gone like that!'

He snapped his fingers.

'When was all this?' asked Fidelis.

'Back in October, at the start of the month.'

'So the bag lay undiscovered in the ditch all that time. It is fortunate you heard of the discovery.'

'I was travelling across Warrington Moss when I stopped at an inn. A Penwortham man was there, talking about how the vicar of Penwortham had spoken from the pulpit about a large purse of money being found, and if anyone claimed it, they should come forward in a timely manner. I discovered the vicar was cautious. He never said how much was in the purse or who the finder was, or even where it was found.'

'What did you do?'

'What do you think I did? I almost broke my horse's legs riding up here to tell the reverend gent what road I lost the purse on and how much was in it. That was yesterday morning. I then heard that Limmington had piked it just last week, and there was to be an inquest. My money was gone, and I resolved to attend your hearing in the hope of finding out where it had gone to.'

'Did you not go to Mr Fleetwood, the squire at the Priory? You should rightly pursue your claim through him, as he is magistrate here.'

'That girl had been kicking up a lot of shitty straw about me with her tale-telling. We got an earful of that this morning. I knew better than go near the beak. He might arrest me for breach of promise.'

'Well, that is understandable. So, how can I help you now, Mr . . .? I don't know your name, sir.'

'My name is Sigginho. Jaime Sigginho. My father was a Portugoose who engaged in the wine trade.'

'Then what service can I do you, Mr Sigginho?'

'You have investigated the death of Limmington; you know the facts behind the facts, if you follow me. So tell me, are you sure the party of rebels really found my money? I have an inkling they did not and that the gold is still hidden in Limmington's house.'

'You heard the evidence about the wainscot panel. What makes you doubt it?'

'I mistrust that old woman. She'd sell her daughter into kennels for the right price. I sense dishonesty in her.'

'I'm afraid there's nothing I can tell you more than you heard in the inquest.'

Sigginho leaned forward across the table and suddenly his face seemed transformed, hideously. His eyes glowed with intensity. His mouth distorted.

'I think you lie, Mr Coroner.'

He was snarling. He grasped my forearm.

'And if you're withholding something from me that might help me find my money, I swear I'll—'

I snatched his hand from my arm. 'You won't threaten me and get away with it, Jaime Sigginho,' I said. 'You've heard my answer and must be satisfied. Now, off you go.'

I snatched the bottle from the table and thrust it into Sigginho's arms. The man rose and stepped back.

'Very well, if that's your very best answer, then I shall follow your most kind advice.'

He stalked away and out of the room. Luke, who all this time had been watching Sigginho intently, clapped his hands together in admiration.

'Bravo, Titus! That was well done indeed, and not without hazard to yourself, I may say.'

'Oh, I don't think so, Luke. But I am rather amazed at his threatening me. The man seemed so smooth and almost agreeable at first. He even made me feel for him, losing such a large sum in that way.'

'I never believed his story. It doesn't cohere. This tale of a loose saddle strap! Does a man tie two hundred guineas to his saddle and not check it is secure? I say he is riding piggy-back on the case. The money was never his, but he saw a way of claiming it by concocting this tale. It is all as false as the name he is using.'

'The name is an unusual one, certainly. Portuguese, he says.'

'That is entirely ridiculous.'

'How can you be so sure?'

'Because I happen to know who he really is, Titus. And the name is an anagram, by the way. Sigginho. Think, and you will get it.'

I did think. Gohising? Hogsingi? Sognighi? Snighoig? It was no good.

'I am defeated,' I said. 'What is it, Luke?'

'Come, come, Titus! It's O'Higgins, of course. His forenames: Shamus Fingal.'

'Oh, my Lord!' said I. 'That's Jim Fingers.'

SIXTEEN

J im Fingers, Prince of Flicks, was the most notorious highwayman that the north-west could boast of. He was also sometimes called the Cheshire Turpin, and for the last five years he'd been liberally plundering the roads anywhere between Carlisle and north Wales.

The legend of the Prince of Flicks, or (by his true name) Shamus Fingal O'Higgins, was known from end to end of our region. The man had more aliases than the devil, and as many disguises, and the tales of his exploits passed from mouth to mouth as fast as the breeze. Twice he had escaped from captivity at Chester Castle, the second time dressed as a woman and on the very eve of his hanging. Once he had held up the carriage of Lord Derby himself, and relieved her Ladyship of her jewels, some of which he gallantly returned the next day, along with a single red rose. He was a notorious womanizer, rake and sportsman. He had entered his horse Pirate in a stakes for fifty guineas on Lord Egerton's course in the Wirral, won in a canter and galloped straight on and over the horizon before he could be apprehended. He was handsome, daring, a deadly shot and, when he chose, a charmer. In short, people (not excepting some of those he robbed) loved the fellow.

O'Higgins had been born in County Kildare. He grew up a horse-coper and, as time went by, became a horse thief and then a thief in general. He crossed the Irish Sea to try his luck in Liverpool and, after a year of successful plundering, removed to London in search of bigger prizes. In London he got his nickname, but also received a check to his career. The water in that pond was too hot, and too full of big fish with sharp teeth, so Jim Fingers returned to the north-west where he could be sure of being the only pike in a pool of carp. He flourished as never before. Magistrates and constables had chased him, tracked him, tried to trap him, but always he slipped from their grasp.

And we, just a few moments ago, had been in conference with the man himself. I am not in general bedazzled by glamour, but I now felt pleasure, retrospective pleasure, at our meeting. Many people like to think propinquity with glamour lends glamour of itself. They are deluded. You are not a changed person, and certainly not a better person, after having a passing encounter with fame. But it is undoubtedly a leg-up for your self-regard when you have a good story to tell in the coffee house.

'I am surprised he lost his sangfroid just now,' said Luke. 'He is said to be cool under all provocation.'

'How on earth do you know him, Luke?'

'I saw him at a prize-fight – Hayrick Harrison against the Nottingham Gnasher at Liverpool. I sat behind him in the pit and heard him letting slip who he was. He'd bet on the Gnasher, and whereas most people thought Harrison would pound his opponent to death in ten rounds, the Gnasher wouldn't go down and then *he* put Harrison down after fifty. It was a hellish struggle, but O'Higgins had gained the confidence of both men's trainers beforehand, and he knew the true state of play. By the end he was cock-a-hoop and reckless in his confidences.'

'I wonder he did not recognize you when he saw you today.'

'No wonder. As I say, I was at his back, and all his attention was directed to the ring, not the seats behind. Add to that it was three years ago. There's no reason why Jim Fingers would remember me now.'

We left the inn soon after and, the snow having relented, were riding along the south bank of the river towards the ferry.

'Contrary to your opinion,' I said. 'I think it quite possible that O'Higgins really did lose those coins. If they were the proceeds of a robbery, he would not be in a position to report their loss – I mean not to a magistrate or an insurance official – but he might try to find and get them back in his own way. And it would explain how he knows the amount of the gold, and also precisely where it was found.'

'He may have been told that by someone Limmington had confided in. It's said O'Higgins prides himself on acting only on the best information. As he did, for example, at the prize-fight.'

'On which occasion, by the way, you did not denounce him,
Luke. Were you not tempted? There is a price on his head, I
believe.'

'Denounce him? I won twenty guineas by his tip on the
Gnasher. It would not have been the act of a sportsman to
denounce him. And besides, it would have had no effect. No
one ever knows where Fingers stays. He flits like a wraith in
and out of town – this town, that town. He is never visible
anywhere long enough to be arrested.'

'You make him sound superhuman, but he is just a man,
Luke. Mark my word, Jim Fingers will slip up one day and
face his reckoning.'

'Would you like to bet on it?'

In the evening I sat at supper with Elizabeth, and silence lay
between us. There was still that sadness in her face. She was
not – or did not appear – agitated, or angry over the Marquis,
but she remained reflective and very quiet. She did not raise
the matter with me, or allow me to raise it with her. The matter
was not open for discussion.

Matty was doing all our shopping as Elizabeth would not
leave the house. Nor, within the house, would she go into our
bedroom. She asked Matty to fetch her dresses out and bring
them to the attic, where she continued to sleep. I was in a
quandary. The attic beds were cramped and the mattresses
lumpy. I wanted to go back to sleeping under our own canopy,
in our own spacious room. On the other hand, I did not want
to lie down without Elizabeth next to me. In the end, she
decided the matter herself. She told me she would rather sleep
alone for a while. Her face looked infinitely tired as she spoke
these words, but I was not compassionate: I was angry and
hurt. Of course, I told her, she must follow this inclination for
as long as necessary and come back to bed with me in her
own time. But I said the words coldly, and rather through my
teeth. I did not understand this. What, after all, had happened?
The Marquis had a crack at her and failed. That should be the
end of it, with the woman glad to have escaped – thanks to
my timely interruption. She should not be spurning me. She
should be overflowing with gratitude.

But that, as I now know, is a man thinking. It is not how a woman thinks and, more notably, not how she *feels*.

In every other way our household returned to the usual round, and so did the town. Commerce resumed. Those that had buried their treasures dug them up again. The Whig burghers and the faint-hearted rest who'd fled Preston now draggled furtively back, with tales of how they had been called away on urgent business or to attend the unforeseen death of a relative.

But outside the burgh, the element of disorder and lawlessness that had trailed behind the Chevalier on his military adventure took a little longer to dissipate. There were now more criminals on the highways than ever before. We heard tell of footpads and robber gangs roaming the public roads, relieving travellers of their purses, watches, jewellery and even their clothing. In response, gentlemen took to riding out in companies, while the operators of the Lancaster Flyer and the Chester Belle added a second armed guard to the crews of their coaches.

This epidemic of crime did much to enhance even further the reputation of Jim Fingers. Being a figure of such notoriety, his name was constantly invoked in connection with these incidents, never mind that for all O'Higgins's supposed occult powers he could not easily have carried out a hold-up in Orsmkirk and another in Garstang, on the same afternoon.

Perhaps it was this constant repetition of his name that made me, one night as I lay miserably awake and alone, go over O'Higgins's intervention in the case of the death of Horace Limmington, and in doing so certain ideas, exciting and novel ideas, flowed into my mind. The following day I went directly to Scrafton's Roost, taking Suez with me, to talk them over with Luke Fidelis.

I found him scolding his apprentice, Peason. The boy had taken it upon himself to see a patient during one of Fidelis's frequent visits to country patients and had attempted to treat her with a preparation of boiling mud, which had scalded the woman's skin. A tall, pimple-faced youth, Peason now drooped before his master's wrath.

'You are a poltroon, Peason. What are you?'

'A poltroon, Doctor Fidelis.'

'And remind me, do you not also carry your brains in your buttocks?'

'I won't do it again, Doctor Fidelis, I swear.'

His pimples glowed redder than ever.

'You had better not. Ah, Cragg! You see before you a very sorry specimen, still a distant stranger to the medical arts, despite all my efforts to introduce him to them. Shall we walk out? Our dogs will enjoy a turn on the Moor, I think. Finish making up those poultices, Peason, and do the job properly, for Christ's sake.'

With Suez and Bawty running joyfully ahead of us, we walked by way of Moor Lane.

'Peason is not a bad lad at heart,' I said.

'I didn't say he was bad. I said he was a poltroon.'

'It comes from eagerness as much as foolishness. He wants to prove himself in your eyes.'

'He will only do that by doing just as he is told, not less and certainly not more.'

'It is the essence of strict British soldiering, is that,' I observed. 'Never do anything other than your precise orders. It's an awfully limiting existence. Allow the boy a little leeway.'

'I can't. His leeway loses patients.'

I gestured at the townlands on either side of us. A week previously they'd swarmed with Highland men, their tents and their fires, their bagpipes and their kilts.

'Well, in the case of the rebel soldiers, the looser regime wins battles, it seems. Theirs is the very opposite of the redcoat way of thinking, I find. They are more like irregulars than regimental troops. But they've had some rare successes.'

'I know nothing of the military life, regular or otherwise. Nor do I wish to.'

'Then let's speak about something else. I have been thinking about the Limmington case. Certain details of it still do not fit.'

'Such as the woman Griselda's incoherent evidence?'

'Yes, that in particular. I have come around to your view that she lied. And I have formed some thoughts as to why.'

'I wonder if your thoughts are the same as mine. I too have reached some conclusions on this.'

'Very well, let us see. Point and counterpoint. I will go first.'

Point and counterpoint was a kind of reasoning game that Fidelis and I sometimes played in those days. One of us led off with a partial statement which the other was invited to complete. Then the latter would continue with the beginning of a second consequential statement.

'It's plain for all to see that Griselda was a discontented woman. She was so because . . .'

'Her master was a failure, and poor, so that she was paid . . .'

'Small or no wages for years. She saw the chance of redress, however, when . . .'

'Limmington found, by chance, a large sum of money by the wayside, but she . . .'

'Watched in frustration as the man's honesty led him to proclaim his discovery and try to identify the owner. So, fearing that the money would have to be returned, she . . .'

'Made up her mind to have it for herself and saw her chance when . . .'

'That's it, Luke! That was my very thought at three o'clock last night. When the rebels came calling, and caused the death of her master, she saw her chance. The money was well hidden and the rebels did not find it. Only she knew the place. Cunning old vixen! She made a pact with them to show where to look in return for a percentage of their haul.'

'In which case, I'll wager it was the rebels that helped her to get the dead body up the stairs – and it *was* a dead body, Titus. In which case, the question remains. Why is she lying about the time of Limmington's death?'

'She needed time for herself to . . . to do what? To dispose of her share of the loot?'

'It does not seem logical. Why the need? Limmington was dead. He wasn't going to take it back.'

There we ground to a halt, unable to see the reason for Griselda's lie. We turned therefore to the sport of throwing sticks for our dogs.

The next day, Wednesday, Limmington was to be buried in St Mary's, Penwortham. I asked Elizabeth to come with me as it would do her good to walk out. She absolutely refused, saying she did not know Limmington from the man in the moon, and saw no reason to mourn him. I went across the river without her.

It was not a well-attended funeral service. Among the scattering of mourners I saw the old squire Henry Fleetwood of the Priory. Gibbins, with his wife, was also there, assuaging his guilt at having directed the Highlanders to Limmington's house. Of the women, there was Griselda, who came by herself, and two others that I did not recognize.

'Who are those women?' I asked Gibbins when we had debouched into the graveyard for Limmington's burial.

'That's Mrs Limmington and her sister,' said Mrs Gibbins. 'From Macclesfield.'

'They have taken rooms at the Swan,' Gibbins added. 'Mrs Limmington refuses to enter her former home. She is standing the funeral refreshments in our private parlour.'

After the burial we therefore trouped down the road to the Swan for a glass of spiced wine and arval cake. I stood at first with old Fleetwood, who was in a truculent humour.

'Were you a particular friend of Limmington, sir?' I asked.

'No. Used to be. Latterly, I couldn't stand the fellow. He had fallen too low and it changed him. He did nothing but complain about illness, which deprived him of sleep, and poverty, which deprived him of new clothing. He wore the same frayed old coat every day, never changing it. His company was tedious, extremely.'

Fleetwood himself was formally dressed, even smart, in his black coat and stock. He did not look well, though. His hand trembled around the glass, spilling wine over his knuckles. He was there out of duty, I supposed.

'By the way, sir, has anyone made themselves known as claimants for the treasure Limmington found by the Liverpool Road?'

'The money, you mean? He came and consulted me on the matter. I told him to report to you, Cragg, as it may be treasure trove and must go to the King.'

'That did not turn out to be the case,' I said. 'I judged that the gold had been carelessly lost, and that it belonged to its owner, should that person be found or, if not, to its finder – to Limmington.'

'Not treasure trove, you say?'

I explained, as I often need to do, the true meaning of treasure trove, and then repeated my question.

'No,' he said. 'I have had no application of that kind. I do remember the vicar making an appeal in the church one Sunday. No one came forward.'

Another mourner approached to speak to the old man, and I took the chance to detach myself and to speak with the widow. I introduced myself and expressed my condolence, to which she gave a haughty reply.

'You need not express these sentiments to me, Mr Cragg. It is widely known that I had left Mr Limmington as he was no longer capable of supporting me. I've now been told he found a large sum of money just recently only to lose it again, along with his life. That is Limmington in a nutshell. A man who lost everything he ever had, including me. I live with my sister now and we have had an extremely trying journey coming here.'

'Oh?'

'The rebels were all over the road. They invaded Macclesfield – invaded, yes, it is the only possible term – on Sunday night until Tuesday morning when they headed away to the south. But their camp followers made such a crowd even on Tuesday that it was impossible to get on the road without extreme difficulty. I am exhausted, but I insisted we fight our way through because I see an attorney tomorrow who will sell the house for me.'

So the rebels had passed Macclesfield and had evidently still fought no battle with the Duke of Cumberland. Had they eluded him? Were they marching on to London? I put the question aside in favour of another, less momentous one.

'May I ask about Mr Limmington's servant, madam? I mean the housekeeper Griselda.'

Mrs Limmington's back visibly stiffened.

'What do you want to know?'

'Something of the woman's history. How long has she served the family?'

'Twenty years. I would have dismissed her after three, but Limmington would keep her.'

'Was she a widow when she first came to you?'

'Pretended to be, but I doubt she was ever married. She is a hussy and the boy is a bastard, I warrant it.'

'The boy?'

'Her son. He was an ugly disobedient child and is no doubt an ugly disobedient adult.'

'When I questioned her, she said nothing of having a son. Do you know where he is?'

'He went into service. I forget where. I am not much interested.'

I had intended to ask Mrs Limmington if there were any details of the inquest on which I could enlighten her. But I saw there would be none. Anyone less like a grieving widow was hard to imagine.

Shortly after this conversation I made my excuses and left to go home, or at least to go to the office. In those first days of December, as the weather continued cold with much frost, though no more snow, Furzey and I were picking up the threads of my legal practice. I was therefore deep in business every day, which distracted me from my sorrows at home, where Elizabeth continued to mope. More than once I found her in tears, or on the edge of tears. She would hear no questions from me about this and each time left the room without a word.

I had not mentioned it to anyone and found the burden hard to bear. I did not think my wife was punishing me, unless it was for not completely understanding what she was feeling. Then, at the end of the week that had begun with the Limmington inquest, she told me she would go to stay with her parents at Broughton, and that Hector would go with her. Matty would look after me. She did not place a term on her absence.

The next morning she was gone.

SEVENTEEN

The house seemed desolate and I continually sought business – if not in the office, then elsewhere. The work on old Entwhistle's will had long been concluded, but now I received an invitation to dinner from the Parkinsons to look over their enhanced collection of Jacobite objects, and to approve how Entwhistle's items complemented the rest. It was not something I wanted very much to do, but I went for no better reason than to escape the cheerlessness at home.

Catherine Parkinson greeted me happily. She enquired after Elizabeth, in a voice hinting that people around town were beginning to wonder at our estrangement. I merely said her mother was unwell (which actually was true) and that Elizabeth needed to be by her side. I was then taken into the parlour where the sacred objects were displayed in a glass-topped case. I recognized the things Entwhistle had bequeathed – the medals, an engraved glass cup, a lock of hair said to have been snipped from the Old Pretender's head as a boy, and so on. To my eyes, the hair, in particular, was difficult to be excited about, although Catherine was ecstatic.

'Do you see?' she exclaimed. 'It lies next to our own lock of the King's hair, taken much more recently. It is moving indeed to mark his progression from the soft, curly darling locks of a boy to the wise and grizzled hair that he now possesses. Oh! It is like a biography in itself!'

Her husband came in from his chandlery and we sat down to dinner. Jonathan talked gloomily of tallow prices, the near impossibility of obtaining high-quality wax, and the badness of oil lamps which (he said) smoked, smelled and burned down houses.

'The oil lamp is a murderer, Mr Cragg. An arsonist, you might say, and a poisoner of the air, and if I were in charge of the laws of England, I would collect up every one of 'em and send them to the Frenchies!'

'A good idea, Jonathan, very fitting,' I said, though I could not see why his odiferous candles gave any advantage in terms of cleanliness or safety. However, Jonathan Parkinson was renowned in Preston for being regularly tedious on this subject and I avoided any demurral for fear of elongating his rant.

If her husband was a long-faced merchant of complaint, Catherine Parkinson was full of life. She refused to acknowledge the dark side of anything.

'The Chevalier is in Derby,' she said. 'By now he is probably on his way to reduce London. It is so exciting. They say Lord George outfoxed the Duke of Cumberland by pretending to march into Cheshire, then veering back to join the Prince in Derbyshire. It is all going so well. In Manchester hundreds of men joined the colours and are formed into the Manchester Regiment under Colonel Towneley, who is a brave soldier that served in the army of King Louis. We were lucky enough to have had some soldiers in our house for two nights. Officers, of course, though not very senior. I expect you had a general in your fine house, Mr Cragg.'

'A captain and, um, a colonel, I think he was.'

I said nothing more about this colonel or his comportment as our guest.

'And did you see His Highness at all?'

'A distant view of him, merely. He looked pleasant. Very young.'

'He is so handsome when you see him close to. I fought my way to the front of the crowd when he issued the proclamation, and I touched his hand. Oh! Gooseflesh, Mr Cragg! I was covered in it. He has so many admirers amongst us ladies. I wonder if he has a particular love amongst all of them. Miss Cameron, of course, is very assiduous to him, so they say. Do you know the story of how she was sent by her uncle with a quantity of cattle and barrels of whisky as tribute to him? When she arrived at his tent, she leaped from her horse and told him she was come like the Queen of Sheba to drink at King Soloman's fount of wisdom. He received her with great gallantry, but I do not know if they have become lovers.'

'Of course they have not, woman,' growled Jonathan. 'The

Chevalier has no time for such dalliances. He is inured to the hard soldiering life. He must be pure like Sir Galahad.'

Catherine was indignant at this.

'Well, it is a fact, husband, that he is a fine dancer and musician who plays with special skill upon the bass viol. "If music be the food of love", you know? Even a soldier must have his ténder moments. Mr Cragg, have you seen the new picture of him that has been circulating?'

She rose and went out, coming back with the picture.

'I have it already framed, see?'

I looked carefully at the print, which was no more than a foot in height, yet there was a liveliness about it. The Prince wore civilian clothing and a star and sash, but the emblems surrounding him were martial – a helmet, sword and so on. The motto inscribed below the portrait was *Everso missus succurrere seclo*.

'Do you remember, Catherine?' I said, pointing to the inscription. 'The words are from the poem of Virgil that we spoke of before: "sent to set right the upturned age". The medals that came from Entwhistle, which you have in your glass case, carry allusions to the same passage.'

'Oh, yes, I remember. Wasn't there something about a young man – the Chevalier himself, of course – coming to do that business?'

'That's right. Virgil asks the gods not to prevent the young man – in reality, he means the young Emperor Augustus – from saving the nation.'

'Well, that is what is going on now – is it not, Mr Parkinson?'

She asked the latter question very sharply, for Jonathan had fallen asleep in his chair.

'Now, Mr Cragg, sir, you must take a glass of hot brandy and sugar to see you home on this cold night.'

While she was out of the room, I had another drab conversation with the candlemaker about the dearth of best Italian wicking thread, the importation of which (he explained at some length) had been impeded by warfare on the Continent. At last his wife returned with my drink, and took a chapbook from her apron pocket, which she put into my hand.

'It's just that I thought, as you're so kindly translating the

Latin for us, you would like another book of poetry touching on the Prince.'

The pamphlet was crudely enough printed, and with a very different portrait from the one I had just been looking at. It was a simple woodblock of a lad with long, wavy hair under a Quaker hat, his eyes much too large for the face, and the beard writhing on his chin like a family of snakes. The title printed beneath told me who it was supposed to be: *The Prophecies of Robert Nixon concerning the New Order that will be Made with the Coming of the True King into his Own.*

I turned the pages, looking without much enthusiasm over the many lines of doggerel verse.

'Listen to this!' cried Catherine. 'Could this be more exact concerning the Scotch army?'

She took the pamphlet back and read aloud.

> The pipes will pipe and the drums rattle
> Till they shall win the final battle.

'Ah, Mr Cragg,' said Catherine, as her face assumed an angelic look of pleasure. 'That is true poetry, true inspiration.'

She pressed the book back into my hand.

'Take it home with you, do.'

Fifteen minutes later I was letting myself into my house. In lieu of taking Suez for his nightly walk, I let him into the garden, to run up and down its narrow length a few times. Then I took him into my library and stoked the fire. The dog lay down before the flames as, taking Catherine's pamphlet from my pocket, I found the place she had quoted from, to see how it continued. I read:

> With snow on their hats the Scotch shall come
> With eery pipe and dreadful drum.
> The pipes will pipe and the drums will rattle
> Till they shall win the final battle
> But only rule in England here
> One day more than half a year.
> Then shall the King from Avalon
> Ride home and all our sorrows be done.

The metre was lumpy, and the sentiment at the end – well, 'the chance of that carries no fat', as Gilliflower my barber was fond of saying. I looked to see if the chapbook provided its date of publication. It didn't. But I would have been very surprised if a man called Robert Nixon, who may (or may not) have lived in the time of Queen Elizabeth, ever wrote those exact words. He may (or may not) have written some approximations to them, or some of them, but as I turned the pages, I found that these 'prophecies' looked on the whole like the concoctions of London's Grub Street, where they know how to give John and Jenny Bull just what they want to read at any given moment. Some of those distinguished authors were university men, which might account for the odd passable bit of poetry in the chapbook – phrases such as 'eery pipe and dreadful drum', which I rather liked. But most of what I saw was poetical dross.

Until I came to four lines that suddenly almost stopped my heart.

A crow atop a headless cross
Is rape and murder and fell loss.
The day shall wane, the crow shall fly,
And never tell us why.

I read these four lines once, and again, and a third time. I sat for a while staring into the air. Then, after stoking the fire and shutting up the dog, I went upstairs with a pensive tread, the four lines still ringing in my mind. I felt real ill-omen in them, something dark which made me afraid. Something that would, I knew, prevent my sleeping for some time that night.

The next morning, not greatly to my surprise, James Barrowclough returned to the attack. His messenger, Richard Rudgewick, entered the office with a look of grim determination.

'My client has asked me to draw up a writ of slander against you, sir.'

'He cannot still be sore about the Ribchester inquest, Rudgewick,' I said mildly. 'You know quite well my questions were not by any means slanderous. Indeed, I doubt whether a question can constitute a slander, since it comes out of uncertainty, of not knowing, whereas a slander is a false statement that masquerades as the truth.'

'If that is your best defence, I am sorry for you, Cragg. Your "I put it to you" and your "Is it not the case?" were suggestions of what you wished people to believe about my client, but in fact were not true. Therefore, these insinuations falsely brought into question my client's integrity. That is a slander by any measure.'

He drew a small bundle of documents, sealed and folded together, and insolently dropped it on my writing table.

'You are therefore summoned to answer before the Duchy of Lancaster civil court at nine o'clock on Tuesday next.'

Barrowclough and Rudgewick's use of the Duchy court, rather than before the Mayor of Preston, was because my supposed slander had happened out of town. I picked up the writ.

'Very well, Rudgewick,' I said. 'Let battle commence.'

When the lawyer had slid out of the room, Furzey and I opened the writ of slander. It contained among other things a partial transcript of my questions to Barrowclough at the Ribchester inquest, and copies of affidavits from two witnesses who had heard me speak the offending words. The originals of these would have been submitted to the court and were being held by the presiding judge.

'You have an excellent case,' Furzey told me, then started to jerk his head back spasmodically until he sneezed in a great splutter.

'Are you all right?' I asked.

'A cold is coming. A bad one, I expect.'

'My sympathies. Go on. How do you think I should argue the case?'

'You simply make it a point of court privilege – that a coroner's questions and remarks in the course of an inquest, just like those of a judge in a trial, cannot by custom be held against him personally. That will shut the case down entirely. The judge will stop it.'

'Will he? You know perfectly well that the law is vague and even the status of the inquest is unclear. It's governed by tradition and precedent. Do I, in fact, have the same legal protection as a judge in quarter sessions? I am not at all sure. What if Rudgewick has unearthed some case pursued under Henry the Eighth where a coroner was indeed successfully had up in this way?'

'I know of no such case.'

That was some consolation as Furzey knew ten Almanacks' worth of information about coroners and the law.

'Very well, we'll begin with that as a first line of defence. I see one of these affidavits is by Abel Grant. There seems to be nothing he won't do to serve his master. We had better apply to the judge to see the originals of both these, and make sure our copies agree with them. Will you go in and do that on Monday?'

I wished I could talk it over with Elizabeth, whose good sense normally kept me from any gross errors of judgement. But whatever you might call this time in our marriage, it would not be 'normal'. I went instead to meet Luke Fidelis that evening at the Turk's Head.

'I am being sued for slander by Barrowclough,' I said as soon as I walked in. 'He has taken exception to my suggestion that he killed the two Highlanders and cut off their heads. The hearing is the day after tomorrow, at the Duchy court.'

Luke pushed a pipe towards me across the table and poured me a glass of wine.

'You look haggard, Titus. Are you afraid you may lose? It would not be any way just if you did.'

'I am grateful for your loyalty, Luke.'

'How will you mount your defence?'

'I will fight on the grounds that a coroner's public interrogations are privileged.'

Fidelis considered this for a moment while drawing on his pipe.

'Titus, I believe you should plead justification,' he said at last. 'Think of it in this way: by suing you, Barrowclough is taking a great risk. We both consider he was implicated in the Highlanders' deaths, but because no one will talk, we cannot prove it. Here is a chance to put him on trial in front of a judge. It is a golden opportunity to find out what happened. Don't forget you almost suffered military execution on account of that inquest. You must want to know the true state of affairs.'

'I do, of course. But it is more important to protect myself. I have Elizabeth and Hector to consider as well as myself.'

'What does your admirable wife have to say about Barrowclough's suit?'

'She does not know of it. She is with her parents in Broughton. And now that you have mentioned her, Luke, there is a matter I should be glad of your counsel on.'

'Oh, yes?'

I thought for a moment. Should I involve my friend in this marital difficulty? A man's marriage is very much his own affair, and as Luke was himself a bachelor, it would be much to ask him to listen to my story and not be able to bring marital experiences of his own into the discussion. But I was sorely in need of telling somebody about Elizabeth, and of an answer to why she was behaving in this way.

'I know you are not married man, but I would be glad to hear your thoughts.'

'Spit it out, Titus. I am all ears.'

I took a deep breath, but the words I wanted to speak did not come out, for at that moment the door of the coffee house burst open and was hurled against the jamb. The bang stopped all conversation and each of us looked to see the cause of the disturbance. It was MacLintock.

'News!' he shouted. 'I bring news of the rebels!'

Moments later most of the customers had besieged the Scotchman and were firing questions at him from every side.

'We'd given you up for dead, Archie. How did you get away? Did you give them a bribe or what?'

'Aye, a bribe. By luck I had some money about me that they never found.'

'In your shoe, was it?'

It was known in Preston that Archibald MacLintock took extraordinary care of his money and always had a few banknotes in some unlikely place about his person. The rebels, naturally, would know nothing of this habit.

MacLintock laughed.

'You used to all snigger at me for doing that. But now – you see? It saved my bloody life.'

'Where did they take you?'

'They took me all the way to Derby. We came there on Wednesday night. I'd been interrogated at Manchester but with no result. The officer dealing with me was distracted by some other business, so they put me back in the cart and we set off again to Macclesfield, Leek and on to Derby.'

'So there's been no battle?'

'No. They swerved around the Duke of Cumberland. But the Pretender's received a check. In fact, he's been defied by all his generals and senior officers. By the war council, as they call it.'

The room fell quiet. Every man, whether committed to the Jacobite cause or faithful adherents of King George, wanted to know what had occurred.

'It's like this – or this is how I heard it from the man I paid to release me from my irons and let me go. The Pretender was determined to march on to London. He reckoned they would outstrip Cumberland's army because they move so fast. He thought they could be in the capital by Monday or Tuesday and he'd be lording it in St James's Palace while King George took to his heels.'

'Oh, aye,' said someone in the audience. 'They say he has a ship waiting fully provisioned, ready to sail at a moment's notice.'

'He won't need it, my friends,' said MacLintock. 'He won't need it because the war council has flatly refused to march a single step nearer to London. They say there's not enough Englishmen joining them – none at all since Manchester, apparently. They say all their promises of thousands of recruits have come to nothing. They're marching back, my friends. They're marching back by the same road they went down. They're marching back *here*.'

EIGHTEEN

On Sunday I missed church and rode instead the few miles out of town to the Georges' house in Broughton, to see Elizabeth and the boy. She had by no means returned to her own nature, but was a touch more cheerful (I thought) staying in her childhood home, where she could have again some of the benefits of being a child. Her mother fussed over her and fed her up. Her father took her for walks across and around the snowy common to find where his pig rooted, and to look for mistletoe in the woods. There was something strange and troubling about this capable twenty-nine-year-old woman now submitting herself to her aged parents. In the past she could not spend more than a few minutes in that house without clearing out a cupboard or starting work on a new dress with her mother. Yet now she was quiet and submissive. I looked at her and loved her still, but I was seeing her differently – as a different person, I mean. She seemed no longer to be the wife I had known for almost ten years.

In the house, under old Charles George's tutelage, Hector was learning to take his first steps, and it was difficult to tell which of the two was more proud of himself. Meanwhile, being a devout Jacobite, Elizabeth's mother wanted to know the latest news of the rebels (though she did not call them that) and whether they were likely to fight the German army (as she called it) in the near future.

'It is possible, mother-in-law,' I said. 'However, we have heard that the Prince has abandoned his attempt on London and has turned around at Derby. As far as we can tell, the army is marching back up the same road by which it descended.'

'They are coming back the same way? Oh mercy! Then I may see him again!'

She spoke with wonder in her voice. This woman, usually so sharp-tongued, became soft at the very thought of catching sight of her idol.

'Did I tell you,' she said, 'how I saw the beautiful lad leading his army through this village, with his pipes and his drums?' I laughed.

'You did, mother-in-law, several times.'

'Well, I did not expect to see that rare sight again. But now perhaps I shall.'

'You may be sure of it, if there is no battle first. The Scotch will want to regain their own country as fast as possible, and will certainly come back this way, as it is the most direct. However, they are saying he is pursued by the Duke of Cumberland, and if he catches up, they will fight.'

'Pray God it will not be in Preston again!' she said.

'With luck they will be two steps ahead of the Duke as they pass through and will even be able to stop the night again.'

Then I caught sight of Elizabeth's face. She was sewing fiercely, digging her needle into the cloth and making out her attention was on nothing but that. But she was deathly pale, and her mouth was set tight.

After dinner I walked out with my father-in-law. I wanted to speak with him about this change in his daughter, and whether he had found any key to it. The old man was inclined to deafness, making conversation about delicate matters even more difficult. One had to repeat oneself, and even shout to be heard.

'I am afraid Elizabeth is not herself,' I said.

He cupped his ear.

'What?'

I raised the pitch of my voice.

'Elizabeth. She is changed. Something happened when the rebels were in our house. Has she told you?'

He heard that all right.

'Aye,' he said, 'she told us what happened at Preston – a bit. That French devil took advantage of her. And you're right, son. She is that badly affected we hardly know her. The boy's bright-eyed, mind. He's a great consolation to us all. But you are Lizzie's husband, Titus. You must look to her yourself, you know.'

This was no help. I might look to her, but if she would not look back, what could I do? I did not say this, however, and we passed the rest of our walk more in silence than in conversation. Back at the house, I said goodbye, explaining that, with so many robbers and cut-throats about, I preferred to cross the Moor before dark. I kissed Hector and embraced Elizabeth. She endured my arms but did not yield to them.

On Monday, Furzey sent word that he was laid so low by his head cold that his mother had forbidden him from coming to work, but he promised to be with me for the trial in the Duchy court the next day. I spent an hour at the office quite alone, looking over all the papers from the Ribchester inquest and Rudgewick's summons, in preparation for my own defence.

Reading over the affidavits from Barrowclough's pair of witnesses, I remembered that Furzey had been due to make the comparison between these copies and the originals. Now I would have to do the job myself. I picked up the document case containing the papers and walked, in no more than two minutes, to the courtroom of the Duchy on the other side of Market Place.

The case was to be heard by Edmund Starkey. It was at his house that the Prince – having found Patten House too cold and draughty – had stayed. Starkey had practised Duchy law at Preston for twenty-five years, and the fortune he'd made had built for him a fine house. Starkey was one of those who'd found reasons to make themselves scarce in face of the Prince's forces, so the house had been requisitioned without his consent. Nevertheless, I wondered whether he was not a little proud, having returned to find that his place had been selected over Patten House.

Starkey's chambers, considerably more magnificent than my own, were manned by three clerks, one of whom allowed me a seat at his desk so that I could examine the affidavits, which he then produced. They were not in the legal hand, but in the private hands of the witnesses themselves – the first, Anthony Prior, a tenant farmer on the Barrowclough estate, and the second, Abel Grant, James Barrowclough's personal valet. The farmer's scrawl was difficult to make out at first, but I mastered it and found no discrepancies between it and the copy. Prior recorded simply that he had been at the inquest into the Scotchmen, where he heard me say that James Barrowclough had killed and beheaded the two men and that he, Prior, 'thowt the crowner spawk that way for to purswade the room that this was true thaw as far as I new it wuzznt proof'.

Turning to Abel Grant's statement, I found the writing quite different: small, nicely formed and literately spelled. His thoughts on my supposed slander were also a good deal subtler, and therefore more possibly damaging, than Prior's. 'The coroner proceeded to speak in spiteful accents of my master,' he wrote. 'He did not ask his questions neutrally, but made a number of insinuating suggestions by which I understood that Mr Cragg considered Mr Barrowclough guilty of the murders and mutilations, and that he would like this supposed guilt to be generally acknowledged.'

I did not waste time in resentment. These charges could be refuted. Luke Fidelis would speak for me, and I must surely get a sympathetic hearing from Edmund Starkey who would not, I thought, like to open the way for judges such as himself to be accused of slander when speaking in open court.

There was something else about Abel Grant's statement, however, that compelled my attention. I unlatched the case I'd brought with me and searched through the documents until I found the covenanters' message that had been folded and placed inside the mouth of one of the beheaded victims. This paper had now been thoroughly dried out. I laid it down on top of the original of Abel Grant's affidavit and saw immediately that the hands they were written in were not merely similar but identical. The two documents had been written by the same person: Abel Grant.

I was suddenly filled with excitement. My defence against this charge of slander would go further than merely citing my immunity as president of the inquest. It would argue that the supposals I had put to Barrowclough at the inquest could never have been slanderous at all, and this for the simple reason that they were, in fact, true. The handwriting evidence I had before me made it irrefutable that Abel Grant had been in on the murders, and Abel Grant, if my estimation was correct, was James Barrowclough's right-hand man. In the light of this, it was surely inconceivable that the master was not as closely implicated in these killings as the servant.

I was aware I would need another witness, one who could

establish the nature of the close relations between Barrowclough
and Abel Grant. After a moment's thought, I knew who this
could be. I refilled and latched the document case, returned
the affidavits to the clerk and left Starkey's office. It all
depended on the man's mental capacity and I would have to
go and see him without delay to assess whether he was capable
of batting effectively on my side of the game.

With the rebels now on their way back to us, the return of
Patrick and Goody to the livery stables could not be expected
for a while. Old Jones was still at my disposal, however, and
he conveyed me in his ambling way to Barrowclough Hall by
the time it was midday. I made no attempt to pass the hall
gates but knocked on the door of the right-hand of the two
lodge cottages.

'I believe your name is Joseph Wrightington,' I said to the old
man who opened to me. 'I came to your door some days ago
and you directed me to Mr Grant opposite. Do you remember?'

He stared at me, unblinking, with his grey eyes. His hair
was thick and unkempt, and he had not shaved for many days.

'Aye,' he said.

'I believe you can do me a favour, Mr Wrightington. And
I would not be surprised if doing that favour might be rather
agreeable to you.'

'There's money in it?'

'No, I regret there cannot be any payment because that
would be corruption. I am appealing therefore to your sense
of what is right. Your sense of legal fair play when it comes
to the doings of Mr James Barrowclough, and his man Grant.'

Wrightington regarded me for a few more moments. I could
not tell what he was thinking. Then, it appeared deliberately,
his eyelids closed and opened again.

'You had better come in,' he said.

The cottage had the same arrangement as I had found in
Grant's place but in mirror image – a parlour and scullery
with a wooden stair to the bedroom above. But whereas Grant's
cottage had been in every way neat and clean, Wrightington's
was in every way filthy and – there's no nice way of putting
this – it stank. Dead rodents perhaps. Certainly putrefied food,

dishclouts and long-unwashed clothing. I tried hard not to show any disgust.

There were two ladder-back armchairs on either side of the range. Wrightington shuffled up to one of them and contemplated for a moment the clutter of objects that lay on the seat – a candle-holder, a rolling pin, a small tin box, a leather cap, a broken clay pipe – and then leaned down and swept them all with a single gesture on to the floor. He straightened and indicated with his hand that I should sit. He then lowered himself into the corresponding chair. Thank God he offered no refreshment.

'You may try me,' he said. 'Though I don't say I shall do it.'

I gathered my thoughts. Even before I got Wrightington to agree to testify, I needed to be sure that he would be able to do so. It would be no good at all if he turned out to be simple or decrepit.

So I put the case to him in normal terms, with no attempt to simplify. It was a case of slander turning on the ways in which I framed my questions in the course of the inquest. Barrowclough denied being involved in the deaths of the two strangers, yet it was now beyond doubt that Abel Grant, at least, had participated in the murders.

This last part of my discourse, which Wrightington had listened to dully at first, made him sit up and start to look pleased. I saw then that he did not like Abel Grant – that he liked nothing at all that lay between Grant's toenails and his eyebrows. I began to feel confident that this dislike was going to deliver Wrightington's help on my side at the trial.

'I am interested in your special knowledge of Abel Grant and his relationship with his master. When I visited here on the occasion I've already mentioned, I saw the two of them together, and I felt a peculiar closeness about them. I'll put it plainly to you, Mr Wrightington. They behaved more like two established friends than a master and his servant.'

I now stopped talking and waited for Wrightington's response. He was giving it thought (he gave everything thought), balancing relative advantage with possible loss. The views of his master, Sir John Barrowclough, would be an essential part of this calculation, for no servant could safely

act independently of the interests of his master. But if what
Lord Derby had told me about the Barrowcloughs, father and
son, was true, I didn't need to worry. They may be bound indis-
solubly together by their consanguinity, but they hated each
other. The son saw the father as a crabbed and misguided old
fool; the father saw the son as a traitor.

Having sat motionless for more than half a minute,
Wrightington sniffed at last.

'You want me to say they're in league, or something?'

'Well, are they?'

'They're like a couple of girls sometimes. I have seen that.
They touch each other the way men don't do, not usually. Do
you want me to say all that?'

'You must tell the truth as you see it.'

Another half-minute elapsed while he brooded. Then he
stood up and extended his hand.

'Your terms are acceptable, Mr Cragg. Where and when do
you want me?'

An extraordinary change had come over him. The lugubrious
shuffler was invigorated. He stood more upright and spoke
more rapidly, more incisively.

'I want you in Preston at the Duchy court at ten o'clock in
the morning,' I said. 'I want you to be shaved and wearing
your cleanest clothes. Can you do that, Mr Wrightington? Can
you find your way there?'

And then, most extraordinarily, Wrightington laughed.

'Oh, yes, I can find my way there, Mr Cragg. I shall get a
lift to town on a cart, first thing. I shall not let you down – no,
sir. I shall not let you down.'

By the time Jones had delivered me back to Preston, there
was still an hour of daylight. I sent a note over to Scrafton's
Roost, asking Fidelis to meet me later at the coffee house,
then hastened to Furzey's house to inform him of the latest
developments. Old Mother Furzey made a show of being
flustered by my unexpected arrival. Mr Cragg must have tea.
But was there enough milk? Yes, there was, thank mercy. And
she was sure there were some currant cakes left. One or
two, she seemed to remember. Yes! Here they are. And Robbie

must come down from his bed because Mr Cragg can't be expected to climb them stairs, let alone see Robbie in his nightshirt.

She ran around the little house while I waited for her son to dress and come down. After my experience at Wrightington's place, the spotlessness of the Furzey home was balm to me, and I sat at my clerk's dining table perfectly at ease. Furzey then appeared, his nose heavily bunged up, but lucid and not, he told me, feverish. So we held our conference sitting at the table. I explained about my discovery of the identical handwriting, and how we could use this to turn the tables on Barrowclough. I told him of my visit to Joseph Wrightington and of his readiness to testify that there was more between James Barrowclough and Abel Grant than you would expect between master and servant.

'You mean they're buggers, are they, sir?' said Furzey, whispering to avoid the ears of his mother.

'No – I don't know – and I don't think his evidence needs to go that far. It will be enough to say that they were unusually close, like friends. I don't want to risk scandalizing Starkey. He will take it amiss if he thinks we are foisting a buggery crime on him, when he's expecting to try a civil case.'

'How are we going to present the handwriting evidence?'

'We'll introduce it when Grant is under examination. I mean to use it to show my line of questioning at the inquest was reasonably based. I am not going for the full-scale prosecution of either Grant or Barrowclough – not at this stage. As we know, the question of whether the killing of two possibly hostile rebels, or traitors, would have constituted the crime of murder in this jurisdiction remains open.'

Mrs Furzey's currant cakes were more like rock cakes – hard to break into, harder to chew. I ate mine with the help of softening gulps of tea, and as soon as I could, I took my leave.

'Don't fret,' said Furzey, seeing me out of the door. 'It isn't the first time you've been in the dock, and won't be the last, I would hazard, as you are always getting yourself into pickles. But we'll get you out of this one, never fear.'

NINETEEN

arly next morning something – a cry from outside – awoke me, after which I lay with my eyes closed, listening to traffic passing the house below my window, until I drifted again into sleep and a most memorable dream. In this dream we had no fires in the house, and Elizabeth was angry with me for providing neither coals nor logs to burn. I had gone out to scavenge some firewood on the common – the same one at Broughton where I had walked with Charles George on Sunday – and there I'd come across a gamekeeper's gibbet, from which dangled vermin of different species. One rodent's teeth bared in death made a horrible parody of a grin, as if the whole process of being killed were nothing but a sour joke.

A shout reached my ear from Market Place, which my windows overlooked. A man's voice, and one full of news, bursting to tell. Something about the rebels, about the Chevalier. What? Had there been a battle?

I opened my eyes and jumped out of bed. I went to open the window. It was still not fully light, but I could see a small crowd gathered around the market cross, on whose steps stood the owner of the voice I had heard, evidently a peddler since his burdened mule stood patiently to one side. I raised the window.

'This is the news from the road, kind sirs and ladies,' the peddler was saying. 'Fresh word that came to my ears during my trip up here from Leyland. Yes, that's quite right, madam. The rebels have passed through Manchester, they have, and still come on north. And the Duke of Cumberland's in hot pursuit. The Pretender, or Chevalier, or whatever you will, must turn and fight here at the Ribble, they're saying. There shall be a battle here.'

He whipped off his hat and offered it around for tips. A man walked up and tossed a coin in as he asked the peddler a question.

'Another Battle of Preston?' I heard the peddler reply. 'Aye, that *is* what I'm saying, sir. Better prepare yourself.' And he put his hand up to the side of his mouth and shouted the words as if for the whole town to hear.

'Prepare, Preston, prepare! Another battle is coming!'

Matty had also heard the news. While serving my breakfast, she asked if the town was about to be burned and laid waste. I said nothing was certain, least of all news brought by hawkers and peddlers, but I offered her the chance to get out of the way by joining Elizabeth at Broughton, if she wished. She said she wouldn't think of leaving me and Suez all alone.

After breakfast Fidelis arrived and we walked together with Furzey – still snuffling and with pockets stuffed by his mother brimful of handkerchiefs – to the Duchy court. I felt a moment of sentiment at the loyalty of my friends: Matty refusing to leave me; Furzey and Fidelis rallying to support me against Barrowclough. All I needed now was for Elizabeth to come back to me.

To my relief, Joseph Wrightington was there in the street by the door of the courthouse, having ridden all the way from Ribchester with a load of turnips. Going in, we found Judge Starkey awaiting us impatiently in the courtroom's antechamber, but no sign yet of the plaintiff and his lawyer. The judge was in a terrible scrow, as the countryfolk say. Already robed and wigged, he was walking up and down and wringing his hands.

'I've only just put my house in order and now I hear that bastard is coming back to wreck it all over again!'

'How did he wreck it, Edmund?' I asked.

'He knocked down my great looking glass with the French gilt frame and put an elbow into my father's portrait by Devis.'

I could imagine how Starkey might grieve the loss of the looking glass: he was a notorious dandy whose suits all came from London tailors, trimmed with French lace and lined with Chinese silks.

'Now, look here,' he said as we listened to the church clock striking ten. 'We have to get this trial over and done. I must be away from Preston by afternoon. Where *is* Barrowclough?'

'Here, Mr Starkey!'

It was Richard Rudgewick, with his client close behind, both men somewhat out of breath.

'You are late,' said Starkey. 'Go in and I will be with you immediately.'

The Duchy courts have always proceeded according to their own traditions. For much of their business they are thinly populated unless the judge feels the need for a jury, which Starkey had not done this morning. He would be making the judgement himself, assisted by his personal clerk and the clerk of the court. The only others present, besides Barrowclough, Rudgewick and me, were the recording clerk behind his writing desk, a pair of tipstaffs and the witnesses who waited under the tipstaffs' eyes to be called from the anteroom. Preston was far too preoccupied with the anticipated second coming of the Prince to care about a minor slander case, so the public bench was unoccupied.

Edmund Starkey, now appropriately wigged and gowned, swept into court by way of the door from judge's chambers and on to the dais reserved for him.

'Mr Rudgewick, pray outline your case, please,' he said as he settled his rump in the ornate chair.

Rudgewick took five minutes to say nothing that I had not already heard. He detailed my suggestions, made at the inquest, that Barrowclough had first killed two men and then proceeded to mutilate their bodies. He went on to assert my malice against Barrowclough, which did not (he thought) seem to have any known basis but was an irrational prejudice on my part.

Finally, he said, 'We shall therefore argue that Titus Cragg did wilfully abuse the position he holds in this Duchy solely for the purpose of blackening my client's name.'

He sat down and Starkey turned his attention to me.

'Mr Cragg, you appear for yourself?'

'I do, my lord.'

'Then please state your defence.'

'As you will know, my lord,' I said, 'I am one of the County Coroners. Mr Rudgewick does mention in passing that my alleged slanders against James Barrowclough were spoken in that capacity. However, he omits the point that I spoke them while questioning Mr Barrowclough as a witness at the inquest into the deaths of the two men already referred to. I submit with complete confidence that my remarks were motivated not by malice but by the desire to find out the truth. I further submit that these remarks are protected by privilege as I was acting in a quasi-judicial capacity.'

'Thank you, Mr Cragg. So let us get on: witnesses for the plaintiff.'

Rudgewick took his first witness, Farmer Prior, who repeated the words, more or less, of his affidavit. I did not cross-examine him. Next came Abel Grant, looking confident, as I knew he would. He also stated that I had used words in his opinion intended to damage Mr Barrowclough's reputation, and I also let that go by. My chance to attack Abel Grant would, according to my plan, come later.

Starkey then asked me to produce my own witnesses, the first of whom was Luke Fidelis. He merely said that, yes, he had heard me speak the words in question, and that he did not think they were spoken with malice, but were a reasonable choice of words under the circumstances, and quite in line with the questioning at many other inquests he had attended.

I thanked him, then called Joseph Wrightington. Somewhere in the pigsty of his cottage there must have been a chest containing a suit of clean clothes, as he looked surprisingly presentable. He was also shaved, and his hair combed and gathered in a tail at the back. The man was positively well turned-out. He took his oath in a strong clear voice. I felt sure he would make an effective witness.

My first questions established who Wrightington was and that he lived in a neighbouring cottage to that of Abel Grant. So far so good.

Then the trouble started.

'How well do you know Mr James Barrowclough?' I asked.

Rudgewick stood up.

'Objection, my lord. Is this relevant?'

Starkey decided very quickly that it was not. I tried to change his mind.

'My lord,' I said. 'If I may be allowed to continue, I can demonstrate the relevance.'

Starkey gave me the look a disbelieving parent gives to a child's elaborate lie.

'Just ask your next question, Mr Cragg.'

'Very well. How well do you know Abel Grant, Mr Wrightington?'

Rudgewick was on his feet again.

'Again, relevance, my lord?'

Starkey arched his eyebrows and beamed benignly at the lawyer.

'Quite right, Mr Rudgewick. I congratulate you. If the previous question was not relevant, how can this very similar one be? Next question, please, Mr Cragg.'

I breathed deeply, and concentrated.

'I now want to ask you about the relationship between Mr Barrowclough and Abel Grant. From what you have observed, would you say they are close?'

Before I had even finished the question, Rudgewick had bounced back up again.

'I object, my lord.'

'And yet again I agree with you, Mr Rudgewick. No need to go into the arguments: the question is ruled out. Mr Cragg, what else?'

What else, indeed? I was being harried in the direction of nowhere. The judge had completely withdrawn all sympathy for my case. He was not even bothering to justify his position.

Nevertheless, I stumbled on.

'Please would you tell the court what happened on the night the two Scotchmen were found dead in the district where you live?'

Inevitably, Rudgewick rose once more to object and Starkey agreed with him. After that, all my subsequent questions were similarly ruled out one after another until I had nothing left to put to Wrightington and was forced to let him go. Poor Wrightington. He had come all this way and stood on the witness stand and yet had given no actual evidence at all. The look on the old man's face showed disappointment, and underlying disgust.

'Do you have any more witnesses, Mr Cragg?' asked Starkey. 'I do hope not.'

'I'm afraid I do, my lord. I would like to call Abel Grant.'

'Abel Grant? Have we not heard from him already?'

'Yes, we have, but—'

'I can see no profit whatsoever in hearing from him again.'

'I believe, my lord, that Abel Grant was complicit in committing a serious crime and I would like the chance to confront him with the evidence of that.'

'Oh no! No, no! Have a care, Mr Cragg. You are in danger of compounding the slander that you are here accused of by promulgating another slander. Are you bent on pursuing a career of slander?'

'No, my lord. But one of the severed heads had a note inserted in its mouth and I have proof that it was written in Abel Grant's handwriting. I would—'

'*Mr Cragg!* I shall hold you in contempt if you pursue this any further. Is Mr Grant in court? I should like to know if he has any complaint to make of this.'

'Mr Grant has left the premises, my lord,' the tipstaff told Starkey. 'He did not expect to be needed more.'

'In view of the present emergency,' said Starkey, 'that is very understandable. He must have urgent business, as have we all. So let us have closing arguments, please, gentlemen. Time presses.'

It did indeed. The proceedings were rushing headlong towards a conclusion, and I had no means to slow them or turn them towards my object. It was quite clear the judge wanted the hearing over as soon as possible. Rudgewick, who was as aware of this as I was, got up and more or less restated his opening remarks in very short order. I had no other option but to do the much the same.

'I will deal with this case briefly,' said Starkey when I had finished, and after he'd held twenty seconds of conversation with the clerk of the court, he declared, 'An inquest is not a court of law. I don't see any particular privilege attaching to the words of a mere coroner spoken in the course of such an inquest. On the other hand, I note that two witnesses who heard the words spoken by Mr Cragg found them not only detrimental to Mr Barrowclough's character but entirely unsupported by evidence. I myself find the words highly detrimental as to character. To call someone a murderer is a very dangerous – indeed, reckless – game, unless you can prove it. I therefore proceed to judgement. I find the case of slander against Titus Cragg proven.'

I was astounded, indeed speechless. In his desperate haste to get out of the way of the rebels, Starkey had bundled the entire trial into less than half an hour. He had brutally castrated my defence and treated the entire thing as a farce.

After this travesty, only one piece of business remained to be done. How was I to be punished? Starkey, however, was too much rushed to face the question now.

'As to damages,' he went on, 'I will rule on that matter when I have given it my careful consideration. Under the political and military circumstances of the time, it is hard to predict when we will be able to reconvene. I therefore adjourn this hearing *sine die*. Clerk?'

'All rise,' called the clerk of the court.

And that was the end of that.

The only possible place of resort after that was the Turk's Head. Even Furzey, who preferred different coffee houses and taverns to mine, joined us.

'The man must have been corrupted by Barrowclough,' said Fidelis. 'Do they know each other? Are they of the same persuasion?'

'You mean religion?' I said. 'No, Barrowclough is a fanatical Methodist. Starkey is middle-of-the road Anglican.'

'Some other persuasion, then?' said Fidelis.

'I doubt it, Doctor,' said Furzey, picking up his meaning. 'Edmund Starkey is, as far as anyone knows, happily married. I can tell you for a fact that he and his wife have seven children.'

'I wonder if we're looking at this in the right way,' I said, pouring wine for myself and Fidelis while Furzey helped himself to the coffee pot. He rarely took fermented drink.

'How do you mean?' said Furzey. 'When I say the man's happy with a woman, that doesn't make him an honest man towards the world. No man who will speak of you as a "mere coroner" is likely to be an entirely honest man. Not in my estimation.'

'Thank you, Furzey. I am touched. But my point is that Starkey is obviously frightened. The rebels in their retreat are likely to be here tomorrow. They may still be interested in what happened to their comrades in Ribchester – the very matter on which today's case rested – and, if so, they will want to interrogate him.'

'If he is frightened about that, then so should you be, even more so.'

'I'm aware of that. But Starkey has something else to fear, which I do not. Starkey must expect his house to be requisitioned again for the Prince's use. But this time the Duke of Cumberland is coming along behind. What will he think of Edmund Starkey, the eminent lawyer and judge of Preston, who was selected to play host to the Pretender?'

'Starkey can say he played no part in it,' said Fidelis. 'He can say he was not there.'

'Quite. He must indeed not be there. It was one of the reasons for his rushing through the trial this morning.'

'Why did he not simply call it off. Postpone it?'

'In case he is caught and questioned by the rebels. He needs to be able to point to his finding: that the deaths of the two Highlanders are still unexplained and my assertions about it were slanderous and false. That doesn't help me much.'

'So Starkey is tied in a knot,' mused Fidelis. 'If he pulls one string, the Jacobites may have him, and if he pulls the other, Cumberland may have him.'

'I don't know about Cumberland,' said Furzey, 'but the rebels may have you an' all, when they come back. Shall you not make yourself scarce, like Starkey?'

'No, I won't hide,' I said. 'Everything has changed now. First, they are in retreat. Second, I now know a great deal more about what happened in Ribchester and believe I can easily convince them I am innocent of the crime, in spite of Starkey's manoeuvrings. I have the evidence of the handwriting pointing them away from me and towards Barrowclough, and I can produce a complete copy of the inquest report, of which they only have the last page'

'Quite right,' said Fidelis. 'He's brought this case against you, which he should never have done. You may have your revenge.'

'It is an interesting legal point,' mused Furzey. 'Who is the bigger criminal, the one who kills two rebels, as a murderer, or the one who turns that killer over to the rebels, as a traitor?'

'You are always spotting interesting points, Furzey. And I usually find myself in the eye of them.'

TWENTY

Furzey and I were surprised to find Griselda Bigelow waiting for us at the office, wearing a market-going bonnet pinned with flowers.

'How may I help you, Mrs Bigelow?'

'I need a lawyer, I reckon.'

'And you have chosen me!' I said. 'I am flattered. What is the business? A civil case, perhaps? I very much hope not a criminal one.'

I looked at Furzey. He made a gesture with his hands, out of the woman's sight, a tamping gesture. He was telling me to subdue the effects of the wine. Obediently, I adopted a sober expression.

'Why not come through to my inner office?' I said. 'There is a fairly good fire. Furzey, I shall call you if I need any writing.'

We went through the adjoining door and I showed her into one of my two fireside chairs, then stoked the glowing coals until they were comfortably burning. I asked her again how I might help her.

'Is it right that you made Mr Limmington's will?'

'Yes, some years ago. It's mostly irrelevant now, as he died virtually destitute, though I don't believe he ever brought the will up to date.'

'What happens to the house, then?'

'Limmington's?'

'Aye. The house I live in. Until she tries to turn me out, that is. I want to know if she's got the right. If she owns it.'

'As far as I remember, he left everything to Mrs Limmington. Unless he made some special provision for the property.'

I went to the door and asked Furzey to fetch Limmington's will from the basement, where all our old records were stored.

'That house is my home and I don't want to leave it,' said Griselda Bigelow. 'So I want to buy it.'

'Have you the means, Mrs Bigelow? The sum poor Limmington's widow would sell it for cannot be a trivial amount.'

'I know that. I want advice. What do you think she'd be asking for it?'

'Oh, I don't know . . . a hundred guineas, at least.'

I expected Griselda to be rocked by this, as representing a sum she could never hope to amass. Quite the opposite was the case. She smiled.

'Oh, all right. We can manage that.'

'We?'

'Me and my son. Me, I've a few pounds saved, but he has most of the money.'

'I see. So how can I—'

'Will you write to her to give her my offer? An' do all paperwork. Don't worry. We can cover your lawyer's fee, if it's in reason.'

'Do you know where I can find her?'

'She's back at Macclesfield. She left her address with me. Here it is.'

Griselda drew a slip of paper from her purse and handed it across.

'Very well,' I said. 'I'll write to her with your offer of a hundred guineas.'

'No, Mr Cragg! My offer of *seventy* guineas. We'll see what she says to that in the first place. And I don't want her to know it's me. I want to be a nonny-mouse all the time up till she signs. If she knows it's me, she'll not sell, or she'll drive a harder bargain. That woman's never liked me.'

'As you wish. There's no reason why I would say it was you. Will you give me leeway in the matter of money, though? Suppose she comes back with a higher price of asking. Of course, I shall obtain the house for you at the lowest possible sum, but she may want more than seventy. Am I therefore free to negotiate?'

'Up to ninety, and no further without you asking me.'

Furzey came in with Limmington's will. It had been drawn up in happier times, of marital harmony as well as prosperity, and it confirmed my memory: all the property, goods and chattels including his dwelling house were bequeathed to his loving wife, Esther Mary Limmington.

'We will write to her today. But as your son is underwriting the purchase price, I must have his confirmation. Where may I reach him?'

'Oh, I don't know. That changes.'

'Then will you ask him to call on me here at his earliest convenience?'

Griselda Bigelow said she would, and it seemed our business was concluded for the time being. But she had not quite finished with me. She made shift to depart but then hesitated at the door.

'Mr Cragg, the rebels are coming back to Preston, so I've heard. Might they return to Penwortham? Might they come back on the same business as before, helping themselves to the money of respectable people?'

'I reckon they might go around collecting money, Mrs Bigelow. But there is no reason to suppose they would pay you another visit. They are retreating and will not be here long. The town itself will bear the brunt of them this time, and the outlying places will be spared. My own little son stays with his grandparents at Broughton for the same reason. Much as it pains us to be parted from him, we consider he is safer there than in the town. Penwortham is even further out of their way, so I think you will be safe enough there.'

She seemed satisfied.

'Thank you, Mr Cragg,' she said. 'I'll say goodbye.'

Sitting alone for some minutes after she had left, I began to think again about the Limmington inquest. The complacency I'd felt at the end, waiting for the jury's verdict, had entirely left me, and I was filled with new curiosity about the affair, mixed with indignation over the treatment of the victim which the Highlanders would look back on, if they looked back at all, as an unnecessary accident. It was clear Mrs Bigelow was not terribly unhappy about it. Jack Fingers, on the other hand, had forgotten it if he was wise, and was busy plotting new robberies.

It was then that I conceived an extraordinary idea. Like the octopus I once saw when a student at the Inns of Court, in a glass tank at Culkin's Wild Animal Hall, the idea very soon began to grow tentacles and wrap itself this way and that around the death of Mr Limmington. If this idea came anywhere near the truth, it would mean I must cancel the inquest verdict. I must reopen the case.

I called Furzey in and began to dictate the letter to Mrs Limmington at Macclesfield.

That afternoon the first of the returning rebels, a cavalry unit escorting men from the quartermaster's troop, clattered into town. The latter quickly got to work, first securing the same officers' quarters around Market Place that had been pressed into use before, then visiting the inns and taking up all vacant accommodation. This time it was not Captain Lucas but one Morrison who called at the office to inform me that the Marquis d'Éguilles, Madame Lachatte and Captain Brown would each be requiring the rooms they had previously occupied in my house.

I tried to argue that the Marquis, for one, might be better taking himself elsewhere. Morrison, a polite young Irishman with a studious manner, asked why.

'He abused my hospitality. He tried to take advantage of my wife and I punched him, breaking his nose. In my opinion, he is a scoundrel and no woman is safe in the same house.'

Morrison took this calmly. It was not clear if he knew of d'Éguilles's sexual behaviour, for he now said, 'As I am sure you are aware, the Marquis has a reputation as a most religious, devout man. But perhaps it might be best if your good lady were to stay with a relative for one or two nights.'

'She is doing so. But I have a young maid here, whose virginity she – and I, as her employer and protector – would like to preserve.'

'May I suggest, sir, if she is afraid, though it be needless, that she lock her door at night? It is too late to make other arrangements for the Marquis. And you yourself, sir, should perhaps avoid any long conversation with him – any occasion for further quarrelling, I mean.'

He was a remarkably diplomatic young fellow.

'Before you go, Mr Morrison, may I ask you a question about your quartermastering?'

'You may ask, sir.'

'I understand your tax collectors work under the direction of General O'Sullivan.'

'I am afraid I cannot confirm anything about our senior officers and their part in our operations.'

'Will you confirm a negative, then, which does not involve your superiors? It is a question of which parts of this area were visited by the Prince's tax-collecting parties. Am I right in saying that when such a party visited the village of Penwortham, on the south side of the river here, it came away with nothing?'

Morrison thought for a moment.

'I was one of those who posted the tax-gathering parties, and no, sir, we received no money gathered in Penwortham. We did not expect to. Our intelligence told us that, of the two excise officers living there, one had died and the other retired to some other place. We do not waste time where we cannot profit.'

'Thank you, Mr Morrison. I congratulate you on your memory for detail. In return for that information – which is of no military significance, I do assure you – I shall try to endure the Marquis's presence in my house. I shall restrain myself from giving him another bloody nose.'

'We would be grateful.'

Morrison bowed, collected his hat and left. There had been no mention of my arrest, my having been transported to Wigan and my escape. These actions, I presumed, belonged to another part of the army – those in charge of military execution.

As soon as Morrison had left, I told Furzey I was going to Dr Fidelis's house to warn him to hide his horse once more.

'You will let me go home early,' he said. 'I must be with Mother when they come knocking. You can never be sure they will be the same pleasant young men as we had before.'

'Very well, Furzey, you may go now.'

'I can call at Doctor Fidelis's for you, if you like.'

'No, thank you. I shall go myself.'

Fidelis had already installed the horse in his neighbour's pig-house and was, with the help of Peason and his housekeeper, preparing a cauldron of soup over an open fire in his yard.

'Turnip and kale,' he said. 'I also got twenty loaves at the bakery and five dozen sausages. I reckon if I feed them, they'll behave themselves. They'll be grateful. What news from town?'

'The most interesting news you will hear this week. It may mean I need to nullify Limmington's inquest and restart it.'

'Based on what?'

'Based on the fact that Mrs Bigelow has suddenly got a lot of money.'

We sat in Fidelis's laboratory, perched on stools on either side of a bench where he carried out his baffling chemical experiments. First, I explained Griselda Bigelow's visit and her design of buying Limmington's house.

'So who is this son of hers who's so rich?'

'I haven't met him. I've been told he's in service. How he can comfortably lay his hands on the balance of a hundred guineas to make this purchase, I wouldn't know. I've asked her to send him to me so I can find out, ostensibly.'

'The son may just be a decoy. What you've told me must mean our Griselda did what we thought – a deal with the Highlanders.'

'A very advantageous one, Luke. There were two hundred and twenty-seven guineas in that bag of treasure. Griselda told me this morning she would be able to pay a hundred for the house. She must have persuaded four men, tough and armed, to let her keep almost half the loot! Or had she already taken a hundred out of the bag and thought to satisfy the soldiers with the remainder?'

Fidelis drummed his fingers on the surface of the bench.

'I haven't mentioned this idea with you, Titus, but I have long thought we should consider whether such a party of Highlanders ever went to Penwortham at all. Whether they were invented.'

'That occurred to me,' I said, 'and I've found a bit of evidence to support it. The rebels' billeting officer who came to my house this afternoon is also in the tax-collecting section of the quartermaster's office. He says they knew there were no excise officers still active in Penwortham and considered it a waste of time to go there. If that is true, there was no official tax-gathering mission to Penwortham at all.'

'One difficulty, Titus: Constable Gibbins at the Swan. His account of the Highlanders was detailed and convincing. So was he suborned? Has he been paid to tell the story? If not, there must indeed have been a party of Highlanders that day.'

'If you ask me, Gibbins is honest. And I can't see him and Griselda in partnership together. Which leaves what conclusion? Come on, Luke. Point and counterpoint.'

'The point must be that the rebel party did indeed exist, and did go into Penwortham, but . . .'

'But the counterpoint is that it was not an official tax-collecting party sent by the quartermaster.'

'It was an unofficial gang of soldiers out to make profit for themselves. That sounds right! It is plausible.'

'It doesn't explain how Griselda Bigelow is suddenly rich.'

'Perhaps her son will tell you that.'

'There's no knowing if I shall ever see him. But perhaps the rebel army will provide the answer instead.'

'How will you do that?'

'I have an idea. When I next see you, I shall know if it worked.'

Before I went home, I called on the home of Pip Simpson, a boy who often ran errands for me. I used him because he was clever enough to hold word-of-mouth messages in his head, and this was one of those. I gave him sixpence to run to Penwortham, then added threepence extra as it would be dark coming back.

Approaching Cheap Side, I found the bulk of the rebels were now arriving, coming into Market Place in informal groups, having been marched up in formation to the Church Gate bar and there stood down with orders to go to wherever they had previously laid their bonneted heads. By comparison with the men who had marched away so bravely two weeks earlier, this lot were dejected and unfriendly. I speak of the ranks. The officers, such as Captain Brown, who had already arrived at the house with his baggage, remained courteous, although he, like all of them, looked harassed and tired.

I sat waiting for Madame Lachatte with mixed feelings, but certainly with a heart beating more rapidly than normal. She was, when she arrived, in a quite different frame of mind from the troops in whose train she had followed. She swept into the house seeming to be full of life.

'Oh, isn't it exciting! The Duke of Cumberland is in hot pursuit of us. We are racing him to the border. Have you ever seen the Duke, Mr Cragg? He is said to be vastly fat. If so, we should outrun him as we ourselves are lean and fit.'

I could not help my spirits being lifted by her girlishness. I asked her what had happened at Derby. Why did the army turn around?

'There was a great war council,' she said, 'just like the one they had here, and the one in Manchester. Oh, they went over the old ground again. The generals, especially the Scotch, and most of all Lord George Gordon, were banging the table, asking why there were so few English rushing to the flag. Why had the French not landed its army on the south coast? The Prince was magnificent. He would not retreat, he said, and all we needed was a battle and a victory on English soil, because the people would come over to us as soon as they knew we were truly strong. But this time the generals were having none of it. They all lined up and told him one by one that they must turn back. The men would fight for Scotland but not England. They had had enough and did not want to die so far from home.

'How did the Prince take it?'

'I've never seen him so angry and then so dejected. He's a very dear man, an exceptional man, but when people start to contradict him, he hates it. He now says he'll never trust any of 'em again. He likes only O'Sullivan and his Irish friends, those flatterers!'

She seemed very well informed.

'How does the Marquis stand with the Prince?' I said.

'Badly. Very badly. The Marquis boasts always that King Louis's army is on its way, but it never comes. If the French army would come, he would be certain of victory, so His Highness thinks. But now that we are going back the way we came, the Scotch mostly curse him, and His Highness barely speaks to him anymore.'

'Good,' I said. 'He deserves it.'

'I know. I hate him for what he did in this house, and what he does everywhere. But *voilà*! I alone do not satisfy him. He says he loves me above all, but he must have other women.'

'By force?'

'*La!* As I said, he is a disgusting beast. But I no longer care. How is your wife, by the way?'

'She is not here. She is, of course, extremely upset about what happened.'

I almost confided in her – about Elizabeth's new coldness, her refusal to sleep with me. I might even have mentioned my feeling that she was being a little disproportionate. We were alone in the parlour drinking tea, but I told myself that Madame Lachatte might think that I was angling for her sympathy if I started talking like that, and perhaps, even, that I wanted more from her than sympathy. And if I looked hard enough into myself, I would have had to own that perhaps I did want that 'more'. But I could not reconcile this with my love for Elizabeth, and so the subject frightened me. Yes, I am a grown man of middle age, and I am still afraid of a woman's sexual allure.

The Marquis d'Éguilles came in after I had shown Madame Lachatte her room (into which I was careful not to go). His nose had reverted to its usual size, though it was now a little crooked, and he wore an extraordinary smile, which I could not quite construe. Was it ingratiating or complacent? Either way, he seemed to think, after my first outburst of rage, that I would no longer be terribly aggrieved over Elizabeth. That I would even understand and make allowance for his appetites.

I tried my best to convey to him this was not so, telling him as coldly as possible that he would sleep in the same bedroom as previously, and there he would be provided with meals. If he preferred, he might eat with Captain Brown and Madame Lachatte in our dining room, but that I myself was not prepared to sit down at table with him. He listened to me, still smiling and nodding his head. Was there perhaps a hint of contrition? His eyelids were heavy and folded, and the eyes were watery. I could not tell.

That night he did indeed take supper in his room, a supper

got up with ingenuity by Matty, who was coming along greatly
as a cook. However, when the boy Pip came in to tell me my
message had been delivered, I gave him another penny to make
a very different delivery – of the Marquis's meal tray into his
room. I was not going to play at hazard with young Matty's
virtue.

Later, before going out with Suez, I bundled the girl off
upstairs with a stern warning to keep the key of her room
turned and not range about in the night. The house was quiet
when the dog and I returned. My rebel guests had retired, and
though I had invited Fidelis to have a bed as before, he had
opted to stay near his horse. I hoped he was not sleeping in
a bed of pig manure.

Not feeling sleepy, I went to the library to write my journal.
I gave myself the task of remembering, or rather reliving, the
strange dream I had had in the morning, in order to record it.
I had pieced some fragments together when suddenly I realized the meaning of it all – the argument with Elizabeth,
the firewood and, above all, the gamekeeper's gibbet, with the
dead animals hanging from it. The gibbet in the dream, as
most of them are, was formed from an upright stick hammered
into the ground with a crosspiece nailed to the top, making a
T-shape.

In other words, Robert Nixon's headless cross.

TWENTY-ONE

We woke to a morning sun, the first in weeks. No human being, whatever the circumstances, is not lightened by such winter mornings. They make the heart feel for the briefest time young. They ungloom the soul with a fleeting promise of light and spring.

Gibbins certainly felt it. He was in his nature a jovial man, and the day met his nature on equal terms. He strode into my office and wrung my hand like an old friend.

'Lucky it was, Mr Cragg. I have business in town this morning, so when I got your message, I had no difficulty. What was it you wanted to ask me?'

'This may seem strange, Gibbins, but it is about the plaid worn by the men who came to the Swan on the day Limmington died,' I said.

'Are you still looking into all that, Mr Cragg. I should have thought you'd drawn a line there, with your inquest over and done.'

'It is hard to draw a line completely, when one becomes enwrapped in a case.'

'But the matter is decided, is it not? The verdict is given.'

'It is open to me if new evidence comes my way to re-inquest, though I will only do it if I feel the truth has been badly served. There were some details that didn't quite – and still don't – satisfy me, and one of these concerns the troop of Highlanders that came to the Swan and subsequently went over to Limmington's place. Now. Can you picture them still?'

'Oh, aye, I can remember them well enough.'

'I would like to identify their clan, if possible. Were they all wearing the same design or pattern of tartan?'

'Yes, they were. I think so. Yes, I'm sure.'

'Well, Mr Gibbins, the town is full of Highlanders this beautiful morning. Shall we go out and see if we can spot a plaid that matches your memory?'

Gibbins meant to see the brewer about his order for Christmas ale and, to save time, I agreed to walk along with him while we spied out likely tartans. First, we made a tour of Market Place. One group of soldiers gathered around a seller of oranges, some of the first of the season to be seen in Preston, now brightly reflecting the sunshine. Next, we examined another group encircling two men practising swordplay, shouting encouragement as the combatants danced around, their blades catching the sun's rays in flashes. But none of the plaids these men wore were right. We passed along the Strait Shambles and I caught sight of Starkey's house between buildings. The windows were open and a maid scrubbed the step.

While crossing Church Gate in front of the church itself, and walking towards the top of Stoney Gate, we saw at least three dozen more rebel soldiers. They were going this way and that in groups. One group trundled a cannon on its carriage behind a mule. Another walked in file, carrying sacks of stores. A third was coming out of Barkworth's Bakery with armfuls of bread that they certainly had not paid for, since Barkworth stood at his door in his apron, calling after them despairingly.

'We were cheering and praising them when they first came down,' said Gibbins. 'Not now they're going up again. They're costing us. The price of bread's gone sky-high for those that have to pay for it – unlike that lot, who just take what they want.'

'How about that fellow over there – coming out of the barber?'

This officer, rubbing his newly shaved chin, was smartly turned-out. He crossed the road to join a waiting detachment of common soldiers in charge of a cart. They all wore the same tartan, but it was not the one Gibbins remembered. So we turned down Stoney Gate and then left into a cross lane that connected with School Lane. Here stood Thomas Lacey's brewery, one of four in town. We found the brewer in his business room, highly agitated and uncharacteristically voluble.

'They've bloody found my horses,' he said when I enquired after his well-being. 'I thought they were well hid, but someone informed, and they've found them and taken them, with both the drays. How can I sell my beer if I can't move it? I ask you, Mr Cragg, how?'

Gibbins, realizing he had come at a bad moment, did not stay for a discussion but handed over a paper on which his Christmas requirements were written.

'Happen you'll have your dray and horses back soon,' he said without much conviction, while Lacey cast a negligent eye over Gibbins's order.

'I'll not bet on it,' he said. 'Likely you'll have to come and fetch this lot yourself come Christmas.'

We left and headed back up Stoney Gate before turning left into Fisher Gate. The wind had got up, and new clouds were riding in from the east to get across the sun. A few yards along the street we passed my tobacconist and opposite him the goldsmith's, which was open, though the shop window and the shelves and cases inside seemed almost empty of wares. Taking Gibbins by the arm, I crossed the street to look in. It had been just three years since old Hazelbury, previously the chief clerk, had taken over the shop in his own name, with legal advice from me, and I wondered how he'd fared with the rebels. I soon found out for, as we approached, the shop door flung open and a Scotch soldier burst out at a run, with Hazelbury shouting after him from within.

'Stop thief!'

The thief himself had slightly misjudged the shop's threshold and stumbled over it, breaking his stride and making it a simple matter for Gibbins, now just two yards away from him, to dart forward, extend his leg and cause the fellow to trip. As he went down, a small silver pepper pot bounced out of his hand and landed at my feet. I picked it up while Gibbins made the fellow prisoner. He had struck his head on the paving as he fell and was too dazed to resist as Gibbins pushed him back inside the shop.

'Here's the loot – just a bit dented,' I said to Hazelbury, handing across the pepper pot. 'Is it all he took?'

'I reckon so, Mr Cragg. How do, Mr Gibbins. I am fortunate you were passing.'

'What happened?'

'The fellow came in pretending to be a customer, until he whipped this out of the window in full view. It's not the first thing that's been thieved from me by rebels.'

He took me aside and murmured out of the thief's earshot. 'Most of my stock's in a safe at my house.' He winked. 'Which they've never found.'

At this moment the bell swinging from the street door tinkled and the door swung open. A second Highlander stood there, a massive red-bearded ogre who growled something in Gaelic. Having come to himself, the prisoner reacted quickly. He twisted from Gibbins's grip and ducked as I took a step forward and tried to grab him. All I got was a fistful of his plaid. The man himself was gone, through the door and sprinting away, leaving all three of us gaping after him.

'Don't blame yourself,' I said to Gibbins. 'I should have got him myself. But we would have had to let him go anyway, eventually. The good thing is you've still got your pepper pot, Hazelbury.'

Gibbins approached me and touched the plaid that I still had in my hands.

'That's it,' he said.

'That's what?' I said.

'That's the same tartan as the Highlanders wore when they came to the Swan.'

I had taken hardly any notice of the cloth in my hand. I did so now.

'My God!' I said. 'I know this one too.'

'What is it?'

'This plaid belongs to the Clan MacGregor,' I said. 'The same clan that the two murdered men came from. The same clan that took me prisoner.'

'MacGregor?'

'Aye,' I said, remembering my first encounter with the Scotch sergeant on Playhouse Green. 'You'll have heard of Rob Roy.'

Back at the office, I wrote a note to Fidelis.

> The men that killed Limmington are Clan MacGregor, like the two murdered at Ribch'r. Most of the MacGregors are riding under the Duke of Perth, as we know. I think I shall go and see the Duke as I now have two matters to take up with him. Shall you come with me?

I sealed the note and strolled over to Pip Simpson's house off Friar Gate. Pip's father was a weaver and I heard the clack of the loom as I entered the house. His mother was nursing a baby beside the thin turf fire. Without the need for me to ask, she yelled.

'Pi–ip! It's Mr Cragg got postman work for you.'

From somewhere in the backyard Pip shouted he was coming.

'He's with his pigeons,' she said. 'Potty about them, he is.'

'Really? They are excellent for taking messages, I've been told. But I doubt they are better than Pip is.'

She enjoyed my flattery of her son, but this did not prevent her entering a sly enquiry as to my most recent troubles.

'We heard you've been had up again, Mr Cragg. I hope you had a good outcome after your being taken away by the Scotch to Wigan.'

'I had a mixed outcome, Mrs Simpson, if truth be told. But I shall appeal if need be. These times are not really amenable to the smooth operation of justice.'

Pip appeared and took my letter away at a run.

'Is it true the Scotch were keen to hang you at Wigan?' his mother asked.

'Hang me?'

I laughed. I couldn't quite tell if the idea of my dangling appealed, or did not appeal, to Mrs Simpson.

'Their real intentions were not clear, but I had been informed at least that my death would not be by hanging. I never found out what it would be by, because Doctor Fidelis followed behind me and discovered where my prison was, and so helped me escape in the middle of the night. I couldn't have done it without him.'

'Aye, he's a good man, is Doctor Fid. He does our doctoring when we need. You'll be grateful to him for getting you out of the crib. And your wife – how is she doing?'

The voice was definitely in the key of prurience now. Good God! Was there no one in town that didn't know she'd almost been raped?

'She is with her parents in Broughton, with our boy. Best out of the way during this period of . . . of occupation, we

thought. Now, I must be on my way, Mrs Simpson. Good day
to you.'

I waited impatiently at the office for Fidelis to appear, or at
least to answer my note. I did not much fancy the idea of
going into the lion's den on my own, but after twenty minutes
Pip was back to say that the doctor couldn't come this afternoon but would be at the Turk's Head this evening.

I went into the house. None of our guests were there and I
had sent Matty to Broughton to fetch some ham, vegetables,
milk and eggs from my parents-in-law, the Georges, as food
was almost impossible to obtain in town. I dined quickly on
some old cheese and an apple, and went directly out in search
of the Duke.

During their first visit, the rebels made their headquarters
at our largest inn, the White Bull, and assuming it would be
the same this time, I went there first. Two very severe English-
speaking sentries stood at the door, with rifles at the ready.

'Wha'd'ye want?'

'An audience with the Duke of Perth.'

'Have ye intelligence? Information?'

'Yes, I do.'

'In ye go, then.'

This was astonishing. Could anyone claiming to have intelligence get in? Surely that would be too easy. However, I met
a second, harder, barrier once I went inside, in the form of a
civilian clerk sitting at a table, with a list of names in front
of him and an armed Scotchman at his side.

'Your name?'

'Titus Cragg.'

He looked at his list. Not finding my name, he said, 'Your
business?'

'To speak with the Duke of Perth. I am the Coroner here,
you see, and—'

'The Duke is very busy.'

'I understand that. But I have—'

'The Duke sees no one without an appointment. You have
an appointment?'

'No, but I—'

'Then you can't see him today. Off you go.'

I was trying to frame a new line of persuasion when a young officer of the army came in. He glanced at me as he swept past, but five paces into the hall he stopped, turned and came back to the entrance clerk's table.

'Good God! Is it Titus Cragg? It is! Our intrepid runaway.'

It was one of the young officers I'd met in the hallway at Wigan, the one that had given me the mock interrogation prefacing my real interrogation by the MacGregor. I was both terrified and most peculiarly glad to see him.

'But you've got a nerve, coming here, Cragg. We thought you'd be a hundred miles away, in Yorkshire or somewhere.'

'I prefer Lancashire to Yorkshire,' I said. 'The cheese is better.'

He laughed.

'Well,' he said, sounding encouragingly friendly, 'to tell the truth, if you've come back to us for your military execution, you may be disappointed. We are rather busy on other business now. So what is it, really?'

He took me a little way into the hall, away from the clerk at the table. 'I hope it's not justice for your wife vis-à-vis the Marquis d'Éguilles. I believe I explained the position to you when we last met. He is above the law, understand? He can't be touched.'

'It isn't about that,' I said. 'It's the Duke of Perth. Can you get me in to see him?'

'The Duke? That's a tall order. He's got a mountain of work. What do you want to see him for?'

I explained. I mentioned the two men, one at least from Clan MacGregor, who were assassinated and beheaded not far to the east of Preston. I said I had information which might lead to who did it.

The officer scratched his head.

'Strange. That's precisely the matter we arrested you for, if I remember correctly. *You* were supposed to have done it yourself, or more likely ordered it.'

'I did neither thing.'

'Then why stick your head back inside the hornet's nest, man?'

'I want to find out what happened – who did kill those men. I think I know, but I want to be sure. It's my job.'

'Very well,' said the officer.

He went over to the clerk and spoke in his ear, then returned to me.

'I'll see what I can do. I'll come back with a yes or a no shortly.'

The clerk wearily motioned me to sit on a bench against the opposite wall.

Of course, it wasn't shortly. I sat down (by my watch) at just before two. Forty minutes went by. Numerous soldiers came and went, carrying papers in many instances, some of which I could see were maps. Some civilians also came in, and a proportion of these was admitted, but more were turned away. Almost all of the latter wanted to petition the Prince, only to be told to come back the next day. They were being brushed off. It was inconceivable, with the Duke of Cumberland on their heels, that the rebels would still be in Preston then but, even if they were, they would have to stand and fight. Either way, the Prince would not be receiving any petitions.

But to my amazement, after only another quarter of an hour, the young officer was back.

'He'll see you,' he said. 'He's intrigued. Come with me.'

We went up the inn's great oak staircase to its Great Room, where ordinary dining usually occurred, but which was now full of men, many in Highland dress, who used the dining tables in various ways – holding meetings, counting money, working over calculations and lists of figures, consulting maps. The hubbub was considerable.

I was stood beside the wall, between the portraits in oil paint of two sour-faced old mayors, and told to wait. I looked around the room, naturally hoping to see if the Prince was there. At one point a couple of soldiers came in, escorting Mayor Priestley, who had only in November taken office. He had evidently not made himself scarce, as had most of the Corporation. I watched as he was brought before a man in a wig and civilian coat. Mayor Priestley from time to time puffed himself up, and was from time to time deflated, as the conversation waxed and waned.

It may have been about victualling. It may have been about the
rebels' need for money and the town's unwillingness to
part with it. It may have been about prisoners. Whatever it was
about, within ten minutes they had finished the discussion and
Priestley was escorted away. He passed the place where I stood
and noticed me.

I suddenly thought how this might look. Priestley, as the
legitimate power in the town, could quite legitimately treat
with the enemy. In a sense it was his job to do so. It wasn't
mine. If word got around that I had – as had just been said
– 'put my head in the hornet's nest', I might be in serious
trouble. Treason, consorting with the enemy, giving *comfort*
to the enemy: these were all charges that might be levelled
against me.

My one consolation was that, as I had just found out from
Mrs Simpson, much of Preston knew already that the rebels
had arrested me and were even aware that I had been sentenced
to death. This made it quite plausible that I had been called
in for further questioning. The look Priestley had given me
might have indicated he thought I was heading for the scaffold
at the hands of the rebels. On the other hand, he could have
had the scaffold at Tyburn in mind. My fate was, it seemed,
an open question.

A civilian came for me eventually, a pasty-faced middle-aged
fellow, very small in stature.

'I am the Duke of Perth's clerk,' he said and beckoned me
to follow him.

TWENTY-TWO

The Duke was a tall man of about thirty years. He wore a black velvet cap on his head, which gave him a brigandish appearance, and over the back of his chair (to reinforce this impression) hung his sword, a long, curved weapon with an unusual pommel, rolled up like a scroll. I had never seen such a sword before, though now I suspect it was a Turkish scimitar.

'Who is this man?' the Duke enquired.

'County Coroner, my lord,' said my escort.

'I have no idea what that is.'

'I look into doubtful deaths, my lord,' I said. 'In Scotland the same job is done by the Procurator Fiscal. In England it is a separate office.'

'I see. And your name, Mister County Coroner?'

I told him.

'Cragg! You are that prisoner who escaped from us at – where was it? Macclesfield?'

'It was Wigan,' I said.

'You escaped from us at Wigan after you had been sentenced to be shot. You killed my young emissary William Sinclair and his comrade.'

'No, my lord, I didn't. I—'

The Duke held up his hand.

'You will have a chance to speak in time. But first let us see what we already know about you, monsieur.'

He spoke with a curious accent, and the way he ordered his words suggested someone for whom English was not quite his mother tongue.

He turned to a large leathern chest that stood beside his table with its lid thrown open. It contained several ledger-like volumes. He selected one of these and, laying it on the table, started to leaf through it, licking his thumb to catch up each page.

'Capthorne,' he murmured. 'Castleton . . . Chapman . . . Clayton . . . ah! Here we are. Cragg, Titus, lawyer of Cheap Side, Preston. Husband of Elizabeth (RC). Is that you?'

'It is. How do you know my wife's religion?'

'We always are on the – how would you call it? – the *qui vive*?'

'The look-out?' I suggested.

'Yes, the look-out for possible sympathetic people. Catholics are always a little bit more possible. I am one myself, you know.'

He turned back to his book and read some further information on me.

'It seems you have a life of adventure, sir. Sometimes arrested, many arguments with the authorities of your town. Yet you are not known as a Jacobite. Hmm.'

He now untied the ribbons of a document file and sorted through the contents until he came to a small bundle pinned together. I noticed my name on the top page, but the Duke was more interested in one of the pages below it. He read from this paper aloud.

'"I am it must be admitted the man who ordered the killing of the two Highlanders . . . this-and-this-and-this . . . signed Titus Cragg." Is this your signature, Mr Cragg?'

'Yes, it is.'

'Then I cannot see why we don't shoot you. These men you killed . . . William Sinclair, and Jock MacNab to mind him, set out with letters from the Prince to certain Catholic landowners in this county. Not only did you kill them, but you cut off their heads. That was barbarous of you.'

He made a downwards chopping motion with his hand on to the table surface and looked at me angrily.

'William Sinclair was a sweet youth and a faithful servant of the cause. I loved him dearly, and so did His Royal Highness. His death was shocking for us. Jock also. He was famous among his fellow clansmen. He was a man as strong as stone and immovable as a mountain. Why did you do it, Mr Cragg?'

'I didn't, my lord.'

'Major-General MacGregor of the Clan MacGregor told me you did and that he ordered your death when you were tried at Wigan. You then escaped. Why should I not carry out your punishment now that I have you back again?'

From his point of view it was a good question and, as an insurance policy, I had furnished myself with our filed copy of the Ribchester inquest report I had delivered to Lord Derby. I now drew it from my pocket and handed it to the Duke. His eyes drifted over the words until they came to the final page, when they lit up again.

'Here it is again! Your confession and your signature.'

'If I may, my lord.'

I leaned over the table and swivelled the report so that we could both see it. I turned to the penultimate page and pointed to the last line: *no one is likely to be more surprised than*

I then turned the page and showed the continuation: *I am. It must be admitted the man who killed the two Highlanders, and all of that, would be the essence of villainy etc etc.*

'Do you see? There is a full stop after "I am" and a comma after "and that". You need this punctuation to get the correct sense.'

The Duke shifted the cap to the back of his head and rubbed his forehead. He looked tired.

'Well, I've met a few Jesuits in my time, but this is equivocation to beat any of 'em.'

'No, damn it!' I said in a sudden burst of outrage. 'What prevents you people from understanding? It's the truth.'

Suddenly, Perth hammered the tabletop with his fist.

'Mr Cragg! I have Mrs Morag Sinclair to account to. William's mother entrusted the boy – he wasn't much more than a boy anyway – to me. I chose him to carry this letter and therefore she will accuse me of sending him to his death. All I can hope is that I can tell her what happened – exactly what happened – to her child and, if it is in my power, punish his murderer. The clan headed by the MacGregor naturally want the same for the killer of their man. Do you understand now why it would be very expedient for someone to die for this, Cragg? Not only me, but an entire clan wants the killer dead. And at this moment that means you.'

'My lord, if you read that report all the way through, you will understand why I must live. I can provide you and Clan MacGregor with the names of those who really did do this.'

The Duke slumped back in his chair and closed his eyes.

'Very well, I will read it, but not now. Later. I will see you when I have done so, but I advise you to spend the meantime saying your prayers, Mr Coroner.'

He snapped his finger at the soldier that had brought me in.

'Take him down to the cellars, will you? Lock him up.'

The White Bull's cellars were, in happier times, happier places: brick-vaulted caverns pleasantly spiced with the scent of wine butts and ale firkins. Five or six of the cellar bays, which contained bottles of the more valuable old ports and clarets, were equipped with barred gates that could be locked to prevent pilfering. They made perfectly serviceable prison cells, and it was in one of these that I was locked. There was nothing in there except a bucket, a pile of sacks in one corner, a quantity of sawdust covering the floor and a pitcher of small beer with a pewter cup. I poured some of the beer out and tasted it. It was sour.

But someone – having, I guessed, been asleep – had heard the chink of jug on mug and the liquid pouring.

'Who's that? Who's there?'

The voice was calling, though it was more like croaking, across the cellar.

'Water! Is that water? I can hear you drinking. Bring me something to drink, for pity's sake!'

In the space between us was a table on which stood an oil lamp, of exactly the kind so hated by Jonathan Parkinson. By its light I could see the bars of another of the bays opposite mine, from where the voice was coming. I could see the white hands of the prisoner holding the bars. And I knew the voice well.

'Hours since I emptied my jug,' Oswald Mallender was saying. 'Hours and hours. I am thirsty. Confounded thirsty. How long are they going to keep me here? Meanwhile, will I die of thirst?'

'I haven't any water,' I said. 'Just beer, and it's no good. It's turned.'

'Give me some!'

'I don't see how, Mallender. We are locked up.'

'I am. Are you? They manacled me – me! – and threw me

in here. They captured me on the road. I was on my way to
. . . somewhere. Did they manacle you, whoever you are?'

'No,' I said. 'They didn't manacle me. But I am locked in.'

'We can expect no better from them. Savages. But give me
a drink, I beg you.'

'If I could.'

He fell silent and I took a tour of my cell, during which I
prodded my toe into the heap of sacking. It met something
hard, which clinked. I pulled the sacking away and found that
it hid some bottles of wine, overlooked when the bay was
cleared. Picking one up, I read the affixed label: *Douro red
port wine. Messrs Clark, Thornton and Warre, Importers.*

'I've found some wine in bottles,' I said. 'I might perhaps
try to roll one over to you.'

'Yes! Anything! Anything!'

I took one of the bottles back to the front of the cell and
laid it down on its side on the flags outside. If my aim could
be made true, I could roll the bottle right across the cellar to
Mallender on the other side.

The first bottle started in the appropriate direction, but I
hadn't put enough force into it, and it stopped somewhere
underneath the intervening table. The second deviated from
the start and ended out of reach of Mallender's desperate grasp.
The third, like a perfect shot at bowls, ran straight and true
and pulled up a few inches in front of Mallender. His face
was still shadowed but I heard the rattle of a chain and saw
his manacled hand reaching out, snatching the bottle up and
drawing it in.

'Got it!' he croaked. 'You are a lifesaver, whoever you are.'

'Cragg,' I said. 'Titus Cragg. The County Coroner. Remember?'

'Ah! Cragg! So it's you.'

There was a long pause.

'How in thunder do I open this?'

There was another extended pause.

'Have you got a corkscrew?'

'No,' I said.

'A knife?'

'No.'

'I'll smash the top off it then.'

I heard the heavy jingle of Mallender, in his chains, moving round the cell, then the shattering of glass and the gulping sound of the wine flowing out. He must have broken off the neck of the bottle but not wanting to drink directly through the jagged neck was decanting the wine into his jug. Finally, I heard his throat gulping down the wine, and gasping between gulps, like one in the water learning to swim.

I kept an eye on my watch. It was almost three o'clock. At ten minutes past, Mallender asked me to roll another bottle across, in which I obliged him. By half past he was growing bumpsy and singing snatches of song, in between cursing the rebels.

'What do they think you have done, Mallender?' I asked.

'It's not what I've done. It's who I am.'

'The Sergeant of Preston?'

'That, of course, but, even more importantly, it is my connection! Or one of my connections, to be precise. Look, Cragg, I wouldn't want this to get around. May I rely on your honour as a gentleman?'

'Implicitly, Mallender.'

'There is an actress, Fanny Mallender, who is – ahem! – a distant relation of ours.'

'I remember her. She is your brother's child.'

'My, er, niece, yes. A distant niece, you understand.'

'And Fanny is an actress in London?'

'Just so. But – and here is the significance – she is friendly with the Duke of Cumberland.'

'Friendly?'

'Oh, yes. She is very friendly. With the Duke *himself.*'

'Do you mean she is his mistress?'

He did not react to this word but carried on in tones I can only describe as pleased. Drunken, but pleased.

'Fanny is accompanying His Royal Highness on campaign. And because of their close, close friendship, you see, the rebels may therefore put me – her uncle, you see – up as a hostage. My exchange value is high, sir. High as the sky.'

'The Mallender family must be very proud indeed of Mistress Fanny. Who will they exchange you for?'

'Oh, it will be a very important person. A titled person, no doubt of it. No doubt at all. And then I will be out of here at last.'

Silence fell between us, until Mallender began humming.
I sat on one of the sacks and thought about my own situation.
How, and when, was I going to get out of there? My own
'exchange value' was a pittance, at best, unless I could
persuade Perth that my information on Barrowclough was
worth the purchase of my life and freedom.

Then I heard Mallender's curious flat and dirge-like voice
coming from across the cellar. He had started to sing a common
ballad.

> Old Dancy was a Lord
> A Lord of High Degree
> All mighty with the sword
> As he was thought to be . . .

The broadside ballad is the lowest debasement of literature,
in my opinion. Not only is the so-called poetry lame but the
ballad's stock-in-trade is often the trivial and salacious treatment of violent human nature. And ballads will run on and
on – and on – a rule to which Mallender's was no exception,
though he appeared to recall every word. Lulled by the continuous, almost tuneless droning of his voice, I fell into a reverie
while idly listening. I may even have been briefly asleep.

> A count from o'er the water
> To Dancy Castle came (I heard)
> Black-hearted was his nature
> And Blackheart was his name . . .

The words started faintly to tickle my interest, though the tune
was indifferent and the poetry was dross. But some of its
verses were another matter. They had me stirring, and then
sitting up, and listening.

> The Lady Elinor Dancy
> She had a beauty rare.
> Count Blackheart took a fancy
> To have her, then and there.

Could Mallender be singing this particular song on purpose? Could he possibly know what had happened at Cheap Side and was in some way mocking me? However it was, as the ballad advanced, it became more and more painfully pertinent.

> He went into her chamber
> Where she lay fast in bed
> And straight away did blame her.
> 'I am bewitched,' he said.
> 'Your beauty makes me do this.
> Your beauty makes me sin.
> It's you that drives me to this.'
> And straight he did begin.

'Mallender! Mallender!' I shouted, feeling horribly distressed by the story the ballad told, but powerless to stop it. 'What is this? Do you do this by design, you blackguard? Stop your mouth! Stop now!'

But Mallender, in his drunkenness, sang obliviously on and, if anything, more loudly.

> But now the door did open
> Lord Dancy strode inside,
> saw Elinor's honour broken
> and heard how Elinor cried.
> 'Oh foul and fell Blackheart,'
> He said, 'unclasp my wife
> And come with me apart,
> For I must take your life.
> Black your blood will flow.
> Black will be its clots,
> And black will be the crow
> That on your gibbet squats.'

Was I going mad? The song was too hard, too close – not just the rape of the wife, but the crow and the gibbet that I had seen in my dream. I clamped my hands to my ears, thinking only of Elizabeth now. Perhaps I was imagining this. Perhaps I really was becoming mad. But gradually, increasingly, I

became convinced of this ballad's malign power over me. I
was receiving a message through the drunken mouth of a man
who did not wish me well. A man who had always been my
enemy in Preston.

'Stop!' I shouted. 'Enough, Mallender, enough of this!'

The light was becoming dim. The oil was low in the lamp.
Soon it would run out entirely and we would be in the dark.
I did not think that Mallender was paying any heed to my
shouts; more likely, the wine was overpowering him at last.
Before he reached the end of the song, his singing dwindled
and finally lapsed into silence, and then, soon, into snoring.

I slept myself then, deeply, and was awoken – I don't know
how much later – by the door banging and men coming into
the cellar with lamps. There was a confusion of voices. I got
sleepily to my feet and went to the bars of my cell.

'Where is the man?' someone said.

'Not that side.'

'Who is this, then?'

'That's the fool Mallender. Look across from him.'

'Here?'

The lamp had a shiny metal disc behind the flame, which
reflected the light forward, directly into my eyes. It was held
steady for a few moments but, of the men behind it, I could
see only looming ghostly faces, without features.

'Yes,' said a voice, a light and vaguely familiar voice, it
seemed, though I could not place it. 'Yes, indeed, this is the
man. This is Cragg. Do you not know me, sir?'

'I might,' I said, 'if I could see you.'

The man stepped forward and the lamp illuminated his face.

'My God!' I said. 'Is it? Is it Mr Burnet? What the devil
brings you here?'

Another voice growled from the darkness in Scottish accents.

'You're impertinent, man. Don't you know who you're
speaking to?'

'Oh, yes, I do,' I said. 'It is Mr Burnet, my acquaintance
from Manchester, whom I met last year. I hope, sir, your
awkward difficulties at the time you left the town were soon
solved.'

Burnet laughed.

'No, no. They are still not entirely solved.'

I had not thrown off the effects of sleep. My understanding was misted over, as one looking through a window in winter.

'But I still don't understand how—'

'Oh, you will, soon enough,' said Burnet. 'Now, you men. *Allez vite!* Let's get this good gentleman out of here and across to my lodging, where we may talk with him of old times.'

Burnet moved away and headed for the stairs, while the rough Scot stepped forward and keyed the padlock open, releasing the cage door.

'All right, Cragg. You heard His Royal Highness. Look sharp.'

'His Royal . . . What are you talking about? You can't mean that is—'

'Aye, ya fool, ya gowk,' he said. 'That is the royal Prince Charles himself who wants to speak with you.'

TWENTY-THREE

J udge Starkey had in his home a large chamber solemnly furnished according to the time it was built, with oak panelling, half-blackened boards, a huge oaken wardrobe and a great fireplace. The room was lit and warmed with blazing logs and innumerable candles

The Prince received me from a high-backed chair beside the fire.

'You are welcome, Mr Cragg. I have fond memories of our acquaintanceship during my visit last year to this part of the world.'*

I hesitated, not knowing how to greet him. I made a movement halfway between a nod of the head and a courtier's bow. He gestured me into a chair.

'This is astonishing, sir,' I said. 'I cannot think of you as any other than Mr Burnet the silk merchant who fled his creditors in Manchester.'

'Please be at your ease, Mr Cragg. It was a disgraceful impersonation, I confess, but you will understand my reasons. I had no army and could only go incognito among my father's people.'

'I wonder why you chose to be a Huguenot of London.'

'Why, as a contrivance to get around the touch of the foreigner in my manner of speech. And under this pretence it was easier to meet my supporters in Manchester without drawing attention. By the way, you should know that those meetings bore fruit. Unlike the other towns we passed through, men rallied to my standard there and we now have the Manchester Regiment. So much for Sir Watkin Williams Wynn's promise of three hundred horse! We never saw one. And the Duke of Beaufort who promised to raise South Wales and occupy Bristol. He did not stir a stump for me. I saw

* The story of Titus Cragg's visit to Manchester is told in *Rough Music*.

others that pledged me their support last year in Manchester – Lord Barrymore, Sir John Barrowclough. Where are they today? Hiding from me.'

'Is this why you are withdrawing to Scotland?'

'What other reason can I have, except that I have been treated no less shamefully by my own high officers? They would not go with me past Derby. London was three days away and they would not go. They say the English will not support me, which I know to be a lie. I say nothing of the bloody Welsh, but I am certain the English people love me.'

He smiled, as a man smiles who finds nothing to joke about.

'But I will speak no more of that. Divert me by telling how your investigations proceeded last year in Manchester, after I left you, and if you got up to any more adventures with your dog – strangely named Suez, if I recall.'

I described the conclusions Fidelis and I reached on that occasion, a farrago of crimes and accidents that I shall not go into here. He listened with interest at first, but his attention wandered as soon as I began speaking of the dog, no doubt reverting to his own farrago of troubles.

'I am glad the dog is well. A characterful little hound. But now, I regret, we must talk about my young friend Sinclair and his comrade MacNab. I have just mentioned Sir John Barrowclough. Those two carried a letter from me to him but were assassinated either before or in the process of delivering it. I understand you have looked into the matter.'

'That is so, sir. I convened and presided over the inquest.'

'Is that a trial?'

'Not exactly. It is an inquiry before a jury into the truth, as can best be established.'

'And what did your inquest conclude?'

'That the killers were unknown. The jury did not possess all the facts.'

'And do you have these facts now?'

'I have some ideas which are not facts, but which I believe to be true.'

'Then tell me. I must know what happened to my faithful men.'

'I made a full report to Lord Derby, a copy of which I have

presented to the Duke of Perth. The ideas I mention are written there.'

'Ah, yes! The report. Perth has passed it to me. I have looked through it.'

He had, of course, not read it. But that he'd had it in his hands, that he'd *looked through it,* was good enough.

'Then you understand that I myself had nothing to do with those deaths? Some of your men have accused me of this. The last loose page of the inquest report was found by your men while searching Lord Derby's house and this was misread, leading to the misconstruction that I accused myself of the murders. You can easily see how this happened by reading the loose page together with the preceding page that I wrote.'

He nodded.

'Yes, Perth has shown me this.'

'Did you know that one of your officers ordered my death because of this misapprehension?'

'My dear sir, be of comfort. I have countermanded that order.'

'I am relieved.'

'Now tell me in your own words what this report has to say.'

'It records my belief that the murder was committed, or else commissioned, by James Barrowclough, Sir John's son. This happened after the men had come to Barrowclough Hall bearing your letter, which they innocently misdelivered to his son. I should add that the son's religion and politics are grossly at odds with those of his father, whom he hates. There is also a servant to James named Abel Grant who, as I have reason to think, was also culpable. He and James were not just master and servant, but close friends.'

'Very well, I see you have reason. But do you have proof?'

'The evidence against Grant is strong. The note found in the mouth of Sinclair is certainly in Grant's hand. I regret I do not have any proof of Barrowclough's guilt.'

'Then you had better read this.'

There was a low table beside the Prince's chair and on it a heap of papers. From this heap he selected one and handed it across to me. It was a letter addressed to him from London.

Your Royal Highness, It is with infinite regret that I have been confined here by illness & unable to assist Yr Royal Highness's passage thro' Lancashire. I have also been grieved to learn that two of your men were murdered in the vicinity of my house in the Parish of Goosnargh, & their bodies disgracefully mutilated. My informant is my faithful servant Jos. Wrightington, who identifies the guilty men in a letter to me which I here enclose. Howsoever they be related to me and my household, I would not have these murderers & traitors escape justice and I therefore commit Wrightington's letter to you that you may pursue the men he names as you wish. I send it by hand of a trusted messenger. I am, Sir, etc. John Barrowclough, Bart.

The enclosure, which the Prince now handed to me, was rather less literate.

Sir John: I greet you. I rite to tell you of a wicked murder dun here of 2 rebels that were dun by yore sun an his frend as I must call him not survant Abel Grant who got sum of the village to help but it were the 2 of them did the deed by inviting them in & when the Scotch were at dinner at the Hall they shot wun and bashed the hed of tother. I did not see it but have hurd witness by Marion the skullery maid hoo surved table & butler Crockett sore it after an all. & then yore sun cut of there heds. As God is my witness this is trew. Jos Wrightington.

'May I ask, sir,' I said after I had deciphered this. 'Shall you pursue Barrowclough and Grant?'
   'I have done so. We've collared the son but not yet the servant.'
   'You have arrested James Barrowclough?'
   'Yes, Mr Cragg, the cur is in the next room. Would you like to see him?'

James Barrowclough was in a bad way. One of his eyes was blacked and his face was decorated by swellings and bruises. He was also very frightened.

'Cragg, you must tell them that they have got it all wrong. I am innocent of the death of those two Scotchmen.'

It was a small side room off the large chamber. Barrowclough's wrists were bound in front of his belly and he shivered even though he was sitting beside the fire.

'If that is true,' I said, 'you must disclose what you know. You must explain, for example, how a note in your servant's hand was found in the mouth of one of the victims.'

'That is what I'm telling you,' he said. 'It's my man that they should be interrogating, not me. It was Abel Grant's doing. All of the mischief was his.'

'I thought Abel was your friend, sir. Shall you betray him?'

He gave me a look between desperation and defiance, but made no reply. I glanced at the Prince, who had been standing apart, watching us.

'Carry on, Mr Cragg,' he said. 'Asking questions is your trade. Please ply it. I, however, have much to do and must leave you for a time. We shall speak later.'

He went out, leaving the door a little ajar. I turned back to Barrowclough.

'I ask again, Mr Barrowclough: if you will not give the truth to the Prince or the Duke of Perth, will you give it to me?'

Barrowclough stared at nothing in particular, while thinking hard. By comparison with our last encounter in Judge Starkey's court, it was I that had the whip hand now and he knew it. I pressed my advantage.

'May I suggest you compose yourself and make the fullest possible disclosure?'

I could see from the way his mouth unset that he had made up his mind.

'If I must, then,' he said.

He sighed and rested his spine against the chairback. I sat down in an identical chair placed opposite him.

'I am pleased,' I said. 'Now, you have already told me that the two Scotchmen came to Barrowclough Hall.'

'Yes,'

'Did you meet them?'

'I did.'

'Who were they?'

'They went under the names MacNab and Sinclair. Sinclair was a young gentleman and MacNab, as your friend Doctor Fidelis ingeniously guessed, was his servant, or more accurately his protector. MacNab wore the Highland dress including that blanket or cloak you showed at the inquest.'

'Did they state their business?'

'At first they were evasive. Made out they were wayfarers. Asked for my father who, as I told them, was away in London. I then invited the youth to sup with me, which he did. MacNab went down to the servant's hall for some porridge. Sinclair had pheasant stew with me.'

'What did you talk about?'

'He would speak only of general matters. Horses. Guns. That sort of thing.'

'You did not speak of the rebellion?'

'I raised the subject. Sinclair coloured like a girl – bright as a radish, he was – but he wouldn't admit any knowledge of it. And it was then I saw he was lying and must have been sent by the Pretender to my father. He came, I discerned, as a spy to gather intelligence.'

'What did you do?'

'I accused him outright and he denied it hotly. I challenged him, and it was then we agreed to settle the matter with guns.'

'And?'

'I loaded a pair of pistols and handed one to him. We took up our positions and he shot wildly over my head. My shot hit home. It went in at the heart and within less than a minute he was dead.'

'So you admit you killed this Sinclair.'

'Of course I do, but it was in a duel.'

'And what about MacNab?'

'He must have heard the shots, for he came up to the dining hall almost at once. But he was quite unprepared for what he found. As he knelt to try to assist his master, Abel Grant came into the room behind him, also carrying a pistol. He brought its butt down with force on the back of the Scotchman's head and the man went down. He was seized with shakes and twitches, his eyes turned up and froth came from his mouth. A few moments later he was dead.'

'And who was it that separated the two men's heads from their bodies?'

'I did. I fetched my medical kit and cut the heads off with a bonesaw.'

'Why did you do this?'

'Grant insisted. He said they were rebels against their anointed king and that is what happens to traitors: they are beheaded as an example to others not to traduce the state. He said we must do it to insure ourselves against being held common murderers.'

'Did anyone help you in these beheadings?'

'I needed no help with that. But when I had done the amputations, Grant wanted the bodies to be found, and their treachery exposed. The servants took them as far as it was possible in half an hour, both in different directions. It was intended to leave one in an exposed place – outside an inn, for example – and put the other in the river to be recovered at some point downstream.'

'Why were they stripped and what did you do with the clothing?'

'They were stripped for the same reason they were beheaded: as an awful example to others. Grant told the men to dispose of the clothing, and I believe some of it was burned and some thrown into the river. Grant himself retained the Scotch servant's weapon, a knife. He also kept the two men's horses.'

'And why were the severed heads exchanged so that they did not correspond to the bodies they were found with?'

Barrowclough shrugged.

'I don't know. A jumblement occurred. Does it matter?'

'Whose idea was it to post a message inside the mouth of one of the victims?'

'Again, Grant's. He said it would further exonerate us in the eyes of the law.'

'Yet by your own admission you're a guilty murderer. Why should you not face the gravest penalty?'

Barrowclough shook his head.

'No, no! This is my point, Cragg. I killed the man Sinclair, yes, but I feel no guilt. Indeed, I expect to be handsomely rewarded once the Duke of Cumberland arrives.'

'How so?'

He leaned forward and lowered his voice.

'Because this was a duel entered into as an act of war, sir. It was done in defence of the realm and therefore cannot in any way be called murder. I signed the covenant that had gone around the county. I bound myself to defend the King and his crown.'

He was almost whispering now.

'By the same token, I am a prisoner of war. I should be treated as one. Instead, they make a common criminal of me.'

'And yet you have been behaving like a common criminal. You have just betrayed your accomplice and friend, Abel Grant, assuming that in return, as is usually the case, you will receive a lesser penalty, or no penalty at all. You are a regular Peachum out of the *Beggar's Opera*. You are a Jonathan Wild who, under the guise of being a friend of the law, spent his time breaking it.'

'How dare you, sir, compare me to those blackguards? As for Abel Grant, he is no friend of mine, not now.'

'Yet you were on the friendliest of terms. Why are you estranged?'

'He has left me, Cragg. The dog . . . the bloody dog . . . the bloody beautiful *dog*! He is gone. Says he has no need of me now. Was that his plan all along? To use me until he had no more use for me?'

As Barrowclough bowed and cupped his face in his hands, the door of the oaken wardrobe swung open and the Duke of Perth's little clerk stepped neatly out, carrying a candle and writing equipment. The Duke came in with an armed guard and held a whispered conference with him. He ordered Barrowclough to be taken down to the same lock-up in which I had been detained, below the White Bull.

'Cragg,' said Barrowclough as he was bustled away. 'Speak up on my behalf, I beg you. You alone can help me now. Save me or these . . .' He mouthed the word he meant: 'savages'.

'Unless you intervene, they will do for me, Cragg! Please!'

The soldiers, one on each arm, took him bodily away. I listened to his protests until he was too far away to be heard. Perth sank with a sigh into the chair Barrowclough had occupied.

'An incorrigible villain,' he said. 'My clerk has transcribed your conversation, except for some parts which he could not hear. No matter. He heard enough. We know from Barrowclough's own mouth that he himself killed young Sinclair, and that he saw Abel Grant bludgeon MacNab without mercy. It is a confession. I don't believe his story of a duel, however.'

Nor did I, but I didn't think it was on this that Barrowclough had pinned his hopes of survival.

'James Barrowclough expects the reward of his life for turning evidence. He means to be what is called an approver.'

'Approver? What is that?'

'A man who confesses to a felony but, by naming his accomplices, gets off lightly.'

Perth shook his head

'Oh, no. He cannot get off lightly. We shall shoot him.'

'If you cannot consider him an approver, then I expect he will try to argue the case as a duel, or he may plead that he is a prisoner of war. I have heard, my lord, that your Scotch army is notably humane in how it treats its prisoners.'

Perth shook his head.

'Not this one. We shall shoot him for this barbarity. William Sinclair's and MacNab's mothers demand no less. He shall get no mercy and nor will his associate Grant, when we catch him.'

He stood up and extended his hand.

'Mr Cragg, I wish you well, particularly as His Highness says you were of service to him once. I now have the honour of letting you go about your business. Good day, sir. I have much to do; we march at first light.'

On my way out through Starkey's stately room, I looked for the Chevalier. Everywhere there were signs of packing up and preparations to leave. The Duke of Perth was overseeing the closing and roping-up of his leather chests. Soldiers were lowering the Stuarts' coat of arms that had been hung on a wall, maps were rolled up and bagged, and musical instruments that had been played to soothe the courtiers were put away in their cases. But there was no sign of Charles Edward.

The church clock struck six as I came out of Starkey's house under a black, starless sky, crossed the Shambles and entered

Market Place. Deeply inhaling the freezing air, I became almost intoxicated by my freedom. Today was Thursday, a day with no official market, but the scene was still lively. A few soldiers had lit a bonfire, fuelled by sticks of furniture they must have helped themselves to from nearby houses. A bagpiper played a jig to which a few danced and a chestnut roaster nearby was doing brisk business.

I spotted a fellow, in dirty worn-out clothes and a tattered hat, strolling about with a satchel bulging full of paper.

'Come, buy!' he was calling in a hoarse voice. 'All the latest! Tuppence apiece. Direct from London town, the latest ballads, and all the old favourites I have too! You know the tunes, now get the words. Best London ballads, tuppence apiece.'

I looked around to see there was no one of my acquaintance close by, then approached the man.

'Do you happen to have the one called "Lord Dancy and Count Blackheart" or some such?'

'Yes indeed, sir.'

Seemingly able to locate any required sheet without recourse to light, he whisked a ballad out of his pouch and handed it to me.

'A great favourite is that one,' he said. 'I congratulate you on your taste, sir. A great favourite, is that.'

I took the sheet, folded it and gave him his tuppence.

'May I interest you in another, kind sir?' he rattled on. 'I have "Lady Godiva's Ride". That might suit. And let's see. Oh, yes! "The Sad Ravaging of Lady Castlehaven" – that's a very good one.'

I cut short his pattering by turning on my heel and walking briskly away. I was ashamed to be taken for some sensation-seeking ballad-fancier in search of wanton songs to drool over. Yet I had to know how the story of Lady Dancy's rape turned out.

TWENTY-FOUR

At home, poor Matty had been harassed continually as Highlanders came and went, demanding food and wine, smoking their pipes in the parlour, consulting maps on the dining-room table and arguing loudly in military language she could not understand. As an ally, she had cajoled Furzey into coming in from the office to the kitchen to sit with her, in case of trouble. Ignoring the voices I heard from the dining room and parlour, I went straight there, finding them huddled over cups of tea.

'Oh, Mr Cragg! Wherever have you been?' cried Matty as I walked in. She fell into my arms and I let her hug me for a few moments, then detached myself.

'I have been the guest of the Chevalier himself,' I said.

Matty's mouth fell open.

'Have you met the Prince?'

'Yes. And incredibly, Furzey, it was he that we . . .'

I checked myself. Furzey too had known 'Mr Burnet' in Manchester in the previous year, but I now felt for some reason reticent to tell him of the supposed silk merchant's true identity.

'But what was he *like*?' cried Matty. 'Is he as handsome as they say?'

'Yes, Matty, he is handsome. And he treated me handsomely. You will both be glad to know that he has lifted the sentence of death against me. I shall not after all be subject to military execution.'

Furzey's face twisted into that enigmatic smile of his.

'Then the Pretender is good for something,' he said. 'It would have been a sorry waste of good bullets.'

I asked after my wife and son, but there had been no word from Broughton.

'But I wish they would come home!' said Matty. 'Will you not go and fetch them, sir?'

'They will return in their own good time,' I said. 'What about Doctor Fidelis? I need to see him. I shall go to the Turk's Head, and if he is not there, I must send for him.'

As Furzey was ready to return home, I asked him to go by way of the Simpson place and send Pip to me. When the boy arrived, I took him with me to the coffee house where, not finding Fidelis, I wrote a note asking him to join me and sent the boy to deliver it at Scrafton's Roost. Then I took a table and ordered pipes and port wine.

The humour of the coffee house this evening was one of wariness and noise. The wariness was on the part of the Prestonians in the room, and the noise came from a small group of drunken Scotchmen – young officers, I guessed – who had collected in a corner and were carousing and shouting defiant slogans against the Duke of Cumberland and the Elector of Hanover.

I was just lighting a pipe when a shadow fell across the table and I looked up.

'MacLintock!' I cried. 'This is wonderful! Sit down, have a pipe and tell me how you escaped.'

'It was *you* that escaped, Cragg, or so I've heard. They merely let me go.'

He accepted a pipe and told me his story. The cart containing the group of prisoners from Preston had reached Manchester, where the rebels stayed two nights. MacLintock was inter-rogated in much the way I had been at Wigan, and was shown a letter he had written from Preston to his brother during the rebels' advance into England, which the rebels had intercepted on its way north and thought might be evidence that MacLintock was a government spy. Unable to make up their minds about him, they kept him with them all the way to Derby, MacLintock continuing to argue that this letter was not of military interest and that it gave no secrets away.

'The irony of it is, Cragg, that my little letter to my brother Douglas would actually have been useful to the rebels. Yes, I moaned about their coming and I wrote one or two uncom-plimentary things about the Pretender. But from their point of view, what was more important was that I described the mood and disposition of us in Preston as we waited for the rebels to come. It was not my intention, of course, as I never thought of the mail being seized. But it gave them fresh intelligence of the town. I told them this, but they are suspicious of any Glaswegian and they held on to me unreasonably long before they finally saw sense and let me go.'

'Have you just got back? You took your time about it.'

'I had not a penny of money and so I walked and begged bread until I could get to Knutsford where there is a man I deal with, who took me in and lent me the means to go the rest of my journey. I was forced on to byways, for the road had their army on it, retreating by the same way that they came.'

'And now they are here again. Do you have any news of Cumberland?'

'I met a group of his scouts on the bank of the river at Warrington. They are frustrated because the bridge was broken down by the Liverpool militia; if it was usable, they would gain half a day on the Prince and likely catch him up. But Duke Fatty moves only sluggishly. They laughed about his mistress who lives in the baggage train unless he calls her to his tent, which he does each evening.

'Fanny,' I said.

'Who?'

'Fanny Mallender. Niece of our Sergeant here in Preston.'

'Is she indeed? The actress? Well, she is doing the Scotch a service by slowing Fatty down. With her in his army, some say he's too distracted ever to catch up with the Pretender.'

MacLintock's friends were calling to him, so he left me just as a Highlander came in from the street carrying a fiddle. The newcomer joined the young officers and began to play, though not the joyful jigs and reels we had heard so often during Charles Edward's earlier incursion into Preston. Tonight his tune was solemn, full of melancholy and with many notes of yearning. The shouts and challenges we'd heard earlier faded away under the spell of this music. The officers sat silent, lost in thought. They were young men a long way from home, a long way from their sweethearts and their mothers, whom they may never see again after the winnowing of the battle that was bound to come soon.

I thought of the soldiers who, as Mrs Bigelow had told it, bullied Horace Limmington to death and took his money. They might even have been some of the same men. I knew little enough about soldiering, but I suspected this double capacity for cruelty and fondness, which we all have, reaches the extreme in the members of an army.

I felt the wet muzzle of a dog pushing my hand and saw that it was Bawty. I looked around. At last, Luke Fidelis had arrived.

'How did your Highlanders enjoy their soup?' I asked.

'They couldn't have enough of it, Titus. They had it for supper and they had it for breakfast. Better than any broth from their own field kitchen. Not better than their mammies', of course, but that's to be expected. What have you been doing, Titus?'

I poured him some wine and gave a full account of my meeting with the Duke of Perth and the Pretender, and how the latter was the same as Mr Burnet the lace merchant. Fidelis, who had chased Burnet across three fields the last time we'd seen him, laughed.

'That is astonishing. But he took an extraordinary gamble, coming into the kingdom like that.'

'He is an extraordinary gambler, Luke. This whole exploit is a gamble, and so far a lucky one. But it seems the cards are beginning to run against him. He no longer trusts his generals, it seems, as it was they who made him turn around at Derby.'

'I fear I cannot match that for news,' Fidelis said. 'But nevertheless we – that is, Bawty and I – have seen something interesting today.'

'In regard to what, Luke?'

'In regard to our friend Mrs Bigelow. We have visited my patient in Penwortham this morning.'

'The dropsical one?'

'The same. And on the way back, as you know, one passes the former house of Mr Limmington. In doing so, I noticed two men watching the place. They were on the opposite side of the street.'

'Did you approach them?'

'Certainly I did. I suggested they were loitering with intent, and they did not deny it. Said they were bailiffs collecting a debt. I told them they'd get no satisfaction as the householder was six feet underground, and they laughed and said, "It's not with the corpse we got business. It's with the old baggage."'

'Mrs Bigelow? Could this be to do with the money she has got to buy the house from Widow Limmington? Has she borrowed from moneylenders?'

'If she has, they want it back before she's had a chance to spend it.'

'What did you do?'

'I left them to it. They were not doing anything wrong and their story was not too far-fetched. But later I put my mind to the conversation, and in particular to this supposed loan that Mrs Bigelow has acquired to buy her house. Why should it be a loan? Why should it not, as we supposed, be the golden guineas that her master found beside the Liverpool Road?'

'In which case, who were those two men?'

'Who indeed?'

I did not have time to reply, for now I was aware that a boy was standing beside me. It was Pip, with a sealed letter in his hand.

'Here is a letter for you, Mr Cragg. This man brought it to your house, but Matty said you were at the coffee house, so he asked what boy ran messages and I was sent for to bring it to you.'

Pip showed me with his finger two words on the cover, written in capital letters beside my name.

'Matty says it says here "Most Urgent".'

'Why did he not bring this urgent letter himself, if he'd learned where I was?'

The boy shrugged his bony shoulders.

'The man didn't say. But he told me a house here in Preston that I'm not to repeat out loud.'

'Well, this is all very secretive. Is it to that house you will take my reply?'

'I don't know.'

I turned the letter over and examined it. The wax was impressed with a plain seal and there was no indication who my correspondent was. I broke the seal and read the letter.

'What do you make of this?' I said handing it to Fidelis. Fidelis read out loud:

> If you are curious to know how Horace Limmington died, come to me at the house the boy brings you to. He is sworn only to show you my whereabouts, and not to repeat the address, and he knows I will break his bones if he discloses or shows the place to any except yourself and the doctor. I will, of course, serve you both in like manner if you blab about my whereabouts. J. Sigginho.

He looked up, noticeably excited.

'Underhand dealings, Titus! Secret addresses! The highwayman's lair! This has the makings of a first-rate adventure. We must go without delay.'

I stood up.

'Yes, but we shall return to my house and collect a pair of pistols first.'

The boy led us to Back Weind Court, which was not far behind Friar Gate, yet a part of town into which the burghers of Preston and their men – Sergeant Oswald Mallender and his like – did not venture. The houses were ancient and in a state of advanced decay. Their timbers sagged askew, their thatch moulted and hardly any of their windows had glass. About halfway along, Pip pointed.

'In there,' he said. 'The door with the knocker.'

In response to my triple knock, a villainous black-bearded and very fat fellow opened. He had a sharp, broad-bladed knife stuck through his belt

'You're Cragg?' he grunted.

I said I was, and without another word he stood aside to let us in. We squeezed past him into a passage and, ignoring the doorway to an uninhabited ruinous room, went up to another closed door which led into the back of the house. Going ahead of me, Fidelis opened it and we stepped into a warm, candlelit room where a fire burned and the air was aromatically fogged with pipe smoke. In a high-backed chair at the head of a dining table lounged Jack Fingers, drinking wine. With him sat two other men with tankards before them, one wiry and hollow-cheeked and the other much muscled, with the thickest neck I'd seen since I'd last attended a match between wrestlers. On the floor lay another creature with a neck almost as thick – a bulldog, who sprang up and growled at us. We had left Bawty outside in the care of Pip, but I rather wished we had brought him in to balance the canine equation.

Jack Fingers did not get up but acknowledged us with a waft of his hand.

'Will you look here! The legal and the medical profession have arrived. You are welcome, learned gentlemen, to our commodious apartments. Paddy, you lazy dog, fetch glasses and wine for our guests.'

The giant shambled through an inner door where another voice was heard, followed by his growling reply.

'Sit down,' said Jack, indicating the two unoccupied chairs. 'I have the pleasure of introducing you to my associates, Stumpy and Joe.' He did not indicate which was which.

Fidelis and I took our places opposite these two.

'In your letter,' I said, 'you still try to hide under the alias of Sigginho. But I should warn you, we know quite well who you are.'

'You solved the little anagram, did you? My congratulations.'

'That letter spoke of Horace Limmington,' I said. 'You claim to know how he died?'

'I do know how he died. And I know who did it. The culprit is here, in this house, under close arrest, ain't he, boys?'

Joe and Stumpy nodded as one.

'Oh, aye, we got 'im,' said Joe, or Stumpy.

'We got 'im,' echoed Stumpy, or Joe.

'Who got him, you pair of addled sots?' O'Higgins jeered.

'No. I mean ter say, you got 'im, chief,' said one of them, hurriedly.

'Yer. You did. You got 'im,' chimed in the other.

'Of course I did, and never forget it.'

He tapped a finger against his temple.

'These idiots would be lost without me,' he told us. 'They're good enough as brawn, but I have the genius. If a question arises, I give consideration to it and I find the answer. The question here was how and why Limmington's life was snuffed out.'

'And you say you have found the answer?' I said.

His mountainous disciple now emerged from the back room with two glasses and a bottle, which he put on the table. O'Higgins filled both our glasses and pushed them towards us.

'You will remember I told you I did not trust that old woman. That distrust burned in me. Yes, it burned. So I watched her house and saw a certain young blade – one that I didn't know – coming and going. I didn't follow him into the house but instead followed him when he was leaving it, and he led us straight to this salubrious apartment, the hidey-hole where he had laid his nest. Within a few minutes of our entering, we had persuaded him to give up the thing he had hidden here.'

Without leaving his seat, he reached up and behind him and drew down a pair of saddle bags that hung over the back of the chair. In a moment he had unlatched one of the buckles and drawn out a bulging leather pouch, which he planted on the table before him. I recognized the bag. I had last seen it in the house of Horace Limmington, and then it had been full of golden guineas.

It still was. Jack Fingers unlaced the pouch and thrust his hand inside, coming out with a fistful of glittering coins, which he trickled back into the bag, his face suffused with pleasure at the act.

'So, you see, I have my money back. Do you want to discover who returned it to me?'

He snapped his fingers.

'Fetch him out, Paddy. Keep a good hold on him, mind. He's a slippery one, like all snakes.'

Paddy made his laborious way out of the room and again there was a voice raised in complaint.

Fidelis nudged me with his elbow.

'I believe I know who we are about to meet, Titus,' he murmured.

The door swung open and Paddy was there, with his huge hand around the upper arm of a tall, slim fellow, smartly dressed but otherwise drooping woefully in the giant's clutch.

I did not recognize him at first. Released from Paddy's grasp, he was looking from one face to the next while desperately trying to regain composure. He somewhat straightened his back, but he could not make his face straight. It was badly disfigured, not unlike the face of James Barrowclough as I had seen it at the rebel headquarters only that afternoon. One of the eyes was bruised, puffed and almost closed. The nostrils were caked with blood and the lips were swollen. The man had taken a heavy beating, and recently.

Then, with a jolting shock, I saw through the disfigurement and grasped who the man was. I was looking at Abel Grant, James Barrowclough's servant.

TWENTY-FIVE

'Come and join us, young man,' said Jack Fingers, as if inviting him into a party.

Grant was dragged shuffling through the door, evidently suffering many bodily injuries beside his facial ones, and brought to stand next to Fingers's chair. I looked at Fidelis. I didn't see how he could have known beforehand, but the satisfied smile on his face told me my friend wasn't in the least surprised. In response to my glance he gave an acknowledging nod of the head towards the captive.

'Greetings, Mr Grant,' Fidelis said. 'But should I not perhaps call you Mr Abel Bigelow?'

There were three or four seconds of silence and then Jack Fingers slapped the tabletop in sudden pleasure.

'Ha-ha!' he cried. 'Upon my word, that is good! What a subtle mind you have, sir. I had meant to spring a surprise, but you have smoked out the truth even without my helping you to it.'

Fidelis's complacency did nothing to soften my own surprise. To me, the sudden appearance in the room of Abel Grant (or whatever his name was) remained incredible. And why Fidelis had addressed him as Bigelow was even further beyond my comprehension.

'You have me wrong, Doctor,' said the man. 'I am not Bigelow.'

'Grant is not your alias?' said Fidelis sharply. 'It is not your *nom de guerre*?'

'No. It's the name I was born with.'

'Then . . . let me think,' said Fidelis. 'In that case, your mother was Grant before she was Bigelow. You are her bastard!'

'I am her son,' he said. 'I do not say bastard.'

'No matter. And are you, then, the son who was at Limmington's house when the poor fellow died?'

'I have no brother, if that is what you're asking.'

'Your mother doted on you, of course. That was why she falsified the time of her master's death. To give you time to get away.'

'Yes, sir, I suppose so,' Grant muttered, glancing sideways at Jack Fingers. That glance told me much. He was more afraid of the highwayman than he was of telling the truth.

'It was not very clever of her,' observed Fidelis, 'as what matters is not the moment when Limmington breathed his last; it is when he received the injury that caused to him die. And at that moment you were indeed present, weren't you?'

Grant's single visible eye narrowed. His contused lips opened to give an answer when I butted in.

'Wait a minute, I have a question before we get into all that. How did you come into the service of James Barrowclough, Grant?'

'Sir John Barrowclough,' Grant said. 'He's got a parcel of land at Penwortham. And he knew old Limmington. Politics in common, they had. He was sometimes at the house when I was young.'

'So Sir John was your first benefactor.'

'Called me a likely lad and said I could start at the Hall as pantry boy.'

'A charming story and all beside the point,' cut in O'Higgins, who had been listening closely to our exchanges. 'The man's a murderer. He killed his mother's employer, which is petty treason by my reckoning, all for this bag of gold.' He pointed at the bag. '*My* gold.'

'But it isn't the only killing he's accused of,' I said. 'By a wonderful chance I have heard him denounced this very afternoon not only for the assassination of a Highlander named MacNab on Sir John Barrowclough's estate, but also having a hand in the beheading of MacNab's corpse and that of his companion. The result is that the rebel army is out for Abel Grant's blood.'

I said this as much to inform Grant as O'Higgins. I looked at Grant. He answered me with a look of controlled alarm. O'Higgins, however, chuckled in delight.

'Well, well, well, what a pickle you are in, Abel Grant. What a doleful dilemma, between the military execution and the bloody assize. And it is a dilemma from which you are indeed going to die, on one side of the horns or t'other. People want to hang you, whichever direction you look.'

'I have to go to the privy,' said Grant.

'Are you beshitting yourself?' jeered O'Higgins. 'Not surprising, I will admit. Paddy, take him out to the jakes and never take your eye off him.'

'The question is what do we do with him?' I said when Paddy and Grant had left the room, followed by the bulldog.

'Who is this "we"?' asked Jack Fingers. 'It seems to me, as to what is done with him, that the call is mine.'

'And yet you sent for me and Doctor Fidelis. Why?'

'Pride. I must prove to you that I was right. That I am not to be treated with the contempt you showed me at the Swan Inn.'

'Very well,' said Fidelis. 'We grant that you were right about the money. It was never taken by any Highlanders. What do you propose to do with him?'

'I am undecided between a quick death and a slow death. Or I may spare him altogether. He is nobody's fool, not even mine, and he held out longer than most under the fists and boots of my men.'

We had been talking for five minutes or more when the bulldog came back in alone. O'Higgins said, 'What the devil are they about back there? It never takes as long as this for a condemned man to void his bowels. Joe! I say, Stumpy! You couple of dozey dimwits. Get out there and see what's what.'

Both of them seemed to have fallen asleep over their ale. Now they woke up with a start and scraped back their chairs.

'Yes, chief,' they said in unison.

They went out and we heard them calling for Paddy. Then, 'Oh Christ! Chief! Chief! Come out here.'

We all went tumbling out. The backyard of the house was covered in paving. This was itself covered in black ice and we scarcely kept our footing so that it took a few seconds before we were secure enough to see the great mass of Paddy lying on his back athwart the threshold of the privy, with the bulldog snuffling at him. Paddy was groaning and breathing in rattles and whistles. Fidelis, stepping forward, pushed the dog aside and knelt beside the fallen man.

'He's been stabbed in the belly. A deep wound. I doubt we shall save him.'

O'Higgins thrust his head through the door of the privy.

'That little windfucker's gone! He's flit.'

The wall at the back of the yard was five feet high. Even in his enfeebled state, and spurred by desperation, Grant could have vaulted it. O'Higgins ran at the wall, skidded for a moment, then hurled himself over. Joe and Stumpy got over the wall more laboriously and disappeared into the dark beyond, following after the sound of their chief's curses.

We heard a woman's shriek and the highwayman's stream of blasphemy and invectives fading. Fingers had already gone through the house opposite and into the street on the other side. There was a moment after that when the only sound we heard was Paddy's laboured breaths, which by now had turned into an unearthly snore. Seconds later, the snoring stopped.

'He delivered a hefty stab,' said Fidelis, feeling for a pulse. 'And I fancy it was with Paddy's own knife, as it is not longer in his belt.'

He concentrated briefly on what he was doing and then stood up.

'Well, he's dead. It seems we now have a three-times murderer on our hands.'

'And quite an actor,' I said. 'I would say Mr Abel Grant was by no means as badly injured as he pretended.'

'Very likely. And a fat man, taken by surprise while standing on iced flags like these . . . No, Paddy wouldn't have had a great chance.'

'Come on, Luke, there's no time to lose. We must leave while we can.'

We went back into the house and through the room in which we had taken wine with O'Higgins. Acting on an impulse, as I passed the back of the highwayman's chair, I lifted the bag of gold and hid it under my cloak.

'Titus!' Fidelis hissed. 'What in God's name are you doing with that bag?'

We had come out of the front door into Back Weind Court,

pulling it shut to keep the bulldog inside. Pip appeared from the shadow of a doorway, accompanied by Bawty.

'This money can be put to better use,' I said. 'I mean to see that it is.'

The scene at my house was one of social and military confusion. A group of officers had come to hold a conference with the Marquis and Captain Brown. Soldiers stood around on our steps and in the hall, conversing and showing each other papers, while messengers came and went, running across Market Place or along Fisher Gate, bringing orders, lists and rolled-up maps.

Opening the dining-room door, I found the meeting was in progress, with half a dozen bottles of my best French wine open. Presiding over this committee, the Marquis d'Éguilles sat in my chair, enjoyed my wine and burped with satisfaction after making a successful frontal attack on my food. His back was half turned away and he did not notice me as I smartly shut the door again and went into the kitchen, where Fidelis and Pip had gone ahead of me. Bawty's reunion with Suez was a noisy affair until I ordered them out into the back garden to sniff around for rats.

Matty was washing dishes with the fury of a woman driven to the limits of her tolerance.

'They are without shame, master. They thrutch into the house asking for the Marquis and Captain Brown, and when I show them in the dining room, they demand bread and cheese and wine and soup and I don't know what. I wish the mistress was here, that's all. I wish she was.'

'I wish she was here too, Matty. You must give them nothing more now, which you will say is by my own orders, and I trust they will respect that. They'll be gone from Preston first thing tomorrow and then we can forget about them.'

I told her we would go into my office. Luke and I took candles with us and went through. I unlocked my safe, put the bag of coin inside and locked it again.

'When he finds it gone, he'll come straight here demanding it back with threats,' said Luke.

'Of course, he will, but this is not the best night on which to threaten us. We have a dining room full of well-armed soldiers.'

'He will come anyway. You saw his temper. He is a man of violent action, which he conceals under jests and irony. He will not, however, find the loss of his gold amusing.'

I went back into the hall to lock the front door. The arrivals of rebel soldiers had ceased by now, and though the dining room was still full of them, the hall was deserted. But just as I was turning the key, there came a furious hammering from outside.

'Who's there?' I said.

'Titus! It's Elizabeth.'

There was something in her voice, a catch in the throat, an unnatural pitch, that did not sound right. I quickly unlocked and pulled open the door. Elizabeth was there in travelling cloak and bonnet, her eyes narrowed in anger. Behind her stood Jack Fingers.

'My dearest Elizabeth,' I said, 'what in all thunder is this?'

The highwayman answered me before she could.

'Mr Cragg, I feel most fortunate to have met your pretty wife just as she was mounting the step of this house. Naturally, I did not waste the opportunity to have her help me inside, so I—'

Elizabeth interrupted him angrily.

'I was coming home. This scoundrel accosted me, found out who I was and put a pistol to my back. He promises he will discharge it unless you admit him to the house.'

I had been ready to repel Jack Fingers, but I never foresaw that he'd have my wife as a hostage. I took a step back, forcing myself to be calm.

'Then so I must. Come in, sir. I believe I know why you're here. Elizabeth, may I present Mr Jack Fingers, alias Shamus Fingal O'Higgins, alias Jaime Sigginho, et cetera, et cetera.'

Elizabeth maintained her steely composure. She tossed her head back.

'The highwayman? I might have known. You are a man notorious for his contemptible treatment of women.'

'I regret the need to have you play hostage, madam,' said O'Higgins smoothly, 'but your husband has a thing of mine, for which – if he does not give it back – someone must die. If that be you, no one will be sorrier than myself. Is that clever doctor here, by the way? I should willingly kill him in your stead.'

Fidelis stepped out of the shadows at the back of the hall and gestured towards the dining room.

'Release Mrs Cragg and come through, sir,' he said. 'There you shall see how we may satisfy you.'

Fingers pushed Elizabeth a step or two forward, but a burst of laughter was heard from the dining room and the highwayman froze in alarm.

'Ah! If you have company in there, then so shall I out here. Open the front door again, Cragg.'

He started to move backwards again, pulling Elizabeth with him. I opened the door as requested, and as O'Higgins reached it, he gave a piercing whistle. Seconds later Joe and Stumpy came running out of the dark and up the steps to back up their chief. Joe (or perhaps it was Stumpy) held a pistol while Stumpy (unless it was Joe) brandished a long and pointed knife.

'I will not be tricked a second time,' said O'Higgins. 'Give me what's mine here and now, and I'll be on my way.'

Fidelis and I exchanged glances. With a slight movement of the head, Fidelis indicated the door that connected the house with the office. I said, 'Then you must come into my business room, where my safe cupboard is.'

I opened the door and led the way through, followed by Fidelis and O'Higgins – with Elizabeth still in his clutches – and finally Joe and Stumpy, who were ordered by O'Higgins to guard the door.

'Now,' I said. 'Shall we all sit and lay down our arms and have a civilized conversation?'

'There'll be no laying down of arms,' snarled O'Higgins. 'And no civilized conversation. I simply require you to give me the sack of gold coins.'

'Shall we light some more candles first?'

I took a taper and went to the sideboard, in one of whose drawers there were fresh candles.

I had lit three when the door from the house opened and

Matty stood there holding a lit candle of her own. Joe
and Stumpy, both stationed on the hinges side, were tempor-
arily shut out of affairs by the swinging door.

'Sorry to disturb you,' she said. 'But the Marquis wants
to see the master.'

D'Éguilles stepped past Matty and into the room, his figure
splendid in a silver-threaded coat which shimmered in the light
of Matty's candle. I heard a gasp from Elizabeth.

The Marquis looked from myself to Fidelis, then interroga-
tively at O'Higgins, who scowled at him.

'What's this popinjay doing in here? Get rid of him, Cragg.
I want to get on with the business.'

'*Monsieur*,' the nobleman began, addressing me, '*je veux
bien vous entretenir au sujet de—*'

But whatever it was he wanted to talk about, we never knew,
because quite suddenly Bawty and Suez, who had been re-
admitted to the house by Matty, burst into the room behind
the Marquis, barking angrily. In the way that dogs can, they
immediately saw the human threat facing them and launched
towards O'Higgins. Before they could reach him, there was a
deafening explosion as Joe (or perhaps it was Stumpy) pushed
the door back and fired his pistol out of the shadow. The
consequence of this was a squeal and a thump as Bawty went
heavily down. Suez, however, was not deterred. He leaped at
the wrist of O'Higgins's right hand, which was holding his
pistol, and snapped his jaws around it. O'Higgins let go of
his gun with a yell and at the same time loosened his grip on
Elizabeth who, with a twisting of her body and a stamp on
the highwayman's foot, was able to release herself entirely
from his hold.

Fidelis jumped forward to deal with O'Higgins, who was
hopping on one foot and cursing as he was still seized by the
bite of Suez's mouth. Fidelis wrestled him to the ground and,
to pacify him, punched him once or twice in the face before
removing Suez from his wrist. I myself swung around to deal
with the remaining threat, the knife wielded by Stumpy (or
possibly Joe). With as hard a chopping motion of my hand as
I could muster, I struck the man's forearm and was rewarded
with a grunt of pain and the blade clattering to the floor. His

head went down towards his wounded arm and I brought my knee up sharply to crack it against his chin, which collapsed him entirely. I then remembered I had a pistol of my own, took it from my coat pocket and held its point against Joe's (or conceivably Stumpy's) forehead, forcing him down to join his comrade on the floor.

This small engagement was not quite finished, however. For a brief moment everyone was still, as in a tableau. Then there came a quick movement by Elizabeth towards the Marquis, and almost at once a second gunpowder explosion. The Marquis squealed – it is the only word for it – and fell to the floor, his hands both going to his groin. I turned in astonishment and looked at my wife. She was standing above him with Jack Finger's pistol smoking in her hand.

TWENTY-SIX

Gruff interrogative cries were heard in the hall; then the pounding of feet, the swishing of swords unsheathed. Two pistol shots had been more than enough to interrupt the council in the dining room and bring the soldiers tumbling out to see what the matter was. Shouldering Matty aside, they packed the doorway to view the scene in my business room.

On the floor lay the writhing, shrieking figure of the Marquis, who was bleeding copiously from the groin. Fidelis knelt beside him, trying to see the extent of the wound, while on the other side of the room Jack Fingers struggled to his feet and glowered at my dog, who stood guard before him, his teeth bared. Joe and Stumpy, disarmed and discouraged, made no attempt to rise, while Bawty could not have done so. She had been shot through one haunch. Elizabeth, meanwhile, had stepped away from the Marquis. The gun that she'd snatched up off the floor – O'Higgins's gun – hung from her hand, still oozing wisps of smoke.

'Will someone go into the dining room and clear the table?' said Fidelis. 'And give me a hand here, you men.'

Three of the officers came forward, hoisted the suffering Marquis and got him out of the room, leaving a thick trail of bloodspots. A fourth at my request drew his pistol and covered the three highway robbers, who were now gathered together in a corner of the room. Then I went to Elizabeth and, with my arm about her shoulder, guided her out of the room.

I took her into the kitchen and sat her on the rocker by the fire. I knelt before her and took her hands in mine.

'My dearest, what brought you back?'

'To do what I have now done, husband. I knew that man would again be in our house. I came back home to punish his rape to the utmost of my ability.'

'I do not say he is not deserving, but should you not rather say "would-be rape"?'

She looked at me steadily. Her face – pale as wash, grave, unregretting – looked astonishingly beautiful.

'No, Titus. It was not a "would-be" rape, and he is not a "would-be" rapist. You do not understand what you saw that night. You were certain when you came into the bedroom that you'd interrupted him *before* his attack began. You thought that you had saved my honour in the nick of time.'

'Dearest, did I *not* do that?'

She shook her head, then spoke to me very slowly and quietly.

'He had penetrated me, Titus. He had been *inside* me. When you came up to the room, he had already finished forcing me. It was over and done with.'

'Oh, God!' I said, laying my forehead on her knees. 'Why did you not tell me, Lizzie? Why did you not let me help you?'

'I was ashamed, Titus, quite terribly. But also I was full of disgust for everything sexual, and I did not know how I could tell this to you, my loving husband. But after staying a few days with Ma and Pa, not talking about it, but thinking, thinking about it, I came to a firm decision. I saw no hope that the man might be arraigned by any lawful authority, but I was not going to let it rest there. I would not be able to sleep, and I would never be reconciled with you, dear Titus, until I had punished the Marquis before the world. I have tried to do so tonight. How well have I succeeded? Will you go through to where they have him in the dining room, and find out for me, Titus, how well I have done?'

I got to my feet and went into the dining room. The Marquis, gasping from pain and swearing a string of French oaths, lay on his back on the table, which was covered with oilcloth. One soldier held him down at his head and another at his feet. Fidelis, now wearing a professional wig, had fetched his medical bag from the kitchen, where he had left it prior to our setting out for Back Weind Court. He got out a pair of very large scissors which, when he saw them, made the wounded man flinch and stare with eye-bulging fear.

'*Ne vous inquiète pas,*' Fidelis said reassuringly. '*Seulement pour couper le pantalon.*'

He fit actions to these words by cutting away the, by now, blood-drenched breeches, and examining what he found beneath. Handling the Marquis's wounded flesh, he produced more agonized squeals, which were abruptly followed by silence. The Marquis had lapsed into unconsciousness.

'How is he, Luke?' I said.

'He's taken the ball full in the balls,' said Fidelis. 'They are beyond saving, but I believe I can stop him bleeding to death.'

'Shall we all agree to call this an unfortunate accident?' I said, looking around at the rebel officers present. 'The fellow O'Higgins was holding my wife at pistol-point when he was attacked by the dog and accidentally discharged the gun, hitting the Marquis in his genitalia. Shall we call it a peculiarly providential accident?'

'Aye,' they said. 'An accident, it was. Nae blame on your wife, o' course, but the Frenchie deserved it, nae question.'

I went back to the kitchen and told Elizabeth what I'd seen and heard. She closed her eyes and smiled.

'I am glad. There is no need for him to die. But he will rape no more women now, and with that I am satisfied.'

We were interrupted by Matty who was followed in by one of the kilted officers who was carrying in his arms, with some effort, the great wounded mastiff bitch. Matty laid down an old sheet in front of Elizabeth and Bawty was placed on it. I knelt and looked at her wound, which had almost stopped bleeding. By contrast with the Marquis, Bawty had been lucky. The bullet had passed right through her upper thigh, missing, as far as I could tell, any bone. Elizabeth began to tell Matty what to do – how to wash the wound and bandage it – and her voice sounded so much more like her own, full of renewed spirit and purpose, that I felt I could leave her without anxiety.

I went back to the business room to speak to the highwaymen. To my surprise, I found Madame Lachatte had come down from her room and, under the armed eye of the sentry, was deep in conversation with Shamus Fingal O'Higgins.

'Good Lord, Mr O'Higgins,' she was saying. 'What an agreeably exciting life you do lead. Ah! Mr Cragg! I have been making friends with this handsome Irishman, though I must forgive him for being a Dubliner. Cork does not hold with Dublin, you know.'

'I am no Dubliner, madam,' said he. 'I am born and bred in Kildare and that's the God-honest truth. But I have lived in Dublin and found it a fine city, very fine, and the second city of the kingdom. Dublin is London in all but size, and I am fond of it.'

She fluttered her eyelashes and gave a coquette's laugh, a penetrating high-pitched trill.

'Cork is finer. Dublin may be the London of Ireland, but Cork is the Venice of it – as you must know, sir, if you pay any attention to such matters. Cork is the *Serenissima* of Ireland.'

'I regret I have been to neither of those distinguished cities, so I cannot judge the comparison,' said Jack Fingers. 'I can only bow to your superior knowledge about the world.'

He was quite at his ease, like a man calling on a lady for tea, in order to flirt with her.

'Mr O'Higgins,' I said, 'I am eager to know if you caught up with Abel Grant?'

'No,' said the highwayman. 'He disappeared entirely. Perhaps he has gone to ground in the house of some confederate. A pity. I had been thinking quite soberly that, instead of killing him, I would invite him to join our fellowship and try his luck on the road. He has the makings, you see. He has the qualities.'

Madame Lachatte wanted to know who we were talking about.

'Oh,' said O'Higgins, 'it is a young fellow who is all athwart the law. He killed a man, then stole from me, but since he no longer has the money, I am prepared, or at the least inclined, to forgive him.'

'Yet this evening he viciously murdered again – your man, Paddy,' I said. 'Do you not hold that against him?'

'Oh! Mercy!' said Madame Lachatte. 'He did a murder this evening?'

'Not two hours ago,' said O'Higgins with smooth complacency. 'But I couldn't tell you how many times I've wanted

to kill Paddy myself. So there's another point in Mr Grant's
favour. He has done me a useful service.'

O'Higgins was one of those who tries to make his mark
with a lady by playing the devil. And in this case, more than
a little chagrined, I could see how well he was succeeding.
Madame Lachatte's eyes were transfixed on Jack Fingers, and
they were shining.

'I doubt Grant will throw in his hand with you,' I said. 'You
have beaten him and put him to the torture. He will hardly
believe you are sincere.'

'The torture!' whispered Madame Lachatte in something
like a rapture. 'Can this be true?'

'Yes, it's true, I regret to say, but necessary,' said O'Higgins.
'As to his joining up, I can be very persuasive. Would you be
kind enough to convey my invitation when you see him next,
Mr Cragg, to join me in infamy?'

The door that connected to the house opened again and this
time Captain Brown entered. I had not seen him all evening,
and he had evidently come in late, only to hear of the events
that had happened in the meantime. He looked aghast at them.

'I am very concerned, Mr Cragg,' he said. 'We move out
in only a few hours, and I cannot possibly leave the Marquis
behind. Will he be fit to travel?'

'You must ask Doctor Fidelis. He is confident of saving the
Marquis's life, at all events.'

'Thank God for that. But he must be fit to travel.'

'They are in the dining room,' I said. 'You must go and see
for yourself.'

It was past one o'clock and the visiting rebel officers began
one by one to excuse themselves, hoping to get three or four
hours' sleep at their billets prior to the muster, which was to
be an hour before dawn.

One of these was the man who had been watching over the
Cheshire Turpin, with Joe and Stumpy, in my business room.
Madame Lachatte had reluctantly said her own goodnights
half an hour before, and now the soldier, too, said he must
get some rest. I thanked him for his service and he went away,
leaving me alone with the three criminals.

'It's time for a decision, Cragg,' said O'Higgins. 'What to do with us? That is the question.'

'And I've decided it,' I said. 'I'm going to let you go your ways.'

'That is courteous of you,' said O'Higgins, with a raising of his eyebrows. 'It is the act of a gentleman.'

'It is not meant to be. The plain truth is the times are so disjointed that I have no means of detaining you. Our Sergeant, whom I would normally call out, was this afternoon lying imprisoned in a cell below the White Bull Inn, drunk as a stickleback in a brandy flask. I doubt they have released him, or that they will before they march away. Everyone holding judicial office in Preston has run from the rebels like rats from a burning barn. Therefore, you get the benefit.'

'Are you not interested in the great sum promised as a reward for my capture?'

'Let's say I already have it, in golden guineas. This is the price you pay for your freedom, O'Higgins, and I trust you are glad to pay that price and will banish that bag of money from your mind.'

'I have done so, I assure you,' he said.

'Then come this way, if you please.'

I led the trio into the deserted outer office and unlocked the street door.

'Goodbye,' I said, pulling it open and letting in a gust of freezing wind and powdery snow. 'In some ways it has been a pleasure, and in others not.'

'It has been interesting, at all events,' said O'Higgins. 'I hope our paths cross again. Goodnight.'

And, with a tip of his hat and bared teeth in face of the weather, he was gone. Stamping down the steps after him went his acolyte Stumpy, with Joe going after. Unless, of course, it was Joe followed by Stumpy.

I locked up and returned to the house. The patient had been removed to his bed upstairs, and Matty was wiping clean the table, watched by Luke Fidelis and Captain Brown. The two men were in conference.

'I tell you he ought not to travel,' Fidelis was saying.

'I have sewed his wounds as finely as I can, but the jerks and bumps of the road—'

'There is no question of leaving him,' said Brown. 'The Marquis must not be captured by Cumberland.'

He lowered his voice.

'We all know – though it is unofficial and not spoken of – that the Marquis is the personal representative of King Louis. His capture would give the government in London something big to brag about. The French king would have to beg to have him returned. He would lose countenance and appear duplicitous and weak.'

'I don't see why,' said Fidelis.

Fidelis had a powerful mind, but it was too straightforward to grasp the political arts.

'Because,' I broke in, 'instead of sending an army to give support to this rebellion, he has sent a single man. And that man may be more spy than ambassador. These are things our rulers would publish to the world, holding France in contempt. Is that not right, Captain?'

Brown nodded.

'Add to that, there must be harm to the Prince's credit with King Louis. We cannot take the risk.'

Fidelis shrugged.

'Instead, you take another risk – that the Marquis may die before you reach Carlisle. So be it. As a doctor, I prefer to vindicate my skill and save him; as a man, I think Mrs Cragg may have done the world a service by giving him that wound, and I would dearly like him to live with its consequences. But if you insist on his travelling, I can take no responsibility for his death.'

He swept off his wig and dropped it into the case, with the rest of the medical equipment.

'I will therefore say goodnight, Captain.'

Brown bowed to him, and then to me, and went up to his bed.

At the door, Fidelis said, 'I must leave poor Bawty here with you, Titus. But I'll come tomorrow early to look at the Frenchman and bring a salve for the dog's leg. I have given the Marquis opium, by the way, so he will sleep.'

I locked the door and stood for a moment in the hall, listening. The house at last was quiet, though I knew Elizabeth was still sitting up in the kitchen. I found her drinking ale, spiced and mulled, with Matty. I accepted a glass myself. 'A Christmas drink,' I said. 'There has been so much going on that I had quite forgot the season. And it is my favourite time of the year, I think.'

Shortly after that we went up to our attic bed and lay down together for the first time in a fortnight.

'Will you tell me how it was?' I said after we had stared companionably at the ceiling for a while. 'I mean your suffering, Lizzie. I know it was terrible, but what form did it take?'

I knew I was being a little importunate, a little pressing. The right thing was probably to let the matter rest for a while, but I couldn't stop myself. I couldn't wait to have my Lizzie back as she was before. And I was impatient to understand.

To my surprise, she was willing to talk about it without reserve. She talked as freely, in a way, as she might on the subject of some other woman to whom these things had happened.

'It was like being possessed by a demon,' she told me. 'It sat smack down on my spirits with its great sooty arse. It blackened my light; it soured my food and drink. I could do nothing without it being in the way.'

'That was horrible. Have you exorcised it now?'

'It was my intention when I came back to Preston. It was something Father said to me that started me thinking of it. As you know, he never has much to say at the best of times. But like many taciturn people, when he does say something, it is worth attending to.'

'What did he say?'

'This was when we were out walking, just the two of us with the dog. Quite suddenly, he said, without us having led up to it in any way, "You know, lass, the man as can only misuse it should lose it." He said it in such a way that I felt he was giving me his permission.'

'How were you planning to do it? You couldn't know you'd get the chance to shoot him.'

'The carving knife,' she said. 'I thought I would cut him with the carving knife.'

To my amazement, though very quietly, Elizabeth laughed, and it was then that I was sure she was my Lizzie again.

After a few more minutes her breathing settled into a regular pattern, and I knew she was asleep. As I turned to snuff the candle, I saw, on the bedside table, the sheet of paper I had put there after clearing the pockets of my coat. It was the ballad I had bought in Market Place that afternoon.

I unfolded it, thinking to myself I did not know how the fight between Lord Dancy and Count Blackheart turned out.

TWENTY-SEVEN

I n the first hour after dawn, it stopped snowing, but the swollen clouds looked ready to burst again at the slightest provocation. As the vanguard of the rebel column started along the northern road, these ashen skies were a match for its mood. The martial jubilation, the skirling pipes, the muscular songs had all gone. Sullenly, the soldiers marched away to a lone drumbeat on every fourth step.

The first arrival of the Pretender in Preston had been greeted with celebrations by his many supporters. There was no corresponding outburst from his enemies now, only a restrained but universal feeling of relief, as with the puncture of a boil. In the last few days, fear of a fight between the rebels and Cumberland had swollen to painful proportions. But now we knew there would be no street fires, no holed roofs and demolished walls, no dead babies. There would no new Battle of Preston in 1745, thank God.

The withdrawal was still only half accomplished when, at nine o'clock, Luke Fidelis returned to have a look at the Marquis. The wounded man would be leaving us prostrate on a litter, to be loaded on a mule-cart and trundled along behind the army, in company with the ladies' coaches and the baggage train, taking his chances on the jolting road, trusting to the fastness of Fidelis's stitches. Before he was carried away, the doctor unpacked the wound and, having repeated his advice that the Marquis d'Éguilles ought not to travel, said that the closures he'd made last night were holding.

As Brown's men were manoeuvring the patient down the stairs and into the street, I wondered why we had not seen Madame Lachatte. Neither Captain Brown nor Elizabeth had seen her. No more had Matty. I sent the girl to look into the lady's room.

'She's not there,' said Matty. 'I've looked in the press and under the bed, just to be sure. She's gone. Her box is gone an' all. There's only this.'

She handed me a book and I recognized it at once. It was *Roxana*. Slipping it into my pocket, I walked into the garden to see if the privy was occupied; it was not. There was really nowhere else she might be. She must for some reason have left early, before the rest of the house was awake. I could not imagine why.

Elizabeth had avoided getting anywhere near the Marquis but was otherwise cheerful. I even heard her singing once or twice – just odd phrases – as she set about changing the beds with Matty and airing the rooms.

Even the dog Bawty gave reason for optimism. She had a decently cold nose and seemed not to be in pain, except when she tried to stand up and walk. Fidelis, having given Matty instructions for the use of his ointment, said she would be fit enough to return home to him in a few days. The only shadow for me, therefore, was the continued absence of Hector. I wanted my son with me. Elizabeth said he ought to stay with his grandparents until after the Duke of Cumberland and his army had come through.

'If they choose to billet here, as the rebels did, we can do nothing to stop them, and we'll be all at sixes and sevens again. Best leave the boy where he's settled for the time being.'

'Very well,' I said, 'but he must be back for Christmas.'

At half past nine I walked out to see what was happening. Along the whole length of Friar Gate, a column of soldiers stood waiting to start. Many stamped the ground and hugged themselves against the cold, but they were quiet, like cattle. I strolled across to Lawyer Starkey's and saw the Prince coming out with a group of officers. They mounted horses and rode away without ceremony to join the column. The Chevalier's expression was sulky, intransigent, and quite unlike the young man of the world he seemed when we'd spoken just the day before. Nor was he the brave young warrior who had led his men south on foot. He looked more like a mardy boy.

Waiting in Church Gate for the Friar Gate column to start were the camp followers, a livelier, less disciplined mob of old men and women of all ages, trying as ever to make last-minute sales – Charles Edward's portrait prints, little wooden soldiers whittled for children, trinkets and tawdry objects they'd stolen or looted along the way. Among this throng were the baggage vehicles and three or four coaches, the nearest of which I recognized as Lady Ogilvy's. I approached and, rising to the step, looked in.

'Is Madame Lachatte with you?' I asked.

There were only two women inside: Lady Ogilvy, I presumed, and the younger and more beautiful Mrs Murray of Broughton. A third seat was occupied by a fat middle-aged civilian with one of his feet bandaged and resting on the empty seat opposite – a victim of gout, obviously.

'We have not seen her,' he told me. 'She will be in one of the other coaches.'

Without a word, he reached out and abruptly pulled down the blind.

I walked down the street until I reached the next coach waiting amidst the seething throng, its horses snorting and stamping the cobbles. Here I enquired again. Madame Lachatte was not there, and nor was she in the next coach. While standing on the step of this last, I could see one more coach thirty yards further down.

'Who is in that other coach?' I asked the driver, a slovenly fellow wearing a dirty cauliflower wig. 'The one coming after you, I mean.'

'That coach is special for His Highness's lady friends,' said the coachman. 'Miss Jenny Cameron, and the rest of 'em.'

I stepped down and, thinking she could not be in that one, began walking home. I felt sure that Madame Lachatte must have plans to rejoin the coach of Lady Ogilvy later on, though what she was doing in the meantime I could not imagine. Then I passed the window of Sweeting's shop, with its packed array of tempting volumes. I remembered the book that Madame Lachatte had bought there in my company only two weeks before, and took it out of my pocket. I flipped the cover back idly to expose the title page and immediately saw, above the words *The Fortunate Mistress*, a line written by hand: *page 94 if you please, Mr C!*

The book had been new when she'd bought it, so the author of this message must be the lady herself. And 'Mr C'? Myself, presumably. I hurriedly turned to the page referred to. At first nothing in particular appeared but, looking more closely, I saw some lines had been marked by a few very light ink-dots down the margin. They read as follows:

> To be courted by a prince, and by a prince who was first a benefactor, then an admirer; to be called handsome, the finest woman in France, and to be treated as a woman fit for the bed of a prince – these are things a woman must have no vanity in her, nay, no corruption in her, that is not overcome by it.

Good God! The message she was sending me could not have been clearer. Somewhere on the road between Preston and Derby she had found herself in the Pretender's company. He was dazzled. He flattered her, courted her and, finally, seduced her. She had no need now for the faithless d'Éguilles. The career that had begun among the milk cows of Cork was now on the march to greater and greater things as she sat with Miss Cameron in the coach 'special for His Highness's lady friends'. Madame Lachatte had become a royal mistress.

I felt immensely glad about this. The fatuous Marquis, with his criminal roving eye and false religiosity, would never be of good use to such a fine and intelligent woman – even less so now that he was, thanks to Elizabeth, frankly a eunuch. I returned the book to my pocket, thinking that although it was not the sort of title I normally keep, I would award it a permanent place in my library shelves as a memento of a remarkable woman – and one who may, if fortune continued in her favour, become even more remarkable still.

By midday the soldiers, drummers and pipers, the hawkers and harlots and cannons and carriages, and all the bluster and swell of the army, had gone from our streets. Preston was quiet, suspended as if between two storms. *How far away is the Duke of Cumberland?* was the question in the Mitre and the Turk's Head. *A day away* was the answer most commonly heard. Twenty-four hours and he'd be here.

We went about our business, but we couldn't concentrate. I picked through some papers concerning a disputed will and soon laid them down. Then I saw the draft of my letter to the Widow Limmington in Macclesfield. I wondered if I would be hearing more from Mrs Bigelow, now that her son's bag of ill-gotten money was sitting in my safe cupboard. Finally, my thoughts turned to my own son. It had been too long since I had seen Hector. I decided that, as business was impossible for me, I must go out to Broughton that very afternoon.

The cloud-fast snow had still not descended, but the wind blew in icy blasts. Old Jones, in no more of a hurry than usual, carried me across the Moor at an amble. We soon began to come across a few remnant followers of the rebel army, over-burdened walkers or crippled stragglers who had already found it impossible to keep up with the soldiers' pace.

We came to a place where the Moor dipped and began to rise again, and here a ghastly sight reared up on the skyline. It was a single stout wooden post, thick as a young tree, and set in the ground in such a way as to be visible from every direction. This post was topped with a crossbeam, and from each end of this dangled a human shape, suspended by his neck and swinging to and fro in the wind.

Reaching this grim gibbet – which immediately recalled the gibbet of Nixon that I had seen in my dream – I dismounted to take a closer look. Neither of the victims would be recognizable in themselves. The faces were grotesquely swollen above the tightened nooses, and they wore no distinguishable clothing, being both dressed in nothing but a dirty shift. But handwritten papers were nailed to the post, one on each side, presumably placed there by the disgraced men's executioners. I put on my spectacles.

John Bellasis, said one, *declared enemy of the true King and shouter of damned lies about the same. By military order done to death this day 13th December 1745.*

Bellasis. I remembered him – my fellow prisoner in the cart between Preston and Wigan. No doubt he had driven his captors mad with his unceasing reckless scurrility against them, until they reached breaking point and hanged him. Well, he had asked for this, if that is how he behaved. I moved around to the other side of the post.

James Barrowclough, it read, *who murdered William Sinclair*

*and did then mutilate the same by beheading after his death and
also the beheader of John MacNab, two faithful souls who met
their deaths violently while serving the True King. Hanged by
military order this day 13th December 1745.*

I remounted Jones and rode away from the dismal scene,
trying to regulate my thoughts about the end of James
Barrowclough. His father had betrayed him; that was the most
horrible thing about the matter. Nothing, no earthly persuasion
or unearthly terror, would ever allow me to do the same to
Hector. I felt my love for him to be iron-bound in faithfulness,
and though I did not think that, even as he grew to be a man,
we would or could ever disagree as the Barrowcloughs had
done, I would nevertheless stand by him even though we were
in mortal dispute. It is a law that though a son do sin, a father
does not sin against his son. How old Sir John could break
that law of fatherhood I would never comprehend. These
reflections occupied some of the forty minutes it took us to
reach the house of my parents-in-law, the Georges. When I
finally arrived, and walked into their cottage, I found the place
in uproar.

There was a strong smell of burned food, the source of
which was a tray of potatoes charred black and another equally
blackened pudding. Mrs George was on one side of the range
shrieking and sobbing alternately. Mr George sat across from
her, obviously in a state of bewilderment. He was casting his
eyes this way and that, as if looking for help from somewhere,
anywhere. Help there was, of a kind, for at least three sets
of neighbours were with them, including the constable of
Broughton, Simon Rackshaw, a kindly soul and in my estimation not a fool. He had his arm around old George's shoulders
and was bent down to his ear shouting questions, which
he had to do to defeat the old man's deafness.

'Did you know them? Tell me about them. Can you describe
them?'

Two women posted on each side of Elizabeth's mother were
holding her hands and attempting in high-pitched tones to
reassure her, though she took no notice. Her apron was thrown
up over her head, and she was crying and keening and calling
on Jesus and his mother and all the saints to come to her aid.

Whatever had occurred, I had evidently arrived too late to prevent it.

I clapped as loudly as I could. I banged my fist on the table. In the end, I simply bracketed my mouth with my hands and bellowed.

'WILL ONE OF YOU TELL ME WHAT THIS IS ABOUT?'

It had the effect I wanted. Rackshaw stood up straight. The two female neighbours looked around. They all stopped talking.

'Mr Cragg!' said Rackshaw, after a moment. 'Am I pleased to see you! What a good chance.'

'What on earth's happened, Rackshaw? Why all this caterwauling?'

He came forward and took my hand, as in a handshake, but there was something else about his touch, something of pity and condolence that all at once made me shiver and grow cold. An appalling thought gripped my heart.

'Hector,' I said simply. 'Where is he, Rackshaw? Where is Hector?'

'That's just the thing, Mr Cragg,' said Rackshaw. 'We don't know where he is.'

My first act was to tear through the house looking in the rooms, behind the doors, under the beds, in the blanket chests and every other possible hiding place. I went outside and ran around the house, first clockwise and then the other way, calling my son's name. I searched the chicken coop and the goat house. I searched the midden and the privy. Hector was not there. He was not anywhere to be found.

I stood outside the cottage front door for a moment and stilled myself, drawing deep breaths of air. Then I went back inside and guided Rackshaw into the parlour, a small room used for particular gatherings only. If any gathering was particular, it was this one. I took some more deep breaths to calm myself. It was no time to give way to panic. It was a time for rational thought and rational action.

'Tell me what happened, Rackshaw. Everything you know, and everything you suspect.'

'From what I can gather, Mr Cragg, men came. Carrying

pistols, they were, and had cloths like kerchiefs tied over their faces. Under their hats, only their eyes showed.'

'Who was here?'

'Just Mr and Mrs George and the little man himself.'

'Did the intruders say who they were?'

'Mrs George keeps saying it were Jack Fingers, Jack Fingers, over and over. I can't make out if she's just convinced herself of this, or if one of them admitted he was Fingers.'

'Well, I have some reason to think it may very well be him. What happened next?'

'The two old folk were tied up. They were found trussed up to their chairs and gagged with leather belts.'

'When was this?'

'Half an hour ago they were found. The neighbour Mary Crutchley came in for some reason and that was what she saw.'

'But do we know when the men came? What time it was?'

'No. We don't know how long the Georges sat there tied up. But the room smelled strongly of smoke from their burned dinner.'

'So it was before dinner-time. And did Mrs Crutchley send for you?'

'Yes, right away.'

'And you looked for my son?'

'Yes. He was not to be found. Not in the house, and not in the yard, as you've seen for yourself. He was taken, sir. I wish I did not have to tell you this, but he was kidnapped. It's the only explanation.'

I went back into the main room. Mrs George's storm of emotion had subsided.

'Mother-in-law,' I said. 'There is no use in unreasoned grief. You must know we may quite reasonably expect Hector is well looked after. I am sure these men who took him do not want to harm him, but to exchange him unharmed. So I must know exactly what happened here today.'

She nodded her head, seeming to take this in.

'I am glad you are here, son.' She was speaking now in a hoarse whisper. 'The leader, he said he was Jack Fingers the highwayman and he'd come for the son of Titus Cragg.'

'What time was it when he came?'

'Almost dinner-time. Happen twelve o'clock. The food was still in the oven. We never got it out till now.'

She gestured at the ruined food on the floor beside the range.

'Did the men come on horseback?'

'Yes.'

'Was there anything about the way the leader spoke?'

'He spoke roughly. But there was a bit of the gentleman about his way of speech too. Just a bit.'

'And did he say why he wanted to take Hector? Did he leave any writing, any letter, explaining himself?'

'No. He just told us we'd be hearing from him. We were to wait to hear from him, he said.'

'My guess is that it will be me who hears from him,' I said, 'and not here, but in Preston. Therefore, I must go back there at once. Jack Fingers might already have sent me his demands. Elizabeth may have opened them. I hope not, but if she has, I must go home at once to reassure her and get started on the business of bringing Hector home again.'

I turned to Simon Rackshaw.

'Will you go around and find anyone who saw these men? If you can get any description at all, I would be very obliged. You must write to me as soon as you have any intelligence.'

'I will that, Mr Cragg,' said Rackshaw, 'even if we're all night looking.'

I went out and mounted Jones.

'You must run like a horse ten years younger,' I told him. 'We have little time.'

TWENTY-EIGHT

J ones did his best, but by the time we reached Cheap Side, it was dark and the long-threatened snow was already falling. I went in by way of the office and found that Furzey had not yet left work. I asked if any letter had been received. None had.

'You may go home now, but I'd be glad if you would call on your way at Scrafton's Roost and ask Doctor Fidelis to come as a matter of urgency.'

Furzey looked at me with that ironic pity that he often assumed to assert his independence of me, and of the business of the office.

'What's happened? You are not yourself.'

'Why would I be myself, man? My son has been abducted.'

I hurried through to the house, where I found Elizabeth in the parlour. She put down her sewing and shook a paper at me.

'This letter has come. What does it mean? Something about someone's money and you have it.'

I took the paper from her. It was very much as I expected.

I have him. And you have my money. I will take it back in return for him. You will receive your instructions tomorrow.

Tomorrow! I couldn't wait until tomorrow.

'When did this come?' I said.

'A quarter of an hour ago. It was pushed under the door.'

'Only fifteen minutes? My God, if Jones had been ten years younger, I might have caught him!'

'Caught who, Titus? And who is "him" the letter talks about?'

'Matty!' I shouted at the door. 'Run out and get Pip Simpson. I want him immediately.'

I headed back towards the door connecting the house with the office. Elizabeth called after me.

'Titus, you are beginning to frighten me. Tell me what this is about.'

'Hector. It's about Hector,' I said, opening the door.

She followed me through as I went to the safe cupboard.

'But Hector's with my parents. Haven't you just seen him this afternoon?'

'No, I haven't. I found the house had been attacked. Your mother and father were tied up and gagged, and Hector was not there.'

Elizabeth clapped her hands to her cheeks, eyes wide.

'You can't mean that he . . . what the letter is about . . . that Hector has been . . .'

'Yes. The letter is a ransom demand. A man went to Broughton at dinner-time today and took our son away.'

'Dear God in heaven! Who, Titus?'

'The highwayman, O'Higgins.'

'O'Higgins, who was here last night, whose pistol I shot?'

'The same.'

'And you have this money that he wants?'

I pulled the safe cupboard open and took out the leather bag. I held it up in front of her eyes.

'Yes.'

'Then you must give it to him!'

'Of course I must. I wish I could do it tonight. But I don't know where O'Higgins is.'

We returned with the bag of money to our living quarters, where I placed it square on the mantel in the parlour, ready to ransom Hector.

'I thought I had convinced O'Higgins to give this up. Damn him! I should have known he was lying. "Show me a thief and I'll show you a liar"! Damn him to hell!'

Pip came in with Matty.

'Will you find Barty?' I said. 'I need him as soon as possible.'

Barty was the orphan boy who used to do the jobs that Pip now did, running messages for me around town and gathering information when I needed it. Now a big sixteen-year-old, he was no longer the urchin sleeping in the hay barn at Lawson's Livery, but he still refused all regular employment and remained closer to the lowlife of the town than anyone else I knew.

Pip said he reckoned he could find him, and off he ran.

'What are you going to do, Titus?'

'Find this ruffian and rescue Hector. But first I mean to muster our forces.'

Forty minutes later most of these forces had come together, and we formed a committee around the dining table: myself, Elizabeth, Matty (her eyes overflowing with tears), Luke Fidelis and Robert Furzey who, to my surprise and pleasure, had returned with the doctor – 'returned to duty', as he put it. Pip had still not reappeared. I took the head of the table.

'You all know what's happened,' I said, 'but I will summarize the emergency anyway. Today at about noon three masked men arrived at the house of Elizabeth's parents and gagged them and tied them up. The leader identified himself as Jack Fingers, also known as Shamus Fingal O'Higgins, the Prince of the Nicks, the Cheshire Turpin, et cetera – you have all heard of him. Last night O'Higgins was running around town trying to recover a bag of money. This bag.'

I rose and lifted the bag of guineas from the mantel, opened it and spilled some of the coins on the table.

'I had taken possession of the money since its origin and ownership were questionable – quite possibly it was the accumulated profits from O'Higgins's robberies and thievery up and down the county. O'Higgins eventually came here, late in the evening, and held Elizabeth at pistol-point, in order to extort the money from me, but was frustrated and overcome. As we could not safely detain him and there was no lawful authority in the town able to do so, I was obliged to let him go, which I did after making him promise no longer to pursue this money. And now we see what his word is worth. He is using a child of not two years old to get it back.'

The rap of the doorknocker was heard and, a moment later, Pip and Barty came in, brushing off the snow. I invited them both to take their places at the table.

'This is a council of war,' I said. 'Like those the Chevalier or Pretender held when he was here in Preston, it is about how to defeat the enemy, who in our case is Shamus Fingal O'Higgins, and to bring Hector back to us as soon as we possibly can. Now, we have had just one message from

O'Higgins, which is this: *I have him. And you have my money. I will take it back in return for him. You will receive your instructions tomorrow.*'

I looked from face to face.

'Tomorrow? Fiddlesticks! We want Hector back tonight, but first we must locate O'Higgins's hideaway, or wherever it is that he is keeping Hector. Remember that the child is not two years old, walks unsteadily and does not talk continuous sense. Who has anything to say that might be helpful in finding him?'

Elizabeth, after the first shock, had, as I had done myself, suppressed her emotions over Hector's disappearance in favour of the practical business of getting him back.

'What is a highwayman going to do with such plunder as a small child?' she said. 'Look after it himself? I don't think so. He's going to find a woman, and one who knows how to do the job.'

'That's good reasoning, is that,' said Furzey. 'O'Higgins's thieves' hideaway, wherever it is, may not be where he's keeping your boy. So even if we do find it—'

'He might've just as well have brought such a woman in,' said Fidelis.

'What women do we know of who associated with O'Higgins?' I asked. 'I seem to recall a Molly Binks, a few years back.'

'Binks was arrested and transported in forty-one,' said Furzey.

'Babs Cuffley . . . I remember that name too, and her sister – what was it?'

'Annie,' said Furzey, enjoying the chance to show off his knowledge of the lower end of Preston society. 'Babs died of smallpox five years since. Annie Cuffley married Jeb Knights and they moved to Manchester.'

'And there's Fanny Garnish, so I've heard,' put in Barty.

Here Furzey's omniscience received a check. 'That family's hard to keep track of,' he muttered, 'there's so many.'

The Garnishes lived in Back Water Street and were a well-known disorderly family with nobody knew how many members. They lived in an extraordinary house known, because of its great height above its neighbours, as Garnish Tower.

'Thanks, Barty,' I said. 'Fanny Garnish looks like one possibility. What other women does O'Higgins dabble with that we know of?'

'The man's had scores of women,' said Furzey. 'Hundreds, even. Filthy beast.'

'Well, we shall start by paying a visit to Back Water Street. Does anyone have any ideas about where else O'Higgins likes to hang his hat in town?'

Barty raised his hand.

'There's the Black Crow Inn on Ribbleton Lane. It's not much better than a common mughouse, but it's got stables of some sort and they say Jack Fingers is friends with the landlord and keeps a horse there. And sleeps there too now and then. The landlord's Jerome Kerly. He's Irish, like Jack is.'

'That's good, Barty. If one is hiding a child one has kidnapped, a closed room at your friend's inn must be a prime choice.'

'So long as nobody hears the babby crying,' said Furzey.

'Robert Furzey,' said Elizabeth sharply, 'don't speak easy as that about my child in distress.'

It was agreed we would form three parties. The inn was a mile out of Preston, so Luke Fidelis, who had a horse young and fit enough to manage in the snow, undertook to go there with Barty. Elizabeth and I would walk the short distance to Back Water Street, which lay just on the other side of Church Gate, while Matty and Furzey formed the base party, with Pip as their messenger, staying at home in case news came from Constable Rackshaw. Both of the out-going parties carried loaded pistols.

'These Garnishes,' said Elizabeth as we set off. 'The Ladies' Committee of Relief had them on its list as being a poor family and likely to starve. But when we went there to give out our bread and pickled fish, we found them all drunk and feasting on roast stuffed chitterlings and custard tarts. We never went there again.'

'Shall we use that as our pretext for this visit?' I said. 'Shall we pose as scouts for the Ladies' Committee.'

'I think not,' was Elizabeth's frosty reply. 'This is not a laughing matter.'

'Forgive me, Lizzie,' I said. 'I cover my fear because I cannot bear to look at it.'

Garnish Tower was in considerable need of repairs, both outside and in. We found it teeming not only with adults but with children – an excellent place, in other words, to hide a child, just as one hides a button in a button box, and not a biscuit box, or a hen in a hen house, and not a pigeon loft.

It happened to be Fanny who met us at the door – a pretty slattern, well rouged in the cheeks and lips, and with an alluring sway and undulation in her manner of walking. No wonder Jack Fingers fancied her, I thought. She brought us into a large room, of the kind called a hearth-room, in which all the life of the family and their friends ebbed and flowed like a great sea. There was a score and a half of people here: a fiddler with a children's dance circling around him; games of dice and cribbage; discussions and arguments and playful mock fighting; cooking and eating, pouring and drinking. No one seemed to notice our arrival.

The heads of the household, Tom and Bridie Garnish, were holding court over this hubbub. Old Garnish was a man of the last century. He smoked a long clay pipe and wore a countryman's smock, leather laces crossed up and down his legs and a bush of a beard that almost entirely covered his substantial rounded belly. Gold earrings pierced his broad and fleshy earlobes – a token of his time as a sailor in his long-ago youth. Neither he nor his wife looked in any danger of starving. Bridie, fat as a ball of butter, sat surrounded by a mob of her offspring, and her offspring's offspring, with a jug of ale in one hand and a large slice of plum cake in the other, her flesh quaking with laughter at the slightest amusement.

Elizabeth asked for a word alone with Fanny and she took us through to a small inner room with nothing in it but a pair of cots in which four babies slept. None of them was Hector. Elizabeth came straight to the point.

'I believe you know the man O'Higgins,' she said, 'well known for committing robberies in this part of country.'

'I know *a* Mr O'Higgins. I s'pose there's more than one.'

'There is only one Shamus Fingal O'Higgins, and that is the one I mean.'

260

'What of him?'

'Is he here?'

'No, he has not been here any day this month, or last.'

'May we verify that he isn't in the house?'

'How do you mean?'

'By going through it.'

'He's not here, I say. Who are you that's asking?'

At this point I excused myself, saying I wanted a word with old Mr Tom Garnish. I returned to the thronged room but went nowhere near the old man. Instead, I sidled unnoticed (so I thought) as far as the stairs and crept up to the next floor. One by one I looked into its rooms, before proceeding to the rooms on the second floor. All these rooms were in a state of extreme disorder and decrepitude, inhabited only by a few sleeping infants, none of whom was Hector.

Having seen the last of these rooms, I returned to the staircase leading to the attic floor, and found two beefy young men with violently red hair waiting for me on the landing. They were clearly twins.

'You've looked your fill, then, Mr Cragg?' said one.

'Pryers,' said the other. 'Nobody likes 'em.'

'Neither do they like peepers,' said the first.

When you meet a person (or in this case two people) for a second time, differently dressed and in a different place, there can be a blockage in the memory. I knew that I had seen these men before, but I couldn't at first say where. Then it came back to me.

'You two,' I said, 'I remember now. You're the twins that are – or were – in service at Barrowclough Hall, yes? Well, well, this is a coincidence indeed. I am afraid I have melancholy news to tell you.'

They looked at each other, uneasily.

'What news is that?'

'Of your master, Mr James Barrowclough. I saw him this afternoon. He was swinging by his neck from a gibbet on the north side of the Moor.'

Again the men exchanged glances.

'A gibbet, sir?' said one.

'Who was it that hanged him?' said the other.

'Possibly he was shot first,' I said. 'At all events he has suffered military execution by the rebels. They are very aggrieved at his part in the killing of two Highlanders at Barrowclough Hall on the third or fourth of November last. I wonder what you two boys know about that event?'

This set the twins aback even more. No longer interested in confronting me for nosing around their home, they were astonished at the grisly fate of their master and wondering what I knew that might lead them to suffer the same.

'It were nowt to do wi' us, were that,' said one.

'No more were it,' said the other, standing aside to allow me to pass down the stair. 'You'd best be off, Mr Cragg, and say no more about it.'

I rejoined Elizabeth, who was still talking with Fanny in the back room, and told her we were leaving. The girl led us back through the large room, where the uproar had not abated. For the first time, as we hurried on our way, I looked around at the company as a whole. The twins were talking, rather urgently it seemed to me, to a man whose back was turned. Whatever they said to him, his response was to raise the glass of negus in his hand and (as I thought) speak a toast before draining the glass. Then he turned slightly and I saw his bruised and swollen face.

'I have learned a thing or two,' said Elizabeth as we slipped and slithered away through the snowy streets. 'Fanny feels she has been jilted. O'Higgins called her his sweetheart and the silly girl believed him. Now he won't come near her and she is full of rage against him. He has other women, but she is too proud to tell me their names – if she even knows them.'

'If it's true, and the highwayman no longer comes here—'

'Oh, I'm quite sure it's true. The girl isn't clever and real indignation is difficult to dissimulate.'

'Well, it means we're looking in the wrong place.'

'Yes. However, Luke and Barty may not be. Fanny mentioned the Black Crow Inn as being one of O'Higgins's favourite foxholes. She strongly insinuated he might be found there.'

'Then let's hurry back to Cheap Side in case of any news.'

There was indeed news. A note from Mr Rackshaw had come.

Dear Mr Cragg, My enquiries have established that there were three men in the kidnap party. All on horseback. They wore hats pulled down over their brows and neck-erchiefs tied across their faces. They had pistols. Two or three saw them come up, but no one recognized them. No one saw them ride away, so I can't tell what direction they took. The horses were nondescript bay geldings. That is all I can tell you.

'It sounds like Jack Fingers had Joe and Stumpy with him,' I said. 'I am sure it is the extent of his gang, now that fat Paddy is no more. Good. Three is not too formidable a number.'

'There may be others that you haven't seen.'

'Jack Fingers is not Robin Hood, leading a whole fellowship of merry men. A couple or three confederates are all that he requires.'

I sent a reluctant Pip home to his mother. We drank tea and grew anxious, but hopefully anxious, as no news came from Ribbleton Lane.

'They must be on to something, else they'd be back by now,' said Furzey.

Another half hour passed and midnight struck.

'What is keeping them?' Matty said.

'On to something,' said Furzey again. 'Mark my word. On to something.'

He had no sooner spoken than we heard loud raps on the door. Matty ran to allow Luke Fidelis in.

'We've seen him!' he cried. 'O'Higgins is stopping at the inn. I'll warrant Hector is there too. Let us all go together and fetch him home.'

TWENTY-NINE

On his way back to Preston, having left Barty to keep a watch on the Black Crow, Fidelis had worked out a plan of attack.

'We cannot attempt the rescue while the inn is full of customers. We must go there at closing time and, if possible, have more guns than O'Higgins can muster.'

I showed him the dispatch from Rackshaw in Broughton.

'According to this, O'Higgins had two men along with him when he came for Hector. Is it the extent of his power now?'

'There was no sign even of those two at the Black Crow,' said Fidelis. 'If we take Furzey and Barty both armed, we will be four against one at the worst.'

'No, we will be five,' said Elizabeth. 'I'm coming with you. Hector will need me.'

'Must I stay in this house alone?' wailed Matty.

'Someone must,' I said. 'And there may be more pistol play there, Matty. You will be better out of it.'

Between Fidelis and me there were four full-sized pistols, but I had another pair of pocket guns, which I loaded, giving one to Elizabeth and the other to Furzey. My clerk treated his piece with the caution of somebody handling a polecat.

'Have you ever fired a pistol?' I asked him.

'No, and I always hoped to die before I have to. If I must shoot tonight, it will be to stop myself dying.'

'That is a good policy.'

We put on cloaks and hats against the weather – the snow had stopped but the wind was icy – and at the last minute I grabbed the bag of money, Hector's ransom, and packed it securely in Jones's saddle bag. Fidelis put Furzey up behind him, while I took Elizabeth on the rump of Jones.

'So, what happened?' I asked as we rode down Church Gate, past the Bull Inn, the church itself and Patten House dark and shuttered. 'Tell how you saw O'Higgins.'

'We went in like two thirsty passers-by. It was busy, being a Friday night. The landlord looked suspicious and at first didn't want to serve us, but I insisted. After we'd been sitting for a while at the back of the room with our ale, O'Higgins came bouncing down the stairs, as bold as you like, and into the room. He was calling out to Kerly and greeting one or two other drinkers without a trace of fear. You would think he was at home. No one would guess there was a price on his head. But I did notice Kerly calling him over and whispering to him, tipping his head towards us.'

'Does Kerly know who you are?'

'No. I've never met him before.'

'What did O'Higgins do after they'd spoken?'

'Went out immediately.'

'Without recognizing you?'

'I think not. I was sitting in the shadow. And he would not have left if he knew I was there. He would have confronted me. He must have seen us as what we pretended to be – passers-by.'

By half past twelve we had gone through Church Gate bar and were well on our way. I was giving Fidelis an account of the Garnish house and my meeting with the two footmen from Barrowclough Hall. Before I reached the point where I spotted Abel Grant, he interrupted me.

'There's the Black Crow up ahead,' he said.

The inn was set back from the road, sheltered within a stand of trees. The windows were still lit up, but customers were leaving now, calling out their goodnights, their voices slippery with ale just as their feet slid precariously on the packed snow.

'Look!' Elizabeth pointed to one of the curtained upstairs windows, which was lit. A shadow passed across the drapes – a human figure, so it seemed.

'Oh!' she said. 'Please, Jesus, let Hector be all right!'

We dismounted within the trees where Barty, shivering and rimed with frost, greeted us.

'Has O'Higgins come back?' I whispered.

'Not a sign of him,' said Barty, his teeth chattering like a ratchet. 'I stood at the side of the house watching both doors, front and back.'

'Good lad,' I said, and handed him one of my pistols. 'Now,

we must wait until the last of them comes out and Kerly's ready to lock the door. Then we go in. Furzey!'

I gestured for him to go forward and spy through the parlour window, but he looked at me, appalled.

'What me? By myself?'

'Yes!' I hissed.

His body gave an ungainly jerk in the direction of the inn, as if he wanted to go but could not. Then we all heard Kerly's voice booming across the snow.

'Out you go! You're the last and d'you think I've got all night to lock up?'

A befuzzled old drinker staggered out, impelled by Kerly's hand on his back.

'Come on!' I said, starting immediately forward. 'Before he turns the key!'

The inebriated old codger gave us a queer, disbelieving look as we stumbled past him and attacked the door. Fidelis and I reached it together just as it was closing, and he got a boot between door and jamb.

'What? Who's there?' shouted Kerly, still trying to shut the door.

'Push!' I said.

We shoved the door with all our weight until Kerly was forced to sprawl back and allow it to crash open. The next thing he saw was Fidelis's pistol aimed at the bridge of his nose.

'Furzey, Barty, your pistols,' I said.

Barty came forward and showed me his was ready, while Furzey, delving into the folds of his greatcoat, laboriously produced his own little gun. I closed and locked the inn door.

'Aim squarely at his heart. Shoot him if he tries to run away and give a hollo if anyone comes.'

Elizabeth, Fidelis and I crept up the stairs. Without having expressed the thought, we were doing what O'Higgins had made his career from: gaining advantage by springing a surprise. We found that the corridor ran the length of the inn and had five doors. Only one of these showed light beneath it, corresponding to the lit window we had seen from outside. We crowded around this door, Fidelis having a hand on the knob. I counted down: three, two, one. Fidelis turned his hand and swung the door open.

It was a bedchamber. The first sensation was its warmth and the second was the scent – burning pinewood from the fire and a French perfume. The woman herself was undressed to her linen and stood with her back to the door, arranging the fine tresses of her hair in a mirror. She was in the room alone

'Shut the door, *cheri*,' she said, still titivating. 'There's such a draught.'

And she turned round.

Surprise? I don't know who was the more unprepared for this meeting. She gave out something between a shriek and a squeak. Elizabeth said, 'Oh!' and I swore. Only Luke Fidelis, who had a genius for staying cool when others were lost in shock, retained his presence of mind. He stuck his pistol into his belt and walked into the middle of the room.

'Madame Lachatte,' he said. 'You will oblige us by saying where the child is.'

'Child? Did you say *child*?' said Madame Lachatte, looking wildly at each of us in turn. 'What child? I know nothing of a child, and I don't understand why you are here, Mr Cragg, Mrs Cragg, Doctor. Do you have business with Mr O'Higgins? He is not here. He left more than an hour ago. And anyway this is a strange time to be—'

'It is my son, Hector, who is two years old,' I said. 'He has been abducted this day and we have excellent reason to believe it was done by O'Higgins. Do you mean to say you know nothing of it?'

'Nothing at all. And nor does Jack.'

'Hector isn't here,' said Elizabeth, having already looked in the bed, and behind it, and into the clothes press, and every corner of the room. 'Not in this room.'

'The others, then!' I said.

In no time we had looked into the four bedrooms alongside, and found all dark, and neither with fires nor any other signs of occupation.

'I will interrogate the landlord,' said Fidelis, when we were back at the door of Madame Lachatte's room. He headed towards the stairs. Elizabeth and I went back in to see if Madame Lachatte could say more. She could, but not on the subject of Hector.

'What you did last night to the Marquis, Mrs Cragg,' she said. 'It was nothing short of magnificent. You fired that shot on behalf of so many women that he's raped, or tried to rape – including myself!'

'He attacked you?' I said. 'And yet you stayed with him?'

'It was temporary. I had enough of his bullying bedroom ways a long time ago, but I couldn't see how to leave him until now. It's beyond belief really that I ever liked him. His fate was so perfect and just, but it needed someone with courage like you to visit him with it and put a stop to all his activities on behalf of all our sex.'

'I didn't do it for our sex,' said Elizabeth briskly. 'I did it for myself. But it seems a long time ago, now. I am thinking only of Hector. Tell us where he is, for pity's sake.'

'Jack did not do this thing, Mrs Cragg, Mr Cragg. He was here with me all of the day, in this room, in that *bed*.'

She pointed, and if one believed her, which I did, it was easy to see it all. A beautiful woman of the world flees at dawn to the bed – at a friendly inn – of a new man. This man is a rake, but no matter. His being a rake makes it all the more plausible that the pair lose no time in getting to know one another, spending the best part of the same day in that bed, engrossed in their pleasure. This vision dissolved my certainty that O'Higgins had kidnapped my son – though, if he had not, I couldn't imagine who had. I looked at Elizabeth. She was frowning. I could see she had not yet let go of the suspicion.

'He needed you, though. He needed a woman to look after the little boy. Is that not why he lured you to him?'

'No, where do you get that idea from, Mrs Cragg? I was his fancy; that is the only reason why. And he, of course, was mine – as soon as I saw him. There was nothing about looking after a child – not his, nor yours, nor anybody's!'

'She is telling the truth, Elizabeth.'

The speaker was Fidelis, who now strode back into the room. With him was Shamus Fingal O'Higgins, wearing a somewhat smug smile.

'I regret you've come here on a fool's errand,' the latter said. 'I had nothing to do with any of this.'

'Jack!' cried Madame Lachatte, flinging herself at him to be enfolded in an embrace that lifted her clean off the floor.

'I should have seen it,' said Fidelis. 'A fool's errand is right, and the fool is me.'

'But the kidnapper *said* he was you,' objected Elizabeth, pointing her finger at O'Higgins. 'He admitted it.'

'He was lying,' O'Higgins said, releasing Madame Lachatte at last.

'Yes! Yes! Of course he was!' I saw it all myself now. 'He borrowed the identity because he knew you had a claim on that money. It was so easy to do, and he knew everyone would believe it.'

'So who is he?' said Elizabeth, giving us all a sweeping, challenging look. 'And where is Hector?'

I glanced at Fidelis. Of course he had the answer; but now so did I.

'Come on,' I said. 'We can still get Hector tonight.'

'I am coming too,' said O'Higgins. 'No man borrows my name without charge, and I will see him pay.'

'Where are we going, Titus?' said Elizabeth, as I pulled her up behind me.

'Where we have already been once this evening,' I said. 'We're going back to Garnish Tower.'

Madame Lachatte said farewell to us with a great show of sincerity.

'I hope your boy is safe, dear Mr and Mrs Cragg. And do make sure you lay that knave by the ears, Jack, for there is no excuse for using a little darling in that horrid way.'

The road was deserted at this late hour. Its surface of compacted snow made for easy enough riding and O'Higgins, Fidelis and Furzey set off at a smart pace on their young horses. Elizabeth and I went more slowly on Jones, while Barty ran alongside, so that by the time we passed through the bar, up Church Gate and into the maze of little back streets and alleys on its south side, I had explained the whole plot to Elizabeth.

O'Higgins had already used his skills and let himself into the house by a window. We three latecomers found the door unlocked and were able to walk inside. We found the place very much quieter. Most of the company had left or gone to bed, though two or three members of the family lay around the hearth-room snoring in chairs and on settles. The fire had fallen into ashes. Three or four candle stumps still burned.

I heard low voices from a small back room, the one in which Elizabeth had earlier held her conference with Fanny Garnish. The girl was there now, in her night-dress, having been fetched down by O'Higgins (he knew where she slept) in order to assist in the plan of attack. She was looking at her former lover sulkily, but also longingly. There was just enough longing in it for her to cooperate.

Furzey gave me the gist of what had been said so far.

'The house has twelve bedrooms. That's why we need Fanny to guide us. She says Abel Grant is in one on the attic floor, where you never had a chance to look when you came earlier. The Garnish twins are his accomplices. They sleep on the second floor. We don't know which room your lad is in, but as you never saw him when you searched, it stands to reason it's also the attic.'

'Doesn't Fanny know which room it is?'

Fanny shook her golden locks.

'Abel Grant is a rat, so I keep clear of his business,' she said. 'My cousin Sarah's up in the attic, and she gets on with him, God knows why. Happen it's her that's got the little one in her bed with her.'

'So how are we going to do this?' I asked.

'The advantage we have is that we're in the house and nobody but Fanny knows it, because they're all asleep,' said Fidelis. 'So we have surprise on our side.'

'Let's hope it's *all* on our side, unlike last time.'

'Barty and I will deal with the twins,' Fidelis went on. 'You and O'Higgins, with Furzey and Elizabeth, go up to the attic. The first thing is to find Hector and make sure of him. Then you arrest Abel Grant.'

That was to be the regulation. The reality was a little different. First, the twins were not sleeping in the same room, each having bedded down with a young lady in a different apartment. As Furzey was unprepared to act on his own, O'Higgins agreed to get one twin, while Fidelis dealt with the other, both men having been equipped with lengths of cord that Fanny had found for them. From the second-floor landing, Fanny peeped with a candle into each room and discovered which ones contained the twins. While the rest of us waited near the foot of the narrow attic stairs, Fidelis went into the first one with Furzey as a candle-bearer, crossed to the man's side of the bed and gently whispered into his ear until he rolled on to his stomach. He then put a knee into the small of the man's back and lashed his wrists together, the awakening and howls of protest being muffled in the pillow. The gin-drunk naked girl beside him hardly stirred as Fidelis used a second length of cord to secure a balled hand-kerchief as a gag in the fellow's mouth, and finally bound his ankles and secured them to the bed rail. So far, so good.

O'Higgins had a greater struggle. With Barty holding the light, he entered to find the girl lying wide awake beside her lover and was obliged to whisper threats of immediate death to prevent her from screaming. She still managed to kick the man next to her awake under the covers and he, thinking his girl was being seduced away from him, reared up and attacked the highwayman. Their noisy fight, which O'Higgins eventually finished by knocking the other man out cold with the butt of his gun, did not go unheard by other residents of the household. A girl came down the attic stairs – Sarah evidently. And then a different door opened on our landing and the bearded, night-gowned old patriarch wandered out, scratching himself under his beard.

'What's goin' off?' he wanted to know, muzzy-voiced. 'Noisy for night-time, i'n't it?'

'Someone's having a nightmare,' I said.

'Oh, aye,' he mumbled, 'is that a fact?'

He turned about and wandered back to bed, leaving his door open. Seeing Fidelis and O'Higgins had emerged, having trussed up their respective twins, I was about to head on up the stairs when a small figure tottered out of the old patriarch's room, clutching a tattered piece of old blanket. I was taken so unawares that I gasped and accidentally blew the candle out. I'll never know how but, in spite of the darkness, the child knew we were there.

'Mama! Papa!' said Hector.

THIRTY

Elizabeth gasped and ran forward. Hector held up his arms, spread them wide, took two steps forward and crashed into his mother, winding his arms around her legs. She sank to her knees and hugged him. I joined them, enfolding them both in a hug of my own.

Then Elizabeth wriggled out of our embraces and began running her fingers over Hector's face and body.

'He seems well. I can't find anything wrong. I'm taking him home. Nothing else matters now.'

In one way she was quite right. While our son was beyond our sight, held in unknown hands and exposed to an infinity of dangers, nothing was more important than to find him and make him safe. But for me, now that he *was* safe again, there was another need, which felt as strong. Not having a mother's single-heartedness, I was filled with a father's desire for justice, for the punishment of the black-eyed murderer who had tried to use my helpless young son for his own avaricious ends.

'Yes,' I said, 'You must get him out of this infernal house as quickly as possible, but I have to stay and deal with Grant.'

I crossed the landing to speak to Furzey.

'Will you walk Mrs Cragg and the child back to Cheap Side? Then get yourself home. I'll come with you as far as the street.'

Furzey was only too pleased to do so, and when I thanked him for his loyalty and help, he said, 'What my mother will say when I come drabbling in at half past three in the morning I don't like to think about. But I'm right glad we got your boy back. It's been a good night's work, has this.'

I watched them on their way to the end of Back Water Street, with Furzey leading and Elizabeth carrying Hector wrapped in a blanket. Just as I swung round to go back upstairs, I heard a single pistol shot, several cries and screams, and a hoarse male voice shouting.

*   *   *

By this time the house was generally roused. Gathered on the second-floor landing was a small mob, in which it was hard to tell members of the family from remnant guests. Not that it signified anything, except that our attempt to capture Abel Grant had long ago lost any secrecy and surprise.

'Who fired?' I asked, shouldering my way with difficulty through the onlookers. 'Is anyone hit?'

Fidelis and O'Higgins were guarding the bottom of the stairs that led to the attic.

'It was Abel Grant's shot,' said Fidelis. 'O'Higgins tried to go up, but Grant was watching the stairhead.'

'He missed me,' said O'Higgins, 'but I didn't linger for his next shot. We need a stratagem. He is up there alone now, but who's to say how many firearms and how much powder he has?'

I took a look at Grant's accomplices, the two redheads. Barty had them both under his eye now, trussed up in the same way and in the same room. Their female bedfellows had joined the throng on the landing.

'Let's clear these people downstairs and out of the way,' I said.

We shooed and shepherded them down to the floor below.

'All of you!' I said. 'Keep away. There may be more shooting. Don't come up any higher than this, not until we've taken him.'

I took a lantern into the old man's room, the one from which Hector had emerged. It had once been quite grandly appointed, but now everything was peeling, threadbare, damp-stained. Tom Garnish was lying in his bed under a mound of covers, apparently asleep. I pulled away his blankets and shook him until his eyes, watery and bloodshot, sprang open.

'It's Titus Cragg, the Coroner,' I said to reassure him.

'Eh?' he said. 'What dost yer want? I'm deaf, young man. Tha's to speak up.'

I repeated myself louder and closer to his ear.

'I mind your dadda,' he said. 'He never did me a favour and I never did him one.'

'A missed opportunity on both sides,' I said. 'Tom, listen, I'm here because on the floor above us you have a desperate and dangerous fugitive, Abel Grant, and he is armed.'

'Armed, you say?' said Tom, heaving himself up and balancing on one elbow and blinking. Then he began to issue a wheezy kind of laugh. 'You'll be telling me next he's got legs an' all.'

I ignored this.

'We must take him, Tom. He kidnapped my son – that's the infant you had in your room just now.'

'That little lad? Your son?' He tugged his beard, giving the momentary appearance of seriousness. 'But Abel told me it were his boy, and he put him to sleep wi' t'other lads in my room because . . . because . . . I don't know why else it's that the house is full of folk and I've got the last truckle with any sleeping room in it. It's that one over there.'

He pointed to the bed against the far wall. Two boys, older than Hector, slept peacefully in it. I went over and shook them awake.

'Please tell me about the attics, Tom,' I said. 'Is there any other way of getting up there?'

I pulled both boys out of the bed and pushed them across the room to the door.

'Yer what?' said Tom.

I returned to him and raised my voice.

'The attics, Tom. Excepting the stairs out there, how else can a man get up there?'

'He can't. Unless he wants to go down through the roof.'

'There's a trap-door giving on to the roof?'

'It's a trap all right. It'll probably kill you getting up there.'

He began to wheeze out another laugh as I left him. I ushered the two boys down the stairs, where their anxious mother claimed them.

'It seems we have a simple choice,' I said to Fidelis and O'Higgins, when I was back on the landing. 'We can try to storm him, and risk getting shot, or we can wait it out.'

'A siege?' said Fidelis. 'We have him bottled up?'

'In effect. There's a hatch that opens on to the roof. But this house is that much taller than the ones on either side. If he gets out there, he's got nowhere to go unless he can fly.'

'We might negotiate. That's the best way with an impasse.'

'Negotiate?' said O'Higgins. 'He won't. I'll show you.' He

went halfway up the stair and shouted roughly, 'Grant! You might as well come down. We've got you in a corner like the rat you are. What's your answer?'

From out of the darkness above a wooden stool came bouncing down, which O'Higgins barely dodged.

Fidelis took the stool and sat on it while O'Higgins paced up and down. Half an hour passed, and then another, during which old Tom Garnish wandered out of his room, saying he was damned if he could sleep. It was near six o'clock. I guided him down the stairs and told him to go and find Bridie. Of the members of the household that had been gathered on the landing below, I found that some had now gone back to bed, while others sat on the floor, huddling for warmth, to await developments. I smelled smoke and was told a few had returned to the hearth-room, stoked up the fire and were toasting bread on it. It was still dark, but the day was beginning.

'If he were a naughty ferret refusing to quit a rabbit hole, we'd smoke him out,' I said, returning to the siege with the smoke-smell still in my nose.

'Titus, I believe you've hit on it!' said Fidelis.

He thought for a few moments, then sprang up from the stool.

'There must be a tin bath. I need a tin bath, some blankets and a bucket of water. The stairwell up to the attic will make a fine chimney. Titus, you keep watch while I get the things we need.'

He plunged down the stairs while O'Higgins bustled in and out of the second-floor bedrooms until he had made a pile of six or seven blankets. Fidelis returned with a bath and a boy carrying the water. He placed the bath at the bottom of the attic stairs and put a heap of blankets into it, laid another blanket on the floor and poured water over it, then wrung it to make the material uniformly damp. He found some paper and, burrowing among the blankets in the bath, made a cavity at the bottom in which he kindled a fire with the paper and a candle.

As soon as the blankets in the bath began to catch fire, he covered the whole with the damp blanket to keep the contents merely smouldering, but lifted it up from time to time to release the smoke. Soon, by carefully controlling the amount of air in the fire, he was producing smoke in thick, choking quantities, cloud upon cloud, which obediently drifted up the stairwell and into the attic. From time to time he sprinkled more water to dampen the covering blanket.

We waited, listening for Abel Grant to react. We could hear him moving around restlessly and coughing.

'We could rush him now,' said O'Higgins. 'His vision will be doubtful.'

'No, it's too soon,' I said. 'And he may yet give up or fall unconscious.'

'How will we know if he does that?'

'He will come down before. He will have no choice.'

Fidelis removed the covering and dropped another blanket into the bath, waiting until it was just flaring up before lowering the cover once more. Thick smoke streamed inexorably upwards.

Another ten, fifteen, twenty minutes passed. Outside there was the hint of dawn. The quantity of smoke that had accumulated in the attic was now spilling back out and down to where we were standing. Our throats were scratchy, our mouths felt begrimed. I thought how much worse it must be for Abel Grant crouching in the very thick of it. I imagined him with his mouth and nose pressed to the floor where there were still remnants of breathable air. Still we heard his wracking coughs. I did not feel sorry for him.

We waited a little longer and there came a moment when no more coughing was heard.

'He's passed out, or died,' said O'Higgins. 'I'm going up.'

He undid his neckerchief, wetted it in the bucket of water and tied it around his mouth and nose. Fidelis pulled away the blanket covering the bath and splashed water into the smouldering mass inside to put out the fire, then followed O'Higgins's example. As I began to remove my own neckerchief, he stayed my hand.

'One of us ought to stay down here,' he told me. 'Keep an eye on the stairs in case he breaks out.'

A moment later they had both drawn their pistols and run up the stairs into the smoke.

The condition of the attic was different from what they expected. The smoke was thinner and the air more breathable. Fidelis and O'Higgins set about searching the three attic rooms. They opened cupboards and poked the spaces beneath the beds with broom handles. They tested the windows and found them securely locked. Grant was not there.

This was soon explained. Grant had opened the roof hatch that Tom Garnish told me of, letting the worst of the smoke escape and giving himself a new lease on life.

'He must be out on the roof,' Luke Fidelis called down to me. 'I can see the end of the stepladder that he used to reach the hatch. He pulled it up after him.'

'I'll go down to the street and see what I can see,' I said.

I ran down, ignoring the questions the members of the household threw at me, and reached the street. Looking up while walking backwards, I established a vantage point from where I could see – with the dawn-lit sky behind – all of the near side of the snow-covered roof up as far as the ridge. Against the snow, the open hatch appeared as a dark square through which wisps of smoke still drifted upwards. Lying half across it was the ladder Grant had used. Looking further up, I saw the chimney pot from which smoke was also rising, and to this the figure of Abel Grant was clinging with every appearance of fear. He was looking desperately around for an escape route – a vain hope as Garnish Tower rose two storeys above its neighbours, and there was no safe way of climbing down except to go back through the hatch.

But there was, it turned out, another means of climbing up, for now I heard a splintering sound, and one of the two dormer windows in the roof was forced violently open. Presently, the figure of O'Higgins squirmed out, put a toe on the sill and vaulted with extreme muscular strength upwards to sit astride the ridge of the dormer's own little roof. What followed was extraordinary. O'Higgins drew out his pistol, which he carried stuck into his belt. As he did so, Grant's right hand let go of the chimney and went to draw out his own pistol, which was similarly disposed. Finally, I saw the head of Luke Fidelis poke out of the hatch, surrounded by smoke, and with it his extended arm, and a pistol in hand pointing at Abel Grant.

It was impossible to tell who fired first: all three guns went off as near together as made no difference. Nor was it possible to see exactly why Abel Grant's other hand left the chimney and went up towards the sky, leaving him teetering and unsupported. He did not teeter long but began to slide inexorably down the slope of the roof, gathering speed as he went. As children, we used to go down snowy hillsides on greased sacks in much the same way. But we would pull up when we met level ground. What Grant met was empty space as he launched off the roof, issuing at the same time a terrible scream. The scream was abruptly terminated as he smashed down on to the cobbles not five yards from where I stood. The impact destroyed his skull and broke his body to horrifying effect.

I looked down at this once handsome figure lying before me, gruesomely disfigured and splayed every whichway, like a puppet whose strings have been cut. Earlier I had felt no pity at the thought of him stifled by smoke in the attic. I felt none for him now.

After a few minutes Fidelis and Barty joined me in the street, their faces streaked with soot and sweat.

'We'll need one of those blankets to wrap him in,' I said, nodding at them. 'I suggest the Garnish twins as carriers.'

Fidelis was squinting up at the roof of Garnish Tower.

'Their girls are puzzling over how to get the twins' bonds undone,' he said. 'So there's plenty of time to see first to his safety.'

He pointed up to the roof where the highwayman still sat astride the ridge of the dormer roof, waving his arms and shouting for rescue.

'How did you get up to the roof hatch, Luke?' I asked as we rode out of the maze of weinds and ginnels around Water Street. Ahead of us the Garnish twins were carrying between them the corpse of their former leader. 'The ladder had been pulled up.'

'I put the stool on the upturned bath,' he said. 'It got me just high enough to poke my head and my gun out.'

'You might have followed my lead,' said O'Higgins, riding behind us. 'There was a second window, you know.'

'That was a move to be made by someone anxious to die. Not me.'

'I am no more anxious to die than you, Doctor,' said the highwayman, pulling up his horse just as we came to Church Gate. 'Which is one reason why I must leave you now.'

'What is the other?'

'That I have a beautiful woman waiting for me.'

He wasted no more time saying goodbye but kicked his horse and clattered off down towards the Church Gate bar and the top of Ribbleton Lane.

'You know,' I said, when he had gone out of sight, 'I was convinced Madame Lachatte had become the mistress of the Chevalier.'

I told Fidelis about the passage Madame Lachatte had marked for my attention in *The Fortunate Mistress*.

'It is not surprising you thought that,' he said, 'since it indicates Roxana had fallen in love with a royal prince.'

'But in Madame Lachatte's case it was *not* a royal prince; it was only the Prince of Flicks.'

We put our horses to walk up Church Gate.

'You know what must follow this death, Luke?' I said.

'Obviously,' he said, 'an inquest. And I suppose you want me to cut open the body and tell you whether he was struck by a bullet from my direction or Mr O'Higgins's.'

'You forget,' I said. 'It is not my business. This death happened in the jurisdiction of the town, not the county. But I think if you are called on to do this office, you should consider a third possibility.'

'Which is?'

'That the ball which hit Abel Grant and precipitated his death came not from your gun, or from O'Higgins's, but from his own. That, at least, is my own conclusion, speaking as a witness to everything that happened.'

Fidelis gripped my arm.

'Not for the first time, I am impressed by your tactical acumen, Titus. That suggestion may save me a lot of trouble.'

We arrived at the church, where the verger had risen early to prepare for a special Saturday service celebrating the departure of the Pretender. He was disconcerted when I demanded the key to the vestry outhouse, as I used to do when still Coroner of the town, in order to store corpses prior to inquest. Reluctantly, though, he bowed to precedent and we left Grant's remains behind before going the short remaining distance to my house.

On the step of the house we encountered a man splendidly accoutred in scarlet uniform and cockaded tricorn hat, with two other redcoat soldiers carrying muskets in attendance. He raised his hat courteously.

'Mr Titus Cragg?' he asked.

'Yes?'

'I present the compliments of the Duke of Cumberland. His Grace will require the use of your house for the quartering of some of his officers tonight.'

'Oh? And what if I happen to refuse?'

The officer drew himself up to his full height.

'I'm afraid, Mr Cragg, you would regret that happening. You would regret it very deeply indeed.'

EPILOGUE

The Crime of Count Blackheart:
A Broadside Ballad

Old Dancy was a Lord
A Lord of High Degree
All mighty with the sword
As he was thought to be.
A Count from o'er the water
To Dancy Castle came;
Black-hearted was his nature
And Blackheart was his name.
Young Lady Elinor Dancy
She had a beauty rare.
Count Blackheart took a fancy
To have her, then and there.
He went into her chamber
Where she lay fast in bed
And straight away did blame her.
'I am bewitched,' he said.
'Your beauty makes me do this.
Your beauty makes me sin.
It's you that drives me to this.'
And straight he did begin.
But now the door did open,
Old Dancy strode inside,
Saw Elinor's honour broken
And heard how Elinor cried.
'Oh foul and fell Count Blackheart,'
He said, 'unclasp my wife
And come with me apart,
For I must take your life.
Black your blood will flow,
Black will be its clots,

And black will be the crow
That on your gibbet squats.'
'Old man, speak not too soon,'
The Count did straight declare.
'Come with me to your doom.
Come down the winding stair.'
And so they both descended
Into the castle court
And there the pair contended
A battle bruised and fraught.
The castle walls resounded
As Blackheart's ball and chain
Lord Dancy's scutcheon pounded
Again and again and again.
Lord Dancy strove to answer
Count Blackheart's fierce attack.
He feinted like a dancer
While turning not his back.
He strove with all his might
To give the Count reply
And with a swingeing smite,
He made his helmet fly.
But his old sword was blunted,
His breath would soon abate.
'Old man,' Count Blackheart grunted,
'Prepare to meet your fate.'
Elinor at the casement
A hundred feet above
Looked downward in amazement
And feared for the man she loved.
She leaned out in alarm
As tiring Dancy dodged
Then all at once her arm
A potted herb dislodged.
It toppled off the sill
And fell at a rapid rate
Down through the air until
It smashed on Blackheart's pate.
The Count spoke not nor cried

Robin Blake

Nor gave a deathly rattle.
He just fell down and died
And so ended the battle.
Lord Dancy he was spent
It took him half an hour
To gather up the strength
To climb again the tower.
But then, with tears and laughter,
The husband hugged his wife,
And happy ever after
They lived and loved their life.